INTO the DARK

INTO the DARK

Into the Mists Trilogy
Book Two

Serene Conneeley

Blessed Bee Books

INTO THE DARK: Into the Mists Trilogy Book Two

First edition copyright © Serene Conneeley 2014
Second edition © 2018

All rights reserved. No part of this publication may be reproduced,
stored in a retrieval system or transmitted in any form or by any
means, electronic, mechanical, photocopying, recording or otherwise,
without the prior written permission of the publisher.

Conneeley, Serene
Into the Dark by Serene Conneeley
ISBN: 978-0-9945933-3-7

Website: www.SereneConneeley.com
Email: serene@sereneconneeley.com

Published by Blessed Bee Books
PO Box 449, Newtown, NSW 2042
Australia

Cover artwork: *Storykeeper v2* by Selina Fenech
www.SelinaFenech.com
Illustrations: Daniella Spinetti and Justin Sayers

"In the midst of darkness, light persists."

Mahatma Gandhi,
Indian civil rights activist

Contents

Prologue

Rain poured from the sky, thunder rumbled across the village and lightning split the heavens apart. Shaking with anguish, Carlie ran up the stairs, threw herself through her bedroom door and slammed it closed behind her. Crawling into the far corner, she crouched there, knees pulled up to her chin, arms wrapped tightly around them, trying to make herself smaller, trying to diminish herself in an effort to diminish the pain. She rocked, slowly at first, then less gently, as wrenching sobs shook her body.

Through the mist of her tears, her gaze flickered wildly around the room, coming to rest on the altar she'd so carefully constructed with Rhiannon. The huge chunk of rose quartz sat in the north, mocking her with its promise of forgiveness, compassion and unconditional love. Fat lot of good that had done her.

Close to it was her athame, the ceremonial dagger she'd been gifted by a woman more mist than substance. She snatched it up and held it in her hand, its weight a welcome distraction, grounding her in her body, in her pain. Holding the point of the blade to her wrist, she tried desperately to find one single reason not to draw it across the delicate skin, draw out a river of blood, and draw this painful existence to a close.

He'd promised her that he would slit his wrists before he ever hurt her, but that had clearly been a lie. Fury raged through her, red hot, and suddenly the thought of oblivion, of letting herself drown in this swirling crush of despair and never come up for air, seemed the most welcome idea in the world...

Chapter 1

The Promise

A cold, heavy mist snaked around their ankles as the two girls walked silently through the ivy-wreathed tunnel of oaks to the bottom of the hill. Clad in richly coloured velvet dresses, their long wavy hair fell around them like a cloak, and images of wicked witches danced through their minds. Each clutched a small posie of flowers in one hand and a candle in a glass holder in the other. Their mood was solemn. Tonight they were going to consecrate their newly formed coven with a dedication ritual, and excitement and joy warred with nervousness and a shiver of fear within their hearts.

As the path opened out before them they paused, lifting their eyes skyward. In the soft lavender-gold light of the approaching sunset, the silhouette of Summer Hill rose tall and imposing above them. It was a full moon tonight, the perfect lunar phase for their ceremony, and they wanted to be at the summit in time to watch the moon rise in the east as the sun set in the west. This was a potent moment of magic, and of energy and balance in nature.

The girls smiled at each other in the gathering gloom, then turned away. They'd decided to each take a different path to the top of the sacred tor, to symbolise the individual journeys they'd been on until this point, and the varied experiences they'd had before they met. Then they would join together at the summit, representing the deepening of their friendship and the beginning of their magical partnership.

"Wait," Carlie said. Her friend turned back, her eyes shining with a light that seemed to come from within.

"Maybe we should swap our flowers, so we have something of each other's to bring with us on our climb, to lend each other a bit of strength and support?" she suggested hesitantly.

Rhiannon smiled and nodded, pleased with the suggestion, and Carlie realised that the light in her eyes was just a reflection of her candle flame. And there she'd been, romanticising it all, adding magic where there was none. Reaching out to take her friend's bouquet, she mentally rolled her eyes at herself. Awkwardly they swapped, juggling flaming candles with delicate blooms and trying not to spill wax on themselves. Then they whispered a blessing and turned away from each other again. This was it.

Silky dark hair falling protectively around her, Carlie drew up her shoulders, straightened her back, and took her first step along the path up the hill, the first step on her new magical journey. There were butterflies in her tummy, mostly because she was nervous, but she was excited too. She smiled as she walked – until suddenly she pictured her old friend Emily's reaction to all this, and the look of ridicule that would have been etched across her face if she could have seen her now, draped in purple velvet and climbing an ancient hill to worship the moon. She faltered for a moment, then shook off the thought, lifted her chin and took another step.

A thick swirling fog materialised in front of her, and she drew in a sharp breath, remembering the strangeness of the mists she'd walked into the first time she'd wandered around this place. Perhaps this one was here to comfort her. To shield her and encourage her.

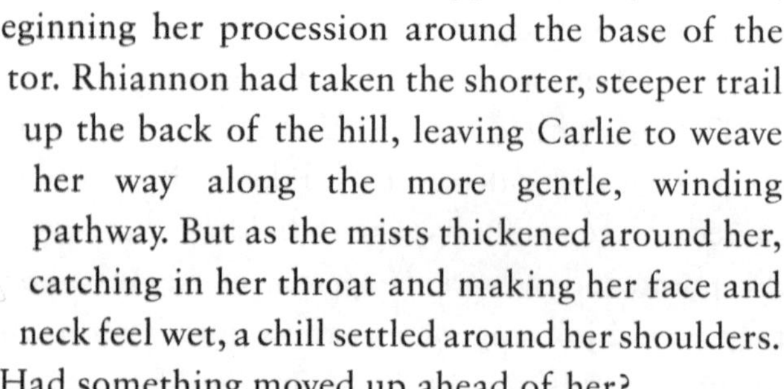

Smiling at the thought, she stepped slowly into it, beginning her procession around the base of the tor. Rhiannon had taken the shorter, steeper trail up the back of the hill, leaving Carlie to weave her way along the more gentle, winding pathway. But as the mists thickened around her, catching in her throat and making her face and neck feel wet, a chill settled around her shoulders. Had something moved up ahead of her?

Focusing on her breathing again, she told herself to calm down. It was probably just one of the rabbits that burrowed its way into the soft ground on the sides of the hill, or maybe it was a raven or a bat. They liked the full moon too.

She took another tentative step, then froze. Something was coming out of the mists ahead of her. A shiver snaked up her spine as she peered into the damp, swirling air ahead of her.

Slowly a form started to emerge from the whiteness, seeming to be half in the hill and half out of it, a natural part of the earth. It was the figure of a woman in a green gown, her eyes gentle yet strong, and the very air that she breathed out, nurturing and comforting as Carlie breathed it in. But how could a creature materialising out of the mists be comforting?

"Just breathe," the figure seemed to whisper, although Carlie would have sworn her lips hadn't moved. "There is no need to worry. I know you have met my sister of the heart, the one you called the woman in blue, and that she gave you a message that you know in your heart to be true," she continued.

Carlie nodded, sensing as she did so the familiar wash of peace and contentment coming over her, the spell that made it hard to think straight or concentrate properly. "Who are you?" she asked, her voice barely a whisper.

"I am the beating heart of this hill, and of the nature and landscape of this country," the woman replied. "I have no name, and no need of one, yet some have called me Brianna. To others I am simply the Keeper of the Hill. I am older than humanity, as old as the land itself, and you can call on me when you need to ground yourself and connect back to the earth, or to feel my nurturing and protection."

Carlie looked at her quizzically. "But I'm okay now," she said, confusion in her eyes and her heart.

The woman stared back at her, head tilted a little to the side, eyes thoughtful, as though weighing up what she should and shouldn't say. "I have been sent to give you a message. Whether you are capable of heeding it or not is of no concern to me," she finally replied, and her voice held a thread of steel and menace. "I am just doing a favour for my friend."

Carlie giggled at the thought of the lady in blue requesting that this stern figure carry out her bidding. She just couldn't picture it. But the look on the green-clad woman's face quickly stifled any sense of merriment she felt.

"I am here to tell you that soon you will have a choice. An important choice. And when you make the decision, you will need to remember how important your friendship is, how much value it has to you, and how good she has been to you."

Carlie stared at the woman. "Of course I know how important Rhiannon is to me," she snapped, bristling at the suggestion that she was not grateful every moment of every day that she had met her friend when she did. "Am I not acting grateful enough?"

"So quick still to anger Carlie?" the woman asked.

"Sorry," she muttered. "Go on."

"Things can change, and people can get in the way," the woman continued, her voice quiet but imposing. "You will be tested. Your loyalties will be divided, and it is within you to betray the people closest to you." Carlie felt a flash of anger bubbling in her stomach, but the protest she wanted to make died on her lips as the woman stared at her, into her, then reached beneath the folds of her gown.

"It is within every person Carlie," she said impatiently. "Now, this is a gift for your friend," she added, offering her a small silver ring. Her eyes flickered to the young girl's pocket as she handed it over, and without consciously thinking about what she was doing, Carlie slipped it inside without even looking at it.

"And this is for you," the green-clad woman said softly, handing over a small package wrapped in deep green velvet. Curious, Carlie unwrapped it, to reveal a small double-edged silver blade with a carved wooden handle. "An athame, a coven gift for you, to cast a circle, to focus and direct energy within that circle, and to remind you to focus on the positive in your life when you are away from the circle, away from your friend. Keep it – and your friend – close to you."

Carlie traced the strange symbols carved in the handle with her finger, feeling the magic that was imbued within this ancient looking ritual tool. Finally she tore her eyes away and looked up, to thank the woman for the strange gift, but there was no one there. She shivered, suddenly aware of the fading light, the cold breeze, and the long walk she still had to make to the top of the hill. Carefully she wrapped the athame back up in the length of velvet and stowed it in the bag that was slung across her shoulder, then she continued up the path.

On the other side of the tor, the steep side, Rhiannon was climbing slowly but steadily. She'd tucked her flowers into the bodice of her dress, so she had one hand free to hold the candle that was lighting her way, and the other free to cling to the earth of the hillside, sometimes pulling herself up a little, other times leaning on it to give herself a boost to continue her upward journey. When the mists started to close in around her, she smiled. They'd always felt magical to her, Otherworldly, and as they swirled around her she felt comforted by their presence, the cool dampness soothing her reddened cheeks and invigorating her just as the climb had started to feel difficult.

She sent a short blessing of gratitude outwards towards the milky wisps, then halted in surprise, her heart suddenly beating a mile a minute as a face appeared to form from the whiteness ahead of her. Nervously she lifted the flowers from her dress and clutched them tight, like a talisman.

A body began to materialise under the head, until a woman finally stood before her. She smiled at Rhiannon, with a look of such love and comfort that her fear slowly faded away.

"Ah Rhiannon, my brave and shining one. You bring hope to me and my kind," she said as she moved forward, without having seemed to move at all, and enfolded her in a hug.

Rhiannon felt a sense of joy and peace come over her at the woman's touch, as though she didn't, and never would, have a problem in the world. She smiled uncertainly at the figure standing before her, dressed in blue, with her long red hair flowing down her back. Was this who she'd met once before, after her mother died, who had held her close while she cried? The one who had shown herself one more time, a few months later, who had taken her hands and encouraged her to reconsider her career plans?

The figure before her inclined her head regally in acknowledgement. "Yes, I am the blue-clad woman, as Carlie calls me, and to Rose I am

Brauna. Others have dubbed me the Keeper of the Well. But my name is of no consequence. I come here tonight to give you a message."

Rhiannon bit her lip. There was so much she wanted to say to her, to ask her, but clearly that wouldn't be welcome right now.

"We are so happy that you are taking this step with your friend, committing to your magic, and to your own growth and inner peace," the woman said, although her lips didn't appear to move, and Rhiannon wasn't sure whether the sound she was hearing was coming from within her own head or outside of it. Could she be making this up, thinking something magical was happening because she wanted so badly for it to be true? Still, she may as well enjoy the moment either way, even if this was just a figment of her imagination. What was she going to tell herself next?

"Rhiannon, I come tonight to remind you of what lies within you. You will need strength for the coming battle," Brauna said.

Battle? She almost giggled. She was going to be involved in a war? "I think you have the wrong person," she whispered. "I'm not strong. I have no weapons, and no will to fight anyone."

"Ah, young shining one. You have the strength of the whole world within you, and then some. And you will need it, because you will be sorely tested in the months ahead. You will need to hold fast to what you believe, and what you know to be true. To trust, even when it seems as though that trust is not warranted."

Rhiannon stared at her. "I have no problem with trusting – some people say I'm far *too* trusting," she insisted.

The woman took her hands and held them tight. "Then remember that. Hold that to you, even when you feel as though betrayal surrounds you. There are things you cannot see, things you cannot know, that will make you doubt the ones closest to you. Remember your faith in them, even when it seems no longer deserved. This will test you as much as them, believe me. And you will pass, if you stay true to you."

Rhiannon shook her head. "I don't know what you're talking about. Tests? Doubt and betrayal? What is this, some kind of quest for the holy grail?"

Brauna's eyes became sad, and Rhiannon felt her heart squeeze at the pain radiating from them. A pain it seemed she was causing.

"The holy grail is symbolic, not real," the blue-clad figure told her. "It is a state of searching that culminates in enlightenment, a state of bliss that results when you can overcome your fears and look into the heart of the world, into the hearts of those close to you — and into your own heart."

Rhiannon tried to understand, to really hear the words and the emotions behind them, and commit them to memory so she could puzzle over them later. Then she saw that Brauna was holding a silver chalice in her hands, and holding it out to her.

"For you, when things get hard," she said, and placed it in the bag slung over Rhiannon's shoulder. "And for your friend," she added, slipping a small object into the hand that held her flowers.

Rhiannon gazed down at it. Even squashed in on itself in her half-closed fist, she could see that it sparkled. "It's beautiful," she breathed, enchanted by the way the candle flame glittered on the crystals. She looked back up at the woman to thank her, but there was no one there. The mists continued to swirl around her, and in front of her. Reaching out her hand, she called out, but there was no reply, no evidence that anyone had ever stood before her whispering messages and prophecy. She shook her head. People said this hill could get into your mind and your heart, play tricks on you, and it seemed as though she had fallen prey to it too.

Yet she felt the weight of something in her hand, a sharp sensation around the stems of the flowers she was still clutching tight. And when she glanced down, her heart skipped a beat. Nestled in her palm was a silver ring, with a delicate silver butterfly on it. This was real, even if the mist-wreathed woman wasn't. The wings were made from sparkling aquamarines, and from the light of her candle she could see the delicate blue crystals reflecting and refracting light. Aquamarines symbolised truth and trust, which seemed to match the message she'd been given.

Wishing that she had a pen and paper, and the time to write down everything that had just happened, she tried to hold on to the words at least, commit them to memory so she could ponder their meaning later. She took a deep breath, then, feeling the ring in her hand, she slipped it into the pocket of her robe and continued her climb.

Carlie was already standing on the summit when Rhiannon arrived, looking as shaken as she felt.

"I have something for you," Carlie said, and put her hand in the pocket of her robe, pulling something small from the folds. "It's from a... I don't even know where to begin. Try it on!" she urged as she handed it over. Rhiannon drew in a breath, part surprise, part awe.

It was a delicate silver ring with a silver dragonfly on it, and tiny pink rose quartz crystals forming its wings. Rose quartz for compassion and love and healing. She held it up to the candle flame, marvelling at the colours and the way it sparkled so brightly. Slipping it on the ring finger of her right hand, where it fit perfectly, she suddenly reached into the pocket of her own dress. Her fingers closed around the matching ring that she'd been given for Carlie, and she pulled it out and handed it to her friend, who looked equally enchanted by it.

"Thank you so much, it's gorgeous. And it matches the butterfly on the aqua aura pendant Mum gave me for my last birthday, so I can wear them together, have you both with me," Carlie said. Then, looking at the butterfly, she sighed. She knew it was a symbol of transformation, of enduring tragedy and emerging through the other side stronger than before – she just wished that stronger side was a bit closer, because right now it seemed as though she was just as broken as she'd been the night her parents died. But she had to stop thinking like this, thinking of loss, because tonight was special, and she had to be in a much better, much more positive, head space for their ritual.

"It's not from me, it's from a mutual friend of ours," Rhiannon offered, voice small and unsure, and Carlie looked up from her hand, where she'd been tracing the pattern of the butterfly.

"A mutual friend? Wait, you met the woman in blue?"

Rhiannon nodded, eyes shining. "And you did too?"

"Well, I met Brianna, the green-clad woman, who said she's a friend of Brauna's. And that she's the Keeper of the Hill, as distinct from the Keeper of the Well. Maybe this means they're happy for us to be here, to be making magic in this sacred place?" Carlie asked.

"Brauna told me that she's glad we're doing this, which was a nice confirmation," Rhiannon agreed. Her smile faded as she remembered her other words. Would her friend betray her? And had the green-clad woman given Carlie a similar message about her? With an effort, she shook that thought off. She needed to think clearly, to put aside any doubts or wondering and focus on the ritual to come.

Deciding to push the unsettling conversations they'd had with women who surely couldn't really exist to the back of her mind, for now at least, Carlie began taking things out of her bag. She and Rhiannon had been talking about starting a group of some kind – she still shied away from the word coven – since the ritual her grandmother Rose had facilitated a few weeks ago. They'd both been spellbound by the magic of the night and of the seasons, and been moved to tears by the camaraderie and nurturing support that Rose, as the high priestess, so obviously shared with the women she wove magic with.

It was the Lughnasadh rite, the festival that marked the beginning of autumn, and the harvest, both metaphorically and in nature. For Carlie, it had been her first experience of group ritual and magic, and it still hurt her brain if she tried too hard to think about it with her usual logic – and her hitherto fairly strong scepticism.

And for Rhiannon, Carlie's new friend and confidante, it had been the first ceremony she'd taken part in since the death of her mother, who she used to attend the sabbats with, so it had been bitter-sweet at times, but had also made her surprisingly happy.

The morning after that ritual, Carlie had started reading the books on Rose's bookshelf, searching for mentions of group work and, although she'd been a little scared of using the word, covens. Rhiannon had begun searching online too, and they'd spent lots of time drinking tea together and making plans.

If she was honest, at first Carlie hadn't believed they would actually form a group, she'd just liked the idea of making a commitment to spend time with Rhiannon. But the more they'd researched and read, and the more she'd thought about the beauty of the Lughnasadh ceremony, the more she'd wanted to do it. And so they'd decided that tonight would be the night to perform their ritual of dedication. Rose was staying with her friend Elsie at her home near Winter Hill, and she'd suggested that Rhiannon might want to sleep over to keep Carlie company. So the two girls had put on their velvet dresses, gathered up their herbs and incense, and made their way up the sacred tor.

Now they knelt together on the lush grass at the summit, looking through their bags by candlelight and the last rays of the setting sun. Rhiannon pulled out the blend of lunar herbs she'd mixed that morning, a piece of charcoal and a clay dish in which to burn them, as well as two thick pillar candles in pretty glass jars and a small glass bottle of lavender-infused spring water.

Carlie placed a large piece of clear quartz she'd borrowed from her grandma alongside them, as well as a few different sized candles and a box of matches, then they reverently set up their altar. They placed the quartz in the north to represent earth, the herbal incense blend in the east to represent air, a gold candle in the south to represent fire, and a small cup of the lavender water in the west to represent water. In the centre were the two large pillar candles, a silver one to represent the goddess, and another gold one for the god.

Rhiannon ignited the incense in its dish, then picked up a bundle of dried lavender and lit one end. She gently wafted the smoke around Carlie and then herself, then walked around the circle marked out by their candlelight, cleansing and purifying the space within it with the sweet smelling smoke.

Slowly, reverently, Carlie unwrapped the athame from its velvet pouch. Rhiannon's eyebrows rose in surprise at the unfamiliar object, and she wondered if it had been a present from Brianna, twin to her gifted chalice. She watched in awe as her once-shy friend lifted it confidently to her heart, blade pointing outwards and upwards, carved handle fitting perfectly in her clasped hands.

Carlie raised her eyes to the darkening sky, inhaled a deep, centring breath, then took a step backwards, away from Rhiannon. She began to slowly pace out a circle, moving deosil – with the sun, or clockwise – her athame tracing the lines of its border. She smiled, because she'd discovered today while studying her grandma's magical books that if she'd been doing this back home in Australia, she would be stepping out her circle the other way, since energy was raised by moving with the sun, which in the southern hemisphere went in the opposite direction.

Focusing back on the present, she took another deep breath and began to speak, her voice shaking only a little.

Within this circle, that our intent will form,
Between the worlds, a safe place born.
Ancient beings of this sacred hill,
We call to you with our deepest will.
Please hold us close throughout this rite,
Reveal the magic on this full moon night.

The air seemed to shimmer as she came back to the place where she had started, and Rhiannon gasped as golden sparks danced around Carlie's head, just as the moon began to slowly rise above the horizon, leaving her awestruck as she felt a sensation of warmth and power slide over her shoulders and warm her.

As Carlie stepped inside their circle and moved towards the centre, Rhiannon picked up her chalice, which she'd filled with the spring water, and raised it above her head as she turned to face the north.

Guardians of the north, and element of earth,
Please ground us with your strength and nurturing,
and watch over our sacred rite.

Guardians of the east, and element of air,
Please grant us your intuition and clarity,
and share your wisdom with us this night.

Guardians of the south, and element of fire,
Please burn away our fears and doubts,
and flood us with your power and might.

Guardians of the west, and element of water,
Please wash away all we no longer need,
and allow us to soak in this magical moonlight.

They both walked slowly to the altar at the centre of the circle, and stood opposite each other, one on each side of the two large pillar candles. Gazing skyward again, Carlie raised her arms.

Goddess of love and compassion, magic and moonlight,
Please bless us with your presence through our sacred rite.

She lowered her arms and closed her eyes for a moment, before lighting the silver candle. To Rhiannon she looked as though she was gathering all the energy of the universe within her. Smiling at her friend, she too raised her hands and eyes to the sky.

God of strength and sunshine, love and might,
Please shine your blessings on us tonight.

She bent over and lit the golden candle, then they sat down on the cool grass, the altar between them. Rhiannon inclined her head slightly in Carlie's direction, signalling for her to go first. Carlie nodded, and lifted a small thin gold candle, bending forward to light it from the central flame. She held it to her heart, then looked towards the horizon as the huge glowing ball of the full moon slipped free of it and began to rise slowly into the darkening sky.

"I light this flame to symbolise the growing flame in my heart, as it awakens to the magic that flows within me, and the sense of ancestry that runs through my blood and connects me to this land. I come before you, goddess and spirits of place, humble in your presence, to commit to learning more, understanding more, sharing more. I am grateful to Rhiannon for allowing me to share this with her, and I promise I will work hard, research well and often, remain open minded, be supportive, and commit wholeheartedly to our Tuesday night study circle."

Placing her candle in the small glass holder in front of her, she looked over at Rhiannon with a smile. Her friend nodded, then took her own small thin gold candle and lit it from the central pillar.

"I light this flame to be a beacon of hope and love, to illuminate the darkness so that Mum can see me from wherever she is," she whispered. A tear rolled down her cheek, and Carlie yearned to lean over the altar and wipe it away, to comfort her friend with a hug. But she stayed where she was, too intimidated by the sense of the sacred that they'd created to break it by moving. Rhiannon smiled at her, as though she'd read her mind, then continued her declaration.

"Tonight under the silvery beauty of the full moon, I promise to honour the Old Ways, to step where my mother once walked, on the path of the goddess, and to pledge my support, my time and my heart to the coven that Carlie and I are consecrating tonight. Blessed be."

"Blessed be," Carlie echoed, as her friend set her candle down in front of her. "I wish I had your gift with words," she added, voice tinged with regret.

Rhiannon shook her head. "It's all about your intent, what you say doesn't really matter," she said, her tone confident and assured. "The goddess reads what's written in your heart. Besides, your dedication was beautiful. I'm so glad we decided to commit to this, and to consecrate it in this way. It makes it feel more real."

A cool breeze set their candles fluttering, and the girls collapsed back onto the grass, suddenly feeling a little light headed. Rhiannon pulled a bottle of fruit juice out of her bag and poured it out between three small glasses. Each girl lifted one up and took a sip, then together they raised the third glass and poured it out on the ground, an offering and libation to the spirits of place, and to the goddess and earth mother they revered so much.

Then Carlie lifted a small container from her bag and offered it to Rhiannon, who took two of the spicy moon cookies they'd baked that day, popping one in her mouth and crumbling the other onto the grass. Carlie did the same, smiling as she pictured the black ravens feasting on the crumbs once they'd gone. They were an important part of nature and of life, and if the goddess wasn't hungry, some of her creatures would surely enjoy their offering.

The girls sat in companionable silence for a long time, lost in the magic of the moment, the beauty of the night, the cleansing light of the luminous lunar orb as it sailed across the dark sky, and the sacred promise held within their vows. The scurrying of a creature down the hillside brought them back to the present, and they smiled as they realised that they'd lost all sense of time and place – it really was like another world within the borders of their circle, a place where time didn't exist. They could have been sitting atop the hill for hours tonight, or just minutes. After another few golden moments, something unspoken passed between them, and they decided they'd achieved what they'd gone up there to do.

Rhiannon slowly got to her feet and took up the chalice, walking back around the circle, farewelling the guardians of the four directions and thanking the elements for their presence. Then they held hands across the altar as they farewelled the goddess and the god, before Carlie lifted the athame and walked around the edge of their circle again, widdershins this time, against the sun. Using her words, her intent and the energy she was directing with the ceremonial knife, she dissolved the energetic bonds that had held them safe and nurtured, closing the space they'd forged between the worlds.

They stood for a moment, suspended in that liminal place between the sacred circle and the real world, heads filled with magic and whirling with promise and potential. Carlie's eyes shone, and her heart felt wide open. She gazed at Rhiannon, gratitude filling her as she pondered the kindness and friendship she had so freely offered to her. She shuddered at how empty and grief stricken she would still be feeling right now if not for her new friend. Rhiannon smiled back. She knew it would surprise Carlie to realise just how grateful she too felt for this growing friendship, this finding of a like-minded soul who understood her grief and was also as open to magic as she was.

Finally the moon headed behind a huge cloud bank, and they knew they wouldn't see it again that night. So the two girls gathered up their belongings, lit another small candle each to guide them, and set off home, walking together down the gentle slope to signify their joined purpose and promise. Once home, Carlie unlocked the back door of the cottage and switched on the kitchen lights. They'd set out dinner before they left, and now they both sat down, suddenly ravenous.

Carlie passed the salad bowl to Rhiannon and bit into a carrot stick. "Did you feel the magic up there?" she asked nervously.

"Of course, it was palpable," her friend said, her face alight with passion. "From the moment you stepped out the circle, I felt a shiver of energy go through me, and it stayed with me throughout our ritual."

"It wasn't just the cold air that made you shiver?"

Rhiannon looked at her friend, her left eyebrow raised. "Really? You didn't feel a sense of magic up there?"

Carlie blushed. "I did, of course, I just… sometimes it's hard for me to believe this is real. You grew up around it, you and your mum went to the rituals that Rose runs, and had energy healings and psychic readings. I didn't know any of this existed until I got here eight weeks ago. And it turns out that I didn't know my mother at all, because she grew up here, grew up like you, surrounded by all of this – then she ran away across the world and denied it all," she sighed, voice sad.

Pausing for a moment, she tried to gather her thoughts. "If I think about it too hard, it doesn't make sense. How can magic be real? How can we feel the breath of the goddess or hear the words that she says? How can we talk to the moon and feel the air around us shift?"

Rhiannon smiled. "Don't try to over analyse it or think it away, just try to feel it. Because really, does it have to make sense? If you hear the answer to your question, does it matter if it was the words of the goddess or your own inner voice?"

Carlie shrugged. "I guess not."

"And if Brauna and Brianna are just figments of our imagination, does that change their wisdom?" she asked. "Although given that we've both seen them, and they've given us gifts that we can physically hold in our hands, perhaps they are real," she mused.

They both looked down at the silver rings on their fingers as she said that, and carefully tried not to think of the messages they'd been given. Carlie didn't want her friend to know she had the potential to betray her, especially as nothing on earth could make her do that. And Rhiannon didn't want anyone to know how damaging her doubts could be, how little faith it seemed she really had.

They jumped as Luther knocked on the window, and broke out of the nightmarish daydream they'd both wandered into. Rhiannon smiled as Carlie stood up to let the little black cat in. "If it's real to you, then it must be real, right?" she said, and her friend nodded. "Now pass me the hommus and let me tell you about the boys who'll be in our class. Can you believe we start school on Monday?"

They chatted about that for a while, but although they'd imagined they'd stay up all night talking, they were soon fast asleep, crashed out on the fold-out couch in the lounge room long before midnight, dreaming of moonlit forests and boys in school uniforms…

Chapter 2

Moon Magic

It was mid-morning by the time they woke up, and Rhiannon had to rush back home to help her little brother get ready for school. Carlie folded up the couch and put the blankets back in the closet, then went out to the kitchen to make a cup of tea. As she stared out the window, she suddenly felt terribly alone, and so far from home. A wash of sadness rolled over her, and tears welled. Blinking rapidly in an attempt to stop them, she wiped impatiently at her eyes – then jumped when she heard a sound behind her. Spinning around, she saw Luther striding across the floor towards her.

He jumped up into her arms, miaowing affectionately, and she laughed as she had a vision of the opening credits for the old TV show *Bewitched*, where Samantha turned herself into a cat before jumping up into her husband's arms. "You're not going to turn into a person are you?" she asked Luther, then shook her head. Yep, she was still talking to the cat, and still expecting an answer...

When she heard the front door open she bent down and gently let Luther go. He looked up at her, haughty for a moment, then seemed to smile, before he trotted back through the house to greet Rose. "Hello Gran! Welcome home. Would you like a cup of tea?" she called out after him, and her grandmother poked her head into the kitchen and smiled. "Thank you Sweetheart, that would be great. I've just got to pop these out in the garden, then I'll be right in."

Carlie watched through the window as her grandmother picked up a small trowel, then bent down with the punnets of young herb seedlings and gently planted them out. Her herb garden was so beautiful, so lush and green, and so powerfully aromatic. Carlie had been learning about herbs from Rose since that first ritual, when she became fascinated by all things magical. What they looked like, and how to identify them by sight, smell and taste. How to care for them too, and what they were used for, both magically and medicinally.

Rose had shown her the amazing book that she'd started writing in while she was at college, with perfect hand-drawn illustrations of the leaves, the flowers, and even the roots in many cases, of countless herbs. There were instructions on how to grow them, how much water they liked, and whether they preferred sunshine or shade. Not that they always had much choice in the matter – England didn't come close to the levels of sun that her home in Australia enjoyed.

Sydney was where she'd been born, and where she'd lived her whole life – until that tragic winter's night a week after her seventeenth birthday, when her parents had died in a car accident. A car accident in which she had been the driver.

Eventually, thank god, she'd learned from Rose that it hadn't been her fault – a drunk driver had run a red light and slammed into their car. He was currently serving time for vehicular manslaughter, and while she was relieved that it hadn't been her actions that had led to the crash, she also felt a little sorry for the driver. He hadn't meant to kill anyone, hadn't woken up one day and decided to take someone's life, or planned out how to commit a murder.

It had just been a tragic accident, and she had no doubt that it had destroyed that man's life, as well as his young family's, as much as it had destroyed hers. And he had to live with the guilt. He'd written to her, via a newspaper, from jail, filled with self-recrimination and remorse. There had been a time when she'd raged at the very idea of him, had wanted him dead, or to have suffered the death of one of his family members so he'd know what she was going through. But her grandmother had helped her find a way forward, find a way to live with the loss – not to accept it, never that, but to survive it, to make it a part of her life that strengthened rather than weakened her.

Her grandmother was an amazing woman. She shook her head as she thought back to how rude and angry she'd been when she'd arrived on her gran's doorstep, sent across the world to live with a stranger. Cursed, she'd believed, to a life more miserable than she could even imagine. Now she just felt terrible that she'd never even known she had a grandmother. She still didn't understand why she hadn't known – she'd learned since the death of her mother that she'd been a woman of mystery and deep, dark secrets. She'd run away from home when she was seventeen, and never spoken to her mother again – never even let her know that she was okay.

And Rose, grieving the loss of her husband, who'd descended into an alcohol-drenched haze following their daughter's disappearance, before driving off a bridge to end his pain, also had to deal with never knowing if her only child was even alive. Carlie cringed as she remembered how unsympathetic she'd been to her grandmother when she'd arrived here. It had seemed justified at the time – surely she must have been a monster if her daughter had run away, to the other side of the world no less, and never written, never told her she was married and had a daughter, and never spoken of her to her best friend, her husband or said daughter.

Yet she couldn't have been further from the truth. She smiled warmly as Rose walked back into the kitchen, her long silvery hair pulled into two loose braids, with tiny chamomile flowers woven into their lengths. She was wearing a pale lavender dress that swished around her as she moved, and while there were deep lines of grief etched into her face, she also radiated a sense of peace and compassion, which she shone on everyone in the close-knit community she'd forged in this small village in England's south west.

Rose was the centre of the community, a kind of wise woman and beloved aunt rolled into one, and Carlie figured that while many who lost their husband and only child would have become bitter and resentful, Rose had turned all the love in her heart, and every mothering instinct she possessed, onto the people around her. She'd created a wonderful healing centre in the town, where she offered crystals, spiritual books, ritual tools, spell ingredients and colourful dresses and witchy robes, along with various methods of alternative healing and energy work, and many fascinating courses. And she was always available with a shoulder to cry on for those in pain, and ears and heart to listen when people needed that. She also ran the beautiful seasonal rituals that seemed to be a big part of the glue that held this community together, and was a high priestess of wisdom, strength and power.

Rose had been stunned when Carlie revealed that she had no idea about the kind of pagan magic she practised, and no familiarity with the reiki or the herbs she used to help the people who came to her healing centre. In her turn Carlie had been shocked to learn that her no-nonsense lawyer mum, who seemed to lean towards atheism if she even gave it any thought, had once been a flowers-in-the-hair, crystal-loving, red-velvet-wearing witch with a gemstone-encrusted willow wand and a love of oracle cards and the psychic arts, who'd worked in her mum's shop on weekends, performing reiki on those who needed healing, doing card readings and divination, and taking a central role in the magical sabbat ceremonies that Rose led.

In Australia, Carlie's mum had seemed to have no interest in mind body spirit topics. She'd occasionally gone to a fortune teller with her friend Sandy, but it appeared they did it as a joke more than anything else, and they never seemed to put any credence in what they were told. Her life there was devoid of crystal jewellery, oracle card decks and purple dresses – she lived in suits during the week and jeans on the weekends, and was strict and conventional. Almost boring.

Even her mum's name had been a shock and a secret. In Australia she was known as Fiona, but it turned out her name was Violet, or it had been. Why had she changed her name? Even more importantly, why had she fled the country of her birth and disappeared forever? The only reason Carlie had discovered she had a living grandmother was that just a few weeks before her mum had died, she'd taken her best friend Sandy to a lawyer and made her the executor of her will, leaving everything to Carlie, with instructions on how best to do this.

And she'd given her the name and home village of a woman in England who she said was her mother, who, in the event of her own death, should be contacted so Carlie could go and live with her.

Sandy had been shocked, and more than a little hurt, that her best friend had kept such a secret from her – had in fact lied and said that her parents were dead. But after the accident left Carlie an orphan, Sandy had tracked down the mysterious stranger, and reluctantly sent the troubled teen to live with her, as requested.

Carlie and Rose had discussed this mystery until they had no more words, turning over every single possibility they could dream up, but nothing made sense. If Rose had been a monster then fair enough – that's what had made Carlie imagine she was a hateful old woman who'd done something terrible to her daughter. But she'd discovered her mum's Book of Shadows, in a cottage in the mists that didn't actually exist, and it left way more questions than answers.

Violet had loved her life in the village, had adored her mother, and been so eager to follow in her footsteps. She took part in Rose's seasonal rituals, and was learning divination, herbalism, crystal healing and more, so that she could work alongside her mum and eventually become her business partner. She loved her father too, and had been dating her childhood sweetheart – a man Carlie had met, who'd looked like he'd seen a ghost when he first laid eyes on her, and who turned out to be Rhiannon's dad. *Yep, slightly awkward!*

As Rose came in and washed her hands at the sink, then took the lid off a jar of fresh cookies she must have baked with Elsie that morning, Carlie shrugged off her circling thoughts. Taking a biscuit when the plate was offered, she smiled as the rich buttery taste, complemented by the subtle mix of cinnamon, ginger and nutmeg, exploded in her mouth.

"Are these for tonight's full moon ritual?" she asked, and Rose nodded, smiling, before putting a question to her.

"Do you still want to come along tonight? You don't have to speak, I promise. You can stay on the edges if you'd prefer."

Carlie nodded too, grateful for how welcoming her grandma was, and how much empathy she had. She'd done so much to make her feel secure and included, despite her shock at suddenly acquiring a granddaughter she hadn't known existed, and had opened her magical circle – and her heart – to her with grace and generosity. Carlie had never believed in gods and goddesses, or thought that magic could be real, but since she'd started living with her grandma, she'd become more open to the possibility. So many strange things had happened since her arrival, which her logical mind couldn't quite rationalise. She couldn't even begin to comprehend the how or the why, but for now she was just going with it. Maybe it didn't have to make sense, or be able to be explained in a few short sentences. Maybe some things just had to be felt and experienced.

Giggling, she pictured her best friend Emily, and what she would say about all this if she told her. She would deny outright any possibility that the magic Rose wove could be real, and Carlie would have too, not that long ago. They'd both been sensible, rational and evidence-based, and had planned to go to university together to become sensible, rational lawyers. But now she had a new friend, Rhiannon, and although they weren't proclaiming each other best buddies just yet, she felt like she'd known her forever. Rhiannon had lost her mum a year ago, so they had a bond there, which made them feel close to each other in a way they couldn't with anyone else.

She was still in touch with Emily back in Sydney, but there was a distance between them now that had nothing to do with the oceans that separated them. Emily just couldn't grasp the depths of grief, anger and regret that were so much a part of her now, and Carlie wanted to protect her from that anyway. But she also needed to talk about it, and Rhiannon was a wonderful listener, and had so much empathy for people, so much compassion and insight. It was those qualities, and how supportive Rhiannon had been of her, that had inspired her idea to become a grief counsellor or social worker when she left school, rather than a lawyer as she'd always dreamed. And while this shared passion drew her closer to Rhiannon, it made her feel even more isolated from Emily, who she'd always planned to live with as they completed their legal studies together.

When Carlie sighed, Rose looked up from the bench where she was grinding herbs in a marble mortar and pestle, the heady scent filling the kitchen. "You okay Sweetheart?" she asked.

Carlie nodded.

"Worried about school tomorrow?"

She made a face. "A little."

"I'm sorry Sweetheart, I can't really help you with that one. But I know you'll be fine, and Rhiannon will be there, and Laura too. And I think you'll be happy there, if you give it a chance," Rose said, smiling reassuringly across at her. "Now, will you be ready to leave in half an hour to help me set up?"

"Of course. I'll just go up and get changed," Carlie replied, and clattered up the stairs to her tiny room at the back of the house.

As she started plaiting golden ribbons into her long dark hair, her thoughts turned back to Rhiannon. She was the daughter of Mike – her mum's childhood sweetheart – which had been a little strange for them all at first. But the strange seemed to become ordinary fairly quickly around here...

Faery lights illuminated the room above Rose's healing centre, and the large east-facing windows were open to track the path of the still-full moon when it rose. Carlie smiled across at Rhiannon, who was standing in the circle holding her brother Brodie's hand on one side and her dad's on the other, then focused on Rose as she paced out the boundary of the circle, much like she'd done herself the night before, albeit on a *much* smaller scale. Then four regal gold-robed women welcomed the directions and the elements, and Rose stood again in the centre, the imposing high priestess invoking the god and the goddess, then drawing down the moon.

It gave Carlie chills, to see her grandmother so transformed. It was as though the goddess really had come into her body, and was speaking through her, imbuing everyone in the circle with a sense of peace and power. Rose led a beautiful meditation after that, then they all broke into an energetic spiral dance, before most of the participants leaped into the middle of the circle for the group howl. Carlie was still too shy to take part, but she giggled when she saw Brodie with his head thrown back and eyes closed, his high-pitched yet wolf-like howls rising above everyone else's.

"Real magic is the magic of the everyday," Rose whispered in her ear as they watched Brodie. "The magic of family and friends, of the strength found in community. There's no need for smoke and mirrors, or grand fireworks. You don't even need prophetic messages from

Otherworldly visitors, although that can be nice. But that's magic right there," she said, pointing to where Mike stood with his arms around his children, all of them smiling widely, content to be together. "The magic of family – that's healing magic," Rose added softly, pulling Carlie into an embrace.

She swallowed over the lump in her throat, and felt the gratitude that she had Rose to anchor her after she'd lost her parents envelop her. As her grandma gently pulled away, Carlie thought her eyes were glittering with tears, but a moment later her face composed itself back into the confident, inscrutable visage of the high priestess, and her voice became powerful as she brought the gathered people back to awareness and calm in the softly lit room.

It was late by the time they'd packed up and gotten back to the cottage, and after a tired hug goodnight, Carlie made her way back upstairs, crawled into bed and pulled her mum's old quilt up over her. She was a little anxious about school tomorrow, but at least Rhiannon would be there. Then her mood shifted, and she smiled to herself as she heard Luther push open the door and jump up onto her feet, curling into a big purring ball of fluff that kept her warm as she drifted off to sleep. The huge golden moon shone into her room and cast beams of light across the floor as it rose higher in the sky, but she was fast asleep by the time it started creeping across her bed.

Chapter 3

Welcome To My Nightmare

The scream woke her up.

Carlie sat bolt upright in bed, heart pounding. Her head was still spinning, and she gasped for breath.

She'd had that dream again, and she shuddered as she realised it was her own scream that had torn her from sleep.

Luther was gazing at her calmly from where he lay curled up on the end of her bed. When she smiled at him, he walked up her legs and made himself comfortable in her lap. She patted his head. He was a patient creature, that was for sure. She'd cried herself to sleep many a night, and woken up screaming a few times too, but he was always there, snuggled up on her bed, watching over her.

The little black cat felt like a guardian of sorts, guiding her gently through her grief, and she was grateful for his warm body on her feet as the nights grew colder, and the sense of calm and companionship he exuded. She was also glad that her grandmother didn't seem to mind too much that her long-time feline friend had deserted her.

Settling back into bed, she allowed her mind to wander. She couldn't believe she'd been in this village with her grandma for two months now, and that tomorrow she would start at a new school, half a world away from her old one. Already her life in Sydney seemed like a lifetime ago, her old friends like people from a dream. She still missed Emily, but everyone else was fading from her mind.

Not her grief for her parents though. Their death in a car accident was still a raw and gaping wound, and there were times when she wondered if she'd ever survive through the day, so real was the ache in her heart, so tangible was its sensation of brokenness. Sometimes she would catch a glimpse of herself in a mirror or a shop window, and be surprised that her outer appearance didn't reflect the twisted pain she felt inside.

If it wasn't for her grandmother and Rhiannon, she didn't think she'd still be here. But the moments when she wished she had died with her parents were getting a little less frequent. And while she knew she'd never feel fully whole again, maybe that was okay. She wanted to keep them in her heart, keep them close, and if that meant she never let go of the pain, that was all right. Part of her still felt that she deserved to suffer anyway, since she'd been driving their car that night, chauffeuring them home after her mum's somewhat raucous but friendship-filled fortieth birthday dinner.

Sighing, she tried to recall what she'd been dreaming about, but already it was hazy. Something, or someone, had been pursuing her deep within the earth, in a tunnel under the hill, but every time she got close to seeing it, it curled away into mist. There was something not quite right about it though, because although she was afraid, and was running from it in terror, there was a small part of her that wanted it to catch her, wanted to feel it holding her close, stroking her cheek, leaning down to kiss her gently on the lips.

Wait, what? She gazed down at Luther. If only he could talk. Sometimes she was convinced that he knew all the answers to the universe – and to her small and petty problems – but he just couldn't tell her. If only she could study cat as a language instead of French...

At last she drifted off to sleep again. She was dreaming of home, her old home, but this time the women from the ritual she'd done were there with her, hands linked in a circle with her in the centre, all of them spinning around and around, long hair flying in the wind. Her arms were outstretched as she twirled, feeling secure and loved in this most basic of magic rites, this most powerful of enchanted circles. As they all turned their faces up to the sun and laughed, she felt her heart soar. Her mother was there too, gazing down on them from the sky, hand reaching outwards to bestow a blessing on them all.

She awoke gently this time, a smile on her face and Luther purring on the pillow beside her head. More than ten thousand miles from her childhood home, had she finally found her real home? Is that what her mum had wanted all along? What she'd cast that desperate spell for as she'd planned to leave home? For her mother and her daughter to meet at last, to be reconciled, to share the love that she'd felt driven to give up?

Her grandma knocked on her door, and Carlie called out a greeting as she jumped out of bed. Today was the first day at her new school, the first step towards her new career dream, and her new life. She was determined to face it bravely and with an open heart and mind.

Chapter 4

Meeting the Goddess

As she opened the front door and walked into the old school building though, she had to admit she was terrified. It did help that Rhiannon would be there too, and that she had met one of the teachers at her grandma's rituals, but the last thing she wanted was to be the new girl, to have to explain herself, and why she was here, living with her grandmother. To have to explain what had happened to her parents. She was sure everyone would be kind, but she just didn't want to be the centre of attention, to be stared at and wondered about. She sighed. There was nothing she could do about it, so she pulled her backpack up onto her shoulders and slowly walked inside.

The school was small, insanely small compared to her last one, and it didn't take her long to find the office and scribble down her timetable, and directions to each of the rooms she'd be in. When the first bell rang she took a deep breath and made her way to the classroom, and by the time the second one rang she was inside, introducing herself to the teacher and being directed to a spare desk. Quickly, quietly, she sat down and pulled out her books, trying to shrink in on herself, to avoid notice. She caught a few curious glances directed at her, but she kept her head down, madly scrawling notes and avoiding eye contact as much as she could.

Her fourth class was with Rhiannon, and she breathed a sigh of relief as she walked into the room and saw her friend's smiling face.

Rhiannon waved her over to the desk next to hers, and Carlie crumpled into the seat, thankful for even a slight reprieve from the pressure. The morning had been even harder than she'd expected, and she was tired of feeling so strange, so other. Everyone here knew each other, knew the teachers, knew where they were up to in each subject. She was tired of feeling so out of her depth. So when the teacher walked in and she saw that it was Laura – or Ms Henderson as she was known here, who she'd met at her first sabbat ritual – relief flooded her. She was even happier when Laura simply said hello and welcome, and got on with the lesson. She'd already had a few "introduce yourself to the class" moments today, and she was all talked out.

Carlie sat up straighter when she explained that this term they were going to study pre-Christian gods and goddesses, and would each choose one to do a project on. "No prizes for guessing who you two will do," Laura said, glancing at the girls as she handed the list of deities she'd compiled around the room. They stared at her in confusion. Carlie had recently discovered that her mum had named her for Kali, the goddess of life, death and destruction, but Rhiannon? They ran their eyes down the list, then raised their eyebrows as they saw her name there too.

"Rhiannon is the Celtic goddess of healing, inspiration and the moon. And she's especially associated with this area," Ms Henderson said. "Your mother named you well."

Carlie grimaced as she felt Rhiannon stiffen beside her. It was a year since her friend had lost her mother, and the pain was still raw and deep. Their teacher touched her hand.

"You'll be honouring her memory as you research this project, and you may come to know her even better too. It was no accident that she gave you a goddess's name. I remember her talking about it at your baby shower, just before she went into labour." She broke off, suddenly aware of all the students staring at her, and the unwanted attention focused on Rhiannon.

"Later then," she whispered, then turned to the rest of the class. "Now, are there any on this list that people know about already? And who will you study, and why? Let's go around the room."

Her voice shaking with nerves, Carlie said she would be looking into the myths and meaning of Kali, as her mother had named her for this deity, hoping to instil in her the qualities of the goddess. "I'm not sure how that worked out though," she offered, and her classmates laughed kindly at her joke.

By the end of the lesson, Carlie had realised this was going to be an interesting term. They would be able to spend some of their class time researching, then do the rest at home, and they would all have to do a presentation on their chosen deity before they broke for the Christmas holidays.

Dropping her bag in the lounge room when she got home from school that afternoon, Carlie walked over to her grandma's bookshelves, deciding to start on her research, since the due date would no doubt creep up on her quickly. After making a mug of tea, she grabbed a notebook and pen, and curled up in one of the comfy armchairs with a pile of books, and began to scrawl down some of the key attributes of her chosen goddess.

According to ancient Hindu tradition, Kali was the mother of all, the giver – and the taker – of life. Carlie was a little confronted by the images she came across of this goddess, so often depicted as a harbinger of destruction who was violent and bloodthirsty, although she smiled at some of the tales of her, and the metaphorical descriptions of her helping people, through death, to experience the joy of rebirth. She wondered how this related to her. She was starting to realise that death didn't always mean literal death, in the magical world at least, but could there be some relationship between the death of her parents and the resulting rebirth of herself and her grandma?

Of course she would still swap anything good in her life to have her parents back, but some of the descriptions were reminding her of what her mum had written in her Book of Shadows all those years ago, long before she'd ever known her, when she'd implored the goddess Kali to bring her a daughter who would somehow take her place, and redeem her actions in deserting her own mother.

... And so, my last act before I must leave everything I know, love and cherish, is a spellcrafting to attract a soul mate to me. Not a lover but a daughter, one who will be brave and strong and loving, and all the support Mum needs. I'll call her Kali, because she will be powerful and magical, and will transform the chaos of her family into something incredible, something love-filled, something better than I can offer...

I send out my call across the universe. Bring me a daughter ablaze with courage, compassion, strength and generosity of spirit. Kali, I implore you to bless me with this daughter, your namesake. I will nurture her and love her, and help her grow into a woman worthy of you, worthy of my mother, worthy of this world she'll be born into. Full of magic and wonder, imbued with wisdom and grace...

For the first time, Carlie realised the emphasis her mum had placed on a daughter to somehow solve her problems. She hadn't asked for a boyfriend or a husband or a knight in shining armour to rush in and save her and make her life all right, she'd cast a spell to bring forth a daughter, a family member, a woman. Although she had been madly in love at the time, and thought that man was her whole life, part of her hadn't trusted him enough, or depended on him enough, to be the one to help her mother, to give back what, in removing herself from her family, she was taking from her parents and their life together.

She felt her heart breaking wide open, and a rush of love and pride for her young, scared mother, a seventeen-year-old girl in the thrall of a much-older man, trusting in the goddess and the feminine over anything else. Rose would be so proud too, and so touched to realise that she'd managed, through her actions and the way she lived her life, to instil that in her daughter, no matter what else of her parents she had rejected.

Once again, Carlie felt so desperately sad that she'd never known this side of her mother. She wished with all her heart that she could have stood by her side in a sacred circle and taken part in a ritual with her. God, imagine if all three of them could have participated in a magical ceremony together. High priestess and matriarch Rose, her loving, compassionate daughter Violet, and herself, Carlie, starting to realise that she was descended from two beautiful, powerful witches, two women she admired and respected and was so inspired by. It made losing her mother when she did, before she'd ever got the chance to know this part of her, even more difficult.

And so she vowed to live up to her mum's expectations for her, to live a life of beauty, magic and grace, and to be there for Rose and surround her with all the love she'd been denied since her daughter had run away more than twenty years ago. Her heart broke for her grandmother. She was so strong, such a warrior woman, but she couldn't even begin to imagine how hard it must have been for her, for all those years, to think that your only daughter had rejected everything you stood for, everything you were.

Turning back to the books, she sought the deeper meaning behind what scholars had written about this goddess, the things described as negatives that she could see were in fact strengths.

◊ Kali has unwavering judgement, strong willpower and penetrative insight, which you can call on her to help you invoke within yourself...

◊ She assists by shedding light on those who seek to undermine you, saving you from hurt...

◊ While her methods may seem drastic and dramatic, Kali will force you onto a new and better path...

◊ This goddess represents awakening, throwing off the shackles binding you to the past so you can move forward...

◊ She brings passion, sexuality, sensuality and feminine strength into your life...

Carlie smiled as she scribbled, noticing a pattern. Yes, Kali brought upheaval and pain, but it was transformative. Each experience, no matter how tough, was to help you – or force you – to break through old patterns and conditioning, or to leave stagnant situations, dead-end jobs or people who were bad for you, and to open you up to a new and better existence.

Making a note of the crystals associated with this goddess – ruby, bloodstone, garnet, tourmaline and smoky quartz – she decided that she'd check them out and maybe buy one next time she was at her grandmother's shop. Then she copied out some of the affirmations people suggested for working with this deity.

"I am indestructible."
"I am strong."
"I am powerful."
"I am a warrior woman."
"I can conquer darkness, sadness and loss."

The last one touched her deeply, and she hurried up the stairs to her room to find some coloured cardboard and a gold pen, and wrote them all out again on neat little squares that she stuck to her mirror and slipped into her school books as bookmarks. When she had just one left she gazed around her room for a moment, then gently placed it under her pillow. Then she went back downstairs and made a start on her essay notes.

Kali has a reputation as a dangerous, cruel force, wielding destruction as Cupid wields his arrows of love, but she is far more complex than that. When she lays waste to your dreams, to your patterns, to your life, it is to make you take a new and better path, to leave behind the things you no longer need, the things you hold on to out of insecurity and fear, so you can recreate your life in brilliant new ways.

Some people say that if your life is spinning out of control, it's Kali telling you that you have chosen the wrong path. Through her strength, her courage, and yes, even her harshness, she helps you – forcefully! – find the right path for yourself, and thus find purpose and meaning in your life. She encourages you to purge your life of people and situations that are no good for you, to get rid of excess baggage and emotions that no longer serve you. So while she may be destructive, it's destruction of the negative in your life in order to create a new and more fulfilling existence – so in a way she's actually a positive force ☺

*C*arlie paused. How much could she write of herself, given that it was for a school assignment? Pondering the meaning of the goddess though, she felt inspired to be brave, to reveal to herself the truth of her life. She trusted Laura – Ms Henderson – and felt it was important for her own growth as well as the success of her essay, to seek the heart of the goddess and her own connection to her, in order to find a deeper connection with her mother as well. And she had to trust herself enough and be brave enough to be honest. Taking a deep breath and screwing up her courage, she began writing again.

I was not only named for Kali, but my mum did a spellworking in honour of this goddess and implored her to bring me to her, so I definitely feel like I have a lot to live up to!

I only discovered this a few days ago, so it's still a bit strange to me (okay, a lot strange!), and I must confess that until I arrived in this town, I had never even considered that all these gods and goddesses could be real. My mum, who worked the spell two decades ago, gave no inkling that she believed in any of this stuff when I knew her, so this assignment will not only be a journey of discovery for me, but a way to connect on a new level with my mum, even though she's gone.

I have to be honest, I'm still not sure I believe that these deities exist, but I'm looking forward to learning more about them – through this essay as well as through my coven research with Rhiannon and my magical workings with my grandmother – and learning more about my mother too...

Chapter 5

Tuesday Night Magic Club

School was a little easier the next day, her fellow students already including her in their discussions, and she was relieved that it hadn't been as difficult as she'd imagined. But she had to admit that she wasn't paying much attention in class – all she could think about was her first coven meeting with Rhiannon that night. She was filled with anticipation, and a little thrill of fear.

When the final bell rang she raced out the door and hurried home, so she could change into something a little more magical and pick up her reference books and her notes to take to Rhiannon's place. On Sunday she'd looked up athames in her grandma's books, as homework for their meeting, while Rhiannon had been looking up chalices, so they could report back to each other and widen their knowledge about the magical objects they'd been gifted at their dedication ritual – both of them crucial ingredients in a witch's tool box.

Skipping up the front steps at her friend's house, she knocked quickly, and was a little thrown when Brodie opened the door. "Where's your pointy hat?" he asked her with a smirk.

Blushing, she was saved from replying when Rhiannon appeared behind him in the doorway and ushered her in. Her friend ruffled her brother's hair as she passed. "You little terror," she said, but the love in her voice made Carlie's heart ache for the bonds of family. "Just for that, you get none of our treats tonight," she teased.

Sticking his tongue out at his sister, Brodie went back inside to "help" his dad with dinner, and the two girls made their way upstairs to Rhiannon's gorgeous room. Looking around her at the neatly cleaned space, Carlie smiled happily and felt herself relax. The pretty window drapes were tied back to let in the late afternoon breeze, and Rhiannon had already created a magical circle with tiny tea light candles, which flickered in the apple-scented air sweeping down from the tor. Within the border was a small altar, and soft, brightly coloured cushions were scattered around it so they could be comfortable while they worked. They took off their shoes at the door then tiptoed within the golden circle of light, mood instantly reverent as they felt themselves transported to that liminal space between the worlds.

"It's beautiful Rhi," Carlie said, taking a deep breath of the cleansing and clearing oil blend her friend had used. She recognised sandalwood, lemon and lavender, and felt their soothing, purifying qualities washing over her, shaking off the stresses of the day and focusing her on the present, right here in this moment of magic and mysticism.

Sinking down onto a huge purple pillow, she pulled out her notebook. She'd decided that she would scribble everything down as it happened tonight, before transcribing it into her Book of Shadows later, when she could worry about being neat and put her jumbled thoughts in order. For now she just wanted to feel everything, rather than worry about her messy scrawl. To be swept away and caught up in the atmosphere of wonder she was feeling.

Rhiannon settled down opposite her and pulled out a pad of paper too. "So, we were planning to dedicate tonight to our studies, is that still cool with you?" she asked.

Carlie nodded. "I researched athames and their use in magical rituals, and I wrote it all out for you too, so you can glue it into your Book of Shadows, or transcribe it more neatly than my scrawl later on, and write it directly onto a page."

Rhiannon laughed. "What are you worried about? That's perfectly neat," she said, then she started reading through the notes.

An athame is a ceremonial ritual knife used by witches and other magical practitioners to store, channel and direct energy, and to cut an enchanted space between the worlds. Casting a protective circle before a ritual or spellworking is often performed with this sacred tool, although a sword or a wand may be substituted if you prefer. An athame can also be used to draw pentacles or other magical symbols in the air, in order to welcome the elements, as well as to cut etheric cords and cast protective spells. This ceremonial dagger is also utilised to symbolise the masculine – to the chalice's feminine – in representations of the Great Rite.

The athame is one of the four elemental tools in magical practice. In many traditions it represents the element of fire, whereas the chalice corresponds to water, the wand corresponds to air and the pentacle represents earth. In Celtic history and myth, these four objects also correspond to the four symbolic weapons – the sword, the cauldron and/or grail, the spear and the shield – and they're also intimately linked to the four suits of the tarot deck – swords, cups, wands and pentacles.

Traditionally an athame consisted of a double-edged steel blade with a black handle, although today there are many variations. There are beautiful ones with sculpted silver handles, some depicting a deity or a magical creature, and others have a wooden handle. Often times magical symbols, deities, crystals or lunar depictions are worked into, attached to or engraved on the handle.

An athame is generally not used to cut physical matter; it is retained for energy workings only. Instead, many witches will use a white-handled ritual knife called a boline to cut their herbs and other spell ingredients. An athame or a boline can also be used for exorcising, banishing and enchanting in magical herbalism rituals. An athame, and indeed all magical tools, should be regularly cleansed if you work with them often. Purifying them by passing them through the smoke of a protective incense blend is a simple yet powerful way to do this.

"This is fantastic Carlie, thank you. I was worried you'd think I was a swot for writing you an essay, but it seems we're as bad – or as good – as each other. I'm really glad you're taking our magic circle as seriously as I am," she said with a smile. Then she paused, blushing. "To be honest, I wasn't sure you really wanted to do this, and I sensed some hesitation when we were talking about it, even at school today."

Carlie laughed. "Don't feel bad, I did have some hesitations," she admitted. "But don't ever think I'm not taking it seriously."

Rhiannon promised not to, then she handed Carlie a sheet of paper covered in her colourful scrawl. "I wrote you out a copy of my chalice research too, so you wouldn't have to focus on note taking tonight," she said, and they both laughed, happy at their many similarities.

The chalice is one of the four major tools used in magical rituals, alongside the pentacle, the wand and the athame. It symbolises the element of water, and may be included on your altar for this purpose. It can be used in the clearing and setting up of a magical circle too, by placing water in it, blessing it, then walking around the circle aspersing the water. It may also be used to hold a libation to the god and the goddess, and to nature and the spirits of place, with a little of its contents poured out onto the ground in outdoor rituals, to give thanks for the magic performed that night. If you're working inside, you could place your offering in a pot plant, or save it to return to the earth later.

In some rites the chalice is filled with water, juice or wine, which is blessed by the group doing the working then passed around the circle, each person taking a sip before passing it on, a ritual which symbolically unites the individual members and helps them slip into ritual consciousness.

As Carlie read this, she looked up, to see Rhiannon offering the chalice to her. She took a sip, then passed it back to her friend, who drank her fill before returning it to the centre of their altar.

The chalice also symbolises the womb of the goddess, and fertility both literal and metaphorical. It's a representation of feminine energies, which is why many are made of silver, since that is the metal associated with the goddess and the moon. Many incorporate magical symbols carved or engraved into their side, and some are encrusted with gems. Our coven chalice has small moonstones around the base, adding to its lunar power, and is engraved with the symbol of the triple moon and triple goddess.

The chalice represents the feminine and the subconscious, whereas the athame represents the masculine and the intellect. Together the two play a central role in the Great Rite, which is performed to symbolise creation and birth, and represents the principle from which all life springs. The athame is placed in the chalice to represent the union of male and female, god and goddess. Like the yin in the yin-yang symbol, it represents the feminine energies of the earth, with the athame as the masculine yang.

This ritual tool also symbolises the Holy Grail in some traditions. Today it's thought by many to be a Christian symbol, representing the cup Jesus used at the Last Supper, and it's often filled with wine to symbolise his blood. But it had been used in magical rituals for thousands of years before Christ, when it was believed to represent the womb of the goddess, and in modern witchcraft and goddess spirituality it still does.

A cup or a cauldron can be substituted for it if you don't have a chalice on hand, and all three can symbolise inspiration and be used for scrying, by filling it with water or another liquid and gazing into the surface seeking symbols and images.

"Thank you," Carlie said, smiling at her friend. "It's all so fascinating." She paused, and Rhiannon urged her to continue.

"Well, I thought it was really interesting that I was given an athame from Brianna, which represents the masculine, and Brauna gave you a chalice, which represents the feminine. It's like they were trying to make our magic balanced and complete, helping us so that together we can make up the whole."

Rhiannon nodded. "Totally! The Great Rite is also known as the Great Marriage, and uses the chalice and athame to represent the marriage of the god and the goddess, the joining of the high priest and high priestess, and the combination of masculine and feminine energy that is at the core of the earth, of people, of all of life."

"Perhaps that's why we were given these two gifts, rather than anything else, so that our dedication incorporated the god and the goddess in a really deep way?" Carlie mused. "I also found a reference, in a very old book, that talked about the Lady of the Lake gifting a chalice and a sword to someone worthy of those gifts. Perhaps that's who you met, the one who gave you the chalice. Lady of water, of blue, of lakes."

Rhiannon's face lit up. "It's such an awesome mystery, isn't it? I mean, who are they? Are they even real? The things they gave us are certainly real, but I can't work out how a person could materialise like that, or have such knowledge about us."

They went back and forth for a while, discussing the gifts they'd received and debating who the beings that they'd met could be, but eventually they both paused, acknowledging that they might never understand, but content for now to leave it as a mystery. Just before they closed circle, Rhiannon held out a piece of paper to her friend.

"I sensed that you're still a bit anxious about this, about us forming a coven. So we can call it something else if you'd rather, Tuesday Night Magic Club perhaps, or you can work through your fear of the word, and realise the only meaning it has is the meaning we give it. And I don't know, maybe you'd like to include this in your Book of Shadows," she offered, voice suddenly shy. "Only if you want to of course…"

A coven is a group of witches who work together to perform ritual and learn and grow together. And while the word itself is not an old one – it was first recorded as being applied to witches in the seventeenth century – the concept of witches working together is. Some simply celebrate the sabbats and esbats (full moons) together, but others are very serious in their dedication to learning more about witchcraft, healing and self-development, and work deep magic together. They meet regularly, and a sense of trust develops between the members which allows them to delve more deeply into witchcraft and magic, developing spells and rituals, exploring magical herbalism and other elements of magic, and supporting each other in rituals and ceremonies.

American eco witch Starhawk described covens this way: "The coven is a witch's support group, consciousness-raising group, psychic study centre, clergy-training program, College of Mysteries, surrogate clan and religious congregation all rolled into one," which is very apt.

Some covens require that all members are initiated into a particular tradition, such as Alexandrian or Gardnerian Wicca, but others form more eclectic groups, with each member following their own spiritual path. Traditionally covens were enshrouded in secrecy and met in private, as there were times when people were executed if it was known that they practised witchcraft. Today, while there is still some prejudice against witches, it is no longer a matter of life or death to maintain the vows of secrecy and silence, and many covens hold open rituals for friends and newcomers, like the sabbat celebrations Rose conducts, along with deeper, more private magical workings for members only.

Carlie smiled at her friend, then reached over and hugged her. "Thank you for this, for taking my nervousness seriously rather than simply telling me to get over it. And I will get over it – I mean, I know from our rituals, both together and with Rose, that there's nothing scary about it, I've just never used the word witch for myself or anyone else – I thought they only existed in faerytales. I've just got to get my head around this whole secret life my mum was part of. I really wish she'd told me about it, shared it with me. It must have been so beautiful when you worked magic with your mum."

Rhiannon nodded sadly, and seemed reluctant to speak about it at first, but finally she shared some of the magical rituals she'd done and some of the experiences she'd had with her mum, some serious, some more light-hearted, and by the end she was smiling a little.

"It actually feels really nice to talk about Mum, to remember the beautiful moments we shared. Thank you for letting me bring her here, giving her a place in our circle."

Carlie leaned over and hugged her again. "Any time."

"And we'll learn more about your mum, and her beliefs and practices, and we can welcome her too," Rhiannon added, and Carlie was grateful all over again that the stars had aligned to bring the two girls into each other's lives. She couldn't think of a better person to be grieving with, or to be picking up the pieces and moving forward with, and she felt excited at the possibility that they could weave together a magical new life for themselves. They had both lost so much, but she was slowly learning to appreciate the things she'd gained too.

They closed their circle, then grounded their energy with chocolate chip cookies and mugs of strong tea that Rhiannon's dad Mike brought up for them at the perfect time. Afterwards Carlie wandered slowly back home, feeling peaceful as the just-past-full moon shone down on her. She was really looking forward to all the things she and her new friend would discover together, about themselves, about each other, about their mums, about the world.

Her grandma had already gone to bed when she reached the cottage, so she was careful to unlock the door quietly and tiptoe up the stairs to her room, laughing silently as Luther greeted her with a miaow and jumped lightly up onto her pillow.

She slid into bed, and when she woke the next morning she had a smile on her face. Drawing the blankets more tightly around herself, she tried to slip back into the dream she'd been having. This was the fourth time she'd had it, and each time it became a little clearer. There was a guy in it, with long black hair that swept down his back in a jumble of loose curls, although she still hadn't seen his face properly. But he was holding her tight, keeping her safe from the thing that was pursuing her, and she was desperate to learn more about him.

As much as she wanted to though, she couldn't get back to sleep, so she lay awake, trying to recall more about him. But it was too hard – a mist seemed to fall over them where they stood together, his arms locked tight around her. A mist that swirled up, thick, white and impenetrable, a mist she'd seen before. Had walked into, and emerged back from, with new knowledge and new wisdom. Perhaps her dreams were a sign she'd eventually feel ready to open her heart to a boyfriend.

Patience, she scolded herself. She was still a grieving wreck, so it was best to guard her heart until it healed.

The following Tuesday night, Rhiannon went to Carlie's house for their coven meeting, and Rose sat with them and shared stories about Mabon, the next sabbat in the Wheel of the Year, which was the celebration of the autumn equinox. She told them the history of the festival and the literal and metaphorical meanings attributed to it, then helped them delve into the herbal correspondences and foods associated with the sacred day, which they scribbled down in their Book of Shadows, eager to catch and capture every piece of wisdom their much-admired high priestess was prepared to offer.

"Now, how about a more practical lesson?" Rose finally asked the girls. "Because surely you've taken enough notes for one night?"

Carlie put her pen down, suddenly feeling guilty. "Is that a bad thing?" she asked nervously.

"No Sweetheart. Knowledge is very important, and traditions are very important, but so is living your Craft. Don't forget to really *experience* the lessons, so you can discover how they relate to you, rather than just taking notes and blindly accepting what someone else tells you – even me. Truth is different for everyone, so be sure to really *feel* the magic within you, and the wisdom within your own heart."

Rhiannon put her pen down too, gazing at Rose with awe as she continued. "All the festivals have a traditional meaning, rituals that have been celebrated for hundreds of years, but the meaning *you* attribute to it is just as important, and just as valid, as anything someone came up with last year, or last century, or wrote in a book. Whatever you feel is right, is right for you, so don't ever let anyone tell you that you're wrong. The magic you create and send out into the world, that comes from you. That's why a spell you dream up will be far more powerful than any you find in a book, because it's imbued with your energy, your intent, your power," she explained.

"In any kind of magic, the physical tools are far less important than your own intent and your own power of manifestation and creation. Ritual tools, herbs, crystals, candles, essential oils, colours – they all have their own innate power to heal and bring about change, and will work on their own in a magical sense too, but it's the magical practitioner themself that really gives a spell or a ritual its power and the added boost to increase the effectiveness of the magic.

"Your visualisation of the outcome you want to achieve, your intent in casting the spell, your charging of the herbs or tools with your own energy, that's what makes the magic happen, that's what gives the spell or the ritual its power. So don't ever give your power away to another person," Rose finished fiercely, looking far more the stern high priestess than the loving grandmother in that moment.

Both girls stared at her, and she laughed at their puzzled faces.

"I'm sorry, it's just one of my pet peeves, people setting themselves up as experts, encouraging others to give away their own power and accept their will, to do their bidding without question. You have as much magic within you as anyone else does, and only you can ever know what is right for you.

"But that's probably enough about that for one night. Follow me," Rose said, mischief in her voice. She stood up and led the way to the kitchen, Luther miaowing at her heels, and started pulling out ingredients from the pantry and the fridge and stacking them on the bench. Switching on the oven, she then took out a mixing bowl, utensils and a silver baking tray.

"Are we going to start making things for the Mabon ritual already?" Carlie asked, surprised given that the sabbat was still two weeks away. But Rose just laughed.

"Sweetheart, you don't have to be so serious all the time! Studying magic takes a great deal of time, dedication and commitment, but it also requires a light heart and a sense of joyous fun. So I thought we'd done enough study for one night, and it was time to bake some shortbread bikkies, brew up a big pot of tea and sit down together and chat about everything and nothing. Life, love and the meaning of the universe... or we could share some jokes, if you have any," she grinned. "Magic needs levity too."

Rhiannon smiled. "I don't know any jokes, but I'm happy to talk about love. Not that I have much experience with it myself – just as I met someone I really liked, well, let's just say I wasn't in the mood to explore that, with Mum being so sick, and then..." she trailed off, misery colouring her voice as she thought of her mum's battle with cancer and her eventual defeat.

Rose poured water from the kettle into the teapot and left it to steep, then walked over to Rhiannon and hugged her. "Sweet girl, there's plenty of time for love. You'll find someone deserving of your time and your heart very soon, you have no need to worry. And he will be a very lucky guy."

Carlie smiled. Her grandmother was amazing – she always knew the right thing to say. Not for the first time, she counted her blessings that she had these two incredible women in her life.

Chapter 6

A Spell For Love

A no-warning maths test a few days later had Carlie feeling a little out of sorts by the time she met up with Rhiannon at lunchtime, but soon they were laughing and joking, and she felt the stress slipping away as their giggles increased. Rhiannon had brought a book of spells to school, and they were flicking through it, wrinkling up their noses at some of the ingredients in the more ancient ones.

"It's the new moon this Sunday – which is the perfect time for casting love spells," Rhiannon said, sneaking what she hoped looked like a casual sideways glance at her friend.

"We could give it a go," Carlie replied with a nervous smile. "I've never done a love spell, or been in love for that matter. But I remember reading in Mum's Book of Shadows that you shouldn't ever cast one on someone specific, otherwise they might fall head over heels in love with you – and then if you ever want to break up with them, they'll just stalk you for the rest of your days, because they can't break free of your spell and will love you regardless of what you say."

"Plus there's no one we actually like here," Rhiannon reminded her. "So it will have to be a general one anyway." She thumbed through the book. "Do you want to cast a spell for love or lust?"

Carlie blushed. "Can't we have both? Or does it have to be one or the other? I mean, obviously love is more important, right? But do you think true love has to be without passion?"

Rhiannon shook her head. "Of course not, I just wondered if you had anything specific in mind. Now, we'll have to work out what kind of qualities we want in a boyfriend…"

"Like that Alanis Morissette song? With the list of twenty-one things she wants in a lover?" Carlie asked. "Although mine would be a lot different to hers," she added, cheeks flaming again. "I'm not so worried about the 'experimental' and 'uninhibited in bed' bit."

Her friend wiggled her eyebrows suggestively. "Really? But you don't want them to be boring in that department do you?"

"Rhiannon!" Carlie exclaimed, face as red as a tomato. "I'm not interested in any of that."

"Okay okay, don't freak out!" her friend laughed. "So we'll switch our coven night to Sunday for this week, and cast a love spell on the new moon, yeah? Do you want to come to my place? I think I have all the ingredients we'll need."

Carlie nodded, then they groaned as the bell for classes rang. "Don't forget to work on your list of things that you do want!" Rhiannon said, as she waved goodbye and rushed off to chemistry class. Carlie giggled as she realised that it would be a very different kind of chemistry they dabbled with on Sunday.

When she got home from school that afternoon, she grabbed some of Rose's magic books then ran straight up to her bedroom, since she didn't want her grandma to know about this particular spellworking. She planned to do some research before their casting, so she didn't come across as too naive or silly. Rhiannon seemed far more worldly than her, and clearly more experienced in matters of the heart. Opening up the closest book, she began to read.

In love magic, and indeed any magic, it is important to never compromise the "harm none" principle, or to influence another person's free will. Love spells are the most popular and widespread magic of all, and in some ways also the most dangerous, because so many people ignore the ethics and cast a spell on a specific person. This is bad news on several fronts.

First, and most importantly, it violates the free will of the other person, causing them to fall for you regardless of their feelings – which would eventually be a hollow victory, for you would always wonder whether they really loved you or it was just the spell. Additionally, such a spell has the potential to backfire on you and cause you great harm. There are many stories about women, and men, who bewitched the object of their affection into loving them, then realised as they got to know them better that they didn't like them after all. But unfortunately they found it hard to escape from the relationship, because they had bound the person to them, so now they didn't want it to end, and would not go quietly.

Instead, you should cast a more general spell to attract love. You could cast it for a type of person – "I want a man who will treat me this way, who does this, believes in that etc" – because a spell is a list of your desires and intent sent out to the universe. Or you can simply ask for your soul mate or true love to appear, for the highest good of all concerned (including yourself!). You can also cast a love spell on yourself, to open yourself up to the possibility of love and let the universe know you are ready, and to allow people to see you at your best and most attractive.

Lust spells and aphrodisiacs can also infringe on someone's free will and violate the "harm none" ethos if that person is not interested in being with you or is unaware they are being fed a potion. Even within a relationship it is not fair to use such spells if your partner doesn't know about it. If lust is your aim, you can cast a spell on yourself to appear more desirable, which will attract someone who wants the same thing. And while if you find infidelity unacceptable it might seem okay to use magic to keep your partner faithful, it is still not right to use magic on anyone without their knowledge, and with the aim of curtailing their free will. If they are cheating, and want to cheat, that is their choice. All you can do is choose to deal with their actions or end the relationship – and make sure you remember to include fidelity on your list next time you cast a spell to attract a partner.

That was true, Carlie thought. She did want someone who was faithful to her, who loved her for who she was, and didn't flirt with other people behind her back or try to make her jealous. Pulling out a pen and a notebook, she started writing. She'd copy it into her Book of Shadows more neatly later, when her thoughts were in order, but for now she just wanted to focus on what was important to her, in a friendship or a relationship, and scribble down everything that crossed her mind.

Finally she narrowed it down – she wanted someone kind, caring, compassionate and open-minded, as in, someone who wouldn't freak out that she and Rhiannon had formed a coven! And she hoped they would be intelligent, interesting, encouraging and motivated, not to mention understanding and patient too. The death of her parents was still so raw and wounding, and she imagined that she wouldn't cope well with anyone who tried to rush her into something before she was ready. *Hmm, how many traits could she request?*

Once that was done, she started flipping through some of the other books so she could figure out spell ingredients. Jasmine would be a good beginning, so she started writing out a page on its properties in the plants and herbs section of her Book of Shadows.

This pretty flower had long been considered one of the most potent ingredients for love spells – Egyptian queen Cleopatra was said to have seduced Roman general Mark Antony with it, and in addition to using it medicinally, Eastern cultures have used it in love spells and as an aphrodisiac for thousands of years, claiming that it penetrates the deepest layers of the soul and opens a person up emotionally, and that it can attract both romantic and spiritual love. As well as increasing love, happiness and relaxation, it is also thought to be helpful in working to heal sexual issues such as impotence and frigidity.

In the Philippines, the name of the jasmine flower, sampaguita, comes from the words for "I promise you", and it represents a pledge of mutual love – young couples traditionally exchanged jasmine necklaces instead of wedding rings. And in India, jasmine flowers represent divine love as well as romantic love, and there the flower is called "moonshine in the garden", with ancient paintings depicting moonlit lovers embracing near jasmine plants.

The scent is extracted from the tiny white star-shaped flowers of the jasmine vine, which are picked at night when the aroma is the strongest, a property that links it to the moon and lunar spells. Not only can you anoint your body with jasmine oil or use it to dress pink candles which are then burned for love rituals, but dried jasmine petals can be added to sachets to attract love, jasmine tea may be served to increase love, and the fresh flowers can be worn in your hair or placed in a vase during ritual.

Hmm, perhaps she and Rhiannon could anoint each other's foreheads with the oil before they began their new moon ritual?

When Carlie walked into Rhiannon's room on Sunday evening, a sweet incense blend was burning on the altar, and the scent took her breath away. Pink and red candles were positioned around the room, flickering warmly against the fading sky outside, and on the altar a large piece of rose quartz sat in the centre, surrounded by pink and white rose petals. The whole scene was so uplifting, and she felt lighter and happier all of a sudden, then sensed the familiar state of ritual consciousness beginning to descend.

"It's beautiful Rhi," she breathed. "And it smells divine."

"I have some jasmine oil too, so we can anoint each other before we begin," her friend said, and Carlie felt a thrill of pleasure that she'd been on the right track with that. Maybe she would get the hang of this witch thing eventually.

"I figured that a simple ritual would be best," Rhiannon continued, as she pressed a few drops of the oil onto Carlie's forehead then handed her the small bottle so she could do the same to her. "If you cast the circle, then we can welcome the elements and the directions, and invoke the goddess – I thought tonight we could invite her in a few of her love goddess guises. Branwen, the Celtic goddess of love and beauty; Aine, Irish goddess of love and fertility; Freya, Norse goddess of love and magic; Hathor, Egyptian goddess of love and beauty; Aphrodite, Greek goddess of love and fertility; Venus, Roman goddess of love and beauty; Ishtar, Babylonian goddess of love and procreation; and Inanna, the Sumerian goddess of love."

Carlie stepped out the boundary of their circle, directing the energy with her athame, then listened, spellbound, as her friend welcomed the deities of love. Then they sat down in the middle of the circle, one on either side of the altar. Each had a red and a white candle, which they anointed with jasmine oil – ah, the beautiful scent – then carved love hearts into with a white-handled boline. Rhiannon handed Carlie a piece of parchment and a pink pen, and they wrote down all the qualities they'd like in the person they were welcoming into their life. They smiled as they envisioned what type of person would make them happy, how they would spend their time together, and what they had to offer to the relationship in turn.

Then at the exact same moment they both put their pens down and looked up at each other, the candlelight sparkling and dancing in their eyes, and together they began to chant:

As a new lunar cycle starts with this magical new moon,
We ask that you send new love to us soon.
Someone whose heart and soul we can fill,
Someone who comes of their own free will…

As they said it for a second time, they gently held a corner of their parchment into a candle flame, and watched as their lists curled up and started to smoke, their wishes released into the cool night-time air and sent skyward to meet the tiny crescent moon.

Just before the paper burned down to their fingertips, they dropped the remains into the small cauldron on the altar, which had a thin layer of sand in the base to absorb the heat. Then they held hands and chanted their verse for a third time, ending with the witchy equivalent of Amen, "So mote it be."

Carlie didn't know if it was the smoke from the incense, the scent of the jasmine oil, or the presence of some of the deities or beings Rhiannon had invoked, who she wasn't sure actually existed, but she felt a tangible shift in the atmosphere of the room, and a strange  altering of her perception. She saw a vision of the guy from her dreams, with his long black hair and deep brown eyes, and for the first time she became aware of his delicate cheekbones and the gentle smile that curved across his features. When he seemed to see her too, she gasped and sat frozen, as he looked deep into her eyes, into the very depths of her soul.

His smile widened as he realised that she'd recognised him, and he seemed to be beckoning to her across time and space, hand out to her in welcome, in invitation. She felt such compassion exuding from him, and a level of understanding and patience that touched her heart. Then a cheeky grin lit up his face, and he winked at her then turned away, fading back into the mists sweeping through her mind.

Feeling Rhiannon's gaze on her, she smiled across at her friend, impatient now to close the circle so they could talk about what had happened during their spellcasting. Imagine if the person she'd been seeing in her dreams and visions was actually real, and imagine if he was aware of her. Could that even be possible? The thought excited her, but it also scared her. The idea that a person could enter her mind of their own accord didn't thrill her, even if he did seem kind and gentle. And, well, really cute.

But the mysterious stranger was all she could think about that night when she climbed into bed, and her heart was full of love as she fell into sleep, and into his arms. Waking up the next morning with a smile on her face, she felt like she'd made a real friend, and she couldn't wait to get to school to tell Rhiannon about her dreams and visions, and the melding of the two.

Chapter 7

A Brave New World

The bright lights hit Carlie first, but they were quickly followed by the sound of tinkling bells being swallowed up by the incredible noise, then the double whammy of swirling colours and intense heat. It all rose up around her as people pushed against her, and she swayed for a moment, not sure if she would be able to remain standing upright. Looking around the big hall crowded with colourful stalls and streams of people, she widened her eyes at Rhiannon in panic. It was a lot to take in.

Her friend giggled, but took her hand. "Come on, I'll protect you," she said, pulling her into the middle of the first rows of stands.

Carlie hadn't been sure about coming to London for the new age Body Mind Spirit Festival, but Rhiannon had convinced her it would be fun to get up in the dark and catch the early train to the city for it. Her misgivings were returning with a vengeance though, as she battled her way through the crowds, overwhelmed by sensation. But it was nice to be having an adventure with Rhiannon, and she had to admit that their train journey had been fun, chatting about school, about tomorrow night's Mabon ritual, and about when and how they might meet the objects of the love spells they'd cast a week before.

"Do you want to book a psychic reading first, so we can plan our day around that, and then we can go and check out the seminars and see what's on?" Rhiannon asked.

"Sure, whatever you want, I'm in your hands. Just don't lose me," Carlie pleaded, only half joking. It was a much bigger festival than she'd pictured, with four halls at the exhibition centre overflowing with stalls – everything from books, clothes and crystal jewellery to aura photos, wax readings, massage, reiki and spirit guide drawings. Leaving Carlie in the safety of a book stand, Rhiannon made her way through the crowd to the reading room and booked them in.

"Two o'clock. I managed to get us both one at the same time," she said proudly when she'd made her way safely back. Then her eyes lit up as her gaze rested on the stand opposite them. "Oh, it's Rowan! Do you want your spirit guide drawn while we wait?" she asked, dragging Carlie over to a stand whose walls were covered with beautiful paintings of various animals, druids, shamans and what looked like faery people.

The man behind the counter looked up as they approached, his face paling as he caught sight of Carlie. He stared at her, his deep brown eyes feeling as though they were burning into her soul, searching out her mind and heart. She felt flustered under his scrutiny, and a little unsettled. Why did he seem so familiar? Had she met him somewhere? Surely she'd remember that though? Yet Rhiannon seemed oblivious to any undercurrent between them, and he swung his attention to her as she spoke.

"Hi Rowan! We'd love to have a spirit guide drawing done today – both of us if you can fit us in?" she asked, voice a little breathless. "You can do my friend Carlie first," she offered.

He glanced at Carlie again. "Okay," he said to Rhiannon. "You first though. Your friend can come back in half an hour."

Rhiannon turned to Carlie, a question in her eyes. Carlie shrugged. "Sure, I'll see you soon – I'll go for a wander."

As Rhiannon took a seat within the booth, the strange man's eyes followed Carlie until she turned into the next aisle. Shaking off the weirdness, she spent the next half hour taking in the more colourful sights, trying a sample of goji berry juice, gazing at the beautiful crystal pendants at one stand, buying a copy of a spiritual magazine to read on the train home that night at another, grinning at the strangeness of some of the products available for sale and the breadth of healing modalities on offer, and wondering wistfully what it would have been like to come to something like this with her mother – the mother who might have been, but who she'd never met.

Once again, she found herself trying to puzzle out whether the lawyer or the healer was the true Violet, and what the young and idealistic, and very spiritual, version of her mum would have thought of the grown-up corporate Australian version. Her mum had definitely been happy in Sydney, she reflected – still deeply in love with her husband, a caring friend to Sandy, proud of her career achievements, and a really supportive mother too, involved with Carlie's school and encouraging in whatever she wanted to do with her life.

Glancing at her watch, she was shocked that so much time had passed, and quickly headed back. Rhiannon was thanking Rowan profusely as she reached them, and excitedly showed her the painting as she stepped into the booth. Carlie smiled. It was impressively done, what looked like a vision of Rhiannon merging with a proud white swan, the details of the feathering so intricate. In the top right corner a small white horse was depicted, with a trail of golden stars travelling from the centre of its brow to the centre of Rhiannon's forehead.

"It's beautiful," Carlie said, surprised at the incredible skill and the depth of emotion expressed in the painting. Obviously the symbols were personal to Rhiannon, but the image still touched her deeply, seeming to draw her into the painting like a scene from *Doctor Who*. Desperately she tore her eyes away, scared that she really would be pulled into it. The man was staring at her again, a question in his eyes.

"I know, it's amazing," Rhiannon was saying excitedly. "Thank you so much Rowan, I really love it!"

The man reluctantly turned back to her as she handed him some money, then she hugged Carlie. "So, I'll go walk around while you have yours done, and I'll meet you back here in half an hour. Bye!" Rhiannon sang, and headed off in the same direction Carlie had gone before. She watched her friend go, then nervously faced Rowan, offering her hand in greeting.

"I'm Carlie," she muttered. "Um, where should I sit? I'm sorry, I'm new to all this, so I'm not sure what I have to do." He was still staring at her intently, and she was beginning to feel a little uncomfortable. "Is anything wrong?" she asked nervously.

He shook his head, his face clearing as he did so. "Sorry, you just remind me so much of someone..." he trailed off, then smiled and indicated the chair to his left. "Take a seat, just here's fine, and try to relax. I'll meditate for a few minutes, connect with my own guides, then start painting what they show me, and passing on any messages if they have some for you, or if yours want to speak to you."

"Sure," she said, and stared curiously at him as soon as he closed his eyes. She couldn't tell how old he was – he could have been twenty or forty. His face was smooth and free of lines as he gazed inward, yet he exuded a sense of wisdom and strength that made him seem far older and more experienced than he perhaps was. She was amused to realise that she found him attractive – she hadn't even looked at a guy in the last three months, since the accident.

His brown eyes opened again and burned into hers, seeming to see things about her that she wasn't even aware of. Then he picked up a paintbrush and started working silently, as though still meditating. Perhaps he was. When he finally spoke, she jumped.

"You've been suffering from migraines for the last few months," he said. It wasn't a question, and so she just nodded, surprised that he could know that about her. "I've got some herbs that will help with the pain, but the migraines will ease as you heal emotionally, and move forward from the accident."

She stared at him, shocked for a moment, then smiled wryly. No doubt Rhiannon had mentioned a bit of her history to him. That's how it worked with these psychics wasn't it, they were observant, picking up on clues, spinning things out from there?

He raised his eyes from the canvas and stared right at her. "No, your friend didn't tell me anything. She was too busy pondering her own messages." Carlie blushed, but Rowan smiled at her, amused, and the warmth finally reached his eyes.

"There are bees around you," he continued, and she thought of the sweet droning sound that calmed her as she worked in her grandma's herb garden. "They're a good sign – they represent the potential within you, and the possibility of transforming the bad aspects of your life into something good. They're all about sweetness, and letting that into your life, even if you don't think you deserve it."

Taken aback by how close to the bone his words were, she stared at him in shock. She certainly didn't feel that she deserved joy, despite her grandma and her friend trying to convince her otherwise.

"The message of the bees is to celebrate life, even though there are dark times," he continued, and even his voice seemed familiar now. "To focus on the sunshine, and appreciate all the things you do have. This is a good time to manifest your ideas and dreams into reality, to get organised, get busy, get committed, and take practical steps to achieve the life you want.

"And they want you to know that it is safe to trust, and that you can call on their energy to increase your confidence, grow your social skills, and start to allow people into your life. Bees are all about creating community and finding joy in the company of others, so they're advising you to stop shutting people out and saying no to new experiences," he said softly.

Pausing for a moment, he gazed at her thoughtfully. "Just be aware of your sting Carlie. Don't push people away, or lash out at them because of your pain."

She nodded, then looked away, embarrassed by the intensity of his gaze. She didn't want him to see everything about her, or know that she hadn't treated her grandmother well when she'd arrived in England, not to mention her friend Emily before she even left Australia. Sensing her discomfort, he changed the subject. "You're just starting to comprehend the magic within you, and within the world," he said gently. "Sometimes it takes a tragedy to split your heart wide open."

Tears gathered behind her eyes as she thought of her parents, thought of them dead. Looking around wildly, she tried to focus on something, anything, that would distract her from her most painful memories. There were beautiful strings of lights on a stand opposite her, which looked like strands of glowing butterflies in flight.

She smiled as she thought of the butterflies that had led her into the mists, into the strange cottage that had revealed to her the Book of Shadows her mother had written when she was seventeen, not long before she'd left home then fled to Australia and made a new life there. Back when she'd loved the spiritual side of life, and had been immersed in this world. Maybe she'd even come to this festival as a teenager, and been enthralled by all the colour, all the fascinating people, and by the wide variety of alternative healing methods being demonstrated.

"Hey, I'm sorry, I didn't mean to upset you," Rowan said, bringing her attention back to where she was right now.

She shook her head. "It's fine, it's not your fault. Just things I don't like focusing on, but which are always there. Apparently it will hurt a little less as time goes on, or so they say."

"Grief is a strange thing, and it affects everyone differently," he said. "Don't beat yourself up about it, or think you have to stick to some schedule, to be over it by the end of the month or whatever. You have to honour your grief, acknowledge it and accept it, and that can take years to do. Or it can happen much sooner, and that's okay too. You can only be who you are, react in the way that feels most natural to you. Don't let anyone judge you on that – and don't judge yourself either," he added, his voice a little stern.

She nodded slowly, half convinced he was right. It didn't actually change how she felt, but it was nice that he'd tried to make her feel better. That was his job though, wasn't it, to provide comfort in the individual way each person could relate to and accept? He was smooth, she'd give him that. And he cared about people. And, well, he was kind of cute. She shook her head, disappointed at where this was going. She couldn't even think of guys, of dating, of really living.

Shock sent a trickle of ice down her spine. What did she mean, she couldn't think of living? She was happy about living now, *wasn't she?* She'd gone through all of this before, and moved past the half-thought of not wanting to stay alive, which she'd never really meant, *right?*

Focusing back on him, she was unsettled to find him staring at her again, eyes frighteningly intense. "Oh Carlie, it's okay. I know how you feel. Like no one on earth could ever umderstand what you feel, how horrific it really was to go through all that you did." She nodded, feeling the numbness start to descend. "You can talk to me about it if you want to.

I know what you're going through. No one else will ever understand you like I do," he said, voice low, urgent, and strangely intimate.

While part of her found that thought strange, suddenly she was pouring out her story to him, all her pain, her rage, her guilt, her fear. She surprised herself as she spoke, because surely she'd reconciled all of this in the last few weeks? She didn't still feel guilty, did she? Or as angry as she sounded right now? She jumped as he moved closer, kneeling down at her feet and holding her hands as she felt the tears spilling down her face. As he put his arms gently around her shoulders, she felt the sobs welling up inside her, and her body shook as she finally let them out.

Eventually her crying eased, but his arms remained around her, and she realised that it felt good. Soothing and comforting all at once. A flash of her dream came to her, of being held safe by the man with the long black hair and deep brown eyes, eyes she could drown in. Oh god, was this him? Inhaling the scent of herbs in his hair, she knew that it was. How did that work? How could she have dreamed of him before she'd ever met him? What did it mean?

Suddenly aware of where they were, she felt mortified. What would people think, to see this man holding her so intimately? She leaned back, away from him, and looked around in panic. But no one was even glancing at them, they were just walking down the aisle between the festival stands, wrapped up in their own little worlds. It was as though she and Rowan no longer existed, that they'd turned into ghosts. He dropped his arms from her and smiled at her confusion. "Protective charm," he grinned, then waved his hand through the air. All of a sudden the noise increased around them, and people looked at them as they walked past the stand.

"Wow," she said, impressed. "That was awesome."

"Well, there are times I don't want to be seen," he replied, and although he smiled as he said it, Carlie felt a shiver of fear. Why did what he'd said suddenly sound so sinister? Surely for someone in the public eye, it made sense to not always want to be on display. So why had it set off alarm bells? As though he sensed her thoughts, he moved away from her, turning back to the canvas and continuing to paint, and a sense of peace descended over her once more.

Part of her was suspicious that he was doing that too, enspelling her, but even as the thought hovered on the edge of her consciousness, accusatory, it flitted way, leaving her unsure of what she'd been about to ask him. It mustn't have been important, she figured.

He continued painting, and she was aware that people glanced at them occasionally, but no one stopped to ask him anything, and she wondered if he'd only dispersed half of his charm. She didn't know if she thought that was a good thing or a bad thing though, because she had to reluctantly admit that she liked being with him, liked him focusing all his attention on her, liked the sense of mystery he exuded. Concentrating on his brush strokes, she suddenly worried about what she would look like in his painting. Not that that should matter, she reprimanded herself. This was about showing her inner self, not her outer, and the guides she apparently had around her.

"You're beautiful Carlie," he said, breaking into her thoughts and making her blush. "And you have so much within you, so much power that you will grow into."

"I don't want power," she replied, her voice quavering a little as the uncomfortable feeling she'd had before returned.

"You will. You're destined for greatness Carlie," he insisted.

"Am not!" she said, giggling. "I'll just be happy to graduate from high school, get through university so I can become a counsellor, and work a little in Gran's healing centre. I don't need to be great."

He came back over and leaned down, taking her hands again. "Oh Carlie, I can see it," he whispered, voice thick with passion. "We've been together in past lives, and they've been incredible."

Stubbornly she shook her head. She wasn't sure about all that past life stuff, it had always seemed a little far-fetched to her. Everyone was always someone great, someone famous – no one was ever the maid or the butler or the criminal, they were always the lord or lady of the house, or of the whole country. No one ever claimed they were a slave during the era of the pyramids, they were always Cleopatra or a pharaoh. What did that say about people, she wondered, that they had to imagine themselves being so grand in a past life?

But he was talking again, and she tried hard not to laugh. They had been King Arthur and Morgaine, he claimed, twin flames and soul mates, separated by jealous people trying to shape the nation, who had no idea of true love. "We had such amazing vision, but we were ahead of our time. But now..." he broke off, sensing her scepticism, and smiled at her.

"Another time," he said, and turned back to the canvas in front of him. She wondered what he'd been going to say, then shook off the thought. It wasn't true anyway, so it didn't matter.

Finally he turned the painting to face her, and she gasped. She'd never looked as beautiful as she did in this portrait. She was about to reprimand him for the artistic license he'd taken in portraying her, but he took a step towards her, grasped her wrist, and whispered that she really was that beautiful. She rolled her eyes, but smiled a little as she turned back to the canvas. Her likeness was surrounded by bees and butterflies, and peeking over her left shoulder was her mother, short blonde hair giving her a pixie-like look. She was smiling, but in her eyes was a definite warning. As she gazed back at Rowan, she shivered. He was staring at her again with that intensity he'd had when they first locked eyes, part question, part fear, part...?

"She looks like she's trying to warn me about something," she said, turning to him. The fear spread across his whole face for a moment, then he quickly masked it.

"She's just saying to trust your intuition," he insisted, but she wasn't sure she believed him. Her intuition was telling her to get away from him, pronto, but that was silly, surely. What harm could he do? She'd never see him again after today, and she'd felt so safe in his arms before. She blushed as she imagined being back in the warmth of his embrace, and turned back to the painting again, emotions a wild mess of contradiction.

With a stab of shock, she saw that he'd painted a male figure over her right shoulder, which looked just like him, but older and even wiser looking. Sneaking another quick glance at him, she saw that he was cleaning off his paint brushes, oblivious to her scrutiny, so she peered at the painting again, and realised that it wasn't him at all. What had she been thinking, that he wanted to be part of her life?

She shook her head, embarrassed that she'd imagined such a thing, and willing her cheeks to stop blushing.

When Rhiannon returned for her she was relieved, and stood up quickly, if a little awkwardly. Her friend looked flustered, and when she glanced at the clock at the end of the aisle she realised why – an hour had passed. She was shocked. It had felt like way less time than that. And wasn't Rhiannon coming back for her after thirty minutes?

"I'm so sorry Carlie, I don't know what happened," she said, panic and confusion in her voice. "I started heading back here after twenty-five minutes, but I just couldn't get here – it was like this whole aisle had disappeared. I know that sounds crazy, but I promise, I wouldn't just leave you here."

Carlie smiled at her friend, trying to reassure her. "It's okay Rhi, I think time went crazy everywhere – and Rowan only just finished my picture, so you're not late at all."

Rhiannon didn't look totally convinced, but her eyes widened as she caught sight of Carlie's painting. "Oh, it's beautiful," she gasped, awe in her voice. "You get better every year," she gushed, turning to Rowan in astonishment.

He smiled, thanking her, but his eyes were on Carlie. She reached into her purse for the money to pay him, just as he reached under the table and drew out a small packet of herbs. "Make a tea from them and drink it once a day, just before bed," he instructed. "It will help your migraines, I promise."

Taking them with a grateful smile, she held out her money in return, but he shook his head. "No charge. My guides told me this one was free, friend to friend," he said. She blushed again, mortified that she had doubted his motives. Clearly her intuition wasn't working that well, if she'd thought he was creepy when he was just being nice to her. Selfless.

Once more she tried to push the money into his hands, but when he refused a second time she gave up, instead holding out her hand to shake his, and thanking him profusely. He took her hand, drew it to him, pressed his lips to it and kissed it, then turned away. Confused, she turned to Rhiannon, whose eyes were wide with surprise and… jealousy? She followed her away from the stand, mind buzzing, until they'd found a seat in the crowded cafe. A harried waitress took their order, then left them alone.

"What was all that about?" Rhiannon asked, eyebrows raised, and Carlie squirmed in her seat.

"I don't know, it was really weird..." She paused, trying to gather her thoughts. "I think he was just trying to be nice – he knew I'd lost both my parents, you must have mentioned it to him, so that makes sense. And I kind of broke down about it when he talked about them. He must think I'm an over-emotional fool. Which is fine of course," she added quickly.

Rhiannon was still looking at her strangely, a question in her eyes. "I didn't tell him anything about you," she insisted. "But he is psychic, so I guess it makes sense that he would have picked that up. The weirder thing is that I'd planned to come back at eleven o'clock to get you, because that's when your session was supposed to be over, but I seemed to be pushed away by something – it was like I was lost in a maze, and the way back to you kept changing."

Carlie stared at her. "That doesn't make sense," she said, but her voice lacked conviction. Her mind swung back to his protection spell, which had made them invisible to everyone. She'd thought he'd meant uninterested, not *literally* invisible.

Fortunately the waitress came back with their order, and by the time they'd put honey in their tea and buttered their scones, Rhiannon had forgotten about the subject, busy talking about the stalls she'd been to while Carlie was having her session, then eagerly showing her the gorgeous dress she'd bought. "I thought I could wear it to tomorrow night's ritual," she said, eyes lit up with excitement.

Later she dragged Carlie back to the shop where she'd bought it to see if she could find a dress too, but while she tried on several pretty gowns, she couldn't decide which one she liked best, so decided not to get one. Undeterred, Rhiannon continued leading her into the next aisle, and they had so much fun checking out all the pretty clothes, incredible jewellery, various arts and crafts, and the amazing array of healing methods on offer.

When they stopped at a colourful stand offering past life readings, Carlie asked her friend if she believed in them. Rhiannon nodded.

"Well, I don't know for sure, obviously, but I love the idea. And it makes sense to me – maybe that explains why we're drawn to some people and not others as soon as we meet them. And just imagine, if you knew that your boyfriend now had been your true love in a previous life too? How romantic would that be!" she grinned.

"Wait," she said, as she saw Carlie blush. "Why do you ask? Do you believe in them?"

"I don't know, I'd never actually thought about it before. But Rowan said something about us knowing each other from a past life..." she admitted, then trailed off.

Rhiannon stared at her. "What did he say? Come on, spill!"

"Well, it's silly really – even if reincarnation is real, this isn't. It couldn't be. He said he was King Arthur and I was Morgaine, his soul mate and magical partner in Camelot, and that before that we'd been high priest and priestess in the Western Isles." She laughed, feeling foolish for even saying it out loud. "But he was just being nice, trying to make me feel better after I broke down and cried on his shoulder."

"You cried on his shoulder?" Rhiannon demanded, her voice higher pitched than usual.

Carlie shrugged. "Sure, I started crying when he was asking about my parents, and he gave me a hug."

Her friend's eyes grew wide. "I think he really likes you! He never touches people, let alone claiming that they've been lovers throughout time," she said, echoes of disbelief and admiration in her tone.

Carlie scoffed at the very idea of that. "That's ridiculous," she insisted, blushing again. But she had to admit that a tiny buried part of her was excited to hear that, and hoping it could be true. "How do you know he never does that? He might say it to every girl he meets," she replied, then was surprised to realise that she really wished her friend's assertion was true.

Rhiannon shook her head. "No way. I've read interviews with him and seen him on TV. He's always private, almost secretive."

The beeping of Rhiannon's alarm brought their conversation to a halt. "Oh, it's time for our readings in the psychic room," she said, anticipation colouring her words. She handed Carlie a small ticket.

"Yours is with Isabella, and mine is with Carmen," she added, as she grabbed her friend's hand and excitedly dragged her through the crowd to the back of the huge hall.

When they finally got there Carlie blinked, surprised by just how many psychics and mediums they'd managed to squeeze into the room, each at a tiny cafe-style table with an empty chair opposite them for the person they were reading for. She didn't know how they could concentrate with all the noise of voices and moving furniture, or the press of bodies and closeness in the room – she admired their obvious focus.

The two girls were each shown into the room, and their tables and readers were pointed out to them. They split up, Rhiannon walking over to a table near the back of the room, where a cheerful-looking woman wearing a gorgeous purple scarf over her hair and holding a deck of tarot cards sat, while Carlie's table was near the front.

Nervously she walked towards her psychic, a woman in her fifties with a friendly demeanour, who was wearing a bright yellow dress and a big smile. She stood as Carlie approached her, firmly shook her hand, then indicated she should sit in the chair opposite her.

"Hello lovey, what can I help you with today?" she asked.

Carlie shrugged her shoulders, suddenly anxious.

"Love-life, work, health, study, problems with your parents?" the woman asked her breezily.

Carlie froze, then forced herself to relax. *Not so psychic so far.* "Just a general reading would be fine," she managed to stutter.

"Okay lovey, give me a piece of jewellery."

Carlie's eyebrows shot up.

"You haven't done this before, had a reading?" Isabella asked her, and she shook her head. "It's for the psychometry reading. I hold something that you keep close to you, and get messages from it. It connects me to you energetically, and helps me to communicate with your guides," she explained gently. "It can be a ring, a necklace, or even a house key will be fine."

Tentatively unclasping the necklace her mum had given her for her seventeenth birthday, Carlie handed it over, then sat expectantly, watching as Isabella held the crystal pendant in her outstretched hand, closed her eyes, and seemed to hum a little as her face moved, several expressions flickering across it in turn – concentration, questioning, sadness, understanding. Finally she opened her eyes.

"This will be a wonderful year for you," she began, voice cheerful. "Much better than the year just gone." Carlie nodded slightly, non-committedly. That wouldn't be hard.

"I see some very close friendships, and success in an area of study that is new to you, but which will bring you great satisfaction."

Carlie smiled happily, admitting to herself that she was surprised that the reading seemed accurate, but relieved too at the message. She had decided to change her planned career, from criminal law to grief counselling, and it was reassuring to hear confirmation that it would work out well.

"And there will be a resolution with your mother," the psychic continued. Carlie gasped, and Isabella looked up and frowned, then closed her eyes again. "Mother figure," she corrected, but this time Carlie heard the hopeful note in her voice.

Sitting quietly, her shoulders slumped, she admitted to herself that while she'd doubted the possibility that the woman really had psychic powers, some part of her had actually hoped that she was genuine. Realising that something had upset her client, Isabella asked if she had any specific questions.

"My grandmother?" she asked quietly.

"Ah, your mother figure," she replied, relief in her voice. "She will have a few small challenges, but there will be an unexpected solution to the major problem, so tell her to be patient and not to worry."

Carlie nodded, but she was no longer quite as interested in what the woman was saying. "And my migraines?" she asked.

"Migraines?" Isabella asked. "Hmm, just a second. Oh yes, they're from the fish," she said.

"The fish?"

"If you stop eating fish, your migraines will disappear," she replied, voice smug.

Carlie sighed. "I've never eaten fish in my life," she muttered. The woman gazed off to the left, a thoughtful look on her face, then replied excitedly. "Oh, it's your fillings!" she announced.

When Carlie looked blank, she added: "The mercury in your fillings, that's what's causing your migraines. You need to go to the dentist and have them replaced with newer, less toxic ones."

Carlie raised her eyebrows, but she didn't say anything to contradict her this time. Yet there was a sinking feeling in her gut that was making her feel sad. Wasn't any of this real?

"I'm getting a message for you too," Isabella added, suddenly far more confident. "There is a sense of betrayal in your future."

Her voice trailed off, and Carlie felt a shiver of anxiety. The woman in green had mentioned that she had the potential to betray someone close to her, and she didn't want that to be true.

"I can't see clearly who it is that will betray you, but make sure you stay aware," she warned. Carlie relaxed a little, strangely glad that it would be her that would be betrayed. Reinforcement that she would betray Rhiannon would have undone her.

"You'll doubt yourself, and doubt a very close friendship, but remember how strong you are, and trust yourself and your intuition. You'll know the right choice to make, when the time comes."

A bell rang, and Isabella thrust her hand out to Carlie. "Well, I hope that helped," she said. "Best wishes and bright blessings!" And she was dismissed.

Shuffling back through the reading room to the entrance area, Carlie was swept along by the other people who were trying to get in or out, and it was a while before she finally caught up with her friend. Rhiannon was all happy and giggly, excited by the prospect of a tall, fair-haired and handsome guy sweeping her off her feet by Christmas. She wondered who it could be, whether she'd already met him or he was so far a stranger, whether he was a student at their school. Carlie let her chatter wash over her, happy to just smile and nod.

When they were both sitting down at the cafe again with another cup of tea though, Rhiannon grew more serious. "She said it would be a nice distraction from my pain, and that I shouldn't feel guilty about it," she sighed. "But it's such a hard balance to strike isn't it, living your life, trying to plan for the future and enjoy the good things that come along, while still honouring your grief and not wanting to forget the one you loved and lost," she said, voice filled with longing.

"I'm happy at the idea that I might find someone to love, and someone who will love me, but it also makes me feel sad and guilty. Mum should be there to help me buy a dress for the school ball, to share my happiness with me. She should be there at my wedding – not that I'm anticipating that happening any time soon!" she giggled, as Carlie's face must have expressed a little shock.

"But she'll never see her grandchildren, which breaks my heart, and I'll never have her there for advice and help. We'll both miss out on so much now..." she trailed off.

Carlie leaned over and hugged her friend, mentally reprimanding herself for judging her for seeming to be too happy about her reading. "You're right, it's so hard to swing between joy and anticipation, and then guilt for feeling those things. But you do deserve happiness," she insisted, and she meant it.

Rhiannon thanked her, then asked how her reading had gone.

"Well, I'm not entirely convinced about how good she was," Carlie admitted. "She told me that my migraines are caused by the mercury in my fillings, and that if I have them all removed and replaced by a dentist, the migraines will stop."

Rhiannon looked at her expectantly. "That's good, isn't it?"

Her face twisting into a grimace, Carlie shook her head. "Not really – I don't have any fillings."

Rhiannon tried not to laugh as she motioned for her to continue. That was a pretty direct and indisputably wrong hit.

"She did say it would be a good year for friendships, and that I've changed my career goal, which is true – but then she said I would have some resolution with my mother, and we both know that isn't ever going to happen."

Rhiannon leaned over to embrace her friend, tears in her eyes. "I'm so sorry, maybe that wasn't the best idea I've ever had. Do you want to try to book another one, or should we just indulge in a bit of retail therapy? I saw some beautiful jewellery when I was wandering around before that I haven't shown you yet."

Carlie smiled. "Thank you Rhiannon, you're so sweet," she said, making an effort to throw off her negativity for her friend's sake. "She was right when she said I have some wonderful friendships around me. And you're right when you say we need to hit the shops. Let's go!" she giggled.

Arm in arm, they walked around the stalls again, pausing whenever something pretty caught their eye. Rhiannon got excited when she saw a pair of silver butterfly earrings that matched Carlie's coven dedication ring, and bought them for her, while Carlie was ecstatic when she found some that matched her friend's dragonfly ring, and quickly returned the favour.

For the rest of the afternoon they tried to lose themselves in the festival, sampling weird sounding new drinks, listening to spiritual teachers and healthy eating experts at the speaker's cafe, having a reconnective healing session to try to understand what it was, then checking the program and realising that Rowan was running a seminar at four o'clock.

"Can we go, can we go?" Rhiannon asked Carlie, who nodded, looking forward to learning more about what he did herself.

The first thing that struck her when they walked in and took a seat was how normal he looked compared to most of the other psychics, healers and artists they'd seen that day. There wasn't a purple hue, piece of velvet or feather to be found, he was just wearing jeans and a long-sleeved black t-shirt, his long hair pulled back into a low ponytail.

Carlie had imagined that he was just going to talk, but the first thing he did was get them all to stand up, spread out around the edge of the room, join hands and take a few deep breaths. Right away they all began breathing in unison, then she felt a strange tingling up her spine, like a wave of energy, as Rowan came around the circle and blessed each of them. Part of her was dying to open her eyes and watch him, curious about what he was doing, but she also wanted to stay in the moment – she didn't want to lose the feeling of connection that was racing through her, so she made herself keep them closed.

She was very aware of Rhiannon, standing beside her and holding her left hand; she felt her presence energetically, like a protective guardian who had vowed to keep her safe. Tears welled in her eyes, and she was overwhelmed with gratitude for her friend, who was holding her together while also trying to cope with her own loss. She felt her heart warming and expanding, and tried to send appreciative thoughts to her. And maybe it worked, because Rhiannon squeezed her hand, and she felt an answering warmth spreading up her arm and into her heart.

Soon they were allowed to take their seats again, and Carlie smiled as she saw the radiance on her friend's face. She desperately hoped that Rhiannon would receive some healing energy today, because she really deserved it, and really needed it.

Rowan took them through a deep meditation, guiding them as they went deep into their own hearts and minds, and journeyed to a place deep in the forest, where a series of animal spirit guides came to aid them with their emotional and physical attributes. Carlie met a sweet little deer, who said she'd help her be ready to accept love; an energetic dolphin, who told her he would help her learn to be playful again; as well as an old grey owl, who swooped towards her and offered its wisdom and insight into people's motivations.

As everyone spent a few moments swapping stories afterwards, Rhiannon told Carlie that she'd encountered a swan, which made her think of the painting Rowan had created for her, who said she'd assist her with clarity and purpose; a condor, who wanted to help her deal with her sense of loss; and an ox, who ordered her to start sharing the burdens of her family with others, and stop insisting she could handle everything. Carlie hugged her friend, blown away by how right that had been. Rhiannon had certainly taken on a huge amount of responsibility since her mum had died, and perhaps it was time she handed some back.

Rowan asked if anyone would like to share the animals they'd met and the messages they'd received, and several people were eager to do so. He glanced at Carlie, but she shook her head, blushing. There

was no way she wanted to talk in front of a bunch of strangers, especially when the messages were so personal. She'd told him about her parents, but no one else needed to know. She was content with the knowledge she'd gained during the exercise –

she didn't need anyone else to validate it. And it seemed that there were people there who really wanted to talk about their messages, or really needed to, to get feedback from him and the rest of the room on what it meant, and she was happy to let them do so.

After some lengthy discussions, Rowan talked a little more about what he did – he preferred no labels, but conceded that he was part druid, part shaman, interested in herbal lore, meditation, working with the seasons, shamanic journeying, energetic healing and art therapy. He had recently had an oracle deck published, and each card had a beautifully drawn herb or sacred tree on it, with its purpose, magically and medicinally, written underneath, and expanded upon in the guidebook. There were also instructions for different ways of working with the cards, and a link to his website, where he had recipes for herbal brews, incenses and foods that could be made with each plant too. He opened up a new pack, shuffled them well, then walked around the room, handing a card to each person in the seminar.

"This is the plant that has a message for you today, which you can take home with you," he said. "There is a basic meaning written on the card, and studying the painting of the plant will also help you understand it, as I've worked hidden symbols into each one. If you want to learn more you can check out the herbs tab on my website, or come down and read the guidebook at my stand after this session. And of course you can buy a deck too, if you like what you see." He laughed self-deprecatingly, and several people smiled and said they would definitely be getting one after the workshop.

Carlie looked at her card. It was tansy, a plant associated magically with the dead, which was used in rites of death and rebirth. She felt a chill, which Rhiannon must have picked up on, because she turned to her and gazed down at the colourful picture in her hand. "Oh, that's a great one!" she said. "Rebirth of the self is a wonderful thing – it really *is* going to be an awesome year for you."

Carlie hugged her friend. She always sensed when she was worried, and knew just what to say to reassure her and turn the situation around, into a better light. "What did you get?"

"Wood betony, a herb of grounding, of home and hearth, of responsibility. But oddly enough, even though I watched him shuffle the deck and distribute the cards, and none were turned upside down, this one was reversed. Which means the message is the opposite of what it says – which ties in with my animal guides, telling me to stop taking on so much responsibility. Not sure how Dad will take that of course, but I guess I can only try," she said, hope in her voice.

Carlie smiled reassuringly. "I'm sure he'll understand, especially as this is our last year at school, and you'll need to be able to do a lot of homework." They both rolled their eyes and sighed dramatically. "He probably doesn't even realise how much you're doing, and will be horrified when he figures it out. There's no way he expects you to be doing it all, he probably just hasn't really thought about it."

Rhiannon hugged her. "Thanks Carlie – you're wiser than you look," she giggled. "It's funny how it's always harder to see the truth about your own situation. It's easy for me to advise other people, but I can't do it for myself."

Their attention was drawn back to the front of the room when Rowan announced they would be doing a quick closing ritual before they had to wind up. They looked at the clock, surprised that two hours had passed by so quickly.

As they put the cards they'd received in their bags and shuffled towards the door, Carlie felt a hand on her shoulder and spun around. "Did I do okay?" Rowan asked her, and he sounded nervous.

"It was wonderful, thank you! I've never done anything like this before, but it was amazing," she admitted.

His eyes crinkled as he grinned at her, which she found particularly endearing. "You're a natural," he said. "So intuitive and wise." She looked at him, puzzled. How would he know that? Before she could wonder aloud, Rhiannon turned, noticing that Carlie had stopped, and made her way back over to her.

Rowan smiled at her. "Your friend here has a big future, although she won't listen to me." His kind eyes dulled the sting of his words.

Rhiannon laughed. "She won't listen to me either, but I think you're right. Maybe we'll have to gang up on her together, see if we can make her understand and accept it."

"Good plan," he replied, turning to Rhiannon and gazing at her so intently that she blushed and looked away. "Hey, I still have a few readings to do here, a few paintings to create, but do you both want to come to the after-party tonight?" he asked them. "Lots of the presenters and exhibitors will be there with their friends – it's always lots of fun."

Carlie shook her head, but Rhiannon ignored her. "We'd love to!" she said, excitement dancing in her eyes as he handed them two passes to get in. "We have an assignment to do on goddesses for school, so we can pick your brain," she grinned.

He laughed. "Sure, happy to help."

Rhiannon put her arm through Carlie's and waltzed her away. "Oh my god, this is so cool! He must really like you," she teased.

"That's crazy, he was just being polite," Carlie said, feeling unsettled by the invitation. "We should head home – if we can catch the last train I'll be able to help Gran in the shop tomorrow before we start setting up for the ritual."

But Rhiannon was adamant. "My cousin was hoping we'd stay with her, so she can take us to the markets in the morning. She's going to the theatre tonight though, so this is perfect. I'll call her now, and let her know we'll be over later tonight. I know where she leaves the spare key."

Carlie tried to argue, but her friend was determined that they should go to the party, and although she was reluctant to admit it, part of her really wanted to go too. She knew there was no way Rowan could actually like her, but he was really cute, and there was something about him that really fascinated her. He was so wise, so compassionate. Imagine what she could learn from him if they did manage to talk a bit tonight...

Suddenly the huge crowd, the flashing lights and the intense noise didn't bother Carlie quite as much. Her friend's giddy excitement was starting to rub off on her, and she practically skipped down the next aisle with her. She even let herself be talked into trying on some more dresses, and secretly enjoyed it.

"Come on, I've been saving up for this for so long, hoping I'd find something really special here," Rhiannon said. "I can't remember the last time I went shopping – I even have the birthday money Mum gave me, back before, well..." she broke off, looking so sad that Carlie hugged her and gave herself over to her ministrations.

In the end they both bought a new dress to wear that night. Rhiannon's was a deep forest green, embroidered with oak leaves in all the colours of autumn. Carlie's was midnight blue, with tiny stars sewn onto the fabric of the skirt, and the bodice emblazoned with ivy leaves, little flowers and two bees peeking out from beneath some petals. Then Rhiannon insisted they each get a matching necklace, and they found the perfect ones, Carlie's a silver bee charm on a strand of yellow obsidian crystals, her friend's a delicate silver chain with a single silver oak leaf charm.

They headed off to a nearby cafe to drink tea and fill in time before the party started, and changed into their new outfits in the bathroom there. But as they headed back to the festival venue, Carlie got cold feet. It was crazy for them to go there. Not that Rowan would even have time to talk to them, since no doubt there would be lots of far more beautiful and interesting women there, but even if he did, what would she say? She had nothing clever to offer, nothing to share, and she was shy around guys at the best of times, let alone with one she admired. Desperately she tried to talk Rhiannon out of it, but there was no changing her mind once she'd settled on something, and she was determined to go to this party.

"Come on Carlie, don't be a stick-in-the-mud," she pleaded. "Just imagine all the awesome people we'll get to talk to! And who knows, maybe the objects of our affection will be there – the ones we called forth with our love spells."

That was partly what she was afraid of, but she didn't want to disappoint her friend. She owed her so much. "Fine, but you can't leave me on my own, okay? Promise?"

Rhiannon laughed, and held out her little finger. "Pinkie swear," she said, grabbing Carlie's little finger and shaking it. "Besides, don't you want to see him? He's gorgeous, admit it."

Carlie blushed and ducked her head. "Okay, maybe he is, but it doesn't matter – I won't be able to talk to him. I'm too shy."

Rhiannon giggled. "Well, we're about to find out," she said in a loud stage whisper, turning to greet Rowan as they walked in the door. He'd obviously been waiting for them, and his face lit up when he saw Carlie.

"Hi girls," he said, and hugged them both. Then he called a friend of his over, an older man with long silver hair and a long silver beard. "Rhiannon, this is Kevin – he works with goddesses and has studied them for years. He's even published a book on them. He's happy to help you with your assignment – and he'll keep you busy while I get to know Carlie," he added. While his tone was light-hearted, almost jokey, Carlie wasn't sure how to take his comment. Was he just being polite and thoughtful, or was it a bit weird that he'd found someone to occupy her friend so he could get her alone?

But Rhiannon was smiling at Kevin and shaking his hand, letting him guide her to the drinks table then settling down next to him on a small couch and chatting animatedly. *So much for her pinkie swear.* Yet she looked really happy, and relaxed. In contrast, Carlie was terrified, feeling awkward and shy, and totally out of her depth. Rowan put her at ease straight away though, talking about some of the readings he'd done that day, and sharing a few funny anecdotes about his clients until she was more comfortable.

Once she realised how easygoing he was, and how sweetly down to earth, she was surprised to find that they had lots to talk about, and that he was an amazing listener. When he asked her if she wanted to talk more about her parents, she shook her head, insisting that she didn't want to bore him. Gently he took her hand, and turned to stare directly into her eyes.

"Oh Carlie, please don't think for a moment that you're boring, or that I, or anyone, wouldn't want to hear your stories. Sometimes it can help to share a burden, and while I know I can never erase your pain, maybe you'll feel a bit of peace by talking about them. Not the accident, if you don't want to, but tell me about your mum and dad. What were they like? What did you like doing with them?"

He smiled at her. "Talking about them, introducing them to people, is one small way to keep them alive in your heart. Believe me, I know. I lost my dad when I was twelve."

"I'm so sorry," she said, and she knew she would give anything to be able to ease even the tiniest bit of his pain for him. She froze. Where had that thought come from? But he was smiling at her, making her tummy flutter, and her suspicions quickly floated away.

"Hugs can help too," he said, eyes mischievous as he took her in his arms again. She felt a little weird at first – she'd never been a big one for touching at the best of times – but slowly she started to relax into it, and was surprised to find herself liking the contact. As soon as she thought that, he held her tighter. Her fear reappeared. Did there have to be another person who could apparently read her mind? It was unsettling.

But he soothed it away, and eventually she let herself go, allowing herself to feel the warmth and safety of being in his arms, to feel the warmth seeping into her heart, the sense of belonging. It was exactly like her dreams. Oh god, he really was the guy in her dreams. But how could that be?

Pulling away, she broke their contact, muttering that she had to go to the bathroom. As she walked away from him, she could feel his eyes watching her still, and a great wave of confusion washed over her. She had felt loved as he held her close, and that was just too weird. She didn't even know him. And it was impossible. Shaking her head, she rolled her eyes at her imagination running so fast and so far away from her. As if he could love her.

He was a healer, a teacher, famous in his world. She was just a silly school kid. He was just being nice to the poor little orphan girl he'd met. She was surprised when she felt disappointment at that thought, and realised she actually missed his arms being around her. That was strange. Maybe she needed to get out of there, because he was making her feel too many things that she just wasn't ready to feel.

When she got back out to the party room though she saw that Rhiannon was still laughing and chatting with Kevin, and it touched her that her friend was enjoying herself. She worked so hard, and so rarely had fun, that she knew she couldn't make her leave yet just because she felt intimidated. She deserved a little levity from her usual responsibilities. Certain that Rowan would be talking to someone else by now, she looked around the room. Maybe she could use this as a chance to practise talking to someone she didn't know, to let go of a little of her shyness. Before she took another step though, she felt Rowan's presence at her side.

"I figured we needed refills," he said, handing her a glass of iced tea. She was ridiculously happy that he still wanted to talk to her, relieved that he'd respected her request for a non-alcoholic drink, and felt really special. There were so many people there who were more interesting than her, more worldly, but he didn't leave her side all night. And she was surprised, and surprisingly sad, when Rhiannon came over to tell her that four hours had passed and they really had to get going. Rowan held her hand, begging her to stay longer, but she couldn't. Screwing up her courage, she leaned in and kissed him on the cheek, then turned and fled, catching up with her friend at the front door and racing up the street to the station.

As they got the train to Rhiannon's cousin's apartment, Carlie was quiet, her mind a whirl of emotions – longing, regret, hope, joy, confusion. Rhiannon didn't seem to notice though, regaling her with anecdotes from her night. Kevin had been lovely, and said so many funny things. She couldn't wait to write down the stories he'd told her about some of the Celtic deities. He'd introduced her to someone else she admired too, and she was going to get some of the books he'd recommended tomorrow morning, before they headed home.

Carlie nodded whenever she paused, trying to seem interested, but her attention was on the things Rowan had said, the way he'd made her feel – and the mystery of the dreams she had been having that involved him. He was definitely the guy she'd seen while they were casting the love spell, and she blushed as she remembered the dream she'd had about him just the night before, where she'd been lying in his arms in an amazing faerytale bed, held so close, feeling so safe and secure and loved.

In stark contrast, she spent a restless night on the cousin's lumpy couch, tossing and turning as she remembered the way Rowan had looked at her, and the beauty of the painting he'd created of her.

On the train journey home the next day she was still preoccupied, and not even the magic of Rose's enchanted Mabon ritual that night erased him entirely from her thoughts.

Chapter 8

Questioning the Gods

The next Tuesday night at their coven meeting, the girls decided to research more gods and goddesses, and they had a lot of fun together flicking through reference books, comparing the qualities and characteristics of different ones, taking note of the similarities and the differences. Inspired by Rhiannon's conversations with Kevin, they focused on Celtic deities to start with, and planned to explore other pantheons in the coming weeks.

Carlie adored all the stories they read about them, the melding of faerytale and history, gods and goddesses being reduced first to fae creatures and later to mere myth and legend, their power and influence waxing and waning in different eras. She also loved the way these deities were so much a part of the landscape here, inhabiting the sacred hills, blessed lakes and holy springs. And she was especially fascinated with how belief in them had changed over the centuries, and the resurgence of that belief in modern times.

She was still pondering it all when she got home from school the next day, and found Rose in the kitchen blending spices. Dropping her bag on the floor, she perched on a stool at the counter and started chopping the vegies Rose had out on the bench for dinner.

"Gran," she began hesitantly, as she carefully sliced into a plump home-grown pumpkin. "You know all the gods and goddesses you pray to, and who you invoke in your rituals?"

Rose nodded.

"Well, um, do you believe in them literally? I mean, are they real? Or is that a rude question? Sorry, if it is..." she trailed off, not really sure how to word what she wanted to know, or whether it was okay to ask about it at all.

Her grandma smiled. "It's okay to ask me Sweetheart, and any of the people at our group workings. But some people do take offence to anyone questioning their faith."

"Sorry Gran."

Rose smiled again, and shook her head. "It's not a bad thing to ask though, at least to me. I think it's really healthy, and really important, to ask questions. If you profess to believe in God, or many gods, you should be able to explain your beliefs, not be scared that they'll crumble to dust with a well-aimed question."

Carlie nodded gratefully, then raised an eyebrow quizzically.

"Sorry," Rose laughed. "I wasn't trying to change the subject. I do believe the Great Mother Goddess is real, that she exists on an etheric plane where we can communicate with her through ritual and dreams. She's kind and loving, and she's spoken to me many times in my life, and guides me in all that I do, in a way." She paused for a moment, choosing her words carefully before continuing.

"It's not that she tells me what to do, or takes the responsibility for my choices away from me in any way, but if I ask, and if I listen, and if I watch for signs, I can understand her messages, and I feel that she shares her wisdom with me from time to time."

Carlie looked thoughtful. "But if that's the case, if she's a wise and kind sort of mother figure, why would she let you lose your daughter, and your husband, especially so close together? How can you be okay with her doing that, taking them from you long before they should have died?"

"Sweetheart, I don't pretend to know the mind of the goddess. And believe me, I ranted and railed at her when I lost them, screamed challenges to her, threatened to turn my back on her. I think everyone of faith does at some point. But I can't accept that their deaths were her will, or her plan. Sometimes terrible things happen, things that go against the plan she has for us, and it's up to us to find the meaning in them. So eventually I stopped being angry at her, stopped turning away from her, and allowed myself to find comfort in her again."

Carlie nodded, reminded of the blue-clad woman she'd met on Winter Hill, who'd also said that sometimes bad things just happen, and there is no reason, no purpose. "But what about all the other ones, the gods and goddesses that you call on in rituals – Ceridwen and Bridie, and Persephone and Demeter?"

"Well, everyone has a different view on that, even amongst our group. To me they are all aspects of the Great Goddess, faces of her if you will. Rhiannon and Bridie are her in her aspect as the young maiden, and we can communicate with them on questions about love and friendship. Arianrhod and Modron are her in her guise as the mother, and we can work with them on issues of nurturing and fertility, be that of family, plans or dreams. And Ceridwen is her in her aspect as the crone, the wise old woman who guides us and challenges us," Rose explained.

"And because she is really without gender, she also comes to us in male form if we need that, as the sun god at Yule, or Cernunnos, the horned god, in spring. For pagan men especially it can help to have a masculine face of the divine, and for women too. The main difference between Christian and pagan religions, to me at least, is that they see the divine as male only, whereas for us it is balanced, it is both masculine and feminine."

Carlie considered this for a while. She thought about the gifts she and Rhiannon had been given, an athame and a chalice, which symbolised masculine, for the athame, and feminine, for the chalice, and the balance of the two.

Breaking in to her reverie, Rose continued. "Of course that's just my view – others believe they're all separate deities, part of a grand Celtic pantheon. Some also incorporate deities from other pantheons into their spiritual life and rituals, like the Egyptian deities Isis, Osiris and Ra, or those the Vikings worshipped, such as Thor, Loki and Freya, or Greek gods and goddesses like Zeus, Hera, Artemis, Ares and Athena, or their Roman counterparts Jupiter, Juno, Diana, Mars and Minerva. There are so many from around the world, so many you may connect with."

Carlie struggled to get her mind around it all. "But how can they all be right? I mean, doesn't each religion say that the others are wrong? And if that's the case, which one is correct?"

Rose smiled. "Ah Sweetheart, the age-old question. I guess each person has to decide for themselves, work out which is right for them, what speaks to them, discover who they can believe in."

"But how can I choose?" Carlie asked, confused by the idea that you could just decide to believe in one or the other, or both. "And what if there are none I can believe in?"

Her grandma came around the counter and hugged her. "It's wonderful that you're asking questions and challenging viewpoints, rather than just accepting what you're told, by me or anyone else. All I can suggest is that you experience as much as you can. You'll get to know lots of Celtic deities when you work with our group, and I know you and Rhiannon are doing research on your own, so maybe you could explore some of the other pantheons together, perhaps work with Isis or Freya or Artemis. And there are often workshops at the centre, everything from Buddhism and Shamanism to Druidry and Asatru, and you're welcome to take part in any of those that touch a chord with you, or just make you curious," Rose said.

"There are similarities as well as differences between all the world's religions, and I think you can choose to focus on either the things that join humanity together, or the things that tear them apart. That's where eclectic witchcraft comes in, people taking a little from each one. Even amongst Christianity there are those who just take the bits they like and believe in them, rather than having to accept every premise of the religion."

"But that's where I get confused," Carlie said, interrupting. "Don't you have to either believe in and accept it all, the good and the bad, or else reject it all? How can you just cherry pick the parts that you like and believe in those, and pretend that the rest, the crueller parts, don't exist?"

Rose paused for a moment to pour boiling water into the teapot, and the comforting scent of chamomile wafted over to Carlie.

"I can't speak for Christianity, but I know people who've been able to reconcile the fact that there are parts of it they don't believe, but other parts they do, and they are at peace with that," Rose said. "And for the pagan religions, or spiritual paths, I think that freedom to choose and experiment and create a belief system based on your actual experiences is part of the joy of it, tailoring it to your needs and wants. But maybe you'll feel more comfortable simply working with nature, with herbs and other forms of healing, without giving it a human face or attributing any form of deity to it. You could look into humanism too, if you're interested." She smiled as she poured the tea into two mugs and added a spoonful of honey, then handed one to her granddaughter. "What brought this on?"

"We were talking about deities at school today," Carlie replied. "The teacher said he's a Christian, so he believes in the 'one true god', as he put it, and then he told us that lots of people around here believe in gods and goddesses. He didn't exactly say it was wrong to do so, but he definitely didn't approve."

Her grandma sighed. "Your school is supposed to be secular, and teaching all different forms of spirituality, not just one, so I'm surprised at that. But I guess he's entitled to his beliefs, as we are to ours. Don't let him make you feel wrong in any way. Spirituality is a personal thing, and you need only follow your own heart and mind. There are many eclectic witches who take a little bit from Shamanism, a little bit from Buddhism, a little bit from Druidry, a little even from Christianity," Rose said.

Carlie was puzzled. "But don't they contradict each other? If you believe in one, don't you have to disbelieve the others?"

"Well, some forms of the Abrahamic religions definitely insist that all other forms of worship are wrong, and some have a mission to convert every unbeliever, but you'd be surprised by how many people do accept other strands of spirituality now. This is definitely a far more tolerant age, and it's a wonderful time to be able to learn about all sorts of different religions and spiritual practices.

"So all I can really suggest is to try to work out the things that bring you peace and contentment, that help you challenge yourself and your beliefs, and encourage you to grow and develop wisdom.

Seek the path that has meaning for you, even if it's an entirely new one," Rose said.

"Thanks Gran. It seems weird now that I never talked about this with Mum and Dad. I couldn't tell you what they believed, or even if they believed anything at all. But Dad did always say the Bible was the greatest work of fiction ever written."

Rose laughed. "I wish I could have met this Oliver."

"Me too," Carlie said, smiling sadly. "I went to church with my other nanna a few times when I was little, just at Christmas, but all I can remember is lots of singing, and a priest with a really droney voice. None of my friends were particularly religious either. There were a few kids at school who went to church and stuff, the Greek families mostly – I remember because their Easter sometimes fell at a different time to the western one."

Suddenly she felt embarrassed that she didn't know more about what her parents had believed. Or maybe they hadn't. "I guess Mum and Dad could have been atheists," she said hesitantly. "But they were good people, always helping our community, raising money for good causes, volunteering their time."

"Oh Sweetheart, I'm sure they were. How religious someone is has no bearing on how good or moral they are. A few of the girls in our ritual circle are atheists, and they're the kindest, sweetest and most caring people I know. I'd argue that they're actually *more* caring and 'moral' than many religious people. As long as you take responsibility for your actions, and do the best you can to live a good life, it doesn't matter whether you believe in a god, or gods, or nothing. Too many people use their religion as an excuse to *not* be the best people they can be, instead of using it to inspire themselves to be even better," Rose said.

She paused. "Now, I need to get these in the oven. Did you want to do your homework before dinner, or are you starving?"

Reluctantly Carlie picked up her bag and climbed the stairs to her room, to get her maths assignment done, before joining her grandma for dinner then having an early night. She had so much to ponder it was exhausting.

Chapter 9

Opening Her Heart

On Saturday morning Carlie woke up early. She felt restless, like there was something she had to do but she couldn't remember what it was. The tor kept popping into her mind, so she pulled on her jeans and a woollen jumper, laced up her sneakers and tiptoed downstairs. Grabbing an apple from the fruit bowl, she quietly let herself out the back door and walked through the garden, smiling at the scent of herbs in the air as the first streaks of colour lit up the dawn sky, and headed towards the hill.

Disappointment shot through her as she neared the top and saw that there was already someone sitting on the summit waiting for the sun to rise, just as she'd wanted to do. But her breath caught in her throat as he turned his head and looked straight at her. It was Rowan. A smile lit up her face, and her heart started beating really fast. Recognising her, he quickly stood up, eyes crinkling with joy, and walked towards her, pulling her close into a tight hug, then spinning her around in a circle. She tipped her head back and laughed as her feet left the ground and the sky spun around her.

"I can't believe you're here," she whispered breathlessly when he finally set her down. She felt giddy from the spinning, and giddy with joy. "I wasn't sure I'd ever see you again," she admitted.

"And it's such an amazing coincidence. I wasn't planning to come up here today – I was just going to sleep in for a while, hang out with my grandma, then make a start on my next assignment before I meet up with Rhiannon this afternoon."

He touched her cheek, and her heart flip-flopped in her chest. "You came because I called you," he said simply.

She raised her eyebrows questioningly.

"I was sitting up here, sending a message to you, my heart to yours, asking you to come up and meet me. Our hearts are obviously attuned to each other," he explained.

Blushing, she shook her head. "How can that be?" she asked him. "We barely know each other." But her voice quavered with hope.

"Surely you felt it too Carlie," he said, voice low and husky. "We have something special. I knew the first moment I saw you – it was like we were meant to be together."

She stared at him in wonder. "How could you be meant to be with me? Surely there's someone really special out there for you, someone more important than me," she said, flustered.

Shaking his head, he drew her close, into the circle of his arms, where she felt the comfort and safety she'd been craving all over again. It felt so familiar, maybe because she'd dreamed it so often. He kissed her forehead, making her knees tremble, then drew her down onto the grass next to him, his arm around her shoulders as they gazed at the spot where the sun would soon rise.

"You *are* important Carlie," he whispered, lips in her hair. "You *are* special. Can't you feel our connection?"

She turned to him, eyes shining with joy. "Yes, I feel it," she admitted. "I just can't believe that you could feel that way about me."

He stroked her hair, then stiffened as a dog bounded up to them and they saw someone climbing the hill, just as the sun burst above the horizon in all its golden finery. He stood up, then took her hand and pulled her to her feet. "Come on, why don't you show me your town?" he asked her.

Smiling, she led him down the steep side of the hill, avoiding the newcomer, and they spent the morning together wandering through the country lanes, talking easily. Carlie was surprised by just how comfortable she felt with him, but she figured that, because she'd poured out her heart to him at the festival, and he'd sensed some of her turmoil psychically, she didn't have to present a happy front or be constantly aware of keeping her barriers up.

That's what had been so exhausting at school, feeling every moment that she had to protect others from her grief, her pain, to ensure they weren't uncomfortable around her or unfairly burdened. That's why she was always monitoring her words before she spoke, conscious of how she was coming across. It was only with Rhiannon, and now it seemed with Rowan, that she felt this amazing sense of freedom. It was so wonderful to be able to say the first thing that crossed her mind, to share her fears when he asked.

"Oh Carlie, don't ever think you're a burden, to anyone," he said, and she smiled gratefully.

As the day progressed she was so touched that he shared things with her too, things he didn't share with anyone, according to Rhiannon. He said he didn't want to dwell on the sad parts of his life, but he'd already told her that his dad had died when he was twelve, and today he confided in her that his father had left him and his mother when he was little, running off to be with a much younger woman, so he hadn't had much of a relationship with him even while he was alive. There was bitterness and anger in his voice, so she didn't press for details, but she felt honoured that he'd shared that much with her.

Changing the subject, he asked her what she thought about her new life in this country, then told her that he lived in a small town just a half hour drive from her village, and that while he sometimes missed the city, he loved being so close to nature. Excitement bubbled inside her when he revealed where he lived – she'd imagined that he was based in London, which was four hours away.

Grinning, he took her hand again. "I know, it's awesome isn't it. I think it's meant to be, us meeting last week, and living so close to each other." She could barely breathe, overwhelmed that he seemed to like her as much as she liked him, and appeared to want to see her again as much as she did too.

Later they wandered back to where he'd parked his car, and he pulled out a picnic basket and blanket. They walked hand in hand along an oak-lined path to one of his favourite places, a small meadow on the edge of a stream, the bank shaded by two weeping willow trees growing close together. She laughed in delight. She'd never been here before, and it was beautiful.

The gentle sound of the running water was so peaceful and soothing to the soul, and when they sat on the bank, backs to the solid, nurturing strength of the trees, she let out a sigh of joy and relief, a breath she hadn't known she'd been holding. She turned to him, eyes soft, a smile lighting up her face.

He opened the basket and started feeding her autumn berries and wedges of cheese with freshly baked bread. Before he ate anything he crumbled up a cookie and placed it carefully on the ground, muttering what sounded like a prayer as he did so, then followed it with a splash of juice. It touched her deeply that he also left a libation to the god and goddess, and she felt like she'd known him forever, and that they would never run out of conversation.

He regaled her with stories about some of the workshops he'd run and the people he'd taught, some funny, some touching, then allowed her in to small glimmers of his past and his complicated family.

Feeling more at ease, she told him about her life back home in Sydney – not that it was her home any more – and opened up to him about her hopes and dreams. She shared what she wanted to do with her future, a bit about school, and about Rhiannon, and a little of her sadness and guilt over her childhood best friend, who she felt so far away from, not just geographically, but also emotionally.

He was so kind and concerned, hanging on every word, really listening to what she said, and responding with practical advice and sweet sentiments. When she got teary as she recalled the last time she'd been with her parents, he drew her into his arms and held her close. A shiver ran through her as emotion flooded her. She'd never felt so safe, so protected, so loved, but she shook her head, knowing she shouldn't jump ahead of herself. He was a teacher, a healer, no doubt he knew how to make people feel comforted, and loved. As if he could love her!

But his empathy made her realise she was falling head over heels for him. A part of her panicked, and wanted to run. Another part insisted that she not be so naive as to think he could feel anything for her. And a third part tried to shut out her doubts and self-criticism, and simply enjoy the feeling of being so nurtured and understood, even if this was the only moment they ever had.

Focusing on the latter, she took a deep breath, and with a great effort her tears finally stopped, and she began to feel like she had her emotions under control again. But at that exact moment, he slowly lifted her chin and kissed her gently on the lips, and all her composure slipped away as she let herself dive down into the sensation.

His kiss was so soft, so sweet, that she sensed herself dissolving into him, felt her soul merging with his. She knew it sounded sappy, and her sceptical side was rolling its eyes at her, but she could feel their energies dancing together, entwining as they connected on the deepest level she could imagine. Then, after what seemed like forever – or may have been just a single heartbeat – he gently pulled away.

"I hope that was okay," he whispered. "I've been wanting to kiss you since the moment I saw you this morning."

Blushing, she tried to calm her racing heart enough to speak. "It was more than okay," she said shyly. "I, um, I loved it."

Slowly they leaned back in and melted into each other again. Time ceased to exist as she lost herself in the sensation of their lips connecting, and his arms tightening around her. They finally broke apart when they heard the sound of a dog barking and a human whistling, and she glanced down at her watch.

"Oh my god, I was supposed to be at Rhiannon's two hours ago," she said, panicked. But it fell away as soon as she gazed into his eyes again. Reluctantly she looked away, trying to steel herself for their parting. "Thank you for bringing me here," she said with a shy smile. "It's so peaceful, like we're in our own little world."

He took her hand, and kissed it gently. "I wish we could stay here always, just the two of us – away from everyone, from friends and family and school and work." Touched, she nodded her agreement, then finally plucked up the courage to ask if she'd ever see him again.

"Oh Carlie my sweet, of course!" he laughed. "Wild horses couldn't keep me away from you."

Chapter 10

Spilling Her Secret

Tentatively she knocked on Rhiannon's door, anxiety at being so late warring with the thrill of euphoria as she replayed every moment she'd shared with Rowan since their dawn meeting.

"Oh thank goddess! Are you okay?" Rhiannon asked, worry in her voice as she opened the door and ushered her inside.

Carlie nodded, still trying to get her breath back after her mad dash from the corner where she'd regretfully said goodbye to Rowan. "I'm so sorry I'm late Rhi, but the most amazing thing happened this morning. You'll never guess who I..."

She trailed off as they walked into the kitchen and Rhiannon's dad turned and said hello. After a hurried greeting while her friend made them cups of tea, the two girls raced upstairs to the privacy of Rhiannon's bedroom. Carlie curled up in the window seat, hands wrapped around her mug, eyes shining.

"So spill!" Rhiannon urged as she sprawled across her bed, tea in one hand, biscuit in the other.

"Well, I woke up really early this morning, like, insanely early, with this desperate urge to get up and climb the tor," she began, but broke off as her friend raised one eyebrow, disbelief etched across her face. "I know! I hate getting up early, especially on weekends. And the sun hadn't even risen, so you can imagine my shock that I was contemplating walking up the hill in the near-dark," she grinned.

"But I decided to follow my intuition, or whatever it was, and went – and there was already someone sitting at the top."

Pausing, she gazed at her friend, unable to stop the smile spreading across her face at the signs of her impatience, as well as the news she was holding so close to her heart but wanting so badly to share.

"It was Rowan," she finally blurted out.

"Rowan Rowan? Rowan from the festival? Tall, dreamy eyes, gorgeous and amazing Rowan?"

Carlie nodded.

"And you've been with him since before dawn?" she shrieked. "What–? Where–? How?"

A blush stained Carlie's cheeks as she nodded again. "It was amazing. He was amazing. I apologised for interrupting him –"

"Oh honey, you have to stop apologising for everything."

Carlie nodded impatiently. "I know, but… he said he'd summoned me, that that was why I'd felt I had to go up there so early. And we sat there for ages, just talking…" She drifted off, a faraway look in her eyes and her mind clearly elsewhere.

When Rhiannon offered her the plate of cookies she jolted back into the present, and saw that her friend's eyes were sparkling with excitement too, and curiosity. "What does that mean?" she begged.

"He said he'd been thinking about me all week, couldn't get me out of his mind, and he knew he had to see me."

"But how did he know where to find you?" Rhiannon asked, a touch of suspicion creeping into her voice.

"He didn't. He knew which village I lived in – you told him, remember? – but that was all. That's why he had to summon me. And so I went to him. And after we'd talked for a while, he put his arm around me and held me close as we watched the sun rise."

Rhiannon gasped, as excited as her friend now.

"Then someone else walked up, which kind of broke the moment, so we left and wandered around town, just talking and laughing, getting to know each other. He's lovely. And I felt so comfortable with him – I could tell him things I've only ever told you before, and he shared things about his life too. About his father, who left him and his mother when he was little. And then he pulled out a picnic basket from his car and took me to the most gorgeous place, on the bank of a stream, and we sat there and ate and talked, and talked and ate, and oh, he's so lovely!"

She pressed on, telling an enraptured Rhiannon every sight, sound, word and glance she could recall, voice full of excitement and joy and wonder, words tumbling over each other as she tried to express everything in her heart.

Finally Rhiannon held up her hand. "What aren't you telling me?" she asked, eyes narrowing with mock suspicion.

Carlie tried to look innocent. "What do you mean?"

"I know you're holding something back. Out with it!"

Carlie blushed. "Um, he kissed me."

Rhiannon squealed. "What was it like?"

"It was really lovely," Carlie said, her blush deepening. "I really did go weak at the knees, as cliched as that sounds," she offered shyly. "But shouldn't we start our assignment?"

Her friend laughed. "Okay Missy, I'll let you off for now, but when are you going to see him again?"

"I'm meeting him tomorrow morning. But would you mind if I told Gran that I'm hanging out with you if she asks me? It's just, well, I thought maybe I should wait and see if anything comes of it before I tell her about him. I mean, we still don't know each other that well, me and Rose, and…"

Rhiannon cut her off. "That's a good idea. There's no point upsetting her with the knowledge that you're dating a much older shaman guru guy, just like your mum."

Carlie paled. "Oh god, do you think…"

"I'm teasing," Rhiannon said with a grin. "Wait and see what happens before you tell anyone else — and that's good advice no matter who the guy is. So, tomorrow I'm getting the bus over to the library at Smithfield, and your grandma will never know you weren't with me. But only tell her if she asks — the less lies we tell, the easier it will be. And you'll owe me one!" she said, only half joking.

Carlie nodded, then turned to pick up her book.

"Wow, Rowan kissed you!" Rhiannon said with a grin. Carlie threw a pillow at her, then turned back to their assignment.

Chapter 11

Falling

The next few weeks passed in a blur of stolen moments. Carlie was flat out with homework, her Tuesday night meetings with Rhiannon and the full and new moon rituals at Rose's healing centre, while Rowan had to travel some of the weekend days to teach workshops, and had commitments with students several week nights. But on a few afternoons he was able to drive over and meet her after she finished school, and they went and sat by the stream at their special place, talking, catching up on their weeks, gazing at the waning moon overhead, and each time spending just a little bit longer kissing each other goodbye.

And the previous weekend Rose had asked her to catch the bus over to Smithfield, which happened to be where Rowan lived, to pick up another herb order for her, so Carlie had managed to plan a lunch date with him, and they'd loved walking around the medieval style town, huddling in a cosy tea shop after they got caught in the rain, shivering against each other as their clothes dried out, the hot tea warmed them, and the heat between them increased a little more.

She was a bit scared at just how much she missed him when they were apart, and how intensely her feelings for him kept growing, but she still didn't really know what was happening between them, so she tried not to say too much to Rhiannon, in case it came to nothing. But it was getting harder and harder not to mention him, when every time they managed to see each other she felt herself falling deeper under his spell.

Finally this Sunday they would have a whole day to spend together – Rowan had no teaching commitments, and her grandmother was running an all-day workshop and wouldn't be around. The day couldn't come fast enough for Carlie, and when it finally dawned she leaped out of bed, hurriedly showered and dressed, then raced downstairs for a quick breakfast. Rose was leaving for the shop soon to get set up, and wouldn't be home until later that evening. Carlie waited impatiently for her to go, nervous that the knock on the door would come before her grandma had left. But finally she hugged her goodbye, told her to have dinner without her as she'd probably be late, and headed out the door. Carlie sighed with relief.

Sipping a cup of tea, she stood at the back door, excitement warring with nervousness within her. She'd been sad that she hadn't been able to join Rowan at his new moon ritual last Sunday night, but they'd met up after school three times this week, Monday, Wednesday and Thursday. She couldn't get out of her Tuesday night coven meeting with Rhiannon, and even though she was desperate to see Rowan, she didn't want to let her friend down, or be one of those girls who sacrificed friendship for boys. She'd made a commitment to Rhiannon, and to herself, to dedicate time to their magical work, and she wanted to be there. Of course that didn't mean she had to be as patient as usual, or that she stopped wishing every other minute that she was with Rowan, so the night had felt much longer than usual.

And somewhat regretfully, she'd promised to spend the Friday night with Rose, grinding up herbs, packaging up little spell bags for the shop, grabbing a quick dinner at their favourite cafe to catch up on their week, then cooking a large vegie and tofu lasagne and a banana cake together for the workshop she was teaching today.

But now, finally, they had a whole day to themselves, and she couldn't wait. When she heard the knock on the door, she flew to the front of the house, heart beating wildly, and wrenched it open. She grinned as she saw him standing there, a bouquet of daisies in one hand. He scooped her up in his arms and held her tight as he kissed her, making her giggle and blush, and drag him inside before anyone saw them. "Come in," she begged, and he handed her the flowers and followed her inside.

Filled with joy, she led him through the lounge room and out to the kitchen, which was so warm and cosy even on this chilly late autumn day. Luther stared up at Rowan from his perch on the counter, eyes wary. Carlie laughed. "Come on Luther, come and say hello to Rowan." The black cat gazed at her for a moment, then jumped down to the floor and sauntered out the back door. "Sorry," she said, embarrassed, but Rowan just shrugged.

"Maybe he's jealous. He probably thought he was the only guy in your life," he grinned, his eyes crinkling in that way she loved.

She giggled, then, suddenly shy again, walked over and put on the kettle. "Tea?" she asked, to give herself something to do.

When he nodded, she pulled out the teapot, cups and saucers and a jar of herbs, while he looked out the window at Rose's garden. "Your grandmother really is a kitchen witch, isn't she," he stated. Her eyes widened, and she was about to leap to her grandma's defence, but he held up his hands in a peace-making gesture.

"Relax, it's a compliment. Her garden is beautiful," he said, and this time she heard the admiration, rather than the imagined censure, in his voice. "My dad healed with herbs too, and I've been studying them for a long time. It's a good thing to be a kitchen witch," he insisted, then grinned as he walked over towards her. "I like witches," he added, voice teasing, as he kissed her on the forehead.

He leaned across to the counter next to her and lifted up the jar of herbs. He unscrewed the lid and inhaled deeply, then his lips widened in a sexy smile. "Jasmine huh. Are you trying to make me fall in love with you Miss Carlie?" he asked.

"No, of course not!" she retorted, blushing furiously, voice a little shaky. "It's just Gran's newest blend, to bring a bit of summer to the cold months."

He pulled her close, hands on her shoulders as he peered down at her, holding her gaze intently. "Hey, relax, I'm just teasing you. Besides, you don't have to cast a spell on me to make me love you."

She stared at him, breath caught, frozen. Had he just said what she thought he'd said?

"Carlie, I love you," he whispered, staring into her eyes, into her very soul. He drew her even closer and leaned down, hands strong on her shoulders as he gently pressed his lips to hers. She was trembling, so relieved that his hands on her shoulders were keeping her from falling. Falling. It was literal and metaphorical. Falling over, falling under, falling for him. Her head spun as she tried to take in that he loved her. A wave of pure joy swept over her, and she felt butterflies in her tummy. He loved her. He wanted to kiss her. He was kissing her.

The whistling of the kettle drew her back from the clouds with a thump, and she blushed as she pulled away and turned the stove off, then lifted the heavy kettle and poured the steaming water onto the herbs in the teapot. She was too scared to look at him, suddenly terrified that she wasn't a good kisser, that he'd changed his mind, that he regretted telling her that he loved her, or that it was all a practical joke and he was just laughing at her.

She felt him step towards her and gently turn her to him. Softly he stroked her cheek, his eyes bright with emotion. "You're so beautiful Carlie," he whispered to her. "Come here."

And suddenly she was in his arms again, held close against his heart, his hands in her hair and his lips on her forehead, her cheeks, and finally her mouth. Time stood still as she fell into him, felt her heart open wider, and her soul leap up to meet his.

Time stopped, and she wasn't sure how long they stood there, her back against the kitchen counter, his arms holding her tight, their lips joined. Gentle. She felt so protected, as though nothing could ever hurt her, nothing could ever sadden her. As that thought registered, she froze. Sensing her pulling away, Rowan released her and stepped back, giving her space. Space she'd wanted, but the moment she had it she craved the closeness again. What was wrong with her? She couldn't even think straight. Being held by him was intoxicating, brain jumbling. She tried to focus again.

"Are you okay Carlie?" he asked, his voice soft, sweet.

She nodded, but he could see the fear in her eyes. "Hey, talk to me," he said, gently raising her chin so that he could look right at her, right into her eyes. The love on his face touched her heart, and she smiled wanly.

"I'm sorry, I just… for a minute there I…" she broke off, but he nodded for her to go on. She blushed. "I just felt so safe in your arms," she whispered. "For a moment I felt so happy that I forgot how much I've lost. I forgot my grief, my anger…"

He poured her a cup of tea and handed it to her. She shivered as his fingers brushed against hers, her tummy tightening as the butterfly sensation returned.

"Baby, it's okay to feel happiness, to feel love. You can't punish yourself for what happened to your parents. And it doesn't mean you've forgotten them, or you love them any less. They'll always be a part of you. But I can't believe that they'd want you to suffer, that they'd want you to cut yourself off from joy, or from love."

She shook her head. "I know, but it's just…" she trailed off again, back into silence.

"You have no reason to feel guilty, I promise you that. And I understand how you feel, I really do," he said gently. Then, putting down their cups, he took her hand. "How about we go for a walk, maybe climb Summer Hill, then we can come back here and you can give me the tour?"

She smiled gratefully. Part of her had been dreading having to show him her room, the intimacy of that a little too much for her right now. She picked up her keys from the kitchen bench and stuck her wallet in her pocket, and they walked out the back door and climbed the hill. Once out of the house and striding along the back lane together she felt the tension lift, and they spent the next few hours sitting in the autumn sunshine, chatting, sharing more about their lives, and their hopes and dreams for the future.

Shyly she told him more about her desire to be a grief counsellor or social worker when she left school, and he was so encouraging, leaving her feeling so touched that he had such faith in her.

Afterwards they wandered into town to grab some lunch, then made their way back to the cottage, where they drank more tea, and Luther finally came over and joined them – and allowed Rowan to pat him for a while.

"Phew," he said, laughing. "I was worried he was going to hate me forever, and try to convince you not to like me either."

Carlie grinned. "Don't be silly, no one could change my mind about how I feel about you," she admitted, blushing a little. "And cats can't talk anyway!"

A serious expression slid across his face as he gazed at her. "Are you sure about that?" he asked, and she was surprised that there was no note of teasing in his voice. Then again, she certainly had wondered a few times over the last three months if Luther was communicating with her in some way.

"I think this cat has magic, and could do anything it wanted to," Rowan continued. "And he's definitely on your side. He won't let anyone hurt you, won't even let them get close enough to you to try." She stared at him, confused. Was he communicating with Luther now? "I love that about him, don't get me wrong!" he added quickly, and leaned down and stroked Luther's head. The cat stared up at him, green eyes still slightly wary, but seemingly content for now.

"It makes me happy to know that you have an animal ally here, someone watching over you," Rowan said, as he drank the rest of his tea. He put the cup down gently, then stood up and took her hand. "So, are you going to show me around?" he asked, a cheeky smile replacing his more serious expression.

Nodding despite her nervousness, she took a deep breath, then led him through to the lounge room, pointing out the books she'd been reading, the pots of basil in the window box – "Ah, for harmony in the home," he said cheerfully – and the vividly coloured crystals hanging from the lamp shade.

"That's Gran's room through there," she said, pointing to her door, "and the main bathroom is in here. My room is upstairs," she added, shy again. Rowan pulled her in close.

"You don't have to show me, I don't want to make you anxious or scared," he said softly. His understanding touched her, and swallowing down her doubts, she took his hand again and led him upstairs.

"That was my mum's bedroom," she whispered, pointing quickly to the room at the front of the house, then turning her back on it. She couldn't think about that right now.

"And my room is in here. Sorry about the mess," she added, although she'd tidied up last night, and it looked fine. She led him inside, leaving the door open, and walked across to the window, staring out at the silhouette of the sacred hill that had so enchanted her the first night she'd come in here. So much had happened since then, it hurt her head to think too hard about it. She'd become close to her grandmother, the woman she'd feared was a monster, she'd made a dear friend who was helping her cope with her loss, and now…

Rowan's hand was gentle on her shoulder as he turned her around and pulled her into his arms. Resting his chin on the top of her head, he held her close. "And now you've met a man who loves you deeply," he whispered. Tears sparkled on her lashes, but they were happy tears, and her heart melted as she gazed up and saw the love in his eyes. She couldn't believe he could feel that for her, but she felt the truth of it as his lips lowered to hers, and hers rose up to meet them.

The world stopped turning as they kissed. She could feel the energy of the brooding tor over her shoulder, sending her strength to anchor her in the room, to keep her from floating away. They sat on her bed for a while, talking, before he leaned in and started kissing her again.

They both jumped, and sprang apart, when Luther leaped up onto the bed, then slowly relaxed back into each other as they realised it was just the cat. But when Luther placed his paw on Rowan's leg, he turned towards him, gazing deep into the feline's eyes before nodding regretfully. Then he took Carlie's hand and leaned over and kissed it, – like that first day when they'd met – his lips gentle, respectful.

He smiled up at her. "I'm sorry my love, but I have to go. Your grandmother is on her way home, and she's not ready yet to meet me, or know how deeply our feelings run."

Carlie stared at him, puzzled. How could he have any inkling about that? "What… How do you know?" she asked.

Cupping her face in his hands, he leaned in to kiss her once more, then reluctantly got to his feet.

"I'll come back on Wednesday, meet you after school?" he asked, pulling her up to stand next to him. "Tuesday is your night with Rhiannon, right?"

Vaguely she nodded, still confused. What was going on? How did he know? Had Luther somehow told him that Rose was on her way back? That was crazy, surely.

Leading her back downstairs, Rowan picked up his jacket from the kitchen table, and drew her into his arms again. Her head was spinning, and it didn't stop when they kissed again, it just spun even faster. They stood together, clinging to each other, full of yearning and regret, until he broke away from her, raced over to the sink with his cup and washed it, dried it, then put it away in the cupboard.

"I love you Carlie, so much," he whispered, as he held her tight one last time. "And I'll be dreaming of you every night until I see you again," he promised. And then he was gone, out the kitchen door and through the garden and the back gate, at the exact moment she heard the key turn in the front door. Carlie looked down at Luther in shock, but his gaze was as serene and unfathomable as ever.

Rattled, she put the kettle on and called out a greeting to her grandma. Rose breezed into the kitchen, then paused, eyes sweeping the room before she focused on Carlie. "Was someone else here today?" she asked sharply.

Carlie shook her head. "No, why?" she replied quickly, then stumbled on before she lost her nerve. "Would you like a cup of tea? I just came down to make one before finishing the rest of my homework," she said, heart racing as she told the little white lie. What had happened to her, that she could lie so easily to her grandma?

But Rose smiled. "That would be lovely, thank you Sweetheart. It was quite a day today – wonderful, but I must admit that I'm kind of glad it's over. I think it will be an early night for me tonight," she added, yawning, before she started to unpack the dishes from the lunch they'd made and refill the half empty herb jars she'd brought home with her. Carlie quickly prepared the tea, then escaped back upstairs to her room. She pulled out her school books, just in case

Rose came up to check on her, but then just sat on her bed, staring out the window, eyes unseeing as her mind whirred and her heart sighed.

That had been weird. She turned as Luther jumped up on the bed and made his way into her lap.

Stroking his head, she wished again that he could talk, and smiled as she remembered his eventual friendliness to Rowan.

Rowan. Oh goddess, he'd said that he loved her. It couldn't be true though, surely. That was crazy! She was reluctantly prepared to concede that she was head over heels in love with him, but how could he love her? She wasn't special enough for him, smart enough, pretty enough – just *enough* in general. Luther put his paw on her arm, breaking her train of thought, and she gazed at him, grateful for the distraction. Then she opened her books with a sigh – she figured she really should start doing her homework, since it was due tomorrow and she hadn't done a single bit of it.

It took her twice as long as it should have though, because she kept pausing, remembering another perfect moment from their day, something he'd said, the way he'd gently stroked her cheek, the way he'd kissed her and sworn his love. And when she finally got to bed and drifted off to sleep, her dreams were full of him, and Luther's green, all-knowing eyes.

Chapter 12

Facing Her Demons

Tray balanced precariously in one hand and school books in the other, Carlie slowly made her way over to their usual cafeteria table. Rhiannon closed the notebook she'd been scribbling in and glanced up sharply.

"What's wrong? You look like you've seen a ghost," she said, then winced. They'd both love to see the ghosts of their lost parents, so it wasn't an apt analogy. "Well, you look pale and worried," she clarified.

Carlie smiled wanly as she sat down and picked listlessly at her salad. "Well, I haven't really told you how often I've seen Rowan in the last few weeks," she began shyly. "Not because I didn't want to tell you, but I just wasn't sure what was happening, and I would have been too embarrassed if it all came to nothing."

Rhiannon laughed. "Don't worry, I've managed to kind of piece it all together. The days you loitered after school, when he came to meet you – I had to stay back to get some history notes one afternoon, and when I finally left I saw you walking along the road by the tor together, hand in hand," she grinned.

"And last Saturday when you got the bus over to Smithfield for the day to run Rose's errands, I ended up finishing with Brodie early and going over there too – I was hoping I could catch up with you and we could go shopping together, or see a movie or something – until I almost walked in on you both in the tea shop."

"Why didn't you come in and say hello?" Carlie asked her friend, genuinely puzzled.

Her friend smiled. "You looked like you didn't want to be disturbed, shall we say," Rhiannon replied, wiggling her eyebrows suggestively.

Carlie blushed. "Well, I'm sorry I didn't tell you – I was dying to, you have no idea. But it doesn't matter now anyway. I just, I can't see him again," she muttered.

Rhiannon touched her hand, offering comfort and sympathy. "What do you mean?" she asked, concern making her words sharp. "I can tell how much you like him. What did he do?"

"Nothing," her friend sighed, then grimaced. "Well, he said he loves me," she finally whispered, inexplicable pain colouring her words, anguish clear.

Rhiannon was confused. "But that's good isn't it? I mean, you love him, right?" she trailed off.

Her friend nodded sadly.

"So shouldn't you be happy? That's really exciting, surely?" She chose her words carefully, but her expression revealed her confusion.

Tears started pouring down Carlie's face. "But that's just it," she sobbed. "He can't love me. How could he?"

Rhiannon stared at her friend, aghast. "I don't understand," she said, standing up and moving around the table until she was kneeling in front of her friend. "Why can't he love you?"

"Because I'm no one. He's so amazing, so brilliant, so powerful. I'm nothing next to him," she choked out.

"Oh Carlie, that's not true," Rhiannon said, heart aching at her obvious pain. "You're amazing too. You're kind and sweet and clever, and you've endured more than most people do in a lifetime, and can still smile, still love."

Carlie shook her head. "You don't understand. He can't love me, because I'm nothing. I'm a fraud. He needs someone clever, sparkling, beautiful – someone else, someone better than me. He couldn't possibly love me, not really."

"But he says that he does love you," Rhiannon insisted, voice carefully calm. "Why would he lie about that? Why can't you accept what he says?"

Carlie took a jagged breath, and her words sounded as though they were being wrenched from inside the deepest, most broken parts of her soul. "He can't love me because that would mean I was worth loving, that I was special," she said flatly. "And I'm not."

Her voice was so matter-of-fact that it broke Rhiannon's heart. She stood up, then fell down into the chair next to her friend and pulled her close into a hug. After a while she released her and took her face in her hands, holding it steady, as she stared into her eyes.

"Now you listen to me Carlie Parker," she said, voice stern but face soft. "You are special. And you are absolutely worthy of love. I adore you, and you mean the world to Rose. And there's no reason on earth that Rowan couldn't love you too. Where is this coming from?" she demanded.

But Carlie was sobbing too hard to respond. Rhiannon let her cry for a little while longer, patting her shoulder soothingly, then she stood up and took her hand. "Come on, let's get out of here for a while," she said, pulling her to her feet. She led her outside, then across the sports field and into the small wooded area behind the school. The cafeteria really wasn't the place for such a distressed and emotional conversation.

Finally Rhiannon paused, sat down on a fallen tree trunk and pulled Carlie down beside her. "So how did you leave it after he told you this? When are you seeing him next? Or did you already dump him?" she asked, voice surprisingly harsh.

"He wants to take me out on Wednesday night, for a proper romantic date," Carlie sighed, fingers making air quotes around proper and romantic. "He said he wants to pick me up after school, drive over to Smithfield to see a movie, then go to some special new restaurant that's just opened…"

"Ooh, I read about that one, that would be amazing!"

Carlie shrugged. "But how can I go? I'm a fraud. I'm not worthy of him. And I don't feel right about telling Rose just yet — older boyfriend, shamanic healer, has a car — and I can't just be out that late without telling her where I'll be," she said, trailing off, voice a mixture of hope and hesitance.

Rhiannon thought fast. "Okay, how's this? You can tell Rose we've changed our coven night for this week, and you'll be at my place on Wednesday night. Dad and Brodie are going up to London for an orthodontist appointment and will be staying over, so they won't know either way."

Carlie smiled hopefully, and Rhiannon realised just how much her friend was falling for the guy, which touched her deeply. She'd had such a dreadful time lately, surely she was due a little happiness.

"I hate to lie, and I'm really terrible at it, so don't make this a regular occurrence, okay?" she warned, face mock stern. "But I think the guy deserves a chance. If he tells you that he loves you, then I believe him. He wouldn't say it otherwise, I promise you. And PS, you obviously really like him, so give yourself a chance too, okay?"

Carlie nodded, overwhelmed with gratitude for her friend.

"And tomorrow night, our real Tuesday night coven time? You will be at home doing your own ritual of self-love and self-acceptance, all right? And I'll be testing you on Wednesday about it, and checking your notes, so don't think you'll get away with skipping it!" she said.

Her sternness soon dissolved into laughter, and Carlie finally managed a real smile.

"Now we really should get back," Rhiannon said, then grinned at Carlie. "You don't want to get detention after school on Wednesday!"

Carlie laughed, and shyly hugged her friend. "Thanks Rhi, for being so sweet," she said. And was surprised to find that all of a sudden she couldn't wait for her date with Rowan.

Chapter 13

Dear Diary...

In the end she never did do her homework from Rhiannon, her ritual of self-love, because when she got home from school that day there was a large parcel with lots of Australian postage stamps on it sitting at the front door, addressed in Sandy's curly writing. Excitedly she scooped it up, raced inside and up the stairs to her room, then threw herself down on the bed. Ripping open the package, she found some clothes she'd never seen before, a few books and what looked like a jewellery box, which she impatiently cast aside as she searched for a note from Sandy.

When she found it she was frustrated by its lack of information, but then she pulled out the last object in the box, a small package wrapped in layers and layers of tissue paper and surrounded with metres of ribbon tied securely with a series of knots. An unsealed envelope was slipped under the ribbons. Curiously she slid it open, and pulled the card out.

A post-it note was stuck to the front.

Dear Carlie,
I guess this is for you. I haven't opened it, so I have no idea what it is, and I pray I'm not causing you more pain by sending it. Know you can always call me if you need to talk.
Love, Sandy xx

Slowly, tentatively, she opened the card.

Dear Future Daughter,
I don't know whether you exist or ever will, but if you do, I want you to have this. I almost burned it, in a ritual of cleansing and closing of chapters, and who knows, perhaps I still might. But it is a cautionary tale of sorts for any young woman, and if you can take anything from this, it will have been worth me living through it...
Tomorrow I marry the man I love, and step from my past into my future. And so I am locking this book away, with a few other things from my former life. I am grateful that it all led me here, but I no longer need the reminders of the things that I regret...

Carlie stared at the package. She desperately wanted to open it, but she was scared. When she'd laid her hand on it she'd felt a wave of sadness wash over her, and she wasn't sure she could survive drowning in the emotions of her mother, who she already missed so much. Curiosity finally won out though, and she cut through the ribbons and tore it open. A purple journal lay amongst the lashings of wrapping. She gently traced the cover with her finger, then, heart in mouth, turned to the first page.

Dear Diary, I'm lonely, won't you send someone to hold me...

That's how I started off my last journal, but this one will begin with...

THANK YOU! I've found the person I was wishing for, and although I can't believe he wants to be with me, apparently it's true! His name is Andre, and he's a healer and a psychic and all kinds of amazing things. And he's gorgeous too, long dark wavy hair, deep brown eyes I could drown in, and such a kind and gentle face. He's so special – people kind of hero worship him, which is why it's been so hard for me to believe he could care about me, because next to him I'm nothing.

I met him in a tarot class – he's the teacher, and he is so incredible. I've been going to his class every week (along with Mike – he wouldn't let me go on my own, sigh), and the first few weeks I was too intimidated and in awe of him to say much at all, but slowly I got more comfortable, and started chatting to him a little bit.

Then last week he asked me to help him set up for the next part of the class in our break, and oh my goddess, at one point his hand brushed against mine and I got goosebumps. And when I looked up at him, he was staring right at me! I blushed of course, and he laughed, and told me I was beautiful. I could barely breathe for a minute, but then I figured he must say that to all the girls – we're all a bit in love with him, and while I desperately wanted to think he meant something by it, I knew it was just wishful thinking.

Except maybe it wasn't, because tonight… I can still barely believe it! He asked me if I could stay back to help him with something. Mike said I couldn't, because he was driving me, but Andre dismissed that right away, and said he'd take me home! Mike didn't want to leave me alone with him, I know that, but he finally did. And then we just sat there and talked – he hadn't actually wanted me to help with anything, he said he just wanted to get to know me better. So we talked and talked, kind of personal stuff, then he drove me home. I didn't want to go inside, and he didn't want to leave – and then he kissed me! And it was amazing! It really did take my breath away ☺

Mike and I have kissed before, but compared to this, that was just two fumbling teenage friends locking lips to see what it was like. This was different – full of passion and love and longing. I could have stayed with him all night, just sitting there in the car with him, kissing, leaning into each other. But then I saw the porch light go on, and our front door opening, so I had to jump out and hurry inside. Mum asked about Mike (of course, she loves him!), but I said he'd had to leave early so Andre had offered to bring me home. Then I raced upstairs before she could ask me any more questions, because I just wanted to relive our kisses.

I still can't believe he'd want to kiss me. Me! I'm not special or beautiful or amazing like him. Why would he want to spend time with me? But he must, because he asked me to meet him tomorrow.

He'll pick me up outside the church at 10am, which gives me time to go to school, be marked off the roll then leave after the first class. I can't wait! I should try to sleep though, so the morning gets here quicker, and hopefully I'll dream about him too...

Oh oh oh! I don't even know where to begin! We had the most amazing day. I guess I shouldn't go into too much detail, just in case someone reads this, but it was incredible! We drove over to Smithfield, since it wouldn't do for me to get caught skipping school, and wandered around all day, holding hands, talking. He actually cares what I have to say about things. He listened so intently to everything I said, it was just awesome. And he's so sweet and encouraging, and has so many wonderful stories of his own to share. I learn so much by listening to him, and I just admire him so much, quite apart from everything else I feel about him. Like, how much I love kissing him...

I was so sad when we had to head back – I could have stayed with him forever! But I had to get home before Mum was finished at the shop. So now I'm just counting down the minutes until the weekend, when we can spend the day together again....

The weekend was so so beautiful, but in a way it feels too precious to write about, like I'm trivialising it by breaking it down into what we did and where we went and what we said, even how much we kissed. It's like, this feeling I have for him is too big to contain, and far too magical and mystical to try to explain. I just, I feel like I'm floating on a cloud, like my heart is about to burst wide open with everything I'm feeling. Knowing what this feels like, I know it's the first time I've been in love, in proper love. I adore Mike, and I love him dearly, but oh goddess, this is just so much more. More intense, more amazing, more joyful, more exciting, more wonderfully love-filled and inspiring and huge. Sometimes I feel as though I can't breathe, because I love him so much, and other times it's like he's my oxygen, and I won't survive without him. Guess they always said love was a paradox...

I really wish I could tell Mum, because surely she'd be happy for me, but some part of me wants to keep it to myself, not let anyone's judgement or misconceptions taint its purity. How could anyone understand what we have? And I couldn't properly explain it, impress upon someone just how much I love him, so I'd rather keep it to myself, guard it like a precious gemstone, a precious moment, a precious heartfelt connection...

It was so good, yet so weird, to see him at class this week. We managed to get a moment alone before it started, when Mike went to make a cup of tea. Andre kissed me, and held me like he never wanted to let me go, then whispered that we have to keep it a secret, because it won't look professional if he's in a relationship with one of his students. YES, HE SAID HE'S IN A RELATIONSHIP! This isn't a one-sided crush, like Mike has been trying to tell me, it's real. And I think Mike must have sensed something, because when he came back he just looked at me, so sadly, then sat in silence through the class. At the end he just muttered that he had to go and Andre could take me home, and I was so grateful. Another hour together, just the two of us.

The moment everyone left we fell into each other's arms, and he said the last few days have been hell, being away from me, that it hurts him physically to be separated from me. I know just how he feels, but I can't believe he could feel that for me too! I mean, he's so amazing. He's so spiritual, so wise, so accomplished, so artistic, so everything! And I'm just a school kid.

Argh, I shouldn't be writing this, because when I think about it too hard, it really doesn't make sense to me that he could like me so much. When we're together I just feel the magic, just FEEL our connection, and revel in it, and in how amazingly he treats me, how precious he makes me feel. But when we're apart, I can't help wondering what he sees in me. I'm nothing compared to him. He could have anyone, anyone at all, so why would he choose me? But then I remember our kisses, remember how it feels to be held in his arms, and I'm just filled with love all over again... Oh, I can't wait until we're together again. The days in between seem so torturously long...

Carlie smiled. She couldn't believe that she was going through the exact same situation that her mother had experienced when she was her age. Hugging the book to her chest, she felt more connected to her mother than she ever had. And it was so comforting to know that her mum understood exactly how she was feeling – the wondering if she was worthy, the battling to understand how someone so spiritually advanced could care about *her*, just a school kid, not especially smart or beautiful or charismatic or enlightened. She still struggled to believe that Rowan could love her, but it helped so much knowing that her mum had fought the same battle.

She closed her eyes as she felt tears well. "Oh Mum, why couldn't you be here now, when I need you?" she whispered. "If only I could talk to you, you could help me understand all this, reassure me about Rowan." Suddenly her door rattled, and she snapped her eyes open, but it was just Luther, coming to comfort her again. He had an uncanny knack of knowing exactly when she needed him to sit with her, curled up in her lap with a little paw on her knee, and purr away her sadness.

Reluctantly she put the diary down. Although all she wanted to do was race through it to the end, to read every single word right now, part of her didn't want to rush it. This book was a last precious link to her mother, her final chance to be close to her, and she wanted to savour every single page. It felt so exciting, so magical, to know that she had more to read, and she vowed to ration it out, no matter how impatient she got. Standing up, she wrapped the book back up in all its layers, retied the ribbons, then buried it in the bottom of her deepest drawer. Until she'd read it all, she didn't want Rose to see it, just in case there was something in it that would cause her even more pain than she'd already suffered.

Chapter 14

A Night To Remember

The minutes crawled by like hours the next day, and Carlie wondered if her classes would ever end. When the bell finally did ring, she hugged Rhiannon goodbye then raced down the corridor to the entrance. Despite her initial hesitation and nerves over being with Rowan, and going on their first proper grown-up date, now she couldn't wait to see him and be with him. And she'd promised herself – and Rhiannon – that she'd try to accept the possibility that he really could care about her as much as he said.

Bursting with excitement, she pulled open the heavy front doors and stood for a moment, eyes darting around wildly until she saw Rowan across the car park, leaning against the big old oak tree in the far corner. She flew down the steps, and his face lit up when he saw her running towards him. He grabbed her and spun her around, laughing, kissing her and trying to speak all at once. Eventually he set her down and led her over, hand in hand, to his car.

"I've missed you so much," he said, voice thick with emotion, as he opened the passenger side door for her.

"Me too," she replied, breathless, her heart spilling over with joy as he kissed her again, then let her climb in to the car.

As they turned onto the highway leading out of town, she grabbed a long black skirt out of her bag and pulled it on under her uniform, then awkwardly peeled that off to reveal the soft purple top she'd been wearing under it. He grinned across at her. "I kind of like you in that school uniform, but I guess it could cause a few uncomfortable questions on a night out," he said. She nodded, grateful that she'd thought to bring a change of clothes, and so happy that her top was the exact same colour as his. They looked like they belonged together.

"You look beautiful," he said, taking her hand then flicking his eyes back to the road ahead. "You were wearing a dress that exact same colour in my dream last night – that's why I wore this shirt."

"No way! You were wearing a shirt that colour in my dream last night," she shrieked, mind racing at the coincidence.

He looked across at her, smiling, eyes lingering a little too long on her neckline before he gazed ahead again. "Of course. I sent that dream to you."

She stared at him, surprise clear on her face.

"Don't believe me? We met at the bottom of Summer Hill, then you took my hand and led me to the top, before pulling me down onto the grass and…"

"Okay, I believe you," she replied quickly, blushing furiously. Oh god, he could either read her mind to see what she'd been dreaming about him, or send the dreams to her, or both. She wasn't sure which was more embarrassing, and she gazed out the window for a few minutes, trying to regain her composure. But he engaged her in conversation, and she was soon feeling at ease again.

Finally they turned off onto the main street of the town, and Rowan gracefully pulled in to a parking spot right in front of the restaurant. Turning off the ignition, he reached over and pulled her across into his lap. "I sent you the dream the night before too," he whispered against her ear, and she shuddered at the urgency in his voice, the sensation of his lips on her cheek, his hands in her hair, and the memory of that particular dream. She didn't know if she'd ever stop blushing.

"Don't worry my sweet, I don't want to embarrass you – I just wanted you to know that I've been thinking of you every minute, no matter whether I was awake or asleep." She buried her face in his shoulder, too mortified – yet secretly pleased – to face him just yet. He lifted her chin so he could kiss her, then opened the car door.

"Come on, let's go watch the movie, and get it over with so that I can gaze at you again over dinner."

Carlie was glad the only movie on at that time was a comedy, because she wasn't sure she could have handled the intensity of a romantic flick. It was hard enough to sit in the darkened theatre with him, holding hands, brushing fingers as they reached into the popcorn they were sharing, shivering as jolts of electricity raced up her arm. But she really loved the closeness she felt with him, and the friendship that was developing between them. Even if nothing else ever happened, she'd be grateful for that. When she'd lost her parents and been sent away to live with a stranger on the other side of the world, she'd thought that her life was over, and she'd never have a best friend again. Instead she'd found a kind, magical, supportive grandmother, and not just one but two amazing friends, two best friends.

Already she felt so blessed, and their dinner together just reinforced her gratitude, increased her love. And she couldn't believe how much she liked talking to him. He really listened to her, and treated her as an adult, not a kid. He was genuinely interested in her and Rhiannon's plans to study counselling together, and had some wonderful advice for other skills she could learn outside of school that would help her – weekend workshops, less mainstream but still important books, and someone he knew who she could do work experience with when it was time for her class to do that.

There were moments that she became embarrassed by the intensity of his gaze, but he always seemed to realise and break away – pause to butter some bread, order another juice, bring up a funny topic to lighten the mood – until she'd managed to compose herself again.

"Thank you so much for everything," she said, getting brave and reaching out to take his hand across the table. "I've never been in love, never really been loved. It means the world to me."

"So does this mean that you do love me?" he asked softly, and she couldn't tell if his voice was shaking with nerves or something else.

Panicked, she stared at him, eyes widening in terror. Oh god, this hadn't all been a trick had it? "What do you mean?"

He squeezed her hand, and his soulful brown eyes told her that everything was okay. "Well, you haven't actually told me that you love me," he admitted. "I've said it a few times to you, but you never reply."

Horrified that she'd hurt him and made him wonder, and realising the courage it had taken him to reveal his feelings to her, she took a deep breath. "I love you Rowan," she whispered, voice small and shy but very sure. "I really love you."

His smile lit up his face. "And I love you, sweet Carlie. No one will ever love you as much as I do," he said, reaching across and gently stroking her hair.

Her heart leaped with joy. It was still hard to believe that he could love her at all – *her!* – but she was slowly starting to feel the truth of it. And his words made her feel so special.

"You *are* special," he whispered, and she blushed again at the reminder that he could read her so well.

They talked and ate, then talked and drank coffee, until the owner finally came over and politely told them that the rest of the staff had already left for the night, and he really had to close up. Suddenly realising that they were the only two people left in the deserted restaurant, they apologetically got up to leave. Carlie couldn't believe they'd been sitting there together for four hours, so wrapped up in each other, so oblivious to anyone else around them.

It was just before 11pm when Rowan pulled up a few houses down from hers and turned off the ignition. He gathered her into his arms again, gently this time, holding her close and stroking her cheek with more love than passion, and she was grateful for that. She loved kissing him, but she wasn't ready to take it any further just yet, and while she was happy that he obviously found her attractive, it meant so much more to her that she could feel he liked being with her, just talking, as much as anything else.

Kissing her gently on the forehead, he reached around her to the glove box and opened it, then pulled out an envelope and handed it to her. Quizzically she raised her eyebrows.

"Two tickets for the festival where I'm doing a workshop this weekend. I thought you and Rhiannon might like to come. It's a two-hour bus ride from here, but I can bring you both home, and it will be worth it – there are lots of different presenters, workshops, healers, bands. And I'll get to see you," he said, cupping her face gently in his hands. "That's the most important thing, but it would be nice to get to know Rhiannon a bit as well – I know how important she is to you, and to your future plans, and I want to be part of them too."

Her breath caught in joyful surprise at his last words, and he stared down at her, a brief flash of annoyance crossing his face.

"Oh Sweet One, you have to stop doubting me, doubting my feelings for you. I love you, and I want to be with you as much as I can, and for as long as I can."

Inhaling deeply, she tried to smile. "It's not you that I doubt, it's me," she whispered. "I can't believe that I'm worthy of your love."

Lifting her chin, he stared into her eyes. "Then I'll just have to spend more time convincing you," he said, and his lips found hers for the sweetest, gentlest kiss. She lost herself in the sensation, clinging to him, and his words, and the feeling of his arms holding her safe. Finally he broke away, regret in his eyes.

"Your grandma has just left her last class, so she'll be home in ten minutes," he said sadly. "But I'll see you on Saturday, right?"

She nodded, kissed him one last time, then hurried inside the cottage. Luther glared at her, then followed her upstairs to her room, leaping up onto her bed and waiting for her to climb in before he could find his favourite spot. She pulled on her pyjamas and brushed her teeth, then switched off the light and fell into bed to relive the night in her mind. Five minutes later the front door opened, and Rose quietly made her way inside. Carlie feel asleep wondering what magic Rowan had to always know what was about to happen.

Chapter 15

Autumn's End

Staggering out of bed the next morning to get ready for school, Carlie was humming happily as she recalled her date with Rowan, and the dream that had followed it. She patted Luther, then slipped on her uniform and trudged down the stairs.

"Morning Sweetheart. Did you have a good time with Rhiannon last night?" her grandma asked.

"I had a wonderful night," Carlie said. Well, that wasn't technically a lie, was it? "And she got us tickets for the Autumn's End festival on Saturday. Do you mind if we go?"

Rose smiled. "Of course not, you'll have a brilliant time. Will you bring me back some of the bath salts from the Lavender Lady stand? They're amazing."

"Of course! Now I'd better get to school, Rhi and I need to start – well, do a bit more – work on our assignment," she quickly corrected herself. Hmm, she'd have to be careful with her stories, because her grandma was very astute. She waved goodbye and raced out the door and over to Rhiannon's. Hopefully she could catch her before she left, so she could tell her dad about their plans. They'd be in trouble if Rose mentioned it to Mike and he had no idea what she was talking about, since apparently Rhiannon had bought the tickets.

Her friend was beyond excited when she told her about the festival, and Rowan's gift, and her dad was happy for them to go. They talked of little else for the next two days at school, but finally Saturday morning dawned. They met at the bus stop at 8am, chatting happily on the long ride there, and planning which bands they wanted to see and which workshops they hoped to do.

They did Rowan's, of course, and Carlie was impressed all over again. But it was the time he spent with the girls afterwards that meant the most to her. It was important to Rhiannon too, as it was the first time she'd seen them together since the day they'd all met. When he had to leave them for a short time to do a couple of readings, she turned to Carlie, eyes shining and hand clutching her arm, and squealed with excitement.

"He's so lovely! Oh Carlie, you're so lucky!" she grinned. "Well, not lucky, you totally deserve it. But you're just so sweet together, always holding hands, smiling at each other. And the way he reaches out to touch your arm, like he's worried you're not quite real, or that you'll disappear, be snatched away from him, it's so beautiful. I can tell how much he cares about you, just by the way he looks at you, and the little things he does – his arm around you so protectively, always checking whether you need anything, giving you the shirt off his back when you're cold," she said, and Carlie smiled, snuggling down into the cosy woollen warmth of his jumper. She loved wearing it because it made her feel closer to him, wrapped up in his scent, in his warmth, almost like being wrapped in his arms.

"He's conscious of you every single moment," Rhiannon continued. "Even when he's talking to someone else he knows where you are, and is aware of how you're feeling and whether you're okay. It's so touching to see you both together. I really hope I find someone who feels this way about me," she said wistfully.

Carlie hugged her. "You will, I promise."

"Maybe I should have used your list when we did our love spell," Rhiannon replied, and they both laughed.

Although Carlie sometimes wished that she and Rowan had the day to themselves, she ended up being really glad that he'd suggested she bring Rhiannon. He'd been right, again. It was important that her boyfriend and her best friend get to know each other, get to like each other, since they were both such a huge part of her life.

In addition, she was pleased that she and Rhiannon would be able to talk about him in more depth now, now that she understood how serious they'd become, and could share her wonder. She hoped she didn't bore her with her love-struck ramblings though!

After the festival wound down that evening, Rowan drove them home, keeping up an easy conversation with Rhiannon, impressing her with his down-to-earth nature and his good humour. Carlie was quiet, content to let them chat as she sat in the back seat, thinking about all the things her friend had said to her today. She was right, he was incredibly attentive to her, and so sweet and protective. Maybe one day she would accept that he could really love her. Rowan and Rhiannon both turned around at the same time, as though they'd both caught her thought at the same moment, and glared at her sternly.

"Sorry," she muttered, and they all laughed.

When they reached their village Rowan dropped Rhiannon home, and Carlie got out to hug her goodbye then climbed into the front seat. "At last! I've hated not being connected to you, not being able to hold your hand," he said, reaching over to her.

They drove around to the bottom of the tor, and he pulled over and turned off the headlights, then drew her into his lap. "God, I've missed you. I'm glad I was able to spend time with Rhiannon and get to know her a bit more, but it tortured me too, being so close to you but not being able to scoop you up in my arms and kiss you, like this," he grinned, and bent over and pressed his lips to hers.

For a long time they stayed like that, enfolded in each other's arms, lips and hearts joined. But eventually the sweeping lights of a passing car brought them back to the present, and Rowan sighed and rested his chin on her head, still holding her tight.

"I'm so sorry I'll be away for the next two weeks," he whispered, voice thick with sadness. "This retreat was booked in before we met. I've never wanted to travel less in my life!"

"I know, but we'll be okay," she said, trying to sound brave. "Surely two weeks will go quickly? I'll try to stay busy, help Gran in the shop during our week off school, then there will be all the Samhain preparations and our rituals to throw myself into. And you'll be in France – surely that will be magical."

He shrugged. "I know, but I'd rather be with you."

Her heart soared with happiness, even in this moment of sadness. Happiness that they had found each other, and connected so deeply. She vowed to remember to be grateful every day, even when she was moping and whingeing about them being apart. Grateful that she had met him, and so filled with appreciation that he cared about her so deeply.

"Me too," she sighed. "And I'm sorry I promised to go with Rhiannon to her appointment on the Saturday you get back."

"And I'm sorry I promised to help Mum out on the Sunday. But I'll be there waiting for you on Monday after school, desperate to see you, and hold you, and kiss you," he said, then proceeded to do just that, until Carlie lost all sense of time, swept away in the sensation of being loved and cherished.

Another car drove past them, the headlights illuminating the dashboard clock, and Carlie gasped. "Oh god, I really need to get home! I'm so sorry," she said, as an ache of regret settled in her stomach. Sadly Rowan turned on the ignition and drove her home, and after a few all-too-brief kisses, she tore herself away and raced inside. She tiptoed up the stairs to her room, pulled on her pyjamas and brushed her teeth, then drifted off to sleep.

It was a restless night, full of dreams where they were cruelly parted – divided by time, or by other people, even by death in one short nightmare. When she woke up she felt grumpy and out of sorts, but she tried to put on a happy face for Rose. She'd promised to help her in the shop that day, and every day of the next week if she needed her. Sighing at the irony of feeling so miserable when she finally had a week of school holidays, she dragged herself out of bed, threw herself in the shower then walked as cheerfully as she could down to the kitchen for breakfast with her grandma.

Grateful that she'd remembered to grab the lavender bath salts she'd requested from the festival – well, Rhiannon had remembered, since she'd been so wrapped up in Rowan – she put on the kettle and had a pot of tea brewing by the time Rose emerged from her room, and she actually enjoyed catching up with her over their muesli, yoghurt and tea. She realised she'd been a bit distracted of late, and promised herself that she'd spend more time with her grandma this week, and be more present when they were together.

Rose looked up at her and smiled, and Carlie wondered just how well she could read her mind. It was scary, the amount of times she'd known exactly what she was thinking. She'd never really believed in psychic ability, and her experience at the Body Mind Spirit festival hadn't changed that, but if it was true, Rose surely had a big helping of it. Which could get her into trouble if she wasn't careful.

Hmm, time to be a little more focused, a little less off with the faeries, wasting away her time wishing for Rowan. He'd be back soon, and until then she was determined to make the most of the time with her grandma, and her days doing healings. This was important to her – this was part of what she wanted to do with her life – so she vowed to dedicate herself to the experience.

"Let's go then," Rose said, placing their plates in the sink and picking up her bag. So they set off for the healing centre together, and Carlie spent a long but productive Sunday doing healings for people and advising customers on the books, crystals or herbs they might find helpful.

The next morning she was grumpy again though. It was the start of her week-long school holiday, and she lay in bed for a while, bemoaning the fact that Rowan was away just when she could have seen more of him. But with a great effort, she shook it off. Regrets were pointless, and she refused to waste her time moping. She'd done enough of that after her parents died. This week she was going to make the most of every moment – catching up on a few assignments, hanging out with Rhiannon, celebrating the full moon with Rose and the wonderful witchy women she was getting to know a little better, reading the books Rowan had suggested for her counselling study plans, and doing reiki every afternoon.

And so the time rushed by, and before she knew it, it was Sunday night, and she was packing her books for school, and feeling grateful that it was only one more week until she'd see Rowan again.

Chapter 16

The Feast of the Dead

Tuesday night, their coven night, was the eve of Samhain, so Carlie and Rose were going over to Rhiannon and her dad Mike's place for a celebratory dinner that sounded more like a mourning rite than anything else. But she knew it was important to the adults that they could honour this day together, and move forward from any weirdness. Mike's wife, Rhiannon's mum Beth, had died a year ago. Carlie's mum Violet – Mike's first love – and her dad Oliver had died almost five months ago.

When Violet had run away from home at seventeen, she'd broken not only the hearts of her parents, but the heart of Mike too. They had been each other's first love, and Mike had been a wonderful support to Rose, even as he mourned her loss himself, and he'd been there for her when her husband died soon after as well. The awkwardness now, came from the fact that Mike was not only still devastated by Beth's death, but also deeply affected by Violet's recent passing, although he was trying to hide it to avoid upsetting Rhiannon and her brother Brodie. And for Carlie, it was strange that everyone in this village seemed to have known her mum – known her better than she had, she sometimes thought – and was mourning her deeply, yet no one had ever met her dad, so he seemed to have been forgotten.

But when they'd arrived that night, Mike had taken their coats and guided them into the dining room, and she'd been shocked by the incredible effort this man had gone to. The long table was beautifully set, with candles glowing in the centre, and the scent of cinnamon and nutmeg burning in an incense holder brought a richness and air of mystery to the room. Pretty name tags had been left at each place setting, and Carlie felt a chill, then a rush of warmth and gratitude, that at one end of the table three places had been set, with crockery and cutlery and a glass chalice at each one, with her mum's name written on one place setting, her dad's name in the centre and Rhiannon's mum Beth's name on the third.

Mike would be sitting at the other end of the table, opposite the three settings of their dearly departed, with Carlie sitting on one side of the table, next to her mum's place setting and with her grandma on her other side, and Rhiannon opposite her, next to her own mum's place setting, with her brother sitting between her and their dad.

Rose didn't look at all surprised, just smiled warmly at Mike as she walked over to hug him, then embraced his two children. It hit Carlie for the first time how strange it must have been for Rose to live in the same village as Mike, to have expected him to be her son-in-law, and the father of her grandchildren, then to have seen him create that family with someone else.

Rose turned to her with a sad smile, but shook her head. "No Sweetheart, not strange. There were sad moments, of course, but I am so grateful to Mike, and to Beth, for letting me share a little part of their family with them over the years, to be invited to Christmas days and school performances, to share their good news and let me offer a little back in the bad times. I've always loved Rhiannon and Brodie deeply, and it fills my heart with joy that you are such close friends."

Mike came over and hugged Carlie hello. "We've been honoured to have you join us Rose, always, and you've certainly given us far more than we could ever hope to give you. But now," he said, turning to Brodie. "Who'd like to help me bring in the drinks while Rhiannon seats our guests?"

Brodie giggled. "I guess that would be me Dad – you're so silly." Mike winked at them as he followed his son out into the kitchen, and Rhiannon guided Rose to her chair before pointing out Carlie's place, then sitting in hers. "I'm so glad to see you both. And I'm glad you wanted to come tonight Mrs Tyler, I know this is such a difficult sabbat for you."

Carlie raised her eyebrows at her friend's strange sense of formality, then turned to her grandmother, who just smiled.

"Sweet girl, call me Rose, please. You always have," she said to Rhiannon, before facing Carlie. "Samhain is the time when the spirits of those who have passed are closest to us, so I always feel so close – yet so far – from Violet and Louis at this time. But I worry about Mike too. He's still mourning his beloved wife, yet also feeling the loss of Violet all over again. I know he's so grateful to you," she said, turning back to Rhiannon.

"Not just for all your practical help, keeping the house going, cooking the meals, being there for Brodie – but for your emotional support too. He knows how much you're hurting, which makes it even more remarkable that you've been such a pillar of strength to him. And I am so grateful to you for being there for Carlie too. You are a remarkable young woman, and your mother would be so proud of you. We all are."

Rhiannon blushed, while Carlie added her thanks and appreciation to Rose's, then giggled with her at how red Rhiannon's face was. She was saved when Mike and Brodie returned with a tall jug and poured the deep red grape juice spiced with cinnamon, cloves and ginger into all the glasses, including the three at the end of the table. Rose's eyes were wet with tears, but she smiled bravely as she lifted her glass.

"Tonight we honour the ancestors who have gone before us, who watch over us and guide our lives. And especially we have joined together to pay tribute to and share our love for three special people. Beth was a beautiful soul, a devoted and loving mother, a loving wife, and a close friend to so many of us. But she lives on in the two children she adored, and I can see her in both of you – her strength and independence in you Rhiannon, and her cheekiness and sense of humour in you Brodie."

She paused as Rhiannon lifted her glass, and Carlie looked around the table at the people who had become her family. Her friend was sad yet stoical, and the tears on her eyelashes only made her seem more fierce, more protective. Brodie just seemed happy to have people around him, and she wondered how it would feel to lose your mother so young. Then she glanced at Mike, and he caught her eye, smiling at her and conveying with the merest flicker of his eye the pride he felt in his children, and his sympathy not only for them but for her too.

For a moment she felt unsettled, as she recalled the strange parallel world she seemed to have fallen into that morning in the mists, a place where her mum was still alive but Mike had been her dad, a bitter-sweet alternative world that still made her feel guilty to dwell on. Shaking off the feeling, she bowed her head, feeling so fortunate to have so many people who cared about her – people who didn't have to, but who cared anyway. It touched her deeply that these people had opened their hearts to her. She knew most people in this situation wouldn't have.

"To Mum," Rhiannon whispered, bringing Carlie back to the flame-flickering darkness of the room around her.

"The best mum ever," Brodie said.

Mike lifted his glass too. "To Beth – my wonderful wife, your beautiful mother. So sadly missed, and yet here with us always."

He took a sip, and they all did the same, then he nodded, with the deepest respect, to Rose. She held up her glass again.

"And to Violet and Oliver. My beautiful daughter, who I have missed every day since she left us more than twenty years ago, and her beloved husband Oliver, who I so deeply regret that I never had the chance to meet. I honour you both for the gift you have given us all, in Carlie, and I welcome you both – you have a special place in my heart, and on my altar, and you of course live on in your daughter, who has brought me so much joy in my old age."

Mike smothered a guffaw. "You will never be old Rose," he said, then lifted his glass, looking serious again.

"To Violet, my dear friend. I regret that I never got to see you grow up and achieve your dreams, and that you didn't get to meet my beautiful family. And to Oliver, a man I wish I could have known and called friend. I honour your memory, and I hope that somewhere, wherever it is you all are, you have met my wife and you can all feel happiness and pride at the wonderful ways you have all touched our lives. God and goddess bless you all."

Carlie was overwhelmed by the emotions the toasts so beautifully conveyed. "God and goddess bless," she echoed, feeling so inadequate in her ability to express her feelings, and so moved by the eloquence demonstrated by Rose and Mike.

Rhiannon smiled. "I feel the same – they word it all so beautifully don't they?"

She stared across at her friend. "You too?" she asked. "You can read my mind as well?"

"Not so much. But tonight all our emotions are close to the surface, and it's not that hard to gather what you're feeling."

Carlie laughed. "Fair enough."

Brodie looked over at her, face earnest. "I'm so sorry you lost your mum and your dad Carlie," he said, and she was shocked at the wisdom and sadness conveyed in his voice. "I couldn't imagine losing both – it was hard enough losing my mum."

As her eyes misted with tears, Mike reached over and grabbed his son in a hug. It was almost painful to watch their closeness, but it was touching too. Then he sat Brodie down and tickled him. "Now you've got to help me with the food. Come on buddy," he said.

Rhiannon jumped up. "Do you want me to help?" she asked, but Mike shook his head. "You talk to Carlie and Rose. I've got a helper." Brodie looked around at them all, smiling his joy and sense of self-importance, then followed his dad to the kitchen. Soon they returned with an incredible feast – golden potatoes, beetroots, turnips and carrots roasted with sage, rosemary and garlic, pumpkin and ginger pie, a delicious nut loaf with rich onion gravy, a lentil and butternut squash casserole and delicious sides. Brodie proudly served up small meals for their three absent friends, then asked Carlie to tell them about her mum and dad, so they could feel they knew them a little bit.

She was so affected by this young boy's sweetness and strength, although for a moment she didn't know where to start. "Well, Mum was a lawyer and Dad was in sales, but that doesn't say much about them, does it?" she began tentatively.

"They still always held hands when they walked down the street. Dad would make lunch for Mum to take to work, and put little notes in it, to make her smile when she was stressed. And she'd surprise Dad all the time, buying him a book he'd been waiting to read or tracking down an album he used to love. They went on a 'date' at least once a week too, encouraging me to stay over at a friend's place, or getting a babysitter when I was younger. They said it was important to have couple time even though we were a family, and it didn't mean they loved me any less.

"At least one of them would always be at my school plays or sports days or whatever. And we took holidays together once or twice a year – nothing fancy, sometimes we'd just jump in the car and drive, and see where we ended up. Some people used to say they were like kids, so spontaneous and unplanned, like that was an insult, but they were happy. They just really paid attention to each other, you know?

"They cared about each other, supported each other. When Mum wanted to do a course, Dad made it easy for her, even taking time off work so he could do everything around the house and she could really focus. And vice versa. She didn't bat an eye when he had to travel a lot for work when the boss was away, but I know she had a friend who refused to let her husband take a promotion he really wanted because it would mean he was away sometimes."

Pausing for a moment, she took a deep breath, then gazed around the room. "I'm sorry, this must be boring for you all," she said.

Rose wiped a tear from her eye, but she was smiling. "Oh Sweetheart, you can talk about them as much as you like. I'm just so glad that she found someone who loved her, and respected her, who she could love and respect in turn. Especially after, well…"

She shared a meaningful glance with Mike, and something unsaid passed between them.

"I'm really glad too," Mike said. "It seems that we both ended up with our true love."

Carlie smiled. "I'm so glad. But could you tell me about your mum?" she asked, turning to Brodie as she remembered what Rowan had told her at the festival after-party. Talking about your lost loved ones, and introducing them to people who hadn't met them, honoured them and kept their memory alive. "What do you remember best about her?"

Brodie grinned at her, a cheeky glint in his eye. "Well, I remember that she always burnt my toast, and when she cut my hair it was always a bit crooked." They all laughed, and the shadow that had been in his eyes all night lifted a little.

"But mostly I remember that she read to me every night, curled up in bed with me, and she'd read a second book if I begged hard enough." He sighed, his mouth turning down with sorrow. "I miss her so much, but I'm really scared that I'll start to forget her. That one day I might wake up and not remember what she looked like, or what she sounded like, or what she smelled like."

"Jasmine," Rhiannon said. "She smelled like jasmine."

Rose and Mike both appeared stricken, but Brodie's sister had it under control. "How about we start a project together," she suggested to him. "We'll make a scrapbook, and every night we will add one thing to it. It could be a memory, like the scent of jasmine that always clung to her, or maybe a photo, or a list of the best stories she read to us, or a song that reminds us of her. Anything at all. We'll be like detectives, building up a case file about her so we never forget a single thing, and we can keep her close to us always."

Brodie enthusiastically agreed, and said he would start by drawing a picture of tonight's feast, and where everyone had been seated in relation to his mum. Mike was trying not to let anyone know he was crying, but the look of love and pride that he directed at his daughter melted Carlie's heart.

It didn't surprise her though. Rhiannon would be an amazing grief counsellor. She'd helped Carlie navigate the worst of her pain and anger and loss, and she was certainly keeping her little brother afloat too. For what seemed like the millionth time, Carlie sent out a prayer of gratitude to the universe for the good fortune that had sent her halfway around the world to a grandmother who adored her, a new friend who was the most supportive person ever, a village and a community that had welcomed her with open arms, her new beloved, of course, and even what appeared to be two guardian spirits, or fae folk, who seemed to be watching out for her.

Her grandma squeezed her hand. "We're lucky too Carlie, to have you here. And we're grateful that you brought us answers about

Violet's life, and the knowledge that she was happy. You have no idea how much it tortured me, never knowing what had happened to her, if she was even alive."

Rhiannon chimed in too. "It's not one-sided Carlie – I'm so grateful to you for being so understanding of my loss, and for not diminishing it by comparing it to your even greater loss. And for helping me grieve and move forward, and finally realise what I want to do with my life, and how I can make that happen."

"I'm grateful to you too," Brodie piped up. "Rhi is much happier now, so she's stopped making my life hell."

Everyone laughed, and trying to retain the lightened mood, Mike asked Rose if she'd tell them a little about the festival they were celebrating, and she gladly changed the subject for him.

As they made their way through the platters of food, then a huge bowl of blueberry cinnamon crumble with ginger-scented custard, Rose shared some of the history of Samhain, to prepare them for the ritual the following evening. Mike and Brodie listened, as rapt as Rhiannon and Carlie as the traditions and legends unfolded, even though they knew the stories backwards. And Carlie had some idea now too, since she'd been preparing with her grandma for the last few days, cooking up apple fritters, grainy breads and fresh berry jams, drying herbs and baking pies.

The evening was far more enjoyable than Carlie had imagined it could be, and far less awkward. But perhaps she shouldn't have been so surprised that Mike was kind enough to make her feel so welcome, and generous enough to include her dad in their honouring ceremony.

Much later, as everyone said their farewells, Rhiannon leaned over to Carlie. "So, we're still on for midnight, yeah?" she whispered. "For our coven Samhain?"

"Absolutely! See you out the back at half past eleven," Carlie replied, hugging her friend goodbye.

And so, after Rose had gone to bed, Carlie pulled a thick jacket on and crept downstairs and out into the garden, slipping through the back gate into the laneway behind their cottage. It was dark, and although the waning crescent moon would start to rise soon, it would be low in the sky and obscured by cloud, so both girls had a small torch to light their way. Tonight would be freezing on top of Summer Hill, so they'd decided to do their ritual in the ruins of an old church just down the road. It had been built on the foundations of a much older temple, and there was an ancient spring that ran right beside it, which would add the blessings of water to their circle.

The cold night air pierced through their clothes and made them shiver, and they both pulled their jackets more tightly around themselves as they lowered their heads against the wind and picked up their pace. Finally they slipped within the crumbling stone walls, grateful that they were partially sheltered from the wind, yet still able to see the cloudy sky above them.

Rhiannon filled her chalice with pure water from the spring, while Carlie lit the large pillar candle they'd brought, secure in its pretty glass lantern from the icy fingers of the wind. They knew the cold would defeat them soon, so they hastily carved out the boundary of their sacred circle with the power of their words and intent, then called in the elements and the directions before sitting down together on the grassy floor.

They joined hands over their makeshift altar as they welcomed the god and the goddess, then they each picked up a black candle. Her hair whipping around her in the breeze, Carlie carefully lit her candle from the central one, hands shaking a little, and took a deep breath to calm and centre her thoughts.

I call on you Ceridwen, goddess of death and rebirth and the waning moon, on this cross-quarter night that marks the end of autumn and the beginning of the coldness and darkness of winter. In your aspect of wise crone and elder, please lend us your wisdom and prophetic foresight, and help us see through the darkness of our hearts and the veils between the worlds to the spirits of our lost loved ones, and let us know they are still with us.

Then it was her friend's turn. Rhiannon's hand was much steadier than Carlie's as she lit her candle from the central pillar, and her voice was clear and strong.

I invoke you Hekate, woman of the crossroads, goddess of death, and of balance. In this midnight witching hour, in this night of the waning moon, please illuminate the darkness and guide us on our soul journey to the heart of your wisdom, in search of answers from the ones we miss so much.

A dark shape flapped across the sky above them, and the girls both jumped, momentarily jolted out of their ritual consciousness. Then, smiling at whatever creature of the night had felt moved to watch over them, they held hands again and let their voices join together, carrying softly in the cold air.

We ask you, deities of darkness and introspection, of the wisdom of the inner mysteries, to protect us as we travel to your realm in search of answers, in search of comfort, in search of some glimmer of hope that our parents are still with us in some way. So mote it be.

Their voices echoed between the stone walls, gradually growing more quiet, then stilling altogether. Finally, their hands still linked, they closed their eyes and went within.

Carlie was walking along a deserted forest path. It was dark, and she felt skittish as she crept along, feet uncertain on the uneven ground, startling in fear as the shadows shifted in front of her and small shapes loomed towards her then faded away. Her heart beat faster, but she tried to remember the breathing exercises her grandma had shown her, and the relaxation steps from her reiki course. Slowly she began to feel more in control, and as she did, the path widened and became more gentle.

Noticing a golden glow starting to filter through the trees up ahead, she picked up her pace, eager to reach the comfort and warmth it seemed to offer. For a moment she wondered if she should be cautious, if it was all a trap to reel her in, but her heart felt lighter with every step, and somehow she knew she would be safe.

When she reached the clearing, she gasped with astonishment as she gazed on the enchanted vista before her. Tiny golden balls of light zoomed between the trees around the edge, and circled the head of a woman sitting on an ancient stone throne in the centre of everything. Her face was porcelain white, her eyes a deep fiery purple, her lips a dark berry stain that gave her an air of drama and terrible power. But despite her gothic visage, she exuded the most beautiful sense of peace, and Carlie felt herself drawn towards her until she could feel the heat of the candles arranged on the lower tiers of the weathered stone seat, and had to take a step back.

The woman had a huge leather-bound book in her lap, which she was writing in with a beautiful old feather quill. But she looked up as Carlie approached her, and when their gaze locked, Carlie froze in her tracks. The woman on the throne? It was like looking into a mirror. But how could it be her sitting there, in the middle of this forest, being watched by herself? Her brain hurt as she tried to puzzle it out, but the closer she peered at her, the more she realised that the woman looked just like her – except for her deep purple, no, violet, eyes, which matched her floaty dress. Was this the spirit of her mum then, returned to her homeland and her daughter?

"Oh Carlie, always seeking answers outside of yourself. You need to look within," the woman scolded.

Carlie smiled wryly. "I don't even know the questions."

The woman on the throne glared at her, and for a moment the mist rose up around her, obscuring her body as it snaked around her. "Wait!" Carlie cried, and the mists lowered again.

"Why are you here then?" the woman finally asked, her voice a sigh, a whisper, an exasperated communication mind to mind.

"I just... I miss Mum and Dad so much," she replied, pain crackling through her words. "And I'm worried that they didn't know how much I loved them before they died, that I didn't say it often enough. I guess I was just hoping that tonight, of all nights, they could give me a sign, or something..." She trailed off, eyes downcast, misery and loneliness swamping her.

"Sweetheart, of course they knew," the woman said gently, and Carlie's gaze snapped up from the ground she'd been staring at to the figure's face, and those vivid violet eyes. She'd sounded so much like Rose just then it was uncanny, yet there was steel and fire in her expression, and the soothing voice seemed like a trick.

She smiled at Carlie, as though she enjoyed keeping her a little off balance. "The important thing is that you learn from this fear you have, learn from this mistake. Make sure you do not leave things unsaid with anyone else. You know more than most that people can die suddenly, unexpectedly. That they can disappear from your life forever in a single moment."

Fear gripped Carlie's heart at her words, and shuddered through her body. There was something sinister in her tone, almost a threat. Did she know something of the future? Was someone else she loved going to die? Or was this about losing Rhiannon, if she betrayed her the way people seemed to think she would? Was she going to bring misery to everyone in her life?

The woman laughed cruelly. "Oh Carlie, you do not have to do something just because it is expected of you, or because someone said you would. You are in control of your actions. Your parents can die, and you can choose to become destructive or compassionate – or anything else. Your heart can be broken, and as a result you can choose to do the same to someone else, or be even more careful with other people's hearts," she said.

Her eyes glittered, hard and serious, as they drilled into Carlie, then she broke the contact and looked down at her lap. "This is the book of your life, and you are the only one who can control the story or change its outcome. Everything you do, you do willingly – not because you are destined to do it, but because you *choose* to do it. You choose every day what you want to do, and who you want to be. You are the sum total of every choice you make, big and small. And you have to take responsibility for your choices, and your mistakes, and the consequences of all that you do," she explained, voice stern.

"If you do not want to betray Rhiannon, do not betray her! If you do not want to regret leaving things unsaid, do not leave them unsaid! Tell your loved ones how much they mean to you. People are reminded of this for a moment when someone dies, and they tell everyone close to them how they feel, but then they forget again. *Do not forget.* You have been through so much," she said, and there was sympathy in her voice now, and compassion. "Use it to be a better person. Be aware Carlie, be conscious. Remember who and what you want to be."

The mist swirled around them, seeming to push them closer together, then Carlie felt herself being drawn backwards, away from the woman. She reached out to her, but she faded away into the mists, just as she became aware of her hands in Rhiannon's, and the warmth and comfort the sensation gave her.

Opening her eyes, she saw her friend gazing at her quizzically, and felt her cheeks, wet with tears she hadn't known she'd cried, and icy cold from the wind. The fear that had gripped her previously rippled through her, then was gone. She smiled, then leaned forward and hugged Rhiannon.

"Thank you for everything you do for me, for all the things we share. For being you. Our friendship means the world to me."

"You mean so much to me too Carlie," Rhiannon said, holding her tight. "And I don't think you realise how much you give to me, and to Rose. It's not one-sided. I know you think you just take from us and give nothing back, but it's not true. You've enriched our lives too. You've given Rose new purpose, a new depth to her existence, someone to love. And you've helped me heal as well. Brodie was right, I am much happier now, much nicer, because I know you."

Carlie felt her eyes water a little, but they were happy tears this time. "Now we should probably get home and get to bed before we freeze to death," her friend said, and she nodded.

Quickly they thanked the elements, the deities and the directions for holding them safe, and closed the sacred space they'd opened between the worlds. Then hand in hand they raced back up the laneway to where they had to part, hugged each other goodbye, then sneaked back into their houses and upstairs to the welcome warmth of their beds.

Chapter 17

In Your Memory

When Carlie got home from school the next day, Rose was in the kitchen cooking up the last few treats for the Samhain celebration at the healing centre that night. Putting on the kettle, Carlie made them both tea, then perched on the bench for a chat, noticing how tired and frail her grandma looked – so different to the powerful priestess she became at the rituals, and even the confident teacher and conversationalist she'd been last night at Mike's.

"I'm okay Sweetheart, don't worry about me," Rose said, and this time Carlie wasn't even surprised that her grandmother knew what she'd been thinking. "This time of year is always hard for me – remembering the dead, feeling the chill of winter as the world gets darker, sensing the energy of the crone so strongly. But how are you feeling after last night?"

Carlie told her she'd been really moved by the whole occasion – touched by Brodie's sweetness and Rhiannon's kindness, and so grateful to Mike for including her and her parents in their honouring of those who were gone.

"Gran, how did you feel when Mum was dating Mike?" she asked, stifling a yawn.

Rose smiled. "I was happy, of course. They'd been friends for so long, and it was really beautiful to watch them growing up together and falling in love – it seemed as though it was the most natural thing in the world. And it was hard to learn later that she'd been seeing someone else, but was too scared of upsetting me or disappointing me to tell me about him, to let me meet him. I regret that so much, that she didn't know I would have supported her no matter what."

She turned sad eyes on Carlie. "Don't ever feel scared to tell me something Sweetheart, or to share your friendships, or your relationships, with me," she said, and there was a question in her eyes. Carlie gulped, suddenly nervous, but a knock on the door interrupted them, and she went to answer it, grateful that she was off the hook for now. Did Rose know about Rowan? Had she really sensed that he'd been there that day he'd come over? She did want her grandma to meet him, and she certainly didn't want to keep sneaking around, because it made her feel bad about herself. But she wasn't sure she was ready to reveal it just yet.

Sighing, she opened the door, but she smiled when she saw that it was Miri, one of Rose's closest friends and a long-time member of her sacred circle. She was holding a huge bouquet of herbs, and had a large backpack slung over her shoulder.

"Hi Carlie, how are you? How's school going?"

"It's a lot better than I thought, thank you," she replied, smiling as she took Miri's bag from her and beckoned her into the house.

"I'm so glad to hear that. And are you coming to the ritual tonight? Samhain is always a really powerful one. And it would be lovely to have you there," she said.

Carlie felt a rush of warmth at her words. She was still so touched by how welcome she'd been made to feel since she'd arrived, and it was a real welcome, she could feel it, not just something offered out of politeness or respect for her grandma.

"Thank you, I can't wait to be there, and to take part in the ceremony – although only as a general participant, not as an active part of it," Carlie added hastily, as she saw Miri's eyes light up. "I'm not ready to help run a ritual yet, or speak in public, or be responsible for a part of it, but we've been baking the last few nights, so there are lots of yummy treats for afterwards."

Together they walked out to the kitchen, where Rose was slipping another plate of mini pies into the oven. "Hello my dear," she said to

Miri, standing up and walking across the room to embrace her. "Did you want to go over the invocations for tonight one more time?"

Leaving them to it, Carlie hurried upstairs to her room so she could start getting ready for the night ahead. At all the rituals she'd been to, she'd been amazed by the beautiful clothes people had worn, and the effort they went to in order to incorporate the season being celebrated into the way they looked, from their clothes to their jewellery, even their make-up in some cases. And while at first she'd thought that people would be leaning to the theatrical side at this one, dressing up in costumes a la Halloween, the modern incarnation of Samhain, her grandma had set her straight about that.

"Personally I kind of like the fact that secular and even religious people dress up as witches and ghosts and go trick or treating on this night, celebrating the energy of the season, even unknowingly," Rose had said, smiling at the thought. "But there's also a part of me that's offended by the commercialisation of the festival, and the simplification of its meaning. The symbolism of the ghosts isn't to scare people, but to honour those that are lost to us, loved ones who have died, as well as the ancestors, those who came before us, who fought so hard for the right to follow the spiritual path of their choice, and gave us the freedom today to do just that."

Picking up a piece of thin orange ribbon, Carlie started plaiting it into her long dark hair, allowing her mind to follow her actions as she added more, seeing it as a meditation of sorts, a slipping into the sacred space of the ritual before it technically began, starting to focus on the upcoming magical state of mind. Once she was finished, she walked over to her wardrobe and reverently took out the beautiful black velvet dress she'd chosen.

When Rose had offered her another outfit from the shop for this ritual she'd felt uncomfortable – she still had the deep red one from Lughnasadh, and the dark orange one shot through with gold from Mabon – but she had to admit that it definitely helped her slip into a ritual head space much more easily when she was dressed in something selected specifically for the night. She'd decided not to wear these clothes on normal days, just on magical occasions, so they retained the atmosphere of the seasonal ceremony, and their "specialness".

Slipping the gown over her head, she turned back to her dressing table, where her jewellery was strewn across the top. As she picked up the necklace she'd bought at the festival, the bee charm on the string of yellow obsidians, she heard a knock on her door. Opening it, she smiled at Rose as she stood there, hand outstretched.

"I thought you might have use for this," her grandma said, offering an orange fabric-wrapped parcel.

Curious, Carlie untied the ribbon, then thanked her grandma profusely. It was a beautiful silver jewellery box, velvet lined, with lots of separate compartments to put different pieces in. "Oh, it's gorgeous! And you're right, I was just thinking that I need somewhere special to put all my jewellery. Thank you so much Gran!"

Rose smiled and left the room, while Carlie took the silver box over to her dressing table and placed it there reverently. She opened one of the drawers to put the silver chain strung with the aqua aura pendant from her mum and the little vial of sand her friend Emily had given her in – then flew back downstairs, throwing her arms around Rose and thanking her again. Inside the bottom drawer she'd found a necklace of black obsidian, with a beautiful heavy pendant surrounded by smaller stones of amethyst and obsidian.

"You're very welcome, and it looks perfect on you," her grandma said, hugging her back, arms warm and comforting, her heart beating strongly against her own. "And it will help keep you safe from negative influences, and protect you from anyone wishing to harm you or hurt you," she added.

Carlie looked up, startled. Why had she said that? Did her grandma know something about Rowan? Or was she simply being paranoid after their earlier discussion?

Rose just smiled, eyes totally lacking in guile. "Now, we're going to head over to the shop, to start setting up. Would you like to come with us, or do you want to stay here a while longer and make a start on your homework?"

Carlie rolled her eyes and scrunched up her face in mock distress, but grudgingly conceded that her grandmother had a good point. She flounced back up the stairs theatrically, calling out a farewell to Rose and Miri, then opened up her school bag and got to work. It was annoying, but she had to admit that she'd definitely feel much happier when she got home from the ritual and didn't have to do it then.

When she got to the hall that night, she was transported straight to a magical land, and was once again in awe of the atmosphere and sense of enchantment that her grandma and her circle of magical friends could create, both physically and emotionally. A few people waved to her and said hello, and some even came over and hugged her as she wandered inside, spellbound by the beauty of the room.

Black velvet drapes covered the walls, and strings of faery lights illuminated the faces of the guests. A deep orange cloth covered the altar, which looked much bigger than usual, and the rich, heavy scent of patchouli hung in the air, providing a strong bottom note to the lighter scents of cinnamon and pine. Pots of bright marigolds made a circle around the edges of the room, and she could also smell rosemary, wormwood and sage.

Laura – or should she call her Ms Henderson now, even out of school? – stood to one side, next to a table piled high with orange candles. She beckoned Carlie forward and handed her two, then directed her to the slowly forming circle.

Once everyone was in place and a hush had fallen over the room, Rose stood up in the middle of the circle and raised her arms to the sky. Carlie watched, fascinated and in awe, as her grandmother slowly morphed into her high priestess persona. She didn't move, yet with every slow breath she took she looked taller, more imposing, more powerful. And then Carlie stopped thinking about what was happening and let herself simply experience it.

She felt a sense of peace come over her, felt a connection to everyone in the room slip into place, and felt her heart open up wide as she listened to Rose cast the circle, welcome the directions and the elements, and invoke the god and the goddess. Her scepticism was swept away as she dove into the sense of ritual and belongingness that washed over her, and let it draw her under.

Then she felt hands brush her cheeks and stroke her hair as Rose welcomed the spirits of all those they'd lost to be with them at this magical time, this first day of winter, of cold and introspection. Last night she'd told Carlie that this was the moment when the spirits of their ancestors and their dead could come closest, when the veils between the worlds were thin and connection was so much easier. She kept her eyes closed, desperate to believe it was her mum and dad standing with their arms around her, holding her close, and safe. Her mind drifted to Rowan, and his mourning of his father, until she heard Rose's voice in her ear. "Be here Carlie, be present."

Her eyes snapped open – and she was shocked to see that Rose was on the other side of the room, not next to her; her back was to her, and she was walking slowly around the circle lighting the candles people held from the central altar candle in her own hands. As though she felt Carlie's gaze on her though, she turned her head, and nodded once to acknowledge that she'd caught her thought.

A shudder rocked through Carlie, and she looked around wildly, confused and slightly, irrationally, afraid, until she caught Rhiannon's eye. Straight away she felt calmer, more grounded, and she smiled in gratitude at her friend and magical partner.

Finally Rose reached her, and smiled sadly at her granddaughter. "For Violet," she said, as she lit the first candle. "And for Oliver."

Tears welled in Carlie's eyes as she realised the significance of what was happening in the room – people were lighting a candle for everyone they'd lost, then bringing them together in a touching ceremony of remembrance. A single tear spilled over and ran down her cheek, but she smiled bravely as she followed the person next to her to the altar, which was much bigger than usual, and slowly filling with the candles placed on it so reverently by the ritual's participants. As she set hers down in two small silver holders, and watched the individual flames flicker then grow strong, becoming a part of the growing spiral of light, she offered a prayer of gratitude to her parents. She found that she couldn't address a deity she wasn't sure was really there, but she knew, deep in her bones, that her parents were with her on this night, were with her always, and that was enough for her right now.

Looking up, she saw Rose staring at her, pain warring with joy and pride in her eyes. She smiled shyly, then turned and walked back to her spot, and the rest of the ritual passed by in a strange haze as she tried to tell her parents all that was in her heart, and listened closely, hoping she would hear them reply.

By the time the beautiful ceremony came to a close, Carlie felt emotionally drained – lighter in some ways, and glad, but heartbroken too. She waited until she could catch Rose's attention, then told her she had to go. Her grandma held her close, then kissed her forehead, which made her blush as thoughts of Rowan kissing her there swept through her body and her heart.

"Of course Sweetheart," Rose said, her high priestess persona slipping for a moment. "Do you want someone to walk you?"

Carlie shook her head. She needed some time alone, some time to process all the emotions that were so rattling her. Her grandma smiled, kissed her again, then bid her farewell.

When she got home, she threw herself into bed, still wearing her dress, and cried. She cried for her mum and dad, and for Rhiannon and the mother she'd lost. She cried for Rose, the bravest person she knew, and she cried because she missed Rowan so much and wished so desperately that he was here with her right now, holding her safe in his arms, soothing her heart, wiping away her tears. She knew that was a selfish wish, in the face of so much suffering and loss, but he always made her feel so much better. Still, she would get to see him on Monday afternoon, after the longest two weeks of her life. Finally managing to smile, she drifted off to sleep.

Chapter 18

The Winter Queen

The next morning at school, Carlie and Rhiannon met out the front and walked in together, still buzzing from their ritual. They paused when they saw a banner across the hallway, announcing the upcoming Yule Ball, which was to have a masquerade theme.

Rhiannon squealed with excitement. "Ooh, they thought they might not have it this year, but I'm so glad they are! They're always such fun, and it would have been awful to miss out on it now that we're finally seniors. We're the oldest this time, so someone from our year will be crowned the Winter Queen and the Sun King."

Carlie grinned at her enthusiasm. She'd never been one for social events, but she figured it would be fun to go to something like this with Rhiannon. "So what's it like?" she asked, and grinned as her friend's face lit up and she eagerly started to explain that it was a huge end-of-term winter ball, which students from several surrounding schools would be attending, since each one was quite small, and a lot of the kids knew each other from weekend sports games, other electives and community groups. This year it would be held in Smithfield, at the school's gymnasium. Carlie felt a stab of sadness, that it would take place in Rowan's town yet he couldn't be there with her, but Rhiannon was oblivious.

"I wonder if they've appointed the organising committee yet?" she was asking, eyes shining with joy. "I'd love to do that. How about you? It will involve some after-school meetings, a few weekend days, then probably every Saturday for the month leading up to it..."

Carlie shook her head regretfully. "Sorry, I promised Gran I'd help in the shop on weekends in the lead-up to Christmas, do some reiki if anyone asks for it, and man the tills so the other girls get time with clients. But I can't wait to hear all about it," she said.

Rhiannon pouted for a moment, then shrugged and rushed off to the principal's office to see if she could sign up. When Carlie met up with her a few classes later, she excitedly announced that she was on the committee, and pulled out a notebook where she'd already started to brainstorm ideas. "Let me know if you think of anything," she said, enthusiasm brimming over, and Carlie laughed.

"You're so cute!" she teased. "I've never seen you this excited."

Rhiannon rolled her eyes and laughed too. "I know, I'm a bit tragic. I just wanted to be on the committee so badly last year, but the timing didn't really work out. But now I finally am!" She paused, face falling. "I'm so sorry though, I'm going to have to rain check our trip on Saturday, as that's when the first meeting is. I'll call today and see if I can postpone the appointment. I hope that's okay with you?" she asked nervously.

Carlie considered teasing her by saying no, but she couldn't do it to her. "Of course!" she grinned, and meant it. Then she realised that this could be a good thing for her. Her grandma knew she was going out for the day with Rhiannon. She could still go, on her own, and spend the day with Rowan. He was returning from his trip late on Friday night, and would be home all day Saturday.

This was perfect. She'd been so desperate to see him before Monday, and now here it was, handed to her on a platter. Suddenly she felt just as happy and excited as her friend.

That afternoon Rhiannon went home with Carlie after school, so they could start planning their Yule Ball outfits. Rose was there when they arrived, and she put the kettle on to make tea while the girls leaned up against the kitchen bench and chattered excitedly.

"We could do a traditional Santa vibe, you know, red dress, fluffy white trimmings, tinkling bells on our black boots, but that seems a bit obvious," Rhiannon said, kicking off their costume planning session. "And not very magical."

"There's the Snow Queen too, from the faerytales, and from the Narnia stories as well, all icy white and frosty, glittering and diamond drenched," Carlie offered.

"And there are the winter goddesses," Rose added. "The Celtic Cailleach Bheur, who rules the dark half of the year, the Roman winter goddess Angerona, Scandinavia's Frau Holle, the Norse goddess Frigga, the Italian witchy figure La Befana, who rides around on a broom delivering lollies, the Hopi's Spider Woman. And the Yule colours of red, green and white too, as well as gold for the sun."

Rhiannon smiled ruefully. "If we had someone to go with, a date, we could go as the sun god and sun goddess."

"Or the sun god and the moon goddess," Carlie said. If only she could take Rowan – that would be perfect for them.

"Well, I guess we could go together, me as the sun goddess and you as the moon goddess," Rhiannon replied with a giggle.

Rose smiled at them as she poured out the tea. "You will both be beautiful, whatever you go as," she said wistfully. "I remember when your mum went to her Yule Ball Carlie, with your dad Rhiannon. They looked gorgeous together, and so happy. A few of the teachers told them they would have been crowned the Winter Queen and the Sun King if they were seniors – and they probably would have been the following year, but Violet left home before that, and Mike didn't end up going."

She turned away, but not before the two girls had seen the emotion on her face. Carlie suddenly felt bad. Was she just a constant and painful reminder to her grandmother of the daughter she'd lost? Was her being here actually making it worse for Rose, bringing up old memories that she'd rather forget, making the pain of her loss fresh again, over and over?

As she stared morosely into her tea she felt a hand on her shoulder, and looked up into her grandma's wet eyes.

"Oh Carlie, please don't ever think that I regret having you here. I know the circumstances of you coming to live with me were terrible for you, but I'm so happy that you're here, so happy we found each other after all this time. Of course it hurts, when I think of your mother and what we both lost, but all these memories you bring up for me are wonderful memories, and I cherish the moments I have with you, as well as the moments they bring back to me of when Violet was young. They're sad, but a kind of happy-sad."

Rose folded her into a hug, and this time Carlie didn't even mind that she'd obviously read her thoughts again.

"You know, I think some of your mum's old dresses are still in her room, and some of our old ritual clothes and robes," her grandma offered. "You should both have a look through them – there might be something you like, or something we could transform into what you'd like, for the ball."

Carlie wasn't sure what to say to that – it would be amazing to see some of her mum's old clothes, but she remembered how hard it had been for Rose when they'd entered that room not so long ago, after it had been locked up and shut away for so many years.

"Gran, had you really not been in Mum's room since she disappeared?" she asked quietly, nervously.

Rose glanced at her, surprise on her face. "Of course not. I spent hours in there, days, after she'd gone, trying to find a clue to her whereabouts, or a psychic link, or something. Anything. And when we called the police, of course they looked through it too, trying to find leads. In the end I locked the door, because I was spending too much time in there, becoming obsessive. It took Elsie to recognise it though – she came down to stay with me after Louis' funeral, and again when I started to realise that your mum was never coming back. She saw what I was doing to myself, and told me I had to stop spending all my days in there. It was her idea to put a lock on the door, and she took the key home with her, so that I wouldn't be tempted," she said.

"Not that it really helped – whether I was sitting on her bed hugging her pillow or downstairs cooking in the kitchen, or even at the shop, Violet was all I thought about."

Wiping the tears impatiently from her eyes, she beckoned the girls to follow her. Rhiannon squeezed

Carlie's hand as she stood up, and together they headed to the stairs. At the top, Rose opened the door – it was no longer locked – turned on the light and ushered them in. Then she went over to the closet and pulled open the door. The girls gasped. Inside was a riot of colour, vivid red velvets next to sparkling silver sequins and cool blue and green silks, with scarves of every shade imaginable, and a variety of styles of shoes spilling out of the bottom.

Rose smiled at them. "Your mum used to love op shopping, and we made quite a few outfits ourselves too. But I'll leave you to it. Try some on, take whatever you like – I can't wear them, and, well... they're all yours," she said softly. The unspoken words, that Violet would never need them, hung in the air between them, but Rose simply ran a hand over the fabrics then headed back downstairs.

"I'll be in the kitchen making a vegie and tofu lasagne if you need me – and Rhiannon, you're more than welcome to stay for dinner if you'd like," she called out.

Both girls shouted out a thank you, then turned back to the wardrobe. They didn't know where to start, but at an unspoken signal, both reached towards the coat hangers and pulled all the dresses out, laying them on the bed, which was now dust-free.

Then the fun began, as they started trying them on. Some seemed a little old fashioned, which they supposed made sense, and others were a bit too loose or too tight. But finally Rhiannon slid into a bright red velvet dress with deep emerald holly leaves embroidered around the hem and neckline, which flared out over her hips and wrists and fit her perfectly. The gown's vivid hue suited her colouring and her personality, and when she spun in a circle it floated out around her, then fell in gentle waves. She grinned.

"This is it! I love it!" she announced joyfully, then stopped abruptly. "Well, if you don't mind Carlie? I mean, it's yours, of course. If you want to wear this one..." she trailed off.

Carlie smiled. "It's totally you, and totally yours – it looks gorgeous on you. And besides, I think I like this one," she said, as she lifted up a long, luxurious swathe of white fabric. She held it in front of her, then slipped it over her head. Like Rhiannon's dress, it fit her like a glove, and perfectly suited her shape and colouring. It had a fitted white brocade bodice, with tiny crystals sewn onto it, then it swirled out into a ballerina-style skirt that was a froth of soft tulle. Bell-shaped white organza sleeves added movement and sophistication, without being fussy, and her long, loose dark hair was the perfect contrast. She looked like a faerytale princess.

"You look amazing!" Rhiannon cried, her eyes widening and her lips turning up. "It's like it was made just for you."

Carlie twirled around, feeling a mixture of joy and sadness. She felt close to her mum as she stared at her reflection in the mirror, seeing the resemblance now, thanks to Rose's old photos, and loving that she was wearing a dress she'd once worn. But it made her sad too. It was like Rhiannon said – their mothers should have been here to share their excitement about the ball, to help them pick out a dress, do their hair, share their secrets and their crushes.

Rhiannon smiled sadly at her, and came over and gave her a hug. "We have each other though," she said softly. "And you have Rose, and I have Dad and Brodie. It could be worse."

Carlie nodded, and made an effort to regain her cheeriness. Reluctantly they changed back into their normal clothes, and carefully hung the rest of Violet's dresses back up. When Rose called out to them that dinner was ready, they were surprised to discover that three hours had passed. Rhiannon hugged Carlie goodbye, then thanked Rose for the dress and the dinner invitation, but said she had to get home before her dad started worrying.

Over their meal, Carlie listened, rapt, as Rose reminisced about Violet as a teenager, sharing stories both happy and sad. And that night they both dreamed of her.

Chapter 19

Tainted Love

On Saturday Carlie woke up early and slipped quietly out of the house before Rose surfaced. She didn't want to lie to her grandma directly, so it was better that she just assume she was still spending the day with Rhiannon. Hurrying down to the High Street, she breathed a sigh of relief as she made the early bus with just seconds to spare. Pulling out her maths book, she tried to study for a while, but finally gave up, too excited by the thought of soon being in Rowan's arms to be able to concentrate on anything else.

Staring impatiently out the window, her headphones in, she daydreamed about spending a whole day together. The last two weeks had dragged by so slowly, but she was trying to see that as a positive, that she'd missed him so much. She certainly knew that she really loved him now, if she'd ever doubted it before.

When they finally pulled in to his village she leaped off the bus and rushed down his road, excitement pounding through her veins. It was only minutes until she'd see him, and she smiled as she anticipated the look on his face when he saw her. Quickly she raced up his stairs, then, heart in mouth, knocked on the door. She'd never been inside his apartment before, and she was so curious to see where he lived, where he spent his nights as they dreamed of each other.

Then she panicked. Oh god, what if he'd forgotten what he felt for her while he was away? What if he'd met someone else? Suddenly nervous, every second she waited stretched out into an eternity, and all her old doubts started swooping around in her head, immobilising her with the fear that she'd lost him, that he'd forgotten her, that he'd gone somewhere else or found someone else.

Desperately trying to shake off her negativity, she summoned up her courage and knocked again. After another interminable wait, she finally heard footsteps echoing down the hallway. As she stood there shaking, part of her wanted to flee, but another part wondered what on earth had gotten into her. They loved each other. They'd been eagerly awaiting the day they'd be able to see each other again. And any second now he'd open the door and she'd fly into his arms, and all would be right with the world.

Eventually she heard the key turn in the lock, then the door was cautiously opened. He stared at her, eyes bleary and momentarily unfocused, long hair messy but adorable. He was wearing a pair of old tracksuit pants and a loose tank top that really showed off his arms and shoulders. Carlie blushed, even as she moved towards him and whispered "surprise".

"Hey baby," he croaked, enfolding her in a hug then pulling her inside. "It's so good to see you. I thought you were spending the day with Rhiannon today. What time is it?"

Oh god, she hadn't even thought about what her early start would mean for him. "Um, it's 8.30," she mumbled. "Do you want me to come back later?"

He shook his head. "No, of course not, but come to bed with me for a while. My car broke down on the way back from London last night, so I didn't get to sleep until after four," he said, voice still cracked and low.

Taking her hand, he led her back to a darkened room at the far side of the apartment, closed the door behind them then crawled into bed. Terrified and deeply unsure of herself, she stood in the gloomy space, halfway between the door and the bed, and stared at him. What should she do? Did he just mean for them to sleep, or did he intend something else with his invitation to come to bed with him? He opened one eye and peered up at her. "Come on my love, I'm not going to try anything, it's just way too early for me to be awake."

Taking a deep breath, she crossed the space between them, kicked off her shoes, and gingerly lay down on the edge of the bed, her back to him, her body tense. She felt him move behind her, and stiffened as he pulled her into his arms and up against him, scooping the blankets over her so they were cuddled up close together. "I missed you baby," he whispered, his lips in her hair, and his arms wrapped tightly around her. "I'm so glad you're here."

And then she felt him relax against her, his breathing slowing and deepening, and she realised he'd fallen asleep. She sighed with relief – then was confused to discover that a tiny part of her was disappointed that he really had meant what he'd said.

Rolling her eyes at herself, she acknowledged how crazy that sounded, then she let go of the breath she'd been holding, and felt herself relax into the warmth of his body and the bliss of being held so close. She could feel his heart beating, his breath in her hair, the strength of his arms as they drew her closer and held her safe against the world. She drifted off to sleep with a smile on her face, and even as she dreamed, she felt his arms around her.

A few hours later, as the sun drifted higher and made the room a little brighter, she was awoken by his kisses on her neck, and his hands running through her hair. He turned her to face him and pulled her closer, kissing her passionately on the mouth, sending a shiver of pleasure through her as his tongue met hers. She kissed him back, wrapping her arms around him and holding him tight, moaning as she felt his hand on her tummy, softly stroking her bare skin. Her breath caught as he inched higher, pushing her t-shirt out of the way, his touch leaving a trail of fire in its wake.

Shivering with desire, she tried to silence the part of her mind that was telling her to stop. She wanted to stop thinking, to simply abandon herself to the sensation she felt in his arms, love and lust mingling powerfully, trying to drive rationality from her mind.

But as he reached around to unhook her bra she froze, suddenly unsure of herself. The fact that no one knew where she was made her feel vulnerable and exposed. Reluctantly she remembered how much it meant to her that he was prepared to wait until she was ready. And in more sober moments –

when his touch wasn't leaving her incapable of coherent thought – she knew that moment hadn't come.

He groaned as she stopped kissing him and pulled back, away from him. "My god baby, you're driving me crazy. Come on, let me hold you," he pleaded, voice still heavy with sleep. "Don't tease me like this," he added, reaching out for her, trying to crush her against him and under him.

Her breath became ragged with fear, and she shrunk in on herself, trying to make herself smaller, more still, trying not to inflame him any further.

Abruptly he opened his eyes, which widened with shock when he saw her expression. He released her immediately, and shame and regret crossed his face as he inched himself further away from her, putting enough space between them that they couldn't accidentally touch.

"I'm so sorry Carlie, I forgot myself for a moment. I've just missed you so much. And I love you so much. I'm really sorry. I promise I'll never try to make you do anything you don't want to do." He looked mortified, and she felt terrible that she'd made him feel so bad.

"It's not your fault," she whispered, suddenly wishing she hadn't stopped him. "And it's not that I don't want to do it," she added, blushing furiously as she remembered the passion between them. "I just, I'm not quite ready, and I'm so sorry about that. I know it's not fair to you."

Slowly he reached out and stroked her cheek, gently, restrained, careful not to scare her. The love and respect in his touch made her ache with longing, and with joy and gratitude. "Oh my love, you have nothing to apologise for," he said softly. "I'm so sorry. I was half asleep, and I'd been dreaming that we were, you know..." he paused, looking slightly uncomfortable. "And when I woke up and felt you in my arms..."

He trailed off again, and she stared at him, suddenly afraid that he'd want to break up with her now, find someone who could give him all that he wanted.

Before either of them could speak, there was a knock on his front door. She stared at him, eyebrows raised in question. He shrugged, and she saw his mind ticking over, then he sighed. "I'd better check, just in case it's Mum turning up early."

They both stood up, and Carlie pulled on her boots as he threw a long-sleeved t-shirt on over his tank top. She blushed again, as she remembered how amazing he'd looked standing in the doorway that morning, and he winked at her before leading her back out into the lounge room. "Make yourself at home," he said, kissing her demurely on the cheek then walking down the hallway and opening the door.

"Sweetheart, how was France?" she heard a woman cry, before she heard the sound of kissing. Carlie's blood ran cold, and she felt herself sinking into the couch in dismay.

"God I've missed you. When did you get back? And how were the ladies across the channel?" the woman was asking. Her voice got louder as she followed Rowan inside – and the expression on his face didn't do anything to reassure her. He looked… Guilty? Embarrassed? Was he blushing? He was uncomfortable, that was plain to see.

When the woman stepped into the lounge room, Carlie's heart sank even deeper. She was gorgeous. Grown-up and sexy gorgeous. And glamorous and confident and self-assured. She didn't bat an eye as she glanced at Carlie from top to toe, then turned back to Rowan with a dismissive smirk. "So I guess you didn't need to find romance in France," she teased. "You've already found my replacement, and you're already in bed with her too I see."

Carlie's hand reached up to her messy hair, and she realised she must look like she'd just rolled out of bed. Which she had. The woman was staring at her like she was someone Rowan had pulled in off the street last night, a stranger who meant nothing to him.

And what did she mean, about her being a replacement? She was mortified, but mostly she was angry at herself for ever thinking he could be interested in someone like her. She felt so young, so unworldly, so naive compared to this woman, and she didn't like it. She had to get out of there. Standing up, she grabbed her bag and walked towards the door.

Rowan winced, and looked over at her with apology written all over his face. "Baby, wait. Don't leave. Tell me what's wrong," he implored her. "This is just –"

"No, don't," she said. "I have to go." She could hear the ice in her voice, as well as the shakiness. He put his hands on her shoulders and tried to draw her to him, but she shook him off and paced down the hallway. He followed after her, but she kept walking, back straight, eyes on the door. "Carlie, she won't be here for long – we can go out, spend the day together."

Feeling she could drown in the sadness she was feeling, she turned to face him. He saw the anguish in her eyes, and tried to reach out to her, but she shook her head. "Goodbye Rowan," she said, a cold finality in her tone, then she stomped off down the stairs.

"I'll see you on Monday," he called out after her, but he couldn't be sure she'd heard him.

Carlie was shaking by the time she collapsed into a seat on the bus, and it took most of the journey home to get her emotions under control enough to focus on her surroundings. She still felt tears welling whenever the face of that woman slid into her mind though, so she decided to climb the tor before she faced Rose.

Her thoughts were a confused jumble – she didn't know if she felt upset that he'd pressured her about sex, disappointed that she'd said no, or angry about the mysterious woman who'd interrupted them. Who was she? Why had she made her feel so insecure, just minutes after Rowan had told her again how much he loved her? Was she just sensitive because the woman had exuded such an air of confidence and sexuality? Did that make her feel guilty about turning Rowan down? Or was she just garden variety jealous that Rowan had another woman in his life?

Oh god, now she really wished she'd stayed to hear his explanation. What if she was torturing herself over nothing? But even if it was all perfectly innocent and it was his sister or something, the woman had made her feel small and uninteresting, and totally naive and not good enough for Rowan – and that was her own issue, not the woman's. And not Rowan's either. Suddenly stumbling on a rock, she gazed around herself and realised with a shock that a thick mist had risen up around her, and she no longer knew where she was. Peering ahead, she could just make out the branches of an apple tree in front of her. She must have weaved her way around the lower slopes of the tor to the far side. A chill settled around her, and the sense of isolation she felt in the alien white landscape made her feel even worse.

Her breath caught when she saw a figure materialise out of the fog. It was the green-clad woman, the Keeper of the Hill, who she'd met the night of their coven dedication. She tried to remember her words. *You can call on me when you need to ground yourself, and connect back to the earth, or need to feel my nurturing and protection...* She smiled despite herself. She did have need of that right now.

Then she shivered as she remembered the rest of the message from that mysterious full moon night. She was going to betray the person closest to her. Yet hadn't *she* just been betrayed by the person closest to her? Had the message been wrong all along? Should she have been guarding her own heart all this time, rather than worrying about how her actions would affect someone else?

The figure glided forward, and shocked Carlie by sweeping her into a hug. She hadn't seemed the nurturing type. "I apologise for that," she whispered. "I was a little out of sorts at our last meeting."

Carlie giggled. Shouldn't these Otherworldly beings or whatever they were be above things like impatience and grumpiness? Weren't they meant to be all love and light and positivity? She felt the woman laugh as she released her. "Clearly immersing yourself in the mysteries with your high priestess grandmother and your magical friend has not lessened your cynicism," she said with a wry smile.

Carlie grinned. "I'm sorry," she replied, but her amusement faded as the face of Rowan's visitor flashed through her mind again, and she sighed. "I thought I was going to betray someone, not be betrayed. Couldn't you have warned me about that instead?"

Brianna smiled serenely. "Patience beloved. Everything is not as it seems. You are so quick to judge, without waiting for an explanation."

"Some things are pretty obvious," she retorted. "Someone claims they'll wait for you, then doesn't. Says they love you and only you, but has someone else."

Suddenly a raven cawed overhead, the mists swirled around them, and a dog barked somewhere nearby.

"I cannot stay," the figure in front of her said, then handed her a green-velvet-wrapped bundle that seemed to materialise from somewhere within the folds of her cloak. "This is for you and your friend – she will know which one is for each of you."

Then she leaned forward and cupped Carlie's chin in her hand, gazing deep into her soul. "Keep your faith. Trust your heart," she whispered, then faded back into the mists. A moment later the sun came out, the sky cleared, and a man wandered around the curving path towards her, a dog at his heels.

"Afternoon," he said politely as he swerved around where she was standing, feet anchored in the earth. She smiled, but was too surprised to respond. There was no sign that the woman in green had ever been hovering there in front of her, comforting her, offering advice she wasn't sure was worth taking. Yet in her arms was the package, wrapped in a green the exact same colour as Brianna's cloak.

She shook her head, mind a whirl of contradictions and questions. She felt unsettled, and even more confused than she'd been before, but at least she wasn't dwelling on Rowan's betrayal quite as much – she was dying to know what the woman had given them.

By the time she got back to the cottage and was making dinner with Rose, her sadness had returned with a vengeance, but she managed to keep a brave face while she was with her grandma, not wanting to have to explain her bad mood.

Later, she jumped when she heard a knock at the door. Heart racing, she went to answer it, her smile faltering when she saw it was Rhiannon, not Rowan. With a sickening thud she realised that part of her had hoped he would come over to explain, to apologise, to beg her to forgive him. To hold her close and promise he would never hurt her again. Sighing, she hugged her friend and led her inside.

"Tea?" she asked, and Rhiannon nodded gratefully.

Rose smiled as they entered the kitchen. "Hello sweet girl. You two are so adorable – spending the whole day together, then still wanting more time with each other at night."

Rhiannon looked blank for a moment, but quickly recovered her composure. "Well, we figured we should do a bit more on our assignment," she said to Rose, motioning to the messenger bag on her shoulder, before shooting daggers at Carlie.

"I'm not complaining!" Rose said with a smile. "I'm just so happy that you both have each other."

Carlie poured water into the kettle, then went to the sink to wash up their dinner dishes, careful to keep her back to Rose. She knew she was a bad liar, and she would find it hard to keep a straight face if she had to look her grandma in the eye. But Rose motioned her away. "You go upstairs and make a start girls, and I'll bring up the tea when it's ready."

The two girls climbed the stairs and collapsed on the floor in Carlie's room, backs resting against her narrow single bed.

"So I'm guessing you didn't tell Rose about my change of plan, and you went and saw Rowan instead?" Rhiannon asked her, and there was a thread of anger in her voice.

Carlie nodded sadly, oblivious to the flatness in her tone.

"Be careful with your lies Carlie, your grandmother isn't stupid," her friend snapped, but her demeanour gentled as she saw the look on her face. "What happened?"

There was a knock on the door, and Carlie jumped up to open it. Rose stood there with two mugs of tea on a tray, and a plate of cinnamon cookies that smelled divine.

"Thanks Gran," she said, forcing happiness into her voice as she took the tray. Her grandma looked searchingly at her, then smiled and left them to it.

"Did he hurt you?" Rhiannon asked impatiently as she picked up her tea and took a sip.

"No," Carlie said, then faltered. "Not really…"

Embarrassed, she told her friend how bad she'd felt for waking him up, and how nervous she'd been when he'd said to come to bed with him – then relieved when it became obvious that he actually did mean to sleep.

Rhiannon smiled. "That doesn't sound so bad, especially as he was probably beyond exhausted after his trip."

Carlie blushed. "Well, we slept for a while, then I woke up to him kissing me, and trying to… I don't know, go further."

"Oh my god! Did he force you to –"

"No!" Carlie insisted. "He tried to convince me, but he finally stopped. But it was weird, it was almost like he didn't realise it was me for a minute."

"And will he keep trying to convince you until you give in?" Rhiannon asked, and Carlie heard the outrage in her voice.

"I don't know. I do feel guilty though. I mean, isn't that what you're supposed to do when you love someone?"

Her friend looked horrified. "Of course not Carlie, you're supposed to respect your girlfriend or boyfriend's decisions, to wait until they're ready, no matter how long it takes."

"I know, and he does, he's usually really good about it…"

"Don't you dare let him pressure you into this Carlie!" Rhiannon said, voice fierce. "And don't make excuses for him. Any guy who thinks that behaviour is okay should be avoided at all costs, no matter how sweet he appears to be the rest of the time. Believe me, I know."

Carlie pasted a smile on her face, then realised how often she'd been doing that today. "I won't. And he won't." She couldn't admit how close she'd come to giving in, not because he was pressuring her, but because she wanted to. Then again, given what happened next, she was beyond relieved that she hadn't let her desire lead to a decision she would have regretted.

"But that's not the worst thing that happened," she finally said, and Rhiannon's eyes widened. "I was saved by a knock on the door. He answered it, thinking it might be his mum, but it wasn't – it was this stunningly beautiful woman, dressed all sexy and glamorous, who kissed him hello, then remarked on how quickly he'd replaced her. It's weird – I realised that I don't know any of his friends. He could have this whole other life I don't know about. He could be seeing other people for all I know."

Tears started to spill over her lashes, and Rhiannon put her arms around her. "I'm sure he's not seeing anyone else," she said, but Carlie could hear the doubt in her voice. Clearly the idea of him two-timing her wasn't a total shock to her friend.

"What did he say about her? Did he introduce you?"

Carlie shook her head. "No – but I didn't stay around to hear it, I must admit. He begged me to stay, and he wanted to talk, wanted to spend the day together, but I was too upset. I didn't want to start crying in front of her. So, I don't know, maybe that's it for us."

Rhiannon shook her head. "You can't just leave it like that!"

"He said he'd see me on Monday after school, so I guess I'll know for sure then. Oh! But I have something for you – I'm so sorry, I was so preoccupied that I forgot about it."

Reaching over to her bag, she gently pulled out the velvet-wrapped parcel. Rhiannon's eyebrows lifted in surprise, all thoughts of Rowan driven from her mind. "You saw her again? When? Where? What did she say? Which one was it?"

Carlie couldn't help laughing, that her friend would instantly assume any gift was from some Otherworldly apparition they had no idea how to explain. Yet she was right.

"I saw her this afternoon. I was in a strange mood when I got off the bus, and I was too scared to come home and face Rose straight away, so I thought I'd climb the hill, see if I could gain any sense of perspective from being at the top," she began.

"But instead I somehow wandered into the mists and found myself weaving around the lower slopes, amongst the apple trees, far from the path to the summit. And Brianna emerged out of the mists, and talked to me for a moment, saying to trust and have faith, and then she gave me this, and told me to give it to you, because you would know which one of us had need of which object."

Carefully, respectfully, she handed the package to Rhiannon, who held it reverently, then slowly untied the silver ribbon and unwrapped the velvet folds. Nestled inside was a beautiful wand made from a tree branch, with symbols engraved into it and tiny crystals embedded along its length. Beneath it sat a round wooden disc, its surface smooth, carved with a pentacle pattern on the top, and with a large rose quartz crystal set in a hollow in its centre. Both were breathtaking, and both exuded an air of magic. "Earth and air," Rhiannon said, awe in her voice.

She held them out to Carlie to show her, then placed the wand on the floor as she took the pentacle to her heart and held it there, eyes closed. Next she put it down and picked up the wand, repeating the process to connect deeply to each of the objects. Then she handed the first of the ritual tools to Carlie.

"This wooden disc was made from a piece of oak, from a tree that had fallen, rather than being chopped down," Rhiannon said, voice serious and still filled with wonder. "Oak is considered the king of the forest, and is revered for its size and great age. It represents courage, strength, stability and endurance, which will certainly be of use to you. It's also good for divination and inner reflection, for connecting you to your inner knowing and your authentic voice. And of course the rose quartz is there to amplify your feelings of self-love, self-healing, self-esteem and compassion to self," she added.

"The pentacle is used by witches as an amulet and symbol of protection, and this piece can be used to represent earth on our altar. The pattern can also be traced in the air, with an athame or wand, or even just your finger, to invoke the elements and the directions in ritual. In many traditions the lower left hand point of the star represents earth, the lower right represents fire, the upper left air, the upper right water, and the topmost point spirit," she explained, and Carlie traced over the pentacle pattern as she listened, feeling grounded and secure despite her sadness.

As she took the ritual tool and held it to her own heart, she smiled, hoping the rose quartz would imbue her with all its qualities. She felt a warmth coming from the disc, a sense of security and grounding that she desperately needed today. "Thank you," she said softly, as she placed it in her lap, then picked up a cookie and sipped her tea.

Next her friend took the wand in her hand, where it sat so beautifully, so elegantly, looking like an extension of her own body.

"It's an elder wand," Rhiannon explained in reverent tones. "It can be used to represent air on our altar, and it can also direct energy in spellcasting as well as carving out a ritual circle, the sacred space between the worlds. The elder tree is considered the queen of the forest, and it has a powerful feminine energy, holding the wisdom of the crone within it," she added, gently stroking the wood.

"It represents renewal and regeneration, and aids in emotional transformation, and it also offers protection and can help deepen visions and visualisation rituals." She traced the symbols carved along its length as she spoke, then softly touched the small amethyst crystals embedded in the branch and the moonstone at its tip.

"Now we have our four ritual tools," she said joyfully. "It seems that we have friends who want to encourage our magic."

The thought cheered Carlie up, and they spent the next few hours planning rituals they wanted to perform and areas they wanted to research on their coven nights. For a little while she was able to lock her sadness away, but when she got into bed and curled up under the covers later, the pain returned, even more sharply than before, and not even Luther's warm body snuggled up in the crook of her knees could bring her any comfort.

Chapter 20

The Betrayal Continues

Her heart raced as she ran down the corridor, the thing that was chasing her filling her with fear and panic as it gained on her. She could hear its heavy foot falls, feel the heat of its breath on her neck. Relief surged through her as she saw Rowan up ahead, and she desperately reached out for him, eager to feel the warmth of his arms around her, as being held by him was the safest place in the world to her. But when he turned around to face her she was shocked to see the chill in his eyes, and the smile he gave the thing standing menacingly behind her. Panicked, she turned around to face whatever had been chasing her – and recoiled as she realised it was the woman who'd knocked on Rowan's door the other morning. Her face was lit with triumph, and a sickly sweet smile twisted her lips upward.

"Aww, poor little Carlie," she said, leering at her. "Abandoned by her parents, and just not enough for the man she claims to love. He needs a real woman," she crowed, thrusting one hip forward and licking her lips suggestively. Horrified, she turned around to Rowan, praying that he'd argue, that he'd deny it, praying that he'd tell this awful woman that he loved *her*, that she *was* enough. But he was fading away into a swirl of fog, his voice mocking as it echoed back to her as if from a great distance. "Oh Carlie, if only you could have shown me how much you love me, if only you didn't insist on holding yourself back, denying me, denying yourself…"

A soft touch on her face made her shrink back in fear, until her eyes snapped open and she realised it was Luther, her little protector. Relief washed over her, even as she realised her pillow was wet from her tears. It had just been a dream. That woman wasn't really tormenting her, Rowan hadn't really abandoned her – it was just her feverish imagination. She patted Luther's soft head, and was grateful when he curled up on the pillow next to her, little paw on her cheek, and started purring. His presence gave her comfort, and the soothing rumbling sound from his chest seemed to lift her spirits, lift her vibration, so she finally drifted back to sleep. And this time she felt Luther with her in all her dreamscapes, a guardian against pain.

In the morning she laughed at herself for letting her paranoia about that woman invade her psyche and her dreams. She had nothing to worry about – she knew how much Rowan loved her, how close they were, how strong their bond was. And he'd be there after school today, and she'd apologise for running off without letting him explain who the woman was, and he'd tell her she was his sister or his best friend's wife or an old workmate or something, and everything would be perfect again.

Except he didn't turn up. The final bell rang that afternoon and she raced down the front steps, eager to fly into his arms, to put her stupid fears behind her. She turned in the direction of the tree he always parked beneath, but he wasn't there. For half an hour she sat on the bench out the front, excitedly standing up every time she heard a car turning off the main road, then sinking back down, deflated, dejected, heart aching with pain and regret, and increasing frustration.

She knew that if this was a normal afternoon she would have just assumed he'd been held up, or worried that he'd been in an accident, but today she had a sinking feeling that he wasn't coming, and her sadness slowly started to solidify into anger. He was in the wrong here, not her. He'd tried to push her into something she wasn't ready for, and he'd invited some pretty woman around to visit him on the day he thought she'd be with Rhiannon and unable to see him.

Her growing paranoia made her start wondering about her dreams too. He'd said in the past that he could send them to her – so had he sent the nightmares last night to let her know how he felt? To warn her away from him? With every extra minute that passed she got angrier and angrier, and by the time Rhiannon came out from her Yule Ball planning committee meeting, after she'd been waiting for an hour, Carlie was livid. She barely saw her friend approach her through her tears, but she felt her presence just before she sat down next to her and slipped an arm around her shoulder.

"I'm so sorry..."

She wiped her eyes and tried to smile. "Silly me, huh, thinking I could date him, that he could really love me, that a silly, naive schoolgirl could ever be enough for him," she hiccuped.

Rhiannon made comforting sounds, but didn't try to argue with her or convince her otherwise. Clearly a big part of her now agreed with this assessment. "I guess it's just hard, with him travelling so much, and meeting so many women, women who clearly all adore him, to know if you can trust him," she offered. "I suppose you'd never know what he got up to while he was away, who he was with. And it's weird – he's a healer and a spiritual teacher, yet he's not honourable with his word."

"What do you mean?" Carlie asked, surprised by how disapproving Rhiannon had suddenly become of the man she'd professed to be such a fan of just two weeks ago. Part of her had assumed that Rhiannon would defend Rowan, would convince her that there was a reasonable explanation, that he had just been held up. That it would all be okay. She deflated even further.

"He can't teach all that stuff, about being honest and honourable, and committing to your purpose and all that, then just stand you up, without a word of explanation. Say that he'd be here, but not turn up, especially after his behaviour on Saturday," Rhiannon said angrily.

"I did run off without letting him explain the other day," she replied quickly, bemused that she was defending him now, despite her hurt.

"Oh Carlie, don't start creating excuses for him. Don't be one of those women who allows herself to be treated badly, who condones or even blames herself for it. He tried to pressure you into doing something you didn't want to do, he invited some mysterious woman over to his place when he thought you were safely off doing something with me, and now he hasn't even bothered to turn up, to try to explain his behaviour."

"Wow, way to kick a girl when she's down," Carlie pouted.

Rhiannon had the decency to look regretful. "I'm sorry, I didn't mean that to sound so harsh, I'm just really mad at him for making you feel like this. You deserve better."

Carlie tried to smile, while Rhiannon looked thoughtful. "You know, after our Samhain dinner, Dad was talking about your mum's shaman guru guy. He was so glad that she had found real love with your dad, because this guy had apparently treated her really badly. He convinced her to give all her power to him – she stopped seeing the magic within herself, and in her connection to the earth, and decided that it would all come from him. Don't do that Carlie, don't give up on our magical workings, on what you're learning with Rose," she said, her voice urgent.

"I'm not saying Rowan's exactly like that, not at all, but there's always a problem when there's such a power imbalance – even when it's only in your head. You think Rowan is more powerful than you, more magical, more *everything* – and he's not. But in thinking that, you're diminishing yourself by being with him."

Rhiannon paused, thinking carefully about what she said next. She looked like she wanted to continue her criticism, then suddenly changed her mind. "What are you going to do?" she asked instead.

Laughing bitterly, Carlie shook her head. "What can I do? I guess he chose the other woman, *woman* being the operative word. So I should retreat gracefully I suppose," she sniffled. "What other option do I have? I can't chase after him – it wouldn't really work by bus," she said, trying to joke, but managing only the faintest of smiles. "Still, I guess it means I'll have more time to help Rose in the shop, more time to study, and more time for our magical work. I guess you're right, I have neglected that a bit. I'm sorry."

Rhiannon smiled reassuringly. "Rose will love that, and so will I. But I feel terrible – I have to go home now and look after Brodie, because Dad has a meeting tonight. Will you be okay? Do you want to come over tomorrow after my committee meeting gets out? We can do our new moon ritual, and you can sleep over – we can stay up all night chatting and eating cookies and moaning about boys – personally I reckon they all suck."

Carlie smiled. "That would be really nice."

"Now, shall I walk you home? You're not going to wait any longer are you?" she asked, disapproval clear in her voice.

Shaking her head sadly, Carlie linked her arm through her friend's and stood up. "No way, let's go," she said. Casting one last glance in the direction of the main road, she resolutely turned her back and started heading home. She managed to maintain a brave face all the way, even forcing herself to laugh at some of the outlandish ideas that had been proposed at the organising meeting for the ball. But relief flooded her as Rhiannon finally waved goodbye and headed home – she couldn't wait to get inside and let the tears that had been building up fall, and she was grateful that Rose was teaching a meditation class after work that night so she had the house to herself.

Pouring in a liberal dose of bubbles, she ran a hot bath and lay amongst the sweetly scented foam, letting her tears slide down her cheeks and join the water swirling around her. Her emotions were whirling too, sadness and guilt warring with anger and shame, a confused mess that was leaving her head ready to explode. She wanted to get out and take some painkillers for the migraine that was starting, but she didn't have the energy or the mental strength to move. And a small part of her wanted to let the migraine engulf her, wanted to feel physical pain in the hopes it would obliterate her mental anguish.

She'd been shivering for ages before she realised the water was stone cold. Grimly she forced herself to get up and get dry, then, too upset to eat, she climbed the stairs to her room, threw herself on the bed and cried herself to sleep. She was relieved that she was so exhausted, so mentally drained, that when she finally passed out into slumber she had no memory of whether she'd dreamed or not.

Chapter 21

New Moon Wishes

The next day, Carlie felt like a ghost as she floated through school, barely present in each of her classes, barely focused on anything that was said. Rhiannon was sympathetic but preoccupied, distracted by her meeting that afternoon. The committee members from the other schools were coming over for a major planning session, and Carlie thought her friend seemed uncommonly eager to spend time with these other students.

When the end of school bell finally rang, Rhiannon raced off with a quick "see you tonight," and Carlie slowly packed up her books – there was no need to hurry out ever again. Picturing a couple of hours spent moping while she waited for Rhiannon to finish, she put her headphones on, cranked up Platinum Brunette's latest album and listlessly headed for the exit. Unusually for her, she was one of the last to leave, and she kept her head down, not wanting anyone to see the tears in her eyes.

So she didn't see his car parked under the oak tree, or see Rowan walking towards her with a beautiful bunch of flowers entwined with ivy. But she felt his presence just before he reached her, and she looked up, confused. He smiled gently as he handed her the bouquet. "I'm so sorry I couldn't be here yesterday my love. Mum got really sick, and I had to take her to hospital. She was too scared for me to leave her alone, but god I missed you," he said, leaning in to kiss her.

Jerking backwards, she stared up at him, and he took a step back too, confused. He couldn't understand the anguish in her eyes. "What's wrong baby, are you okay? You look so sad." Her face crumpled, and he pulled her into his arms, holding her close and stroking her back tenderly. "What is it? Is your grandma all right?"

"Rose? She's fine I guess."

He cupped her face in his hands. "What's happened? Why are you crying?" As the doors to the school opened and a few stragglers walked down the steps towards them, he put his arms around her and guided her to the car, shielding her from sight with his body. Unlocking the passenger side, he lowered her into the seat, then crouched down beside her, still holding her hands.

"Baby, I can't help you if you don't tell me what's wrong. Are you okay? Why are you looking at me like that?"

"You're here," she whispered, and the surprise in her voice tore at his heart.

"Of course I'm here. I was devastated that I couldn't see you last night, and I've been thinking about you every second today. I couldn't wait to get here!" he said.

Some of the pain and stress left her face, and she managed a small, wobbly smile. "I thought you didn't want to see me again," she admitted, voice soft, embarrassed.

Shocked, he stared at her, clutching her hands tightly. "Why on earth would you think that?"

Cheeks flushing red from embarrassment, she looked at the ground. He lifted her chin so he could gaze into her eyes again. "My love, please, why would you think that?"

"Well, it was all a bit... weird on Saturday, and then that woman came over, the one who said I'd replaced her, and she was kissing you..." she said, words tripping over each other in her haste to get them out. "Then when you weren't here yesterday, I guess we just assumed –"

"We?" he asked.

"I was still waiting for you when Rhiannon's meeting for the ball finished, and she saw how sad I was, and, well, she knew about the woman from the other day, and when you didn't turn up it seemed obvious that you'd chosen her, and she convinced me that I couldn't ever really trust you, because you're away so much, and have so many girls throwing themselves at you, and…"

"Come here," he said, pulling her to her feet and into his arms. "I love you Carlie," he whispered fiercely, then unwrapped his arms but kept his hands on her shoulders so they were still connected, holding her still as he gazed into her eyes. "Firstly, Rhiannon has no idea how I feel about you, or whether or not women 'throw themselves at me' – which, incidentally, they don't. And even if they did, it wouldn't matter to me. I love *you*," he said, with emphasis on the 'you'. "And I'm sorry that you were upset about Jay coming over –"

Carlie blushed. "That was Jay, your manager? Your manager Jay is a woman," she repeated, feeling sillier by the minute.

He nodded. "Yeah, I thought you knew that," he replied softly, looking perplexed that it would matter either way.

"I thought you were spending the day with Rhiannon, so I said it was fine for her to drop by so we could finalise the details for our Yule retreat. Which you would have known if you'd waited just five seconds and let me explain."

The red flush on her cheeks intensified.

"She's got a strange sense of humour at the best of times, but she'll be mortified when she finds out how much she upset you with her joking around the other day," he said, tenderly tucking a stray curl behind her ear.

"Please don't tell her," she implored him. "I'm embarrassed enough over all of this, and the conclusions I jumped to. I don't think any of those things on their own would have thrown me, but after Saturday morning and that whole weirdness about me not wanting to, um… well, and then Jay turning up, and then you not being here yesterday…" Carlie's voice faltered, and she felt a tear slide down her cheek. "I'm so sorry."

"Oh baby, *I'm* sorry," he said, and she could hear that there was real pain in his voice. "I had no idea you were torturing yourself over this. I feel terrible that I hurt you, but I didn't know you were feeling any of this. Can you see that from my perspective there was nothing wrong, that I thought we were fine? So I wasn't avoiding you or trying to cause you further pain, even though you saw it that way. And me not being here last night didn't mean I didn't want to see you, I just couldn't leave Mum on her own there."

"Yeah, I can see that," she admitted sheepishly. "So I guess this is the definition of catastrophic thinking, from that book you suggested for my course?"

He nodded. "It's letting your perception – which is not based on the truth – change how you view a situation, and reframing everything that happens afterwards in that light. Taking one tiny thought, one simple misunderstanding, then running with it, allowing it to colour everything else in your world, see events through a different lens, and so judge them more harshly than you otherwise would have, and give certain actions far more weight than they deserve. Getting so paranoid that you spin one incident outwards to mean the end of the relationship, when I didn't even realise you were upset."

Her brain whirred. His words made sense. She remembered thinking yesterday that if he hadn't – in her mind – chosen someone else over her, she would have just assumed he was running late or that the car had broken down, or been worried that he might have been in an accident. God, she'd invented an entire scenario in her head, spent the last three days obsessing over his supposed betrayal and convincing herself it was all over, that he didn't love her and perhaps never had – yet none of it was based in reality. And while she'd been beating herself up and wallowing in pain, he'd been completely oblivious, through no fault of his own.

He tilted her chin up, so she was looking directly into his eyes. "I'm guessing that you felt bad about us not sleeping together the other morning, guilty even?" he asked her gently, kindly. "And that made you much more sensitive to Jay's comments, and started this whole negative train of thought?"

She nodded, squirming a little under his intense gaze, and blushing beet red.

"Carlie, I promise you, I don't mind waiting for you. And I don't feel like I'm missing out on anything," he insisted. "Being with you in a cafe, holding hands and gazing into your eyes as we share what's in our hearts, sitting on the bank of our stream, kissing you and holding you close – that's more intimate than most of the sex I've ever had."

She grimaced, hating to be reminded that there had been girls before her, *women* before her. It made her feel even more inadequate, more insecure. But that was her issue, something she had to work on. She took a deep breath, and tried to put her worries into perspective. It was the least she could do.

"Yes, I've had girlfriends before, and I've had sex before," Rowan said, voice gentle, arms holding her safe. "But what I'm trying to say is that I would much rather spend time with you, just the way we are, than have sex with anyone else."

"But Jay is so confident, so sexy, so overtly sexual, so many things that I'm not," Carlie blurted out, and he sighed.

"Baby, it's you that I want to be with, haven't you been listening? If I wanted to be with someone else, I would be."

The simplicity of that statement left her breathless, and the truth of it slammed through her. Here she'd been, inventing all manner of scenarios, when in the end it all came down to that. He was with her because he wanted to be. And if he didn't want to be, he wouldn't be. She smiled, finally accepting that truth. "I feel like an idiot," she conceded, trying for a light tone, trying not to blush.

"No, I don't mean that," he insisted. "Feeling things doesn't make you an idiot. But if you ever have doubts again, will you talk to me about them? I really wish I could have stopped you on Saturday before you ran off, let you know that Jay is just my manager, nothing more. And I would have come over on Sunday, but I knew that you were helping Rose in the healing centre, so I couldn't go there, and I had my mum arriving. Oh my love," he said sadly, pulling her back into the safety of his arms. "I'm really sorry you felt all this."

She leaned into him, feeling the warmth and security of his embrace, and the love that flowed between them as they stood together, heart to heart, wrapped up together in their own little world. The sound of an approaching car brought them back to the real world, and he hugged her tight then released her. "Shall we get out of here?" he asked her gently. "Go somewhere?"

She nodded happily and climbed back into the car. And they had a beautiful night together, holding hands as they drove back to his village, sitting in a cosy cafe drinking tea and eating scones as they talked, catching up on the two weeks they'd been apart.

Rowan told her about the retreat he'd facilitated in the French countryside, and the ancient standing stones they'd performed a powerful rite within, then showed her photos of the enchanted faerytale forest of Broceliande, the home, according to legend, of Merlin's tomb, and the Lady of the Lake's abode.

In turn Carlie told him about helping Rose in the shop, how much she'd loved doing healings for people, and about their Samhain celebrations – the beautiful dinner at Mike's place, her midnight meditation in the churchyard with Rhiannon, and the ceremony Rose facilitated the following night, that had brought her to tears with its moving candle ritual. She cried a little as she described it, and he leaned forward and tenderly wiped the tears from her eyes.

Carefully she glossed over school though – she hated being reminded that she was so much younger than him – and tried to change the subject whenever he asked about her last few nights of anguish, although judging by his sweet protectiveness and care, she had a feeling he knew anyway. She tried not to feel too embarrassed by that – live and learn, right?

Later they wandered along the High Street hand in hand, browsing through the bookshop, the florist and the witchy store, then they went back to his place, and she was so happy when she saw that he'd set up a candlelit picnic on the lounge room floor. For a moment she felt a pang of remorse that she'd stood Rhiannon up, but Rowan told her not to worry, that she would understand how important this night was to her, this resolution of their misunderstanding.

She wasn't sure that was strictly true, but she forgot all about her friend when Rowan poured out champagne glasses filled with sparkling grape juice, fed her delicate spinach and pumpkin-filled

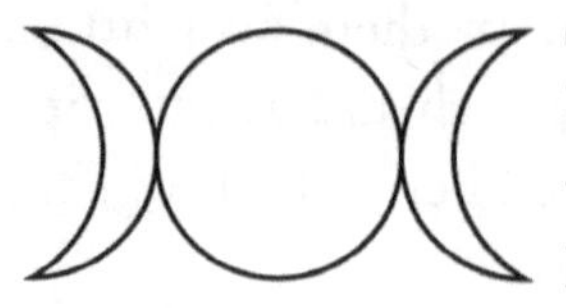

dumplings and other vegetarian delights, then brought out two little pink cupcakes decorated with red hearts and topped with a candle to help cast their new moon wish.

"New moon blessings to you my beloved," he whispered. "I hope we can put this misunderstanding behind us and let tonight's lunar energy mark a new beginning for us."

Leaning forward, she kissed him, slowly and deeply, and they sat there for ages on the red blanket on the floor, in the flickering light of several candles, holding each other close, whispering their love for each other, and feeling the magic of the new moon and their new understanding of each other and themselves.

She knew, if he asked her right now, that she would stay the night with him, that she would happily, even eagerly, give herself to him and take their relationship to the next level. But he didn't ask her. Maybe he was aware of what she was feeling, and wanted to make sure she was absolutely ready before that happened, so she wouldn't regret it later. She tried to be glad that he was proving he wouldn't take advantage of her in her romance-weakened state, but part of her wished that he would. *Poor guy, he just couldn't win with her.*

When the clock struck ten, he loosened his arms from around her, kissed her on the forehead, and whispered that it was time for him to take her home. She tried not to show her disappointment, tried to focus on feeling happy that he respected her so much and was not willing to put any pressure on her, or add any misunderstanding to what they had together, but she laughed inwardly at the irony.

He got her home just before Rose was due to arrive back from her circle, and as he kissed her goodbye she was filled with longing, to spend more time with him, to be closer to him, to make sure he knew how sorry she was – and how much she loved him. "I love you more," he whispered, then watched as she slipped inside the cottage and went upstairs to bed.

Chapter 22

Making Amends

As she got ready for school the next morning, Carlie was suddenly nervous. She knew that missing their coven night and bailing on her sleepover plans would have hurt Rhiannon, and she was pretty sure she'd disapprove of her giving Rowan a second chance too, after her speech the other night. But she couldn't just throw away what they had because of a simple misunderstanding.

Surely Rhiannon couldn't be mad about that? She appreciated that her friend was looking out for her, and that her motivation was pure, but it seemed she'd got the wrong idea from her conversation with Mike about her mum's older shaman guru guy boyfriend – Rowan was nothing like him, yet she was acting as though they were the same person.

Squaring her shoulders, she took a deep breath before walking in to class and sitting down next to her friend.

"Hi," she said shyly.

Rhiannon stared at her for a long moment, before sullenly returning the greeting.

"Please don't be mad at me," she implored. "I know you're upset that I didn't stay over, but I'll make it up to you, I promise."

"Oh my god Carlie, I'm not angry at you, I'm *worried* about you. I didn't know what had happened to you when you didn't come over last night, but I couldn't exactly pop by Rose's and ask her, since

I was probably your alibi again," she snapped, rolling her eyes when her friend blushed.

"For god's sake, I don't want to be your fall back plan, and I don't want to be part of your lies. It's not fair to me, or to Rose. I thought you were better than that, but it seems that your growing deceit doesn't bother you – it appears to be as natural to you as breathing now, which is disappointing," she sneered.

"Rhi, Gran was teaching last night, and didn't get home until after I did, so don't worry, I didn't have to lie to her," Carlie retorted. "And I don't want to deceive anyone, ever. I'm really sorry that I let you down – I didn't plan it that way, it's just that Rowan was waiting for me yesterday, after school, and I figured he deserved the chance to at least explain what had happened."

Her friend looked unimpressed. "So I take it you're back together, and everything is wonderful again – until the next time of course. What was his excuse for treating you so badly on the weekend, and for standing you up the other day?" she asked. "And, more importantly, how could you just forgive him?"

"Because I love him, and he loves me, and because he explained everything, and it was all a misunderstanding," Carlie said defensively. "His mum arrived on Sunday to stay with him for a few days, and she got really sick the next day and he had to take her to hospital. They were there all afternoon and into the night, and she was really scared, so he couldn't leave her. She got out the next day, so he came to meet me straight away – he was waiting for me yesterday when school ended, with a beautiful bunch of flowers wound around with ivy, and he was really apologetic."

Rhiannon rolled her eyes, but motioned for her to go on.

"The woman who was there on Saturday was his manager Jay, which I would have known if I'd stayed around and let him explain – she was just there to sort out some details of the Yule retreat with him, and will apparently be really embarrassed that her bad joke about her being replaced upset me so much."

"That's great Carlie, but what about how bad you felt being compared to a 'real' woman – as *you* described her – and what about that whole forcing you to have sex thing?" Rhiannon said angrily.

"That's not fair Rhi, he didn't force me to have sex – nothing actually happened. And he's mortified that I felt pressured in any way. He'd been dreaming about me, and then he half woke up, and I was lying in his arms, so…" she blushed. "He stopped the second I asked him to, and he knew straight away that I wanted him to back off. And he's finally convinced me that just being together is enough for him – it's *my* paranoia that makes me feel as though I'm not enough, that I'm not doing enough, it's not his fault," she said, and smiled happily as she realised that she actually did believe this at last. She was getting better.

"So you don't have to worry about me Rhiannon, I'm fine. We're fine. He feels terrible about that morning, and he promised it wouldn't happen again."

"That's what they all say," Rhiannon muttered, but she was saved from having to repeat herself, or hearing how Carlie would respond to her dig, when their teacher stepped into the room and class began.

The tension between them defused over the course of the day, and by the time the final bell rang they were back to normal. They went home together, back to Rose's cottage, and drank cups of tea with her before going upstairs to work on their assignment. Carlie carefully avoided the subject of Rowan, but was happy and relieved that she and her friend seemed to be over their spat from earlier that day.

The next afternoon she saw Rowan, but she didn't get a chance to mention it to Rhiannon at school on Friday, because her friend had left that morning to spend a long weekend with her grandma up north. This left Carlie free to help Rose in her centre on Saturday, doing some healings in the morning and helping out in the shop in the afternoon, then spend Sunday with Rowan, wandering around his village, seeing a movie, and just enjoying being together. Holding hands, dreaming of their future plans, sharing precious golden moments that she knew she would treasure forever.

She shivered as a thought whispered through her, to make the most of it while they still could, but Rowan leaned over at that moment and kissed her cheek, then gathered her into a hug, and she forced the sudden fear that had gripped her to melt away.

Chapter 23

Messages From the Other Side

Rhiannon had been away for the whole weekend, then was off sick from school for the next two days, but now it was Tuesday night, and Carlie couldn't wait to get to her place for their coven meeting – and to tell her about her magical weekend, full of such beautiful moments with Rowan.

Her friend smiled as she opened the door and ushered her in. "I'm fine!" she insisted as Carlie hugged her tight and asked how she was. "I stopped throwing up at lunchtime today, so I'll be back at school tomorrow. And don't worry, I'm not contagious," she teased.

"I'm so glad. And I've got so much news Rhi, I've been dying to see you," Carlie said as they settled on the bedroom floor and pulled out their Book of Shadows, notepads and pens.

"Me too," Rhiannon replied, voice sober.

"He really does love me! I've finally been able to accept it – and he wants us to go away together at Christmas!" Carlie burst out, at the exact same time that Rhiannon said: "You have to break up with him, he's bad news."

They stared at each other, shock registering in green eyes and blue.

"Why?" Carlie gasped.

"What?" her friend stuttered.

"You first," Carlie said icily, suddenly not so keen to share her romantic news with her friend.

So Rhiannon poured out her heart. She'd been to a psychic fair at her grandma's village, and had a really intense two-hour reading. The fortune teller had described her mum, and her mum's passing, and delivered beautiful messages from the spirit realm for her. Carlie's heart clutched as she saw the naked pain in her friend's eyes, and the desperate longing for these messages to be true. She knew just how she felt because she felt it too, the intense yearning for connection, for a sign, for some little thing that would make her feel her parents were still with her, even in death. She jumped as Rhiannon's voice broke her out of her reverie.

"But then she said my best friend is in danger, and I have to make sure she breaks up with her boyfriend."

Carlie gazed thoughtfully at her friend. Clearly that was ridiculous, but she couldn't just flat out say the reading was wrong or the woman was deluded, because insisting that this part of the message was unfounded would invalidate the rest of what she'd said, and she knew that Rhiannon needed to hold on to those words from her dead mother.

"Rhi, she doesn't know Rowan, or me. She's never met either of us, or come into contact with us, so she couldn't know anything about us. You don't even know Rowan that well, so she couldn't be picking stuff up from you about him. Besides, maybe she even meant Debbie or Sue," she suggested, naming the girls at school who her friend had been close to before her mum's death caused her to push everyone away.

"Oh Carlie, I wish it was that simple, believe me. I don't want it to be you, but she was so specific. It was my newest friend, my sister of the heart, the one who had just suffered a terrible loss. And it was definitely Rowan who was dangerous – an older man, a shaman, a mysterious weaver of dreams and lies, who can dazzle people and keep them guessing, keep his own darkness hidden. She said he'll break your heart, and cause you deep pain – he'll hurt you in a way you won't be able to recover from."

Carlie stared at her friend. She was touched that she considered her the sister of her heart, but the rest? "I think if I could go on after losing Mum and Dad, and thinking for so long that I had killed them, I can cope with any pain," she said coldly.

"But she's wrong, in that part at least. He's not dangerous, he's the kindest, gentlest person I've ever known. I trust him with my heart, with my life, and with myself, body and soul."

Defiance snapped from her eyes as she glared at her friend. "I can't believe you could just blindly accept that Rhi. You know the woman at the Body Mind Spirit festival was totally wrong during my reading, and she was world-renowned, so why not this one too?"

Her voice gentled a little as Rhiannon stared at her, mute, but she was still infuriated. "I know you want to believe it's true because of the messages she gave you from your mum, but this part of the reading being untrue doesn't take away from that. She might just be wrong about this part – it seems that I'm hard to read for after all," she said, trying to sound light-hearted and jokey, but not being totally successful.

There were tears in Rhiannon's eyes. "Maybe, but she knew stuff about him, about people he'd treated badly in the past. And she saw visions of him Carlie, and of you – she described you both physically down to a tee, like I'd shown her a photo of both of you, and then she talked about moments to come that she was being warned about.

"She told me that she saw a vision of him getting angry at you and throwing you through a glass coffee table, with blood everywhere. She saw him holding you down and forcing you to have sex with him, while you lay there in terror. She saw him berating you and belittling you, extinguishing your light, then hurting you because you no longer shone as brightly."

Carlie was horrified – not at the visions she was describing, but that the woman would say such cruel and obviously untrue, random things to her friend. No wonder she was upset.

"I just don't trust Rowan," Rhiannon continued, eyes sad but defiant. "He's so much older than us – don't you think it's weird that he wants to be with a schoolgirl?"

A wave of anger and betrayal swept over Carlie. Betrayal again. "So you don't *really* think I'm good enough for him, even though you insisted I was. I'm not spiritual or worldly enough for him?" she asked, tears welling in her eyes and pooling in her throat as she tried to stop them falling.

"No, of course not. You know I don't think that. He's lucky to be with you. But he's bad news. I know you don't want to hear this, but I can feel it in my bones about him. I just don't want him to hurt you," she insisted.

Carlie glared at her. "Don't you see Rhi? He's not the one hurting me, *you* are!" she said.

Her friend looked sad, but she didn't stop. "I don't want him to break your heart, destroy your confidence, ruin your life. Force you to do something against your will. How much do you really know about him? Do you even know how old he is?"

"I know everything I need to know," Carlie snapped, hurt. "And I know that we love each other. Are you just jealous that I've found someone who loves me?"

A knock at the door startled them into silence. Rhiannon stood up and opened it, pasting a smile on her face as she took the proffered tray of tea and cookies that her dad handed her. Carefully she placed it on the floor between them, then sat back down opposite her friend. But as soon as the door shut, her face fell.

"Oh goddess Carlie, I'm really not jealous. How could you even think that? I'm scared for you, and I just want you to be happy – I care about you, that's all," she said. "Truce?"

Glaring at her, Carlie considered for a moment, then gave a reluctant nod and picked up her mug of tea.

"So, I guess we should start tonight's coven meeting with a cleansing and space clearing ritual?" Rhiannon asked, one eyebrow raised in question.

Carlie's lips twitched, and although she wanted to stay mad at her friend – and deep in her heart she was – she nodded again, and moved to the dresser to pick out the incense blend they would need. And for the next two hours the two girls lost themselves in ritual and magic.

Chapter 24

Dear Diary...

As she walked down the front steps of her friend's place later that night, Carlie took a deep breath, drawing strength from the waxing moon as it sailed lower in the sky, and the bracing wind that made her pull her coat more tightly around herself. Feeling wound up from her disagreement with Rhiannon, which had never been far from her mind even as they wove their magic, she ran back to the cottage, the physical exertion centring and calming her.

When she got home, she climbed the stairs to her room and paced around between the bed and the dresser, restless. It really bothered her that her friend was so unsupportive of her. If the situation was reversed, she would be so happy for Rhiannon, would celebrate the way she was dealing with her fears, moving through them, learning about relationships and herself, and growing and healing through loving and being loved. Suddenly remembering that her mother would surely understand her, she knelt down by her dresser, slid out the bottom drawer and reverently unwrapped Violet's diary. Curling up on her bed with the precious book, she started reading.

I haven't written much lately because I've been so busy, trying to spend every spare second with Andre. And I'd much rather be with him than writing about being with him ☺ I'm just so happy! He makes me feel so beautiful, so smart. He hangs on my every word, really listening to me, really hearing me, and just treats me so well, like a goddess. At least once a week he picks me up after school and takes me out, to a fancy restaurant or to the theatre or something, which is amazing, but I also love the times when we just wander around the countryside holding hands, or sit by the river, just talking, sharing our dreams for the future, occasionally kissing...

Okay, maybe not so occasionally, but I feel funny writing that in here, because our relationship is so much more than the physical, it's a really deep soul connection, like we've been together forever and keep meeting and coming back together again in every lifetime. The other night he said we'd been King Arthur and Morgaine in a past life – I was his true love, his Queen of the Heart, and his equal in power and influence, although I wasn't always recognised for my contribution. (Women never are!) And more importantly, he said I'm his Queen of the Heart now too. Oh, I love him so much!

Carlie stopped, stunned. That's what Rowan had said, that they had been Arthur and Morgaine, soul mates through time. Could more than one person have been someone from the past? Maybe she and her mum had been more connected than she'd realised, part of the same soul group or something? But did that mean Rowan and Andre were linked? It seemed unlikely – and she was still sceptical about past lives – but what a fascinating thing to ponder...

Then again, it could just mean it was a good line, and that lots of spiritual guys used it. With a shudder, she realised that Rhiannon's words were still making her feel suspicious of Rowan, so she turned back to her mum's hand-written pages.

I couldn't quite believe it – why me? It's so weird, when I'm with him I feel so loved, and he makes me feel important, and worthy of love, but when I'm back home, away from him, all my doubts start surfacing again, no doubt helped by Mike's negativity. But Andre has written me some beautiful letters and cards, so whenever I start feeling that way I re-read them, and am able to regain some of my confidence and remember how I feel when I'm with him. And it's getting a little easier to believe him, the more time we spend together.

Mum knows something is going on – she commented today on how radiant I look, how happy I am, and wondered what it was from. Well, she wondered whether it was because of Mike, because she can't imagine me with anyone else. Poor Mum, I know she's always wanted me to end up with Mike, and I don't want to disappoint her, but this is just so much more! More grown up, more real, more loving.

I did come very close to telling her about Andre, because I want my parents to know him, but something stopped me. Mike suggested that I shouldn't tell Mum and Dad about him yet, because they'd probably freak out since he's so much older than me, and has been married before and stuff. I'm sure they'd love him if they met him, but since it has to be a secret anyway, so no one knows he's dating a student, I'm fine with not telling them for now. We have the rest of our lives together to wait for the right moment...

Ooohhh! We got to spend the whole weekend together, because Mum and Dad were away, staying with Elsie and Daniel for one of their three-day get-togethers. I felt a bit guilty, because Andre cancelled a workshop so he could spend the time with me – he told them his wife was sick and he had to stay with her and look after her! But we had the most amazing time. It was just us, no one else – no students wanting his time, no Mike trying to tear us apart (I'd told him I was going with my parents to see Elsie, so he didn't know I was at home). And it was so beautiful, we got on so well, and he said we should run away and live together for always!

I thought he was joking at first, but he said it again on Sunday, and we started talking about it semi-seriously. I'd always thought I would stay here after school, work with Mum in the shop, study to be a counsellor or something. But I can do that anywhere. And anyway, Andre said I could be part of his work, teach with him, and that would help so many more people than I ever could any other way. I know that Mum would be upset if I left, but she's always said I have to follow my heart, and Andre is definitely my heart... and my soul, and my love.

 Sigh, I really thought that Mike and I were still best friends, deep down. And that he would have grown up a bit by now and accepted that I love Andre, and that he loves me. Yet today I told him that we're planning to live together once I finish school, and he was so mean.

But I guess I shouldn't expect anything else. Things have been awkward between us for a while, because Mike is always trying to convince me to break up with Andre, telling me that he's not good enough for me, that he'll cheat on me, that he'll hurt me.

And he seems to sense whenever I'm feeling doubt, feeling that I'm not worthy, and he tries even harder then. Although that's been backfiring a bit lately, because it actually makes me more determined to stay with Andre, and prove Mike wrong. He obviously doesn't like Andre at all, or trust him, and he spends most of the time we're together, at school or wherever, telling me to end it with him. That he can't be trusted. That he just wants me for one thing. But I know that's not true. He's never pressured me to do anything, and he tells me all the time how much he loves me.

I don't know why Mike is being like this – can't he see how happy I am? How happy Andre makes me? How much he's upsetting me? Why is he trying to ruin it? I wish he'd stop, because sadly it's just ruining our friendship, because his bitterness is getting so frustrating.

I want to find a way to stay friends with him – we've been best buddies since we were kids, before, during (and hopefully after) we were dating – but it feels like he's trying to push me away, trying to make me choose between them. But I don't want to choose, I want them both in my life. Andre says that Mike's just jealous, but surely that can't be it. We've talked about it, and Mike knows we're only ever going to be friends now, Andre or no Andre. Plus I think he's been spending time with Beth, who is so lovely. I hope something develops between them, because he deserves to be happy.

But it's the dark moon tonight, so I'm going to do a ritual to release the pain and sadness I feel about Mike, and the resentment that's building in me, because I want us to be able to be friends again, close friends, to go back to how we used to be, and for him to be happy for me. And I want to banish the negativity I feel from him, *and his jealousy and misunderstanding. It's ironic really – he keeps telling me that Andre will hurt me, but it's him that is actually causing me pain, not Andre.*

Carlie closed the book, shocked. The parallels between her mum and Mike, and herself and Rhiannon, were startling. Rhi was trying to break her and Rowan up, for no good reason – a psychic who'd never met either of them couldn't know what might or might not happen in the future, no one could. And she'd said to her friend just tonight that it wasn't Rowan who was hurting her, it was *her*. Rhiannon was causing her pain, just like it had been her mum's best friend hurting her, not the boyfriend who was meant to be so terrible.

But why? She kind of understood it with Mike – her mum had wanted them to go back to being best friends rather than boyfriend and girlfriend, but he was still in love with her and wanted to be with her. Rhiannon did sound jealous, but she wasn't sure why. She still spent time with her, they still worked magic together at least once a week, they saw each other at school, hung out afterwards. Was Rhi just feeling lonely, and didn't like that she wasn't spending every minute with her any more? Or maybe she was upset because she hadn't met a guy that she liked, so she was feeling left out?

Yet why would that make her want to break her and Rowan up? Try to twist everything and convince her he was bad for her, when he made her so very happy? Maybe she'd have to do a spell to release the pain and hurt she was feeling from Rhiannon?

She was about to turn the page and read on, when she heard the front door open. Quickly she hid the diary back in her drawer, and went downstairs to help her grandma make a late dinner. And by the time they'd eaten, and caught up on their days, she was too tired and discouraged to read any more.

Chapter 25

Meeting the Dead

Groaning, Carlie snuggled down deeper under the covers as she reluctantly opened her eyes. It was so cosy in bed, but she knew she should probably get up soon. After spending a beautiful day with Rowan yesterday, hiking through a nearby forest for a picnic by a lake and a ritual performed in a circle of stones, she'd promised herself she'd spend time with her grandmother today. Rose was teaching her Sunday afternoon herbal class later in the day, so that left the morning for them. Dragging the quilt off the bed and wrapping it around herself, she crept out of bed and peeked out the window – and blinked in surprise. Everything was blanketed in white, and looked so magical in the pale winter dawn. It all seemed so peaceful and soft, the whole world washed clean and pure and bright.

Quickly – well, as quickly as you can with all the layers necessary – she pulled on all her clothes from the night before, wound a scarf around her neck, grabbed her gloves, pulled a beanie over her messy hair, laced up her boots, grabbed a jacket and raced downstairs. She'd never seen snow, and she was as excited as a little kid as she opened the door and tentatively stepped outside. It looked so beautiful, so pure. Jumping down the steps into the tiny front garden, she pulled off one of her gloves and knelt down. Reaching out for the snow, she was surprised by how soft it was, and how clean and sparkly it looked, illuminated by the rising sun as it struggled to pierce the clouds.

Giggling, she picked up a handful of the stuff and squeezed it into a small ball. Her fingers started tingling, although they felt more hot than cold, which she'd always thought was a strange paradox. Grinning, she grabbed some more snow, adding it to the ball, and decided to try to make a snowman. She added and shaped, packed and prodded, until she had a round ball for the lower body, another for the torso, and a smaller one for the head. This last one fell apart the first time she tried to add it to the body, which made her stammer an apology to the poor little misshapen snow creature.

But she persevered, and finally got all three balls compacted and in order, and sitting reasonably neatly on top of each other. She glanced around, finding two small twigs she could use for arms, two pebbles for eyes and a broken piece of rosemary for the mouth.

Carlie stood back, admiring her little creation, then jumped, startled, when she heard Rose's amused "good morning" from the front door. She spun around. "It snowed! I've never seen snow! This is so awesome!" she squealed, hopping up and down in excitement.

Her grandma smiled at her, as though she was a child. "It's not quite so awesome when it snows every day for three weeks, and just getting to the shop to open up is such an arduous task," she explained. "But yes, it can certainly be fun."

And she came down the steps, boots on under her nightdress, and a thick coat over the top. "Bet I can make another snowman quicker than you can," she said, laughter in her voice.

Carlie stared. Seriously, her grandmother was challenging her to a snowman making competition? "You're on!" she said with bravado, and moved a little further from the path to where there was more snow. She began scooping and shaping again, but was amazed to see that Rose already had her snow creature made, complete with twig arms and herb facial features, while she was still on the torso. Shrugging her shoulders, she jumped on top of hers, squashing it into the ground. Her first snowman, imperfect but so sweet to her, would have to do for now. She pulled her gloves back on, suddenly realising how cold her hands were.

"Okay, you win," she giggled. "Guess that means I have to go in and put the kettle on."

Rose nodded. "Absolutely. Meanwhile, I'm getting in the shower before my hands freeze off." Laughing together, they walked back into the house, and Carlie felt a little of the warmth from her hands trickling into her heart. It went without saying that it totally sucked that her parents were dead, but she was grateful every day that she had such an amazing grandmother.

After spending the morning mixing herbs and making incense together, Carlie wandered into town, still smiling as she marvelled at the snow that clung to the trees and cloaked the world in such an immense and comforting silence. When she walked past the graveyard alongside the church though, her eyes misted up. It looked hauntingly beautiful all wreathed in white, yet so achingly sad. She went inside and wandered between the graves, tracing over the names of the dead, touched by the love so apparent in the brief epitaphs, horrified by the youth of some of those being commemorated, and painfully aware that she was on the other side of the world from the resting place of her mum and dad.

She could never bring flowers to their graves, sit by the side of them and talk to them, tell them how much she missed them, ask their advice. She had photos of the funeral, and she knew her mum's best friend Sandy took flowers once a week on her behalf, but it wasn't the same. She couldn't even explain the yearning she felt – she knew the people weren't still there, hanging around in their graves in case someone came to pay their respects, yet there was something comforting about having a place to visit, somewhere to make a pilgrimage of sorts to. To feel that there was somewhere that you could connect with them, even if only in your own mind.

She kept walking, only half-reading the names on the headstones, until a small bouquet of herbs caught her eye. Rosemary, mistletoe and bay laurel – herbs for remembrance, for the dead, for the beloved. Herbs for those who were left behind. Curious, she crunched through the snow to the grave, and as she read the inscription on the stone, she felt her body sinking to the ground of its own accord.

Here lies the body of Louis Tyler – beloved husband of his forever love Rose, adored father of Violet and admired friend of so many – but not his soul, which flies on angel wings to heaven.

Oh god, this was the burial place of the grandfather she'd never met. Rose's husband, who couldn't handle the grief of losing their only daughter, so drank himself to a watery grave via an accidentally-on-purpose drive off a bridge, rather than finding a way to continue on. She felt a sharp stab of regret, to have lost the chance to meet him, and see what had lived on of him in her mother, and even in her.

But more than that she felt such sadness for Rose. What a remarkable woman, to have coped with the grief of losing both her daughter and her husband within weeks of each other. Somehow she had found the strength to remain in the same village, in the same house even, just in case Violet had ever found her way back to her.

Unfortunately she hadn't though, too scared at first to even try to get in touch with her mother, and then, as the years passed, perhaps too mortified by her behaviour to reach out? But she had made provisions that in the event of her death her daughter would find Rose, and for that reason both Carlie and her grandma would be eternally grateful that she hadn't left town.

How strange to think that if her mum hadn't let her friend Sandy finally know – just a few months before she died – that her mother was actually alive and living in England, Rose would still be wondering what had happened to her daughter, and Carlie would be living with Sandy, or with Emily's family, finishing her last year of school and about to start a law degree. She'd loved her life, and would no doubt have been content to continue on the old path, living in Sydney, working for a law firm, sharing an apartment with Emily, bereft of her parents but comfortable in the life she'd planned.

But now, oddly enough, she couldn't imagine how that would have brought her joy. Since she'd moved to England she'd been learning reiki and other healing methods, taking part in rituals with her grandmother and a circle of amazing women, and planning a career change – she wanted to be a social worker or grief counsellor rather than a criminal lawyer. It was amazing to her how so much could change in such a short amount of time.

Her letters to Emily were getting shorter and shorter, and less and less frequent, as were Emily's to her. It wasn't for any particular reason though, it's just that it was hard to maintain such a close relationship from a distance, especially as the tragedy Carlie had endured had changed her so fundamentally. So she was glad that Emily had found new friends, and she was grateful to Rhiannon for taking her under her wing and becoming such a wonderful and supportive part of her life. It certainly didn't mean she could only be friends with people who'd lost someone, but at this early stage, when she felt so raw and burdened by her grief, it had been such a relief to have someone else who understood her, who didn't place any demands on her or feel neglected when she was having a sad or stressful moment.

And indirectly it was Rhiannon who'd made her think about grief counselling or social work. Not because her friend planned to do it – it had been her idea after all – but because having a person like her in her life had made surviving the first stages of her own grief and anger so much easier. Not *easy* by any means, but less difficult. And she was thrilled that Rhi had decided to study the same course, so they could go through it together. She'd be an amazing support to anyone who came to her for counselling, and Carlie hoped that she could be that helpful and comforting for grieving people too.

As she felt the snow melting under her and soaking into her jeans, she looked up at the gravestone again. "Hi Grandpa," she whispered. "You don't know me, and I'm so sorry about that, but I just wanted to say hello, and let you know how much Mum loved you. I know it didn't seem that way, but we found her Book of Shadows, and Mike filled in some blanks too, and it was only ever her fear of harm coming to you if she stayed that kept her away. Although, that happened anyway, didn't it…"

Sighing, she trailed off. She felt a bit silly talking into thin air, but for some strange reason it offered comfort to her to imagine that her grandfather was there beside her.

"Your wife is an incredible woman – she's so strong, and so in love with you and with Mum even now. She definitely saved my life, and

I mean that literally. She pulled me out of the pit of despair I was so self-indulgently drowning in, and helped me see some kind of possibility and purpose to life again. I'm so sorry you didn't feel you could stay and live your life with her Grandpa," she added sadly. Pausing, she reached out and traced his name on the headstone.

"Anyway, I have to get back and do my homework, but it was really nice chatting to you. And I feel close to Mum and Dad while I sit here with you, so thank you so much for that too," she finished awkwardly. "I'll come back again some time."

She saw movement out of the corner of her eye, and jumped, startled and flushed with guilt, as she saw Rose approaching her.

"I'm sorry Gran, I was just walking through the cemetery, and came across Grandpa's grave. Actually I saw the bouquet of herbs first, then I found him," she said, words tripping over themselves as she rushed to explain. "I've never been here before, never even thought to look, but I won't come back if you'd rather that I didn't," she finished.

Rose touched her arm. "Sweetheart, relax, it's okay. It's more than okay! I feel terrible that I didn't think to bring you here before, but it's lovely hearing you say 'Grandpa' – he would have loved that. I would have loved that. I'm sorry that you never got to meet him, or him you, and it breaks my heart that he didn't know that Violet was okay, that she'd found love and happiness, that she'd had you," she sighed.

"I come here every few days, just to say hello, or think about things, and you're more than welcome to come with me, or you can come on your own whenever you'd like to," she added.

"But maybe we should get out of this cold wind – I think it's going to snow again soon. How about we head down to Kylie's Cafe for a hot chocolate?" Carlie nodded, glad she hadn't upset her grandma, and suddenly wanting that hot chocolate more than anything in the world. Simple pleasures – a sweet little snowman, a hot, sweet drink, and a few kind, sweet words.

Chapter 26

When the Moon Is At Its Peak

Carlie and Rhiannon hung out together on Sunday afternoon, doing homework, trying out recipes for the upcoming winter solstice, and studiously avoiding the topic of Rowan. And things seemed to be fine between them at school on Monday, which was a huge relief. Rhiannon was preoccupied with the Yule Ball, which was less than a month away now, and Carlie was happy to let her talk endlessly about the committee's ideas for decorations, food and drink options – Rhiannon had convinced them to include a few pagan offerings – and their negotiations with a local band, so she could daydream about Rowan.

The next day was the full moon – it would become full just after 3am – so they decided to climb the tor for their coven meeting and perform their ritual under the open sky. Winter had set in though, and the nights were freezing, so when her alarm went off at 2.30am Carlie almost switched it off, rolled over and went back to sleep. But she didn't want to miss this special time, or let her friend down again – she knew her patience with her was wearing thin, and she wanted Rhiannon to know how much she valued the time they spent together. Slowly inching her way out from under the covers, she allowed herself a moment of regret for the warm cosiness of her bed, then stood up.

Keeping her warm pyjamas on, she reached for her long midnight blue velvet dress, the one embroidered with stars, bees and flowers, and pulled it on over the top. She followed it with Rowan's thick woollen jumper, and wound the scarf she'd knitted with Rhiannon at their last new moon ritual around her neck, then shrugged into her warmest coat and pulled a beanie onto her head. Picking up her heaviest boots, she tiptoed as quietly as she could down the stairs in her thickest socks, her little black ritual bag and a torch in hand. At the kitchen door she bent down and slipped on her boots, then crept out through the garden to the back gate.

She caught up with Rhiannon near the base of the hill, and they walked the rest of the way together in companionable silence. The serious atmosphere of their rituals always descended as they climbed, as though they left their normal selves behind at the stone that marked the halfway mark of the upward path, and stepped into their magical selves. Their long hair trailed out behind them, Carlie's dark tangle of curls glistening in the moonlight next to Rhiannon's blonde waves. White clouds glowed as they raced across the sky, and tiny stars twinkled, before being covered briefly then revealed again.

They made it to the top with a few minutes to spare. As Carlie ignited a white candle in a tall glass holder, then lit a lavender smudging bundle from the flame, Rhiannon lifted her moonstone-tipped wand and traced the outline of a circle by walking around her friend, wand held up to the sky to capture the energy of the moon as she focused her intent on the ritual they were about to perform.

Once she'd completed the circle, she placed the wand on the altar in the east, to symbolise air, alongside her chalice, which she placed in the west to represent water. Then Carlie took out the small silver god and goddess statues her grandmother had given her the week before, and arranged them in the centre of the altar, with her pentacle in the north to symbolise earth, and a small gold candle next to her athame in the south, to represent fire.

Carlie cleansed their ritual tools with the purifying smoke of her lavender bundle, then smudged Rhiannon, before handing the herbs to her friend so she could be smudged in turn. Once that was done, Rhiannon picked up the small bottle of essences she'd blended that morning – jasmine, sandalwood, lemon and vanilla – and anointed her friend on the forehead. Eyes glowing with joy and connection,

Carlie took the bottle and repeated the process with the richly scented full moon oils. Then, hair loose and hanging around her like a cloak, Rhiannon held her arms up to the sky.

Moon goddess, we welcome you to our circle tonight,
And ask that you lend us your strength and your light on this beautiful night.
Fill us with your energy and intuition, your wisdom and sight.
Please help us know what it is that we need to know, and see what we must see.
Fill us with love and patience, and honour us with your beauty and strength, and all the potential and promise you hold within you.
And help show us what and who we can be.

Carlie gazed at her friend in awe, marvelling at the beautiful words she always came out with, and at the golden moonlight that was flooding her face and illuminating her with an eerie but magical glow. As though it really was listening to them, the full moon had peeked out from behind the clouds just as they'd cast their circle, and now it was sailing across the sky unhampered, shining down on them with its gentle light.

It never ceased to amaze her when the clouds parted at the very moment that the moon became full, as if there really was magic in the world. And she loved watching her friend as she gathered the goddess energies within her and channelled them outwards.

As she basked in Rhiannon's light, she felt herself grow radiant, although she knew that her friend wouldn't see it like that – she'd insist it was her own light she was feeling. "Your turn," Rhiannon whispered, breaking into her thoughts.

Smiling, Carlie turned to the south.

Element of fire, we invoke your strength and passion, your power and compassion. Please fill us with your seeking spirit as we learn and grow.

Then she turned to the west.

*Element of water, of emotion and balance, we invoke you on
this night of intuition, to help us develop our inner sight and
learn to trust our inner knowing.*

Then she turned to the north.

*Element of earth, please ground us and hold us safe, and lend
us your anchoring ability as we fly upward and outward on this
night of magic.*

Lastly she turned to the east, where the moon had risen earlier that
night, and where the sun would rise again a few hours from now.

*Element of air, of insight and new beginnings, please help us
to see what we need to see for the month ahead, to find within
us all the answers we seek outside.*

She paused for a moment, as a memory flooded back to her of the
Samhain ritual they'd done together in the ruins of the church, where
the woman on the ancient, carved stone throne had told her the same
thing. Perhaps she was learning a little after all.

"*Oh Carlie, always seeking answers outside of yourself. You need
to look within,*" the woman had scolded her. "*You are in control of
your actions, and you're the only one who can control the story or
change its outcome. Everything you do, you do willingly – not
because you're destined to do it, but because you choose to do it. You
choose every day what you want to do, and who you want to be.*"

It was true, she realised. She was becoming more and more aware
that it was up to her to create her future, create her destiny, create
who and what she wanted to be. Flooded with new awareness,
she joined hands with Rhiannon in the centre of their circle,
and they threw their heads back so that their faces were
turned to the sky, and to the great golden ball of light that
bathed them in its magical glow.

"*When the moon is at its peak, so our hearts' desires we seek,*" they said in unison, and smiled across at each other.

Then they gracefully sank to the ground and bowed their heads to meditate on the month ahead. Usually they focused on their coven work at this time, the things they were learning individually and together, lessons they wanted to explore. But tonight Carlie felt restless. If it was the desire of their hearts they were seeking, she wanted to focus on Rowan. So she cast out a wish for him on the wind, a fervent prayer to unite them heart and soul. And she smiled as she felt the power of his need for her. It made her feel strong, powerful – almost goddess-like.

Well, Rhiannon did say they were supposed to embody the goddess at these rituals, and for the first time she really felt that within her, within every cell of her body. A connection to the earth, to the moon above, to the spirits of the land and its people, and to Rowan. He was a few hours away tonight, leading a full moon ritual for a group he worked with a few times a year. But she felt connected to him, because she knew they were gazing at the same moon, sending the same wishes to the sky. He'd said to look to the heavens when the moon became full and he would be sending his love to her, and she felt it in a great big rush of emotion that made her sway where she sat.

She felt Rhiannon's hand on her arm, saw her staring at her with concern and a flash of fear as she opened her eyes, then sensed herself coming back into her body.

"Are you okay Carlie?" her friend asked, worry in her voice.

She nodded and smiled back at her. "Just feeling it all," she whispered. "The beauty of this night, the connection we have between us, the moon." She gestured above her, around her. "I never felt this back home. Not because I couldn't feel it there – I'm sure I could have if I'd known about it. But Mum hid all this from me, and from herself it seems, and now it feels like there was always a part of me missing, a piece I didn't even know was lost. I don't know how Mum could have lived that way."

Closing her eyes again, she soaked up all the energy of the moment, then finally opened them once more. It was time to farewell the quarters, to thank the moon goddess for being part of their ritual, to close circle, then to ground themselves with elderflower spring water and the full moon cookies she'd baked the night before.

They poured a little of the drink onto the ground, then crumbled up one of the cookies. Carlie always wondered if it would be a faery, or maybe a big black raven or a small brown bunny, that would partake of their offerings. She'd like to think it was the former, but as much as she wanted to believe in the fae realm, she wasn't totally convinced it was real. Still, she was sure a raven or a bunny would appreciate their little treat too.

She giggled as they sat together on a blanket on the top of the hill, the candlelight dancing between them and fluttering in the wind as they came back to earth, and back to their bodies. It was cold, but they both felt warmed and energised from their ritual, and while they hunched down into their coats and pulled them more tightly around themselves, they didn't want to walk back down to their beds, or back down to the real world, just yet. While they remained up on the tor they still felt a part of the magic of the earth, of the universe; out of step with the normal, mundane world they usually inhabited. And they didn't want that to end.

But eventually they both started yawning, so they slowly gathered up all their ritual pieces and blew out the candles, before letting their eyes grow accustomed to the dark so they could begin their careful walk back down to the ground, and to the so-called real world.

Although the ritual was over, they still felt a shimmer of the magic as they picked their way solemnly to the base of the hill and hugged goodbye, before gliding back to their beds for another few hours of sleep before the alarm went for another school day. Carlie was careful not to wake Rose, although she supposed her grandma would be happy to know she was continuing the magical education she had begun with her.

Chapter 27

A Small Sacrifice

Cursing when the alarm went off again, for school this time, Carlie dragged herself out of bed and pulled on her uniform, grateful that she didn't have to think about what to wear at least. Her brain felt a little foggy, but she focused on the moment the moon had come out and shone down on them last night, and her spirits lifted a little. It was going to be a long day though. Grabbing an apple and a muesli bar from the kitchen, she kissed her grandma goodbye and set out for school.

Her heart leaped when she saw Rowan's car a few blocks down the street. He was sitting in the driver's seat, passenger side window rolled down, shivering as a few flecks of snow drifted in. "Hey, are you okay my love?" she asked, jumping in and winding up the window.

He pulled her into his arms in answer. "Oh god, I just needed to see you," he sighed, squeezing her so tight she could barely breathe. Holding him close, she stroked his back, trying to offer him the comfort and support he always so freely gave her.

"What is it?" she asked gently. "Can I do anything?"

He looked across at her, and the hope in his eyes touched her heart. "Mum had to go back to hospital early this morning," he whispered.

She'd never seen him look so scared, so vulnerable. "Well, surely they allow visitors? Why don't we go and see her?" she offered, and saw his face brighten with hope.

"Really?" he asked. "She's probably in surgery now, but would you really come and wait with me? What about school?"

Shrugging, she took his hand. "It's only one day, and it's important to you. I love you, you know," she told him.

He smiled. "I know. Thank you, so much."

Looking down at her uniform, she hesitated. "Um, is this going to cause problems?" she asked.

He turned and looked in the back of the car. "What about this?" he replied as he reached over the seat then handed her a soft black jumper.

Taking off her blazer, she pulled it on over the top of her school dress. It actually made a big difference – her skirt could be any navy skirt, since the top was now fully covered. She snuggled into it, loving the feel of the wool against her skin, but loving even more the knowledge that it was his, that it smelled like him, and that she felt closer to him while she was wearing it. "Perfect," she grinned.

He leaned over and kissed her, then pulled out from the curb. She felt a pang of guilt as they passed the school, and for a moment she panicked, worried about what her grandma would say if she found out, and what lessons and homework she'd miss. Then she shrugged off the thought as she recalled the look of gratitude in his eyes when she'd offered to go with him. He'd done so much for her. This was the least she could do.

Besides, part of her was really curious about meeting his mother. Rhiannon had started harping on about how little she really knew about him, and insinuating that it was a problem that she hadn't been introduced to any of his friends or family members – although when she'd mentioned it to Rowan the other day, he'd laughed and told her that she could have met Jay, if she hadn't run screaming from his apartment. She still blushed at how silly she'd been that day.

Still, Rhiannon would have to let up a little after she met his mother, surely. She wondered what she was like, and whether she'd approve of her son's girlfriend, or if she'd be on Rhiannon's side, thinking she was too young, too naive, too not-good-enough for her talented son.

"She'll love you," Rowan said softly, and she was touched, as she gazed over at him, to see the pride in his eyes, and to realise that he actually wanted her to meet his mum. Today wasn't just about supporting him while he waited and worried for the outcome of her surgery, but to take their relationship a step further, to let her know how important she was to him – that he wanted her to be a big part of his life, and not be shut off in a secret part where no one else he cared for knew about her.

"Thank you," she whispered.

As it turned out though, his mother was in surgery for much longer than he'd anticipated, and he wasn't allowed to go in and see her until later that night. So after spending most of the day at the hospital together, drinking bad coffee, talking about the upcoming winter solstice, wondering if they'd be able to spend more time together in the school holidays, and debating when they would tell Rose about their relationship, he reluctantly took her home.

Despite the sad circumstances, she was really glad they'd had the whole day together, and that she'd been able to support him in some way, keep his mind off his worrying. And she was even more touched by his confession when he pulled up a few houses down from Rose's, and drew her into his arms.

"Thank you so much for coming with me today," he said, as he leaned down to kiss her. "It meant the world to me that you would take a day off to cheer me up and keep me sane. But I have to admit, mostly I was just so desperate to spend time with you, because I can't bear the fact that I won't get to see you this weekend. Is that silly, that I miss you so much?" he asked. "That I can't face the thought of us being apart for a week?"

She shook her head, smiling joyfully as she kissed him back. "I love that you miss me, that we miss each other, when we're apart. And while I do feel a bit guilty that I took the day off school, I'm really glad I got to spend today with you. Not being able to see you this weekend fills me with dread too."

His arms tightened around her, and he rested his forehead on hers. "I love you so much baby," he whispered.

"I love you too. And I hope you get to see your mum tonight, and she's soon on the mend."

Chapter 28

I'm A Let Down

The joy of her day with Rowan quickly evaporated when she opened the front gate of the cottage to find Rhiannon camped out on her front step, face grumpy and unimpressed. "Where have you been?" she demanded, and Carlie found her happy mood trickling away in the face of her friend's obvious anger. What did it matter to her where she'd spent the day?

"We were supposed to present our goddess talk today, but I couldn't because my partner wasn't there," Rhiannon snapped, disapproval radiating from her. "So I rang, worried that you were sick, but when Rose answered and you clearly weren't there, I had to make up some crappy excuse about why I'd called, so she wouldn't know that you weren't at school."

Carlie had the grace to look sheepish. "I'm really sorry Rhi, I am. I'd forgotten about the presentation," she mumbled.

"That's not the point though, is it?" her friend retorted. "I shouldn't have to lie for you, you shouldn't be missing school, and Rose shouldn't have to be disappointed in you after all she's done to help you."

"Ouch," Carlie said. "That's a low blow."

Rhiannon rolled her eyes. "Sorry to upset you and your plans," she muttered sarcastically.

Carlie put her bag down with a sigh. "I apologise, really," she replied earnestly. "But Rowan came by early this morning, and he was really upset because his mum was in hospital having surgery. He said he just needed to see me, to hold me, before he went in there – so I offered to go with him and wait until she got out of surgery. And he was really grateful, and also happy that I would be able to meet her. He was so afraid for her Rhi, and I figured one day of school wouldn't be too bad to miss." She trailed off. "I didn't mean to miss this day though," she added, looking embarrassed.

Rhiannon stood up. "And did you?"

"Did I what?" Carlie asked.

"Did you meet his mother?"

Carlie blushed. "Well, no," she admitted reluctantly. "She was in surgery for a lot longer than they expected, and he has to go back again now and wait on his own."

"So he didn't really want you to meet his mother, he was just trying to manipulate you again, prove how much power he has over you by having you drop everything and do what he wants," Rhiannon said, and Carlie was shocked by the venom in her tone.

"He was scared Rhi. I'd do the same for you too," she said defensively, but her friend just scowled at her.

"So, can I come in?" Rhiannon demanded, then rolled her eyes again. "I'm not really all that excited to hang out with you either, but we really need to go over our presentation. I'd thought that we could have prepared for it at lunchtime today, but tomorrow we have history first thing, so we'll have to be ready to do it in the morning."

Reluctantly Carlie let her friend inside.

"And just a tip, you might want to tell Rose you came home with a bad migraine or something, because she'll find out for sure that you were absent from school – she knows all the teachers there, especially our history teacher," Rhiannon said. "That's what I told Ms Henderson anyway, so you may as well stick with that story."

Carlie nodded as she led her friend up the stairs to her room. "Thank you Rhiannon, I do appreciate it. And I am sorry you had to lie for me. It won't happen again."

Rhiannon rolled her eyes and got out her school books. "Make sure of that, *please*," she said, stressing the last word. "I'm a terrible liar, so it's more than likely that we'll both end up getting into trouble, rather than me being of any help. And," she added, voice more serious, "I don't want you to risk anything for that guy. He's not worth it. No guy is worth it. I can't believe you're still seeing him for a start, but that you would do something so stupid as skipping school for him is beyond me. Don't risk your grades and your potential future on him. And don't risk alienating Rose."

Carlie nodded, but inside she was fuming. What right did her friend have to tell her what to do? She was just jealous, she'd admitted as much when they'd first met Rowan at the Body Mind Spirit festival, how much she liked him, how amazing she thought he was.

"God Carlie, don't be so stupid!" Rhiannon burst out. "I'm not jealous, not even close, and I wouldn't date him if you paid me. He's an amazing healer, sure, and a talented teacher, but he's a mess as a person, clearly. He's manipulating you and you can't even see it."

Carlie began to retort, but her friend shook her head. "Enough for now, let's just go over our notes for tomorrow and then I can leave you in peace." Realising she'd just read her mind again, Carlie was about to complain about that, but Rhiannon shot her a look of pure anger, and she decided to let it go for now.

She didn't like it though – it felt really invasive, especially now, when they were so at odds over her continuing to see her beloved. And it seemed as though Rhiannon could – and would – use that power of hers to manipulate her, to try to influence her to break up with Rowan for no good reason.

She wanted to scream out her fury, but she realised she'd achieve nothing by doing that. There would be other ways, she mused, but for now she just needed to focus on their project so she could be alone again. They settled down and opened their school books, getting out what they'd each written and comparing notes and theories. When they both felt confident that they had it down, Rhiannon packed up her school bag, moved to the door and offered Carlie a half-hearted wave as she stepped out onto the landing. "I'll see you tomorrow, right?" she asked plaintively, threateningly.

Carlie nodded, then stayed on the floor where she'd been lying, not seeing her friend out. Luther came in and rubbed the top of his head against her hand, and she patted him until he was purring loudly and she had begun to feel calmer. Such a non-judgemental creature. She was so grateful to him. And to Rose.

Then she sighed. Could Rhiannon be right? Suddenly she heard Rowan's words in a different light – that because he'd now be away this weekend, ruining their plans to spend that time together, he'd assumed she should drop everything and skip school in order to spend the day with him, just so they wouldn't miss out on seeing each other when he was busy. Which she'd thought was really sweet at the time – that he was so desperate to see her, and wanted to make up for the time they'd miss out on this week. That didn't mean he was manipulating her though, just that he loved her and wanted them to spend time together. *Right?*

Flopping over onto her back and staring up at the ceiling, she sighed again. If she believed Rhiannon, she'd turned into a horrible person – a liar, a bad friend, a user, a let down – and an idiot too, it would seem, unable to think for herself or make a decision, handing over her will and her power to someone else, and doing only what some guy wanted, being at his beck and call regardless of her needs.

But that wasn't true. She *wanted* to be with Rowan, for a start. And today *she* had offered to go with him to the hospital, he hadn't even asked her to. Plus he'd done so much for her since they'd met, from teaching her healing methods and helping her work towards her career dream, to being so supportive throughout the grieving period that she was only just beginning to emerge out of.

So, in that light, sacrificing a single day to comfort him when he was scared wasn't a big deal. Rhiannon was just looking for the bad in him – she was overlooking all his other traits, all his wonderful traits, and everything he had done for her...

Chapter 29

Dear Diary...

Feeling sad that there was tension between her and her friend again, especially over a guy, Carlie crawled over to her drawers and pulled out her mum's diary. It always seemed to provide some insight into what she was going through, although she had no idea how that could happen. But she was just so touched to be learning about how wonderful her mum's life had been, and how deeply she'd been loved, and in love. She was still puzzled about what had made her move across the world though, leaving her friends and family forever, with no explanation or even farewell...

Dear Diary,

Oh goddess, I've done it, and I don't know how I feel. This morning I left home. It was so hard, but knowing that I'm saving Dad's life by leaving sure made it doable. And it made my last ritual with Mum last night all the more precious. It was Mabon, the festival of Demeter and Persephone, of mothers and daughters, of gratitude and harvest and love. And it was beautiful, really powerful and sweet. I sent prayers to the goddess all the way through it, begging her to keep Mum and Dad safe, to let them recover from me leaving and be happy together.

Mum did ask if I was okay when we got home, but I told her I was just tired, and needed to get to bed, and she believed me. It made me sad that she did to be honest. I think part of me really hoped that she'd somehow figure it out, and stop me going. But I kissed her goodnight, then went up to bed and lay awake all night, too nervous to sleep, too scared I'd miss the train and my plan would be ruined.

But it went off without a hitch. I got up as soon as there was some light in the sky, crept downstairs with my backpack and let myself out the back door. I left a note, saying I was fine but I had to go away for a while, that I'd be in touch. And then I caught the train into the city. Andre was waiting for me when I got there this afternoon, as planned, and he brought me back to the B&B, which is really sweet. I think I'll like it here.

He can't stay tonight because he has some things to sort out with his ex-wife, but I don't mind that at all – I'm feeling a bit sad and mopey, which I guess is to be expected. I'm just nervous, and of course I have regrets about leaving, and not being able to tell Mum and Dad why I'm going. I know they'll be worried, but I had no choice – I couldn't stay there and be the reason that Dad dies. I'd rather never see my parents again, but know that they are well and happy and alive, than selfishly stay there and basically kill my dad.

I'll miss them so much though. I'm not sure I'll be able to cope without them, but I must stay strong. And I worked out the perfect spell to cast before I left, which I've copied into my Book of Shadows, a spell to draw a daughter to me, who will grow up stronger and better than I could ever hope to be, and step in to fill the hole in their hearts. I feel terrible about leaving them, especially Mum, because we loved working together, and I know her dream was to leave her healing centre to me. But I'm not strong enough. I can't challenge the gods and ignore what the reading said, even if it's not true. I'd spend my whole life waiting for some catastrophe to happen, wondering each morning if this was the day I'd do something stupid – or not do something – and cause my father's death.

So, tonight I'm just going to run a bath and read for a little while, then set up my altar and say a few prayers for Mum and Dad. And for me and Andre. And while part of me is really sad about leaving, part of me is really excited too. Lots of people leave home when they're seventeen, to start their grown-up life, to be independent, to grow into themselves... My new life begins now, and I can't wait!

It's been a week since I left home, and being with Andre is everything I could have hoped for and more! He's so wonderful, and he treats me so well. I'm still in the B&B, while he sorts out the house, but he comes by at least once a day, and spends most of his nights here, which is amazing (blush). He's so kind and caring and thoughtful – he brings me over meals or takes me out, and the one time he couldn't be here for dinner he sent his assistant over with food so I wouldn't have to trouble myself going out. Who thinks of things like that!

He's generous too. Until we move into our house (our house!) there's no point me looking for a job, so he's given me some money so I can feel independent – enough to get the bus to the library or go across to the supermarket and get food or whatever. He thinks he might be able to get me a job with his manager too, which would be amazing, although I'd like to keep doing some healing work, like I was doing at Mum's. I'm trying not to think about how much they must miss me, or how much I miss them. Kids leave home all the time at my age, so it's not so weird, right?

When Andre came over last night he said I'd have to stay here a bit longer, as there have been delays with the house or something. Which is fine, I do like it here. It's nice to have a bit of space as I get used to being away from home, although I hope it's not for too much longer. I want to start my new life! And Andre said he'd rather that I don't go out exploring on my own, just for my own safety, which was odd. He assured me it will be different once we have our house and it's my own neighbourhood, but he said he worries about me, being on my own here.

It was a bit weird, I must admit. Yesterday was the only time I've been out on my own, and I just went to the library to see if I could borrow some books then came straight back. I'm not even sure how he knew I'd been gone to be honest, but he was being so lovely, and was so concerned, so of course I assured him I wouldn't go out without him. It's only a small concession on my part, and he has enough to worry about right now, so I don't want to cause him any extra stress.

Today he brought a girl called Jasmine over to meet me. She's the daughter of his manager, and takes part in his local shamanic circle, and she's really sweet. He had to leave to teach a two-day workshop, and he didn't want me to be alone all weekend, so she offered to stay with me while he was gone. I said I'd be fine – I'm a big girl – so she didn't insist, but she told me to call her if I ever need anything, even if I just want to chat. She's so lovely – she's probably around thirty or something, and she's so caring, and kind of motherly almost. I hope we'll be really good friends. I must confess that I miss Mike a lot, much more than I imagined I would. So it was really nice to have Jasmine here for a while, to just have someone to talk to, to joke with, to be silly with. Andre's very much an adult, so I try to be a bit more serious – and a little less goofy – around him…

Sorry I haven't written for a while Diary! We had a few days together when he got back from the workshop, and we spent the whole time here, ordering in food, just staying in, talking, kissing, laughing. It was like playing house, and I can't wait until we can finally move in to the new place. Plus I've been really busy reading and taking notes, which is leaving me no time to write.

Andre gave me all these books to study, really heavy texts about shamanism and healing and soul mates and quantum physics and all kinds of things, and they've been fascinating. It was strange though, once I'd finished reading them all, he grilled me on the subjects, like he didn't trust me that I'd read them – but then he invited me to be part of his main teaching circle. I guess it was some kind of test, to make sure I knew enough about his work, was "enlightened" enough for him. Lucky I passed I suppose!

Words can't even begin to describe how amazing it was to sit in the circle with him, and the other people in the group, and work magic together for the first time. I'd been really missing that, since Mum and I used to do rituals all the time – new moon, full moon, dark moon. Solstice, equinox, cross-quarter day... I'm going to learn so much from Andre, grow so much, I just know it. And Jasmine is part of the circle too, which was such a relief, especially the first time, to have someone I knew there.

I've been a few times now, and Jasmine said the other night how different Andre is with me, compared to past girlfriends, and how much he must care about me and want to be with me. It made me feel all warm and gooey inside. I mean, he tells me he loves me, and I finally do believe him, but he must have been in love with a lot of people before me, so it meant so much to me to know that he's different with me, that I'm special to him in some way. Jasmine also told me that he's never let previous girlfriends or even wives be an important part of the rituals. That just meant the world to me!

Hooray! We've finally moved into our place, and it's amazing! It's sort of a townhouse or something – it's as big as a house, but there are a few other apartments on our floor. When I walked in for the first time I just burst into tears. Happy tears! This is our home, where we will make our life together.

I wish Mike could see me here, see how much I love my life. Then he'd know he didn't need to be suspicious, or doubt Andre's motives. But I've got to stop thinking about Mike – I have to put my past behind me and move forward. Because it's such an awesome life to move forward into. Of course I miss Mum and Dad, and all my old friends, but the time I spend with Andre is so beautiful, and working together with his main circle is just mind blowing. We do rituals together, and it's so much more powerful than anything I've ever experienced before, even with Mum.

Jasmine told me that since I joined the circle, and it's become clear that we're in love and together (it was a secret at first, but Andre finally told them because he said he didn't want to keep it quiet any longer), we've brought a whole new dimension to the group's work – that our relationship and the love and trust we share has pushed the magic further and higher and made it more powerful than it ever was before.

And we're achieving amazing things as a circle – we've done some healing ceremonies that have been incredible, and so many people *have thanked us for making them well. So I'm doing what I always planned I'd do – helping people, doing healing work – I'm just doing it for more people, with even better results. I can't have any regrets about that!*

The sound of the front door opening made Carlie hastily wrap the diary back up in its many tissue paper layers and return it to its hiding spot at the bottom of her drawer, but she was smiling, and feeling so much more peaceful than she had been when Rhiannon had left a little while ago. She knew that something bad must happen to her mum soon – something that would send her fleeing across the ocean to the other side of the world to get away from it – but it made her so happy to know that, for a while at least, she'd really loved her life, her spiritual, inspired-by-Rose life.

She'd found meaning and purpose, and great passion – she'd been loved and adored and cherished by a man she seemed to almost worship, and who others obviously admired so much. And although Violet had doubted for a while that someone so wonderful could love her, she'd finally managed to accept it, which meant that her mum had loved and been loved by three extraordinary men in her lifetime – her childhood best friend and first love Mike, the mysterious Andre, and later Oliver, the man she'd married and had a child with, and spent the rest of her life with.

And maybe it wasn't Andre that had been the problem that made her flee? Maybe it was something else? Either way, it was so lovely to feel that what she was experiencing now with Rowan had echoes in what her mum had had with her "older shaman guru guy", as Rhiannon called him. She herself had felt unworthy of being loved by someone so amazing at first too, just as her mum had, but through her relationship with Rowan she was starting to recognise her own light, acknowledge her own worthiness. His love for her and his amazing kindness and support was making her more confident, helping her see her own potential and how much she could achieve, and the many different ways she could help people.

Most of all, his love was helping her heal. Being held in the safety of his arms was allowing her shattered heart to reassemble itself, or start to at least. His compassion for her was helping to fill the gaping void that the death of her parents had left within her. The sheer happiness she felt when she was with him was a soothing balm to her soul. And the joy she felt in loving him back was giving her the space and serenity to grow, to blossom, to let go of her bitterness and the anger that had been poisoning her heart. She was a better person through loving and being loved by him, and it was even sweeter to know that her mum had felt the exact same emotions and the exact same deep healing with Andre that she was experiencing now through her own love story with Rowan.

As she skipped downstairs to help Rose make dinner, and spend some time catching up with her, Carlie felt light and almost carefree. She still had lots of sad moments, and she regretted constantly that her mum and Rose couldn't have been reunited, that her grandma never got to meet her dad, and that her grandpa Louis never knew that Violet was okay. But she was so grateful for her life here – for her friend Rhiannon, for her lovely grandmother, and especially for Rowan. It might have all turned bad in the end for her mum and her shaman guru guy, she didn't know, but Carlie had a very good feeling about her own future with *her* sweet shaman...

Chapter 30

Meet the Parent

The next couple of weeks flew by, with extra homework as Carlie and Rhiannon prepared for their term gradings and exams, and lots of research being done together on their coven nights as they prepared for the winter solstice. The girls had smoothed over their tension about Rowan somewhat – it certainly helped that Rhiannon was so preoccupied with the Yule Ball planning committee and had extra meetings with them, which gave Carlie the freedom to see lots of her boyfriend without feeling that she had to explain herself to her friend or feel guilty for wanting to be with him.

The Saturday before Yule, she got the early bus over to Rowan's so she could spend the day with him. He was facilitating a retreat over the solstice and would be away for several days, so they were trying to cram in as much time together as they could before that. They went for breakfast at their favourite cafe, then lingered over pots of tea, catching up on their lives, and dreaming about all the time they'd have to spend together over Christmas, when Rowan's retreat was finished and Carlie had two weeks of school holidays.

Finally he looked at his watch, then stood up. "Come on, let's get out of here. Did you want to try those recipes today?"

She nodded, and they wandered back to his apartment and through to the kitchen. Carlie unpacked her bag, which was full of herbs, some fresh, some dried, while Rowan got out a chopping board, some glass bowls, a mortar and pestle and his boline, the special white-handled knife for cutting herbs. He was helping her create some herbal bath oils and potions as part of her Yule present for Rose, because she wanted to let her grandmother know how much she appreciated all the lessons she'd been teaching her, and how dedicated she was to the magical path that she'd been exploring with her and with Rhiannon.

A knock made them both freeze for a moment, remembering the last time it had happened, then Carlie laughed. "Go on, answer it. I won't run away this time," she promised, kissing his cheek then turning back to the herbs she was chopping.

"It could be my mum," he warned her. "She really wants to meet you. And, um, I may have told her you'd be here today."

She pulled a face, but shrugged. "Unless you're worried that she won't approve of me?" she asked, raising one eyebrow.

"My love, she'll adore you. And she's been wanting to meet you for a while now – it's not me who's too embarrassed to introduce you to my circle," he said, then smiled to take the sting out of his words. "Just joking! But I wouldn't care if she didn't approve. I love you, and that's all that matters." He kissed her again, then went to answer the door before the person could knock for a third time.

"Hi Mum," she heard him say, loud enough for her to catch, and a shiver of nerves went through her before he came back into the kitchen with a tall red-headed woman in tow.

"Mum, this is Carlie," he said. "Carlie, my mum Louisa."

Carlie put down the knife and walked over towards her, arm outstretched to shake hands and greet her. "It's lovely to meet you Mrs Dunbar," she said warmly, and she genuinely was happy to finally meet her. Surely Rhiannon couldn't complain any more, after she'd spent the day with Rowan's mum! Clearly he wasn't trying to hide her from the people in his life, as Rhi had claimed.

So preoccupied with thinking all of this was she that it took her a moment to realise that his mother was still standing in the doorway, face frozen, expression blank, as though she'd seen a ghost, or worse.

Rowan turned to her, clearly surprised by her silence. "Mum?" She spun around to him, shock still etched into her features, but when she saw his expression she took a deep breath, made a huge effort to relax her face, smiled at her son, then turned back to his stunned girlfriend.

"Hi Carlie," she began nervously, moving over and taking her hand, then folding her into an awkward embrace. "I apologise, you must think I'm very strange. You just reminded me so much of someone I knew a long time ago." Obviously still rattled, she paused for a moment, trying to regain her composure and steady her voice.

"I'm so glad to meet you at last though. Rowan has been talking about you for weeks, and I've never heard him so enraptured by someone. You really bring out the best in him, and I thank you for that," she said, gently letting her go, and seeming much calmer.

Rowan put the kettle on, but Carlie said she'd make the tea while they caught up. She was desperate to keep busy as she tried to figure out what that had all been about. His mum's reaction to her had unsettled her, but finally she shrugged it off, and the three of them had a lovely afternoon, his mum reminiscing about what Rowan had been like as a kid – cheeky and mischievous mostly, and always wanting to heal the family pets – which embarrassed him, but had Carlie in fits of giggles.

After they finished their third pot of tea, Louisa stood up and told them that she really should go, and let them have some time together. "It was so lovely to meet you Carlie," she said, smiling, and her pleasure was clear this time. Giving her a big hug, his mum lowered her voice and whispered in her ear.

"Thanks again – you make Rowan so happy, and that's all a mother could ask for. I'm so sorry I won't ever be able to meet your mum and dad, but you're a credit to them. You're an amazing young woman, and I can't wait to spend more time with you." Then Rowan walked Louisa down to her car, while Carlie leaned up against the sink, overcome with emotion. Maybe his mum really had liked her.

"She loved you," Rowan said when he returned.

A smile lit up her face. "Really?"

"How could she not?" he grinned, then pulled her into his arms. "Come here. There hasn't been enough hugging today." Carlie melted into his embrace, then suddenly she started laughing, and he let her go, mock glaring as he asked her what was wrong.

"Nothing's wrong, I'm just remembering that incident at your primary school one long-ago autumn equinox," she giggled.

Rowan half smiled, half grimaced. "Well, I'm just glad you finally got to meet Mum. She's been asking me when she could see you for a while now. And she was really happy that she finally got the chance to. And she wasn't joking, she's told me a few times that I've been a nicer person since I met you – more caring, more considerate. And it's true. Loving you, being loved by you, it's changed me. You've changed me. I love you so much Carlie."

Leaning forward, she kissed him, feeling relieved and grateful. "You've helped me be a better person too, and helped me deal with my grief, helped me heal. And I'm really glad I got to meet your mum. Now I feel even closer to you, like I know you a bit better or something."

"Even though some of those stories were a bit on the embarrassing side?" he asked wryly.

"Especially because of that," she giggled. Then her face turned serious. "Rhiannon can't complain now, surely. You're obviously not trying to hide me away from the people in your life if you invited your mum over to meet me."

Rowan shook his head. "I'm so sorry my love, I know Rhiannon's disapproval of me is making things difficult for you. Please let me know if I can do anything to help. I hope she'll eventually realise how much I love you, and lose her distrust of me, because it's killing me to see how sad this is making you. And I'm disappointed in her, that she's hurting you so much."

Carlie smiled, so grateful for his patience. Then she saw the clock and panicked – the last bus was leaving soon, and she had to be on it. They quickly finished the potions and bottled them in pretty glass jars, then Rowan insisted on driving her home, so they could steal a few more precious moments together.

Chapter 31

A Midwinter Night's Dream

School let out early the day of the Yule Ball, so everyone could go home and get ready. Rhiannon had been at the venue all day with the rest of the committee, decorating the place, getting the food sorted and overseeing the soundcheck of the band they'd chosen, but she met Carlie back at her place afterwards, so they could get ready together and psyche themselves up for the night.

Carlie had been floored when she realised how much the approaching festive season was making her miss her parents even more. People often said holidays like Christmas made grieving harder than usual, but she hadn't believed it – it didn't make any sense to her. And yet it was proving to be true.

Rhiannon had been a great support – she'd experienced the same thing the year before, on her first Christmas without her mother, and this year wasn't much easier for her. In addition, she was feeling guilty that she'd been so excited about the Yule Ball and being part of the planning committee, but Carlie finally convinced her to see that she had no need to feel bad – and she was honouring the magic she'd shared with her mum by including their ritual foods in the catering.

Carlie had to admit that she was also feeling shy about spending the night with so many people she didn't know. Although she occasionally chatted to other people at school, she spent most of her time there with Rhiannon, or racing out the door to meet Rowan, and hadn't become close to anyone else. Plus there were a few other schools involved, and all their students would be there too.

"You won't leave me on my own for too long will you Rhi?" she implored her friend. "I know you have to do a bit of committee stuff, but we'll be able to spend most of the night together, won't we?"

Her friend nodded. "Of course, and I can't wait. It will be so nice to be able to hang out together and just have fun. Relaxing, dancing, chilling out – no homework, no coven research, no planning meetings, no boys – just us, having a good time."

Carlie smiled gratefully. It was weird, that in spite of their tensions over Rowan, she felt much closer to Rhiannon than to Emily, her best friend from her old life, and she knew that was in no small part due to their shared grief. Rhi just got her so much more than anyone else could, she understood her pain, her guilt, her fear. But it wasn't just that. She also felt more herself with Rhiannon than she'd ever been before – which wasn't fair to Emily, because she'd really only become her true self after her parents died and she was set adrift, emotions laid bare, and forced to grow up and really comprehend her own self, and the depths, and shallowness, of her own heart.

Rhiannon had gone through her own dark night of the soul, and her own growing up and into herself, when her mother died. And it was through her conversations with her friend, and her observation of her kindness and caring, that Carlie had understood the dream she'd had her whole life – to be a lawyer like her mum – was not in fact her dream, but her family's.

When she'd spent time alone, thinking about her life and her losses, and seen the way Rhiannon was coping with the aftermath of her mum's death while helping her dad and her brother heal too, and the wisdom she'd been able to share with her, she'd realised just how much she wanted to help others in her position, young people experiencing loss, trying to navigate their way through the pain and anger of grief and get to a place of acceptance.

Sometimes she wondered what would have happened to her if she'd still been living in Sydney with her parents – would she have gone to university and become a lawyer as she'd always planned, and have dedicated herself to that? Or would she have still somehow come to the same realisation that she had here, that it wasn't actually what she wanted to do with her life? She didn't know, and she supposed it was no use worrying over it, because her life now was here, and wishing for something else would be pointless.

Trying to shake away this train of thought, she wondered why she was getting so deep all of a sudden, when she should be getting ready for the ball. Did she feel guilty still, guilty that life was going on for her, that she was learning how to laugh again, how to enjoy herself? She would never stop missing her parents, or grieving their loss, but it wasn't all-consuming any more, like it had been six months ago, and while she supposed that was a good thing, it still kept her up at night, making her feel bad.

Wrenching her attention back to the present, she vowed to remember every moment of tonight's rite of passage, even the getting-ready-with-her-friend part. She smiled as Rhiannon twirled around the room in her bright red dress with its holly leaves, laughing joyfully at the way it fell around her, then moving over to the dressing table to start putting on her make-up. Smoky eyes and blood-red lips, with vampy nail polish to match.

They were in her mum's old bedroom, because it was so much bigger than her own. Rose had offered for her to swap rooms, but she wasn't ready for that yet. There were enough ghosts in her life. But tonight they needed the space to get dressed and to spread out Rhiannon's make-up, and room to stand by the large mirror and check out their dresses and do their hair. Forcing a less sombre mood, Carlie pulled her own dress on, then added deep purple lipstick and dark plum eyeshadow, and clipped a few long white hair pieces through her dark curls, adding an extra touch of winter to her outfit.

They both turned as they heard a gasp at the door, and saw Rose there, smiling at them through eyes misting with tears.

"Oh girls, you look so beautiful. And Sweetheart, I remember your mum trying that dress on for the ball she didn't end up going to." She stepped into the room, and handed Rhiannon a red velvet box. "Here's a little gift for you, I hope you like it," she said.

Intrigued, Rhiannon opened the lid, and tears welled in her eyes. The box held a stunning silver necklace that incorporated huge pieces of garnet in variously sized teardrop shapes, and matching earrings. It went perfectly with her dress and make-up.

"Oh Mrs Tyler, they're so beautiful! But I couldn't…"

"Nonsense sweet girl, as soon as this one came into the shop I knew it was for you," she explained. "It's just a small gift to show my appreciation for your wisdom and the friendship and support you've so effortlessly offered to Carlie. Your mum would be so proud of you – not just tonight, seeing you blossoming into a beautiful young lady, but knowing what a fine person you've become, how caring you are, how strong."

Rhiannon walked across the room and hugged the older woman. "Thank you," she whispered. "You have no idea how much I've always appreciated you, how much we all have, and how important you've been to me all my life, not just recently."

Rose was deeply moved, and took a moment to compose herself before she handed a purple velvet box to Carlie. Her granddaughter's eyes widened as she looked inside. Nestled on the fabric was a stunning deep violet amethyst crystal, set amongst several sparkling clear quartzes. "I bought it for your mother, hence the violet, to wear to her Yule Ball, but of course she never went. I thought you might like to wear it tonight, and to have it," Rose said, trying to smile.

Carlie's eyes sparkled with tears. "Oh Gran, it's beautiful. And it goes so perfectly with this dress."

Rose nodded sadly, and watched as Carlie did the necklace up and added the matching earrings. Shaking her head, she tried to clear the image of her long-lost daughter from her mind, but it was hard, seeing her granddaughter wearing the same dress, the same jewellery, having the same long dark hair, the same smile.

"Now off you go, you don't want to be late," she said, voice wavering with emotion, and walked back down to the kitchen to put the kettle on. There was so much sadness in this moment, of what she had lost, but so much joy too, and so much gained. She knew she was lucky, despite the tragedies that had defined her life…

Carlie and Rhiannon pulled their coats carefully on over their dresses, picked up their masquerade masks, and made their way down to the High Street, where the school bus was waiting to take them all to the dance. Their cheeks were flushed with excitement, and they barely felt the cold as they met up with their classmates, who were eagerly chatting about what the night had in store for them.

Despite Rhiannon being on the organising committee, she hadn't revealed any details yet, so speculation began to grow.

"There'll be a band," shouted one girl, who was dressed as a winter faery. "There's got to be a band."

Rhiannon raised her eyebrows coolly and just smiled. "Maybe," she teased. "Who can tell?"

There were catcalls from the back of the bus, and pleas for her to talk, but she refused to confirm or deny.

"Mistletoe – there'd better be mistletoe, and lots of it!" one of the boys, who was dressed as Saint Nick, yelled.

"And spicy apple and cinnamon punch," added another.

"And lots of cute guys from the other schools," said one of the girls. Everyone laughed, but Carlie noticed that Rhiannon blushed at that comment, and she made a mental note to grill her about it later. By the time they arrived at the Smithfield High gymnasium where it was being held, they were all in high spirits. They clattered down the bus steps, the girls giggling in their unfamiliar high strappy shoes, the boys trying to look as dignified as they could in their borrowed suits. There were some wonderful costumes, and when they all slipped their masks on, it added a heightened sense of reality, and a very real atmosphere of mystery and romance.

A few of the guys from their school were in Santa costumes, some were elves, and three had dressed as Zorro, to fit in with the masked ball angle, and there were a couple of Batmans too, which Carlie thought was creative, and brave.

Some of the girls were dressed as angels, with pretty gold masks like the old-style Venetian ones, there were a few Santa and Mrs Clauses, and lots of faeries and woodland sprites. Rhiannon was the only Holly Maiden though, and Carlie was the only Snow Queen, which they were very happy about.

Pausing in the entranceway, Carlie looked around and smiled. She'd seen the gymnasium earlier in the week when she'd come over with Rhiannon, before the committee had started work on it and it was still a bare, draughty room, devoid of all warmth or character. But Rhiannon and her fellow students had totally transformed it. Now it looked like a faerytale realm, with rich red and gold velvet drapes covering the bare walls, a huge golden chandelier casting light and shadows from the high ceiling, and tiny twinkling faery lights strung everywhere.

A beautifully decorated pine tree stood in one corner, giving off an intense, crisp scent, and weighed down with tinsel and red and gold streamers. Silver stars hung from the boughs, and more faery lights looped themselves around it.

Along one wall there were benches, covered in vividly coloured fabrics and groaning under the weight of so many yummy foods – platters of cupcakes topped with green icing holly leaves and red icing berries, cinnamon cookies, mince tarts and chocolate crackles, bowls of candy canes and stacks of faery bread. On a side table there were several bowls of spicy apple cider with cinnamon sticks floating in them – the boy on the bus would be pleased – and some of grape punch, and in the centre was a huge chocolate Yule log cake, which she and Rhiannon had made the night before, and which looked even better, and more festive, than she'd expected.

She turned to Rhiannon and hugged her. "You've done such an amazing job, it looks really awesome! I can't believe the transformation. You guys should go into events management!"

Rhiannon hugged her back, eyes shining with joy. "Yeah, it turned out pretty well didn't it? And now I just have to check in with the committee," she said, before blushing furiously.

Carlie stared at her. "Hey, what's going on?" she asked.

"Well, John is on the committee too, and I really like him," she said softly, suddenly looking shy and unsure of herself.

"Wait, what?" Carlie shrieked, before Rhiannon shushed her. "Who's John? Why haven't you told me about him? Is he nice? Oooh, which one is he?"

"He's the tall fair-haired one over there, dressed as the Oak King. He's from Smithfield High, and he's really sweet. We get on really well, he's so smart and funny and kind, but he doesn't like me like that," she explained, eyes downcast. "I don't think he really noticed I was a girl, to be honest."

"Oh Rhi, how could he not notice you, you're adorable!" Carlie said. "And you look so beautiful, so radiant. Plus you match – did he know you were coming as the Holly Maiden?"

"I'm not sure, but yeah, I guess we do match," she grinned. "But what about you?" her friend asked, voice suddenly hopeful.

"I'm fine, honestly. Now go and say hello to him before someone else does," Carlie insisted.

She smiled as Rhiannon floated over to a group of people she'd never seen before, then she filled a cup with punch and stood on the edge of the dance floor, watching people dance, trying to work out who they were dressed as, and daydreaming about seeing Rowan again. Suddenly she realised a guy on the other side of the room was staring at her. He was dressed as the Stag King, with antlers on his head and an intricate mask, and pale leather pants and no shirt. He was getting lots of sideways looks from the girls there for his amazing physique, and he did look incredible. When their gaze locked he started sauntering towards her, and her breath caught in her throat.

"Hey baby," he said huskily, when he reached her side. He slid his arm around her waist and pulled her in close. "You look beautiful tonight, as always."

"Rowan, what are you doing here?" she hissed. "This is just for school kids. How did you even know it was on, or where it was being held? And aren't you supposed to be at your retreat now?" she asked, looking around nervously, hoping no one had noticed him. Hoping Rhiannon hadn't noticed him.

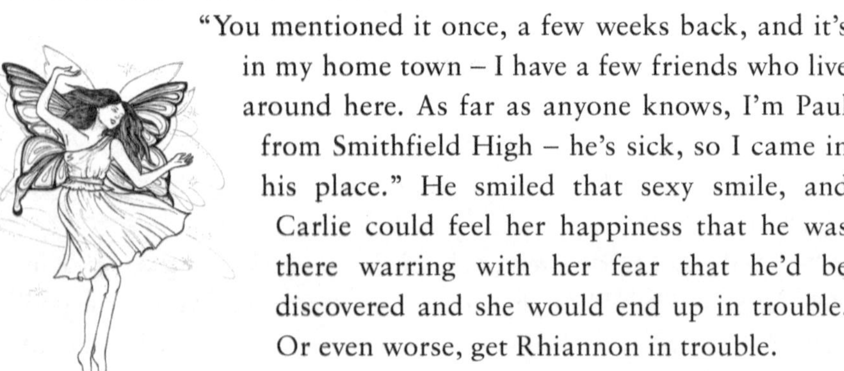

"You mentioned it once, a few weeks back, and it's in my home town – I have a few friends who live around here. As far as anyone knows, I'm Paul from Smithfield High – he's sick, so I came in his place." He smiled that sexy smile, and Carlie could feel her happiness that he was there warring with her fear that he'd be discovered and she would end up in trouble. Or even worse, get Rhiannon in trouble.

"And yes, I should be at the retreat now, but as long as I make it by early tomorrow morning it will be fine," he whispered. "I just had to see you my love, I've missed you so much. I can't bear being away from you. When can we tell people we're together? I need you Carlie."

His grip on her tightened, and while she loved knowing he missed her as much as she did him, part of her was alarmed that he'd turned up. He'd wanted them to be a secret because of his teaching, and she'd told him they had to stay low profile too, to avoid Rhiannon's wrath for a start. God, she hoped his costume would hold up to scrutiny. Then she grinned. It – well, what little there was of it – was certainly being scrutinised by all the girls there, and she had to admit she liked it too. She'd never seen him with his shirt off, it was winter after all, but he really was gorgeous.

Noticing Rhiannon heading towards them, she grabbed Rowan's arm. "Come on, let's dance," she blurted, and dragged him out onto the floor. They danced for what seemed like hours, slow songs and fast songs, and her heart beat a little bit faster every time his hand brushed hers. She felt herself starting to drown in his eyes again, but every time she forced herself to break the intensity of their gaze, the way his mask sat meant that she found herself focused on his lips instead, and imagining how amazing it felt when he kissed her.

Oops, she was getting distracted. She had to pay attention, keep Rhiannon from seeing him. But when he pulled her closer as the music slowed again, she felt herself melting into him. His lips came down on hers, and she felt herself floating away, intoxicated by the magic of the night, the nearness of his body and the connection she felt between them. Head spinning, she kissed him back, only returning to the room when the music stopped and the principals from her school and Smithfield High stepped up to the microphone.

"We just wanted to wish you all a magical Yule and an enchanted festive season, and we're so happy to see so many of you from different schools introducing yourselves, getting to know each other, coming together and having fun," one said.

"We don't want to keep you from the festivities, but we just wanted to thank all of the organising committee – Rhiannon, Tracy, Karen and Peter from Summer Hill High, Lynn, Cameron, John and Annalie from Smithfield High, and Luke, Simone, Helen and Claire from Maryborough High," the other added.

"You've done such an amazing job, in such a short amount of time, and the hall looks magnificent. Everyone, can we give them all a big round of applause?" Enthusiastic cheers rang out around the room. "And you'll all have extra credit noted on your report cards this semester," he finished, to more cheers, especially from the organising committee.

Carlie waved over at Rhiannon, who was at the side of the stage with the rest of the group, blushing a little, but smiling widely. She was relieved to see that she was standing next to John and they seemed to be getting on well – she was happy for her friend, and hopeful that she'd gather the courage to tell the guy she liked him. And, she had to admit, she was also grateful that it was keeping her occupied and away from Rowan.

"Now, it's time to reveal the Winter Queen and the Sun King, and this year it makes us very happy to announce that they are from different schools, furthering the ties we've been hoping to forge in the wider community. These two have the most fitting costumes, being the Snow Queen and the Stag King – either great planning or a wonderful coincidence. So, Carlie Parker from Summer Hill High, and Paul Vickers from Smithfield High, please come forward, and then you can start the next dance."

Carlie stood frozen in shock as the spotlight was angled at them. Bad enough she was being singled out, but to be singled out with Rowan, who wasn't even a student? Now everyone would know, and she'd be in trouble, and Rhiannon would suffer too – or simply hate her. She wasn't sure which was worse.

Incapable of thought, let alone action, she slowly became aware that Rowan had taken her hand, kissing it as he bowed low over it, and was now dragging her forward to the stage. The Smithfield principal shook her hand then placed a diamante tiara on her head, which went beautifully with her necklace, while the principal from her school handed Rowan a gold-plated crown, which he wrapped around his upper arm then squeezed closed, so it sat like an ancient Celtic armband on his impressively muscled bicep.

Then, before "Paul"'s principal could realise it wasn't him behind the mask, Rowan swept Carlie back onto the dance floor and began the dance. They were soon joined by heaps of other couples, including Rhiannon and John, and the whole room seemed to shake as everyone joined in. Relief swept over her, and she finally felt herself relax a little.

When the song was over, Rowan weaved her gently out of the crowd to the back of the room, then towards the back stairs. "Let's go outside for a bit, so we can be alone," he urged.

She shook her head, not sure she wanted to leave the safety of the room, but his grip on her tightened and he steered her out the door and over beside a tree. He started kissing her again, harder and more forcefully than he had before, pushing her up against the rough bark of the tree trunk.

"Stop," she gasped, trying to catch her breath. "We have to go back inside."

He shook his head. "No, we need to be alone together," he said, voice ragged with longing. "I want you to know how much I miss you Carlie, how badly I want you."

Panic flickered through her as she finally realised she was in way over her head. Despite his protests that he was happy to wait, he wanted more than she was prepared to give, and it sounded like he was determined to get it tonight, whether she wanted to or not. Could the fortune teller have been right?

Rowan stepped back suddenly, as if sensing her turmoil and her desire to escape, or her awful final thought.

"Sorry baby, I just miss you so much," he said softly, regret turning his voice husky. "You look so beautiful tonight, and I've been so desperate to see you all week. I just want to hold you, just want to be with you," he pleaded, and she felt the emotion in his words, felt the truth of his feelings.

"And I wanted to give you this, so you know just how much I love you," he finished. And he pulled a small blue velvet box from his pocket and handed it to her. For the second time that night she froze. Her breath caught in her throat, and for a moment she seemed unable to move, or to think. Gently he touched his fingers to hers, helping her open it. "Don't panic, it's just a small thing to remind you of me," he said, as her eyes caught the dazzle of the moonlight on a small clear stone set on a beautifully engraved silver ring.

"It's called a herkimer diamond, but it's just a crystal," he explained softly. "I have one too, its twin," he added, pulling the small stone out of his pocket to show her.

"It binds two people together, joins their souls and makes it impossible for other people to tear them apart, no matter how hard they try. It's a great healing stone too, which is perfect, because you are a healer, but mostly it's a stone of connection, of attuning two people to each other and drawing them to the same planes of consciousness, where they can stand together, equal. You're my *equal* Carlie," he said, emphasising the last bit, voice drenched in emotion as he reassured her that her greatest fear was unfounded. "There is no 'more than' or 'less than'. I love you totally, and fully, as much as you love me, if not more."

He lifted the ring from the box and placed it on the middle finger of her right hand – no connotations of marriage or engagement, she was pleased to note. "It's a friendship ring, if you will, a token of how I feel about you," Rowan said with a wide smile. "A token of my eternal love for you."

Reverently his hand traced her cheek, catching the tear that had fallen from her eye, then moved slowly down her neck until his fingers reached the necklace she was wearing. "This even matches the ring," he smiled. "It's perfect, like you."

"It was my mother's," she whispered, heart swelling with love and making it hard to breathe, let alone speak. "A violet for Violet, Gran said. She gave it to me tonight." He froze at her words, then pulled himself back a step, away from her.

"I thought your mother's name was Fiona," he said sharply.

She shrugged. "Her mum called her Violet," she replied, not wanting to go into it now, just wanting to focus on the beautiful gift he'd given her, on the promise it held. Maybe he wasn't just after one thing, as Rhiannon had been trying to convince her. Maybe he really did love her, as hard as that was to accept. She looked up at him. "Why?"

He smiled shakily. "No reason, it's just that I want you to know that I care about you, and that I do listen, so I was surprised that I'd misheard you on something so important." He held out his hand to her. "I don't only want to have sex with you Carlie, I love just being with you. I love *you*."

Taking a step towards him, hope shone in her eyes. "Really?" she asked. "But I'm not ready to, you know... And I'm so, well, I don't know. I'm nothing special."

Cupping her face with both hands, he stared into her eyes, and she felt her heart open wide with love and joy. "Carlie, you're more special than you know. How come you can't see that? How come you won't believe me?" he pleaded.

She shrugged helplessly. "I don't know. I'm just a normal girl, like anyone else. But you're so talented, so amazing. People look up to you, they learn from you. I'm nothing next to you."

"Oh Carlie," he said, and she felt the pain in his voice at her words, felt the love he had for her as he held her close. Intellectually she still couldn't believe that he loved her, but a small part of her felt the compassion and truth in his words, and responded to that, tried to hold on to that and will it to be true.

He drew her close, and for long moments they stood together, foreheads resting on each other's, heart connected to heart, souls speaking to each other, and she felt so warm and safe there that she never wanted to leave the circle of his arms.

Regretfully she straightened and broke away from him as she sensed footsteps behind her, then spun around when she heard her name being called. Rhiannon was standing there, arms folded against the chill in the air, and an apprehensive look on her face.

"Carlie," she repeated. "I couldn't find you, and I was so worried about you. Are you okay?"

Carlie nodded, and smiled. She was more than okay.

"And you must be Paul?" Rhiannon asked, turning to her companion. "Wait a minute," she said, fury turning her voice cold as she recognised him. "It's you!"

Rowan shrugged. "Hi Rhiannon, it's really lovely to see you again. You look beautiful. And congratulations on the ball, it's been such a wonderful night." Carlie winced. She knew he wasn't being sarcastic, but she also knew that her friend would probably take it that way, and she grimaced as Rhiannon's reply spewed forth.

"I can't believe you'd come here. How dare you? And what about Paul? Does he even exist? Why wasn't the school principal suspicious when you were crowned *prom* king?" she demanded. "You haven't been to school for years."

"Paul's a family friend, and when he told me he was sick and wasn't coming tonight, he offered me his ticket. I figured it would be simpler to just say I was him – with the mask nobody noticed. I thought it would be easier on everyone."

"Easier on *you* perhaps," Rhiannon spat. "What's Paul going to say at school when he finds out that he was not only crowned Sun King, but that everyone saw him making out with Carlie?"

"That is a small complication, but I'm sure he'll live it down – he might even be happy about it. I notice you weren't upset when you thought Carlie was cheating on me with Paul though," Rowan sighed. "Anyway, it's more than two weeks until school goes back, so most people will have forgotten." His arms tightened around Carlie's waist. "But I'm not here to cause trouble. I just came to see my beloved, and tell her how much I miss her."

Rhiannon rolled her eyes. "Missed having sex with her you mean. I saw you two out here."

"Rhiannon!" Carlie was shocked out of her silence. "It's not like that. We were just talking."

Her friend laughed meanly.

"And yes, we kissed once. But Rowan came here to tell me how much he loves me."

"Love?" Rhiannon asked derisively. "He wouldn't know the meaning of the word."

"That's not true!" Carlie said, tears in her eyes.

"Rhiannon, please," Rowan said softly, calmly, beseechingly. "Carlie's right, I came here because I love her, and that's the simple truth. But I don't want to cause any problems, especially tonight, because this is your night. So I'll go now, but please believe me that I adore your friend, and please know that you can't scare me off just because some little old lady who's never met either of us warned you that I was bad news."

Shock swept across Rhiannon's face at his words, but he turned to Carlie, cupped her face in his hands once more and gave her a long, sweet kiss. "I love you baby, hand on my heart, and I will never hurt you. I'll see you soon." And he slipped away into the night, blending into the trees, antlers and all.

Rhiannon turned to her friend to berate her, but paused when she saw the tears in her eyes and the pain on her face.

"How could you do that?" Carlie whispered.

"I'm just looking out for you," Rhiannon replied, but there was a note of hesitation in her voice.

"No, you're not. If you cared about me at all you'd know how happy he makes me, and how much he cares about me."

"He doesn't care Carlie. Remember the reading I had – the woman said he was bad news, and that he would hurt you, physically and emotionally. And remember Dad's stories about your mum's shaman guy too – I just want to protect you from all of that."

"No, you don't, you're just jealous that someone loves me. You're too shy to ask John out, so you just want me to be miserable too." As soon as she said it she regretted it, and the look on Rhiannon's face made her feel awful, but she continued.

"I'm sorry Rhi, I don't want to hurt you, but you have to butt out of this one. I've seen Rowan a lot lately, while you were so busy with the ball, and he really does care about me. He's never pressured me, and he won't. He came tonight to give me a present, look."

She held out her hand, and Rhiannon gasped when she saw the ring sparkling on her finger. "It's a friendship ring, a token of his love – his words, not mine. It's a herkimer diamond, and he has one too, part of a set of two. It means that we are bound together, and it's a promise that we will always return to each other, even if something – or someone – tries to part us."

Rhiannon raised her eyebrows again, but this time she looked less certain, and more impressed.

"I'm sorry Carlie, I really am. It would just kill me to see you hurt, because you've been through so much."

Carlie tried to smile, but it was a struggle. "I know, and I'm grateful for that, but you have to realise that *you* are actually the one who is hurting me. You have to trust me."

"I do trust you, I swear, I just don't trust him."

"Rhi, we've been through this."

"I mean it Carlie. There's something not quite right about him, about this situation, him chasing you, and coming here. You said before that he could have anyone…"

Carlie felt tears well in her eyes again. "So now you agree with me? You think I'm not special enough for him?"

"Of course not! You know I don't mean that, and that I think you're amazing. It's just…"

She broke off as one of the teachers came out the back door and called out to them to come back inside before they froze to death. Part of Carlie was glad their conversation had been interrupted, but another part of her was angry and upset, not at what Rhiannon had said, but at how her friend's doubts fed into her own and were making her question Rowan all over again. Which made her even angrier.

When they walked inside, John was standing at the door, obviously looking for Rhiannon. She hesitated, not sure whether to talk to him or to continue her conversation with her friend. But Carlie was not in the mood to chat, so she shook her head fiercely at Rhiannon, motioned for her to go to John, then turned her back on them and walked back into the crowd. Finding a seat on the far side of the press of dancers, she sat there alone, seething with anger. Looking down at the beautiful ring as she twisted it on her finger, her heart lifted as she remembered Rowan's face as he'd given it to her, the promise he'd whispered to her as he'd slid it on her finger.

Gently she pulled it off and placed it on the ring finger of her left hand, where it fit perfectly. She imagined Rowan smiling at her as he put it there, as they stood under a trellis of white roses and promised to love each other forever.

Then she rolled her eyes at her own silly thoughts. That was certainly letting her imagination run wild. There was time enough for wedding daydreams a few years from now. But she left the ring on that finger, and replayed their time together out under the oak tree in her mind, happiness rushing through her as she recalled his words of love and promise. A guy from her school came over to ask her to dance, but she shook her head and gazed off into the distance, more than content to just sit and daydream until this crazy night ended.

Finally the last song was announced, then people started gathering their coats and filing out to the buses. Rhiannon came over and stiffly told Carlie that she had to stay behind to clean up, and she was glad. She wanted to hold on to her joy, to this feeling of loving and being loved, for as long as possible, and she knew Rhiannon would spoil it. That thought made her sad, but she pushed it away, trying to remind herself that her friend was just concerned about her, as misguided as that worry was.

When the bus delivered them back to their village, Carlie floated home to the cottage and up the stairs to her room. She lay awake for hours in her cosy little bedroom, dreaming of Rowan's kisses – the sweet ones as well as the more demanding ones – and feeling surprised when she discovered that part of her wished she hadn't stopped him as soon as she had.

Chapter 32

Solstice Eve

The next morning she woke up angry, furious with Rhiannon for trying to tell her what to do, trying to ruin her relationship, and mad that she still felt bad about what she'd said to her friend in response, when it was Rhiannon who was in the wrong. But mostly she was devastated that she wouldn't see Rowan for the next few days, because his Yule retreat started that morning. He'd wanted so badly for her to be there with him, and she really wished she was.

Replaying Rhiannon's words from the night before over and over, she got madder with each repetition, feeling the injustice of the way her friend had treated Rowan. Finally she stomped downstairs to get some breakfast, trying hard to shake off her bad mood so she didn't inflict it on her grandmother. Who was smiling warmly at her and asking her how the ball had been.

"It was fine," she said, voice short, but the look on Rose's face snapped her out of her brooding, and she made an effort to smile, and be a little less crabby. It certainly wasn't her grandma's fault that she felt like this. "Sorry Gran, I'm just really tired and not feeling so great. But it was beautiful. Rhiannon and her friends did an amazing job. I danced a lot, and I was crowned Winter Queen, which was a bit embarrassing, but kind of sweet." She smiled at the memory of Rowan's arms around her as they started the dance, of his lips on hers as they stood outside under the oak tree. Then her grandma's voice brought her crashing back to the present, and she hoped she hadn't looked too far away.

"Oh Sweetheart, I'm so happy that you had a great night. I've been worried about you, because you've been so preoccupied. But I know how hard things like Christmas can be when you've lost your loved ones. I didn't even acknowledge the festive season for the first five years after Violet and Louis left me, so just be gentle with yourself. Check in with how you're feeling, and know that you're not obliged to do anything that will make you feel even sadder, even if people think it will be good for you. If you can't face people, you don't have to, no excuses necessary."

Carlie threw her arms around her grandma. How could anyone be so sweet, so kind, so perceptive, all the time? She certainly didn't deserve it. "Thank you," she said, voice choked with emotion. Rose wiped a tear from her own eye and hugged her back.

"I'm off to the healing centre now, but hopefully it will be fairly quiet today so that I can start setting up for the Yule ritual tonight. Did you want to come down and help me decorate?"

Carlie shook her head. "I'm not really feeling very well, so I thought I'd go back to bed for a while, if that's okay? And maybe I'll just go to Rhiannon's tonight and do a ritual with her, possibly stay the night. I don't want to bring the mood down if I'm too sad to be part of it, and I don't want to infect half the town if this is catching," she said, trying to sound sick.

She felt a flash of guilt at the concern on her grandma's face, but she wasn't sure she could face everyone at the ritual, or put herself in the right head space to weave magic. No doubt she'd ruin the whole thing with her anger and negativity, and she didn't want to be responsible for that.

Rose was staring at her, torn, worry in her eyes. "I feel terrible leaving you if you're not well, but there isn't anyone else who can open today. I'm so sorry Sweetheart, I didn't realise you were coming down with something, but I guess it is a lot colder here than you're used to. What can I do? Do you need me to make a herbal remedy, or should I call the doctor? We do have a 'proper' one in town."

Feeling bad that she was lying, Carlie took her grandma's hand. "I'll be fine, honestly. It's nothing serious, so please don't worry. I know how important this ritual is for you, for everyone, and I'll be there in spirit if I can't make it in person."

Rose looked somewhat appeased, so Carlie grabbed an apple and went back upstairs. She was surprised to realise that she really didn't feel that great, and bed sounded wonderful. So she crawled back under the covers and pulled her mum's old quilt up over her. A little while later she heard a knock on the front door, then Rose welcoming Rhiannon and leading her up the stairs. Carlie was relieved that her grandma's voice sounded much less worried than it had before.

"I'm so glad you're here sweet girl. Carlie isn't feeling too good, so she said she might just do her Yule ritual with you tonight, rather than come to the big one. I'm so happy that you two have created such a wonderful magical group. It does good things to my heart watching you both grow and blossom."

Their voices grew louder as they climbed the stairs, then Rose bustled into Carlie's tiny bedroom, kissed her goodbye, wished them both a blessed Yule, then hurried back downstairs and off to prepare for the solstice ritual.

Rhiannon stood in the doorway, clearly uncomfortable, and Carlie felt a moment of pleasure at that thought. But then she relented. This was her best friend after all. "Come in silly," she said, her smile only partly forced. "I hope you didn't have to stay too late last night cleaning up?" She paused as Rhiannon blushed. "Or was it a good thing that you had to stay back, because you got to talk more to John?"

Rhiannon's cheeks went a deeper shade of red.

"And he asked you out?" Carlie pressed. Her friend squealed with excitement, ecstatic that she could talk about it.

"Yes! He invited me to a concert they're having in their village this afternoon."

Carlie forced a smile. "I'm so happy for you," she said. And she was. Her friend might have bugged her last night, but she deserved some joy in her life. "So what's he like?" she asked, and Rhiannon finally relaxed.

Moving into the room, she came over and sat on Carlie's bed, grabbing her hands in excitement. "He's so lovely, and apparently he'd been wanting to ask me out too, but he wasn't sure whether I liked him, or was just being polite when we talked."

"Yeah, being polite can be a bitch," Carlie said, and they both laughed a little, relief mixing with humour.

"It was so nice though," Rhiannon continued. "I guess we were both more relaxed, and it was certainly good to not have a teacher involved in our conversation, like they were in our planning meetings. So we talked a bit, and danced a bit – even a slow one – and during the very last dance he kissed me!" she squealed, eyes shining with joy.

"What was it like?" Carlie asked, trying to sound interested.

"Well, we were both a bit shy – I know I'd been wanting to kiss him all night, and he said later that he'd wanted to kiss me all night too. But we finally did, and it was lovely. So gentle, so sweet," she smiled, and her eyes had the faraway look of someone contentedly reminiscing on a beautiful moment.

"So you're going to see him today?" Carlie interrupted.

"Yes! I mean, if that's okay with you?" she asked hesitantly, the worry on her face revealing that she desperately wanted to go, and that while she was asking her permission, she was counting on a yes. "I thought you'd be doing the ritual at the healing centre."

"Of course it's okay," Carlie said, forcing a lightness into her tone. "And although you've kept him a secret, I've guessed for a while that you like someone, and this is a great time to go see him – discover whether you still like him in the cold light of day," Carlie teased.

"His parents will be there though, and his younger brothers, so I'm a bit nervous," Rhiannon whispered, and Carlie did all she could to reassure her.

They talked for ages, giggling about some of the outfits from the ball, working out how Rhiannon could deal with the pesky little brothers if they tried to tease her, and mentally going through her wardrobe until she decided what to wear. But eventually she broke off, that topic exhausted, and looked uncomfortable again.

"Look Carlie, I'm really sorry about what I said last night," she said, sounding sincere.

Carlie forced a smile "It's okay," she muttered.

"But it's just that I worry about you," her friend blundered on. "I know you think you love him, but you're too young to commit to anyone. He's so much older than you, and… my god, he's so… well, I mean…" she stuttered.

Carlie glared at her. "He's so what?"

"Well, he's a guy, a hot-blooded grown-up guy, as everyone noticed last night with that outfit he was wearing, or not wearing, as the case may be. So he's going to want to have sex with you. If you haven't already –" she broke off.

Carlie was angry, yet calm. "Not that it's any of your business, but no, we haven't. He hasn't pressured me at all, he's happy to wait until I'm ready, no matter how long that takes. He actually likes talking to me, as surprising as that might sound to you," she said, sarcasm making her voice bitter.

Rhiannon looked sad. "I don't mean that Carlie, I promise."

Carlie shrugged, defensive now. "He's twenty-three. That's only six years older than me. Louis was ten years older than Grandma Rose, and they were very happily married."

"But it's a lot right now," Rhiannon argued. "You're in school, and he's travelling the country teaching, meeting hundreds of women who no doubt throw themselves at him. I'd just hate for him to hurt you, especially with what your mum went through, with the older shaman guru guy who treated her so badly."

Fury stabbed in Carlie's chest, and anger flashed across her face. "How dare you talk about my mother? You don't know her, don't know what happened between them." Tears trembled on her lashes, but her voice was fierce. "He was the first man she really loved, and she never regretted any of it."

She felt a moment of triumph as a look of pain crossed her friend's face, but then she just felt bad. "I'm sorry, I shouldn't have said that, of course she loved your dad. It's just that Andre was her first grown-up relationship, and she loved him deeply."

"How do you know this?" her friend broke in suspiciously. "You can't twist it around now to try to justify being with Rowan. Dad said he'd treated her really badly, and was jealous and possessive."

"Sandy found Mum's diary in a safety deposit box, and sent it to me a couple of weeks ago."

Her friend couldn't mask her surprise. "You never told me that. Did it answer any questions, like why she ran away?"

Carlie shrugged. "I haven't finished it yet. I'm saving it, savouring it, trying to make it last so I can feel close to her for longer."

For several minutes they were both quiet as they pondered their losses, and the pain they'd experienced at the death of their parents. Rhiannon was one of the few people who would understand why Carlie wanted to string the diary out. Slowly the anger drained away from both of them, and they sighed at the same time, then looked up at each other and smiled.

"We shouldn't be fighting," Rhiannon said softly. "It's the festive season, the time for family and friends, and forgiveness. I just care about you, that's all. And I'm here if you need me."

Carlie nodded gratefully, then rubbed her hand impatiently across her face to wipe away the tears. Her ring sparkled in the pale sunshine streaming in the window, catching Rhiannon's eye, and her friend quickly reverted right back to her previous objections.

"I just don't trust him," she blurted out. "And I'm only saying this because you're my best friend, and because I care about you — otherwise it would be much easier if I didn't say anything. But the reading was so clear, and according to her visions, he's going to leave you heartbroken, and possibly physically beaten as well."

Carlie stared at Rhiannon, fresh tears in her eyes. "Just go. Go and see John, and have a great time with him," she said angrily.

"Just think about it," her friend insisted. "He's a bad influence on you, and you don't need that. You need to focus on school, not skip classes to be at his beck and call. And you said you wanted to help Rose in the shop, but instead you're lying to her, sneaking around, bringing him into her house to do god knows what behind her back."

She paused for a moment, and Carlie stared at her, speechless. "You don't turn up for our coven meetings, you take me for granted, and you expect me to back up your lies or provide an alibi for you," Rhiannon continued. "I don't think I can be around you, and watch you ruin your life. Watch you betray me, betray Rose, betray yourself

– become someone you don't want to be. Please, you have to break up with him. Otherwise I just… I don't think I can be your friend." And she turned and fled down the stairs.

Carlie stared after her, stunned by the anger in her friend's voice and the ultimatum she'd delivered. How could she expect her to give up the person she loved just because she didn't approve? Expect her to "prove" how much she valued their friendship by making such a huge sacrifice? Especially as she was off to spend the afternoon with the guy she liked, which meant skipping their Yule ritual. So it was okay for Rhiannon to have a boyfriend and stand her up, but she couldn't see Rowan? That was a bit hypocritical, surely.

She wished she'd thought to say that to her friend, but she'd been too shell-shocked in the moment to reply. Now she sat on her bed, dazed, wondering how on earth their conversation had spiralled so far out of control. When Luther leaped up onto the bed and settled down in her lap, she was grateful for the distraction, smiling as she stroked his head and let his purring calm her down.

"Oh Luther, what am I supposed to do now? I love Rowan, but I care about Rhiannon too. She's my dearest friend – she's been so good to me, and we've helped each other so much. And she's always so understanding, which is what makes this so weird. She really loved Rowan when we met him, and when we all spent that time together, the three of us. And I've only skipped school once, and only missed one of our coven meetings. She made it sound like I was never at school, and never with her doing ritual, that I'm not committed to our magical life, but I am. Surely it seems like an overly dramatic response, that I have to choose between them just for that?"

Luther lifted his head a little and gazed up at her, expression serene, aloof, forever unknowable.

"What should I do Luther? I don't want to lose Rowan, and I shouldn't have to, but I don't want to be one of those girls who chooses her boyfriend over her best friend either," she sighed. "Rhiannon and I are so close, we've shared everything, helped each other grieve – and we're planning to go to uni together, study together. I don't want to lose all that."

But the more she thought about it, the madder she got. She knew she wasn't just being defensive – Rhiannon was definitely over-reacting, and over-exaggerating any supposedly bad thing she'd ever done for Rowan, or he'd done to her. And Rhiannon had been so rude to him last night, while he'd been a perfect gentleman, polite and respectful, and leaving the ball – leaving her – just to keep Rhiannon happy. So Carlie lay there, running things round and round in her mind, until she felt her head would explode.

Finally she threw back the covers, stumbled out of bed, and opened the door of her closet. She chose a deep ruby-red velvet dress, pulled on black tights underneath it and a thick black coat over the top, and laced up her thick black boots. Then she pulled down her backpack and shoved a change of clothes, her wallet and her mum's diary inside, and raced down the stairs and out the front door before she could change her mind.

She'd told Rowan she couldn't go to his retreat, partly because she wanted to spend Yule with Rose and Rhiannon, and partly because, well, her grandma had no idea she was even dating anyone, and would no doubt be less than keen to have her going away with him for the weekend if she did know.

But Rose would be out tonight, and would think she was at Rhiannon's, and her friend would be away with John. So no one would ever know if she slipped off now and stayed away until tomorrow. She did have a pang of conscience as she remembered Rhi accusing her of using her as an alibi, but what choice did she have? She was going to go crazy if she had to stay here on her own, obsessing over the ultimatum her friend had given her. And she desperately needed to see Rowan. She couldn't wait until next week, she wanted to see him now. Wanted to continue their conversation from the previous night, and their kissing too. Smiling down at the beautiful ring he'd given her, she remembered how tightly he'd held her as he'd whispered his love to her, how close she'd felt to him as he reassured her that she was special.

There was a bus just pulling in as she raced up the road to the stop, so she took it as a sign. She was meant to be with him. Smiling, she curled up in her seat and pulled her mum's diary out of her bag.

Chapter 33

Dear Diary...

She flicked through it to find where she was up to, and discovered a bunch of loose-leaf pages that had been inserted into the diary, like a letter added much later. Horror engulfed her and her heart broke as she read the pain-drenched words, and finally began to comprehend just how bleak her mother's life had become.

My Dearest Daughter,

Talking to you is the only thing keeping me sane right now, and yet you don't even exist, so perhaps I'm not so sane after all. But I have fifteen precious minutes alone, and I keep hoping that if I can just confide in someone, even someone who only exists as an idea, I'll somehow see something that makes sense, find out what went wrong, and what I'm doing that makes him hate me so much – and hopefully discover why I'm in this hell, and find a way out.

I don't know though, some days I think the only way I'll escape this is through death – mine, his, at this point I don't really care which one. How can I have stopped caring? Mum would be horrified if she knew what I'd become, but even she seems so far away now. Did I ever really know her? Work magic with her? Love life and my family with her?

This did start out as the most beautiful love story ever told though, and I think it's important to remember that. He taught me so much about myself, and for a while I really blossomed in his care, I became so much more than I'd imagined I could be. I thought he would be your father, I really did. When I sent out my spell to Kali to bring you to me, I pictured his face as part of our perfect family. But I can never let that happen now. That would be a fate worse than death for both of us.

But perhaps I should start at the beginning? He was the man of my dreams – quite literally, because I dreamed about him for weeks before I met him for the first time, dreams he told me he had sent to me. And he was amazing – so powerful and magical and strong, so charming and charismatic. He swept me off my feet, and I couldn't believe he could like me, let alone love me. It took him a long time to convince me. And he swore that no one would ever love me the way he did. Which sounded so desperately romantic at the time, but now that thought fills me with bitter amusement and the deepest dread, and I pray that no one else will ever love me like he does. But I'm getting ahead of myself...

I loved him for a long time, admired him, worshipped him in a way. And when he did a tarot reading for me that said my father would die if I stayed at home, then begged me to come and live with him, I was flattered, and excited, and so desperately happy to be with him. I felt sad that I was leaving my parents, but I knew it was for the best if it would save Dad's life, and while of course I wished I could explain it to them, why I was leaving, I always assumed there would be time later to sort it all out.

And it was wonderful at first, living with him, spending all our time together, working magic with him, doing rituals at his workshops around the country, learning from him, so much, about life and healing, and about myself too. I felt so proud to be the so-called love of his life, to watch him work, to know that of all the women he could have had, he'd chosen me. I felt really special, and I loved him so much. And for a while he loved me too, purely and with both passion and compassion. He helped me be a better person, inspired me and challenged me and adored me.

The change was subtle at first. He started to criticise me for the things he used to compliment me on. He stopped welcoming me to his circles as often, letting me take part in his work. Slowly it became clear that he thought I was less than him, that all women were, and that my main job was to cook, clean and look after him, and do everything he wanted me to do whenever he wanted me to do it.

Even then I defended him, twisted it around in my head – I was lucky to be able to care for him, to serve him. He constantly told me that he could have any woman he wanted, that they would beg for the chance to be able to please him, and if I didn't submit, he might just do that. The scariest thing is that this became a new kind of normal for me, and I stopped thinking it was remotely strange. How insane is that?! When we were at his retreats we were surrounded by women who loved him, who wanted him, and who thought I was so lucky to be with him. For a while I thought I was too.

Then he started getting paranoid and suspicious. He became jealous of the guys in our group, who we'd worked with for ages and who were like part of our family. He'd claim I fancied them, and make a joke of it, but I didn't find it funny at all. I became hyper-aware of how I acted around them as a result – I barely spoke to them, too scared to even glance their way in case he caught me looking at them and decided that was proof I wanted them – and that made me sad, because we'd been friends, and here I was treating them like they wanted to be with me but were beneath me, too far beneath me even to talk to them, which wasn't the case at all.

At first I was strangely flattered, that he was so devoted to me, that he wanted me so much and loved me so deeply, but then the suspicion became nasty, and he started accusing me of awful things, things I'd never do. He'd scream at me that he knew I'd had sex with other people, that he'd seen it psychically so there was no point lying to him, but it wasn't true. It was particularly distressing because he was the only person I'd ever slept with, and I didn't want to be with anyone other than him, ever. But his insistence had me doubting my own sanity at times, questioning if I actually had cheated on him, even though I knew that I hadn't.

Even that I put up with and endured without complaint – I figured maybe it was the price to pay to be with someone so amazing? And who was I going to complain to anyway? Everyone around me thought *he was perfect, without fault, a god of sorts. And in between there were still moments where I was happy, where he treated me so well, like he had in the beginning, so I hoped that once he'd learned to trust me, and realised how crazy it was to think I'd cheat on him, it would be okay, it would go back to normal.*

I was a fool. Men who treat women that way don't ever stop, they escalate. The times he treated me well got fewer and further between, and his cruelty increased. He started hitting me, hurting me, and soon he stopped apologising for it, stopped begging me to forgive him and promising it would never happen again, because by then he didn't care. By then we both knew it would happen again. And everything became my fault. I was bringing the punishments on myself. If I only treated him better, if I wasn't such a whore, then he would be nice to me. He was doing it for my own good, apparently…

The letter ended and the diary began again, but Carlie paused, shocked. How had her brave, confident and spiritual mother become such a shell of herself? How had a man done that to her? If only she could have made her way back home to Rose, she would have recovered. But it seemed that the more he tore away her self-esteem, her sanity even, the less she felt deserving of being saved, and that thought overwhelmed Carlie with despair.

She couldn't imagine her mum like that, so scared, so paralysed. She'd been so confident, so assured, when she knew her, the powerhouse lawyer, the family breadwinner. She would never have put up with this. But somehow this man had scraped away the very essence of who she was, had beaten all the strength and self-belief out of her. She wasn't sure she wanted to keep reading – it felt so personal, like she was betraying her mother by learning all this – but she had to find out what happened. And at least she knew, as awful as everything she was describing was, that her mum had escaped. Somehow she'd found the strength to leave, to flee to the other side of the world, and she had found happiness.

Today I returned from grocery shopping to find him sitting at the kitchen table, arms folded, glaring at me. I knew that look, and I quailed inside at what was to come.

"Where have you been?" he demanded, and I told him I'd been buying food for dinner, which I had been. He didn't believe me, so I showed him the docket from the supermarket, and gave him his change. He went through every grocery bag, then grabbed my purse and rifled through that too, but there was nothing to find.

"Where else did you go? Who did you meet?" he demanded.

"I didn't meet anyone," I replied, perplexed.

"Don't lie to me. I called the grocery store, and you were there half an hour ago. Where else did you go?"

I blanched. Suddenly he had me questioning myself, but I hadn't done anything wrong, or anything other than what I'd told him. I explained that the bus had been fifteen minutes late, but even though I showed him the ticket, he didn't believe that either. He screamed "Liar!" at me, and worse, and then he hit me. As I crumpled to the floor, sobbing and clutching my jaw, he rang the bus company – and when they said the bus had been delayed due to an accident, he shrugged and told me to get up and start making dinner.

Carlie could barely breathe. Her mind reeled as she tried to comprehend what she was reading. Her bright, brave, strong mother had been a victim of domestic violence. Of brutal physical and psychological abuse. Her stomach clenched and she felt sick, furious at the man who had done this to her, angry at her friends for letting it happen. Surely someone must have been aware of what was going on? Or was he such a good manipulator that they were oblivious?

It sounded like he'd cut her mum off from her old friends and family, and isolated her from any potential new people in her life, so that she had no one to confide in, no one to help her see just how wrong all this was. She didn't want to keep reading, but she felt compelled somehow. She had to know how bad it got, and also how her mum had eventually escaped. Thank god she knew it had a happy ending, or she didn't think she could continue. She turned back to the diary. A few pages had been torn out, then the entries re-started.

Oh my god! I feel so stupid. I just found out that his ex-wife isn't so ex. That they're still married. And he has a son, who's just a little kid. He'd mentioned doing something with a nephew once before, but no, that was a lie. It was his child. Discovering this made me feel so sleazy, even though I had no idea he was still married, or had any children – he told me he'd been separated from his wife for two years, and that he was glad they'd had no kids because it made it easier to leave her, that the divorce had just been a formality.

But no. She actually thought they were still together, that he was just doing a lot of travelling at the moment for workshops and retreats. Which means that some of those nights that he's been away from me, saying he was working, he must have been staying with them. Tucking his son into bed. Sleeping next to his wife. Sleeping with his wife?

I asked him about it when he got home, and he denied it at first, then he demanded to know who'd told me. I wasn't going to give Jasmine up though, because it seems like she's my only friend now. And eventually he shrugged that off anyway and tried to turn it around on me. That it was all my fault – I was an evil whore who tempted him away from his wife and child, I was a home wrecker. When I reminded him that he'd insisted to me that he was divorced and childless, he just smirked and said that's what I'd wanted to believe. God! It's so infuriating.

And then he turned it around again, and said I was just upset because I was cheating on him. Which doesn't even make sense. He knows where I am every minute of every day, and it's usually with him, or waiting for him, or crying in a heap on the floor after another battle, either physical or psychological, unable to muster the energy to get up, let alone go anywhere. He keeps saying that he can "see" me cheating – he describes it in detail, like some kind of dirty fantasy of his, all the supposed sex I'm supposedly always having, with men I've never even met, even a woman yesterday, apparently. It really does my head in.

At first he made me wonder if I actually had been doing the things he said I did – but I know I haven't. That I wouldn't. And usually that I couldn't, because all the times he says all this is happening, I've actually been with him. It just doesn't make sense!

It's making me question his work as a healer and teacher too – if he is so wrong on this, if he can swear blind that he's "seen" me cheating, does that mean he isn't as psychic as he claims? Are none of his visions true? Or is it just me that he lies to? And if he's prepared to lie and manipulate in his work, to swear his "vision" is true when it is patently false, what does that say about his ethics towards all his students?

But I think I'm the only person he treats like this – I pray I am anyway – because every now and then he gets really upset and implies that I make him behave badly, that he doesn't do this to anyone else, that he doesn't want to treat anyone this cruelly, least of all me. And then he does it all again…

Oh goddess, please give me strength. I've been working in a bookstore for the last few months, so I can earn a bit of money and not feel so totally dependent on him, and it's been wonderful. I've been able to have normal conversations, see again what normal life looks like. But it's all over now – he just rang my boss and told him I wouldn't be coming back. And all for a lie. One of the girls was running late for her shift today, because her mum's in hospital. So I stayed at work until she got there, and she was very apologetic, and very grateful. I was a little nervous about getting home late, so when the elevator was taking ages I got a bit frantic and raced up the stairs. I pushed open our door, and he was standing there, waiting for me. I threw my arms around him in the doorway, kissing him hello, but he didn't hug me back.

"Where have you been?" he snapped, and I took a step back, surprised at the threatening tone of his voice.

"Cathy was running late for her shift because her mum's in hospital, so I said I could stay a bit longer, cover for her. But it was only half an hour, so I didn't think you'd mind," I babbled.

He glared at me, then started hurling accusations again. "You're seeing someone else, aren't you? Don't insult my intelligence by lying to me. I saw you together!" he insisted.

I stared at him, shocked. "I've been at work, call my boss and ask him. You couldn't have seen me with anyone."

"I don't need to call, I've seen you, in my meditations. All the sordid details. Are you trying to say my visions are false? I know you've been with another guy, and you've just been kissing him. Why else would you be so out of breath?"

"I ran all the way from the bus stop then up three flights of stairs," I said, alarmed that he was becoming so irrational even more quickly than usual.

"You're lying!" he choked out, his face red with anger.

I felt a very real flicker of fear. What was going on? "Baby, I'm not lying," I managed to say, but my voice trembled a little. God, would he take that to mean I was lying?

As if he'd sensed my thought, he took a step towards me. "Don't lie to me!" he shouted, arm raised, and I braced myself for the blow.

When it didn't come, I took a deep breath. "I'm not sure why you think I would lie about that. If I wanted to be with someone else, I would be. But I don't. I only want to be with you."

"I know you've been with someone else," he screamed at me. Then he started to tear my clothes off me, right there in the very public hallway, in order to "prove it" apparently, which rocked me out of my daze and made me yell back.

I just don't understand how he can accuse me of things I haven't done? I must have finally got through to him, because after a long time he calmed down a little. And I held my ground, and eventually it was him who looked away. "Okay," he conceded. "But I've been cheated on before, and I know what to look for. Don't think you can trick me. I know what women are like, what you are like."

His words hurt so much, because I'd only ever been honest with and faithful to him, but the mood seemed to be passing him by, so I bit my tongue. And eventually he sighed, and apologised, which was a shock.

"I'm sorry. I'm just getting so many strange messages from you right now, different energies. You're thinking about other men, and it's throwing me. Come inside," he said, then he dragged me in and slammed the door behind us. Okay, so it was an apology of sorts. By that point I was happy to take it.

God I wish I could call Mum and have her come and get me, take me away from this craziness, make everything all right again, like she always did when I was in trouble as a kid. He's told me several times that if I even try to speak to Mum he'll hurt her, or worse, so I can't take the risk. But I don't think I can survive this much longer.

Last night was harrowing, even more so than usual, and the scary thing was that I hadn't done anything to start it. Not that I ever do, but this one came from so far out of left field, without any warning sign so I could steel myself for the storm to come. We'd had a really nice evening – we made dinner together, then watched a movie, curled up on the couch, content. It was almost like old times. And then he turned to me, and there were tears in his eyes.

"I don't want to be with you, I don't want to love you," he whispered, his voice tortured. "I don't want you to have this power over me. I'm always so strong, I'm always the powerful one, the one who is in control. But you make me so weak. Why do you do this to me? Why do you have this power?" he asked, voice ragged, imploring. "What's so special about you?"

"I don't have any power," I replied, surprised and more than a little rattled by his words. I'd never been so powerless.

He grabbed my arm and dragged me into the bathroom, then broke open his razor and held the blade to his wrist. "This is what you make people do," he said, eyes wild. "You make them want to kill themselves."

I sunk to the floor, head against the wall to try to stay upright, and begged him not to do it.

"Why not?" he asked, voice desperate.

"My god, you can't do this. People need you. You need you. You need to be here," I stuttered.

"Do you need me?" he demanded.

I stared at him, terrified. Terrified to say the wrong thing, to set him off, to make him carry out his awful threat. "Of course I do," I replied shakily.

"Do you love me?"

I nodded, too scared to do anything else.

"Say it!" he growled, menace in his voice.

So I said it.

"Like you mean it."

"I love you," I repeated, putting as much force as I could into it, trying to sound as genuine as humanly possible, though my voice shook with the super-human effort.

He smiled, and a look of triumph lit up his face, then he laughed, a horrible, cruel laugh. "You didn't really think I'd do that did you?" he asked mockingly. "You didn't really think that you had the power to make me do it?"

I was trembling, the earlier rush of adrenaline long gone, and a strange hollow exhaustion taking its place. "Of course not," I sighed. And I was suddenly terrified, because the blade was still in his hand, but now it was pointing at me, and his smile had become sadistic.

He pulled me to my feet and dragged me into an embrace, and I tried so hard not to stiffen in his arms, not to inflame him further – tried not to wonder where the blade was.

"I was only joking," he said.

"It wasn't funny," I muttered, voice flat. This rollercoaster of emotions was tying me in knots, and I didn't know what I thought or felt any more. Everything now was simply a reaction to his mood, an attempt to pacify him, to always say the right thing. My whole life was now a delicate balance of tightrope walking and tiptoeing on egg shells. I felt broken, and I knew I couldn't go on like this much longer.

Suddenly his face changed, like another person had taken control of his brain, and he smiled at me.

"I love you so much, you know that right?" he said.

I nodded, numb.

"No one will ever love you as much as I do. They'll never love you the way I do," he continued, self-satisfaction evident.

"I know," I said, conciliatory, plastering a smile on my face. But where once that statement had made me so happy, had made me feel so special, now it just terrified me. God, I hope no one will ever love me this much, in this way, EVER.

As the bus came to a screeching halt, Carlie looked up, panicked, then quickly grabbed her bag and jumped out when she realised it was time to change buses. She felt strange, as though she'd gone through all the awful things her mother was writing about. Taking a few deep breaths, she checked the timetable then walked over to the kiosk and bought a cup of tea and a chocolate bar. She had a few minutes, and she felt the need to ground herself back into her body, back into the present, because reading about the harrowing things her mum had endured was making her head spin and her heart hurt. Sipping the tea made her slightly calmer, and the sweetness of the chocolate soothed her jagged nerves a little.

Her bus arrived then, and she climbed aboard and found her seat, then reluctantly pulled her mum's diary back out of her backpack. Part of her wanted to throw it away, or burn it as her mum had considered doing, so she couldn't learn about any more of her suffering, but something made her open it back up and keep reading.

There were more pages missing, and a large section of the next entry had been scribbled out. She could just make out the end of it...

I know it infuriates him when I won't drink alcohol with him, but I'm scared of losing control around him, of being even more vulnerable than I already am, possibly saying something in the heat of the moment, when my inhibitions are lowered, that will set him off. So I was happily surprised when we were out last night, and he stopped insisting I drink with him, and told me he'd get me an orange juice.

Of course I should have known he would do something awful – he must have spiked my drink, because I came to twelve hours later, aching and bruised, with no recollection of what had happened to me, except that he said, with the sleaziest grin, that he had some wonderful photos of me, and that I'd better not ever upset him or displease him, or else he'd send them to a sleazy magazine to publish, then to my mother. I feel sick even wondering what he did to me, and how it came to this. The worst part of all is that this has become my normal. I'm not even shocked or outraged any more, I'm not surprised by the depths he'll go to. I'm just numb.

I don't know how much longer I can cope with this – I feel like soon I'll break into a million pieces and disappear. Just cease to exist. He "let" me come to his shamanic healing retreat this weekend, and said it was going to be a new start for the two of us. And I can't believe I actually fell for it. That I forgot there would be an ulterior motive.

I met some really nice people on the Friday afternoon, all women of course, I wasn't stupid. I was bunking in with a sweet mother-and-

daughter pair, Maria and Lenore, and I had dinner with them, but as I was heading over to the shower block after that, Andre grabbed me and started kissing me, then begged me to come to his cabin. I reminded him that we had to pretend we didn't know each other, but he was crying, pleading, saying he really needed me to be with him. So I went, and as soon as we were inside, he broke down.

"Oh my god, I'm so glad you're here," he said. "I just can't stand it, all these people demanding my attention, all with their pitiful little problems, all trying to make everything be about them. That woman with the drum, my god! Could she be more annoying?"

"Her name's Maria, and she thinks the world of you," I said, shocked at his lack of compassion.

"They're all the same, they just want someone to make them feel important, someone to tell them how special they are, and what to do with their life."

"They think you're a god," I said, giggling a little at the thought. "Be nice to them."

He stared at me, and it was like a switch had flipped in his mind. I froze, because I knew what that meant. He demanded to know why I didn't see him the way other people did. Said everyone at the retreat, and everyone else he'd ever met, thinks he's a god, and treats him that way. Except for me.

"They respect me totally, but you don't. You question me, challenge me. Why don't you treat me the way I should be treated?" he demanded. "Why don't you think I'm a god?"

My face was still throbbing from where he'd hit me the day before, for saying thank you to the bus driver, so I wasn't as careful as usual. "Perhaps it's because I know you better than they do," I replied, no longer willing or able to bite my tongue. "Or maybe it's because you treat them better than you treat me."

"What?" he shouted. "I treat you better than anyone."

"No, you don't," I said, voice expressionless, like a robot. "You're jealous and violent and cruel, and you don't trust me."

He was shocked. "Of course I trust you. And I'm not jealous, or violent or cruel," he said, genuinely surprised I would say such a thing. "You're my consort, it's because of me that people respect you."

I just stared at him. No one here knew I was with him, because he wanted it to be a secret, and I was glad of that, so there was no way they would think anything of me either way. Besides, how on earth anyone could respect me, now that I'd sunk so low, I had no idea. And how could he even begin to think he was treating me well?

And then he started his usual ranting. I don't appreciate him like everyone else does, I don't recognise his true worth. I'm an ungrateful whore who just came this weekend so I could have sex with another guy, I only wanted him for his money, blah blah blah. Then he tried to drag me into bed, and I tried to get away – his awful accusations never do put me in the mood – but he grabbed my arm so tightly that I know there will be bruises tomorrow, and ripped my jumper off.

"Why do you think I asked you to come," he asked roughly, and I froze, horrified. "I could have any woman here you know, from the youngest to the oldest. They beg me for it. So why do you think you're so special?" he shouted.

My blood ran cold, but I managed to screw up my courage and speak. I had nothing left to lose. "Then you should go and have one of those women," I said. "But be careful, because it would be easy to ruin your reputation if you tried to force someone to have sex."

"I don't have to force anyone," he retorted, anger blazing in his eyes. "They all want me."

"Then go and be with one of them," I cried. My voice shook, but I managed to maintain eye contact. And I saw the moment he deflated, then watched, shocked, as he burst into noisy sobs. He apologised, which he hadn't done for a long time, and begged me to forgive him; implored me to love him. So I tried to reassure him, to comfort him, even though it was the last thing I wanted to do. Sometimes he's like a little kid, so needy. Where was the self-possessed and self-confident "god" they all saw? I tried to explain again how important he'd said it was that I didn't stay with him here, that people thought he was above "petty human relationships" as he put it, but his body started shaking again, and I could feel sobs building up within him. I couldn't believe that I was the mature one.

He dragged me down onto the floor with him, holding me so tight I could barely breathe.

"*I need you,*" he cried. "*How can you reject me when I'm being so open with you, when I'm begging you to stay with me? I'm not sure I'll survive the night if you leave me now.*"

I didn't know what to do. His voice was getting louder, and his state of mind more hysterical, and if I didn't do something soon the whole camp would come rushing in, wondering what was going on, and then they'd all know anyway. Maybe it would be easier to just do what he wanted and stay. So I gave in – and it was the longest nine hours of my life. He raged between begging me to stay, threatening me with violence, then curling up in a ball, crying hysterically and threatening to kill himself if I left. I swung between reassurance and empathy to fear and anger, and a hundred emotions in between.

For a while he was convinced that I was a spy, sent to trick him into revealing his secrets, then that I was a government agent, trying to set him up, trying to destroy him. When his eyes alighted on the small black base of one of the lamps in the room, he swore blind that it held a bug, planted there by the CIA to record his conversations, and he became hysterical until I put the lamp outside.

It was all getting way too crazy for me, and I almost walked out, but as always he seemed to sense when I'd reached my breaking point, and was all of a sudden sweet and conciliatory, full of apologies and a rare moment of candour and sanity.

But then when I said I needed to go to the bathroom, he flipped out again, accusing me of planning to leave him, and sneaking out the bathroom window, off to meet some stranger in the forest to have sex with him. The more I denied this the worse and more paranoid he became – it wasn't until I showed him there was no window in there that he let me go in, and I finally had two minutes to myself.

When I emerged he'd made me a cup of tea, exactly the way I like it, and we talked rationally for half an hour. Then just as I felt lulled into a sense of security, and thought maybe we could finally get some sleep, he turned on me again, saying I was a whore, that I was using him for money, that I used sex as a weapon, then berating all the people who had come to the retreat again, complaining that they didn't understand him or value him enough, that they were selfish and self-obsessed, and that I was the worst of them all.

As I tried to stay calm, he grabbed me again, dragged me into the bedroom, and told me to get undressed, to do what I was there for. But I couldn't bring myself to do it – I felt like I'd been through a psychological war, and the thought of being intimate with him made my blood run cold.

So he ripped my clothes off me and forced himself on top of me, and held me down until he was done. I tried to shut down, to become numb to it all, to escape at least mentally from the most mortifying moment of my life. But my tears just seemed to turn him on more, and he kept going. His hands all over me made my skin crawl, but he didn't appear to notice, or care. And when it was finally over he held me close, and told me how much he loved me, and that just made the whole thing worse. I lay in his arms, frozen with shock, unable to move, to even think straight, just praying, over and over, that I would eventually be able to get out of that room.

When the sun finally rose, I felt relief wash over me. Surely it would have to end now, he would have to let me go. He'd have to pull himself together, sort himself out, and get out there and teach. I crept into the bathroom and stood at the sink staring into the mirror. Horror shot through me as I gazed at my reflection. My skin was as pale as a ghost and there were huge black circles under my lashes, but it was the expression in my eyes that scared me the most. I looked like a zombie, with not an ounce of energy or will left, drained of every bit of whatever it was that made me, me. It was like I had left my own body and gone off somewhere to hide.

Yet when I came back out he was calm, and totally himself again. And he looked amazing, like he'd slept for nine hours and didn't have a care in the world. How come I looked like I'd been tortured for the last twenty-four hours, and he could have walked off the set of a fashion shoot?

"Thanks so much for staying last night," he said, smiling at me and moving forward to hug me. "Now you'd better get back to your cabin, so no one knows you stayed over." And he winked at me, as though it had been me who had begged to stay with him.

"Oh, and here's a shirt you can wear – yours looks a little ripped," he added, with a lascivious grin that turned my stomach. Like it wasn't him who had torn mine off so he could force himself on me. But I put it on and ran out the door, and I'd never been so grateful to see the sun, or people, in my life.

Breakfast was beyond embarrassing. Maria had been worried about me, because I hadn't been in the cabin when she woke up this morning, and because I looked so terrible. I lied though, of course, something about a migraine, and a nightmare, and needing to clear my head, and she seemed to accept it.

And Lenore was bubbling over with excitement. "I had the best dream last night – really meaningful, and for once I actually remembered it. I've had a situation at work that I've been really torn over, but in my dream Andre was there, and basically told me what I should do – then showed me a vision of what would happen with each of the other possible choices, so I could know I was making the right decision. It was amazing! Already he's solved my problem! I told you, this guy is incredible!"

My face ached from the smile I tried to paste across it, and Maria gave me a searching look. "Are you sure you're okay honey?" she asked. I nodded. I hated lying to them, hated being forced to lie, but what could I say? The amazing Andre is a cruel and manipulative bully of a man? A violent sociopath? No one would believe me.

Just then he walked into the breakfast room – speak of the devil – and walked straight over to us. "Thanks so much for spending the night with me Violet," he said, so loud, then leaned down and kissed me, in front of everyone. I was mortified, and shocked and angry too. The hypocrisy and injustice burned in me, but he didn't notice, or care. He simply breezed off and sat at another table, and one of the young girls there jumped up to get him some porridge, while another one got him a coffee.

I looked at Maria and Lenore, and quailed inside as I tried to reassure them. "It wasn't like that, I promise. And I'm so sorry, I didn't want to lie to you, but he insisted no one could know I was there – just talking to him – in case everyone got the wrong impression. Which they have now," I stammered, blushing beet red.

I saw a strange mix of admiration and jealousy in Lenore's eyes, which worried me, but Maria gave me another searching look that made me feel really uncomfortable. It was like she could see inside my heart, and knew the truth, and I hated what she must think of me, of how weak and pathetic I had become.

But I was saved by the bell, so to speak, as right at that moment the retreat organiser stood up and started explaining how the day would work, and people scraped their chairs back as they stood up and stacked their plates, or raced back to their rooms to get pen and paper, or grabbed a last mug of coffee.

Andre began the day with a beautiful ritual, which I just couldn't reconcile with the man he'd been last night. Then we broke into small groups to work on individual issues and activities, and he moved between them all, listening carefully to each one, offering suggestions, explaining concepts clearly, making every single person he made eye contact with think they were the only person in the world.

I watched him, one part impressed by his deception, one part horrified. He'd spent a lot of time last night railing against these people, saying they were stupid and didn't deserve his time or attention, let alone his help, but here he was, making them love him. And it was all a lie.

At one point Maria came and found me, and put her arms around me. She said she was really worried about me, and wanted to know if she could help me, but Andre swooped in and separated us, and kept us apart for the rest of the weekend. And when it was finally over and we had packed up and were heading home, he was his old loving self, saying how much it had meant to him to have me there, how he really hoped I'd come to more of his retreats with him now. And then he said he had to spend the night with his mum, that she was sick and scared, so he dropped me at home then left. I don't know if that means he's staying with his wife, or with some other woman, and to be honest I don't actually care.

I need some time alone, time to think. So now here I sit, trying to make sense of what has happened. He's been violent before – I've lost track of the injuries, the blood, the bruises, the brutal hair pulling that leaves no mark but gives me a migraine that lasts days. And he's been psychologically abusive too many times to count, so much so that often I doubt my own sanity.

Certainly I doubt my worth. But this is the first time he's ever held me down and forced me to have sex with him, and I feel like that should be the line in the sand that can't be crossed. The line has moved several times in the last few months, I know, and I've endured worse and worse treatment from him without complaining – treatment I'd always thought I would end a relationship over immediately if it happened to me.

But I worry that if I can't get away somehow, I will end up accepting this too, and blaming myself. I have to save myself, I have to get away somehow, otherwise there will be nothing left of me. And yet, where can I go? He stopped me from working, so I have no money and am totally dependent on him. And he scares away anyone who wants to be friends with me, anyone who shows any concern for me, so I'm completely isolated. I just don't know what to do...

Chapter 34

A Tangled Web

Carlie was so engrossed in the diary that she nearly missed her stop, but the driver remembered her stating her destination, and called out to her. As she wandered up the road to the cafe where retreat-goers were meeting, she felt dazed, and fear and anger at what her mother had endured warred with the compassion she felt for her. Violet had only been seventeen, the age she was now, and she'd been alone, cut off from Rose and Mike, and from anyone who could have helped her make sense of the situation she'd found herself in. She couldn't imagine ever being that isolated from the people she loved – the ones who were still alive anyway.

Another pang of guilt washed over her, that she was lying to her grandmother again, and she felt nervous that she would get Rhiannon in trouble if anyone found out where she was. But she was so desperate to see Rowan again, to try to figure out what she felt for him, and what she should do about the ultimatum Rhiannon had delivered.

Over a comforting cup of chai she was introduced to an older woman, Cressida, and her daughter Vicki, who offered her a ride out to the retreat space. A wave of sadness shuddered through her as she recognised a little of her grandma in the tall grey-haired woman, and she wondered if, had things been different, it could have been Rose and her daughter Violet at a weekend retreat together – maybe even all three of them. But she made an effort to shake off the gloominess and tune back in to the conversation, and smiled as they raved about how much they were looking forward to the weekend, and how amazing Rowan was, how much he had helped them to heal from a bitter divorce and a crushing lack of self-worth in Cressida's case, and a complicated health issue in her daughter Vicki's.

On arrival they were directed into the large common room where they would have their meals and perform some of their rituals. The moment she walked inside she saw Rowan across the room, talking to a pretty woman who was clearly besotted with him, leaning in close, touching his arm as she made a point, stroking his chest. Her heart lurched, Rhiannon's accusations that he'd find someone else in her absence playing over and over in her head, along with her mum's description of her shaman boyfriend's words. "They all want me." "I could have any woman here." "They beg me for it."

Cressida touched her shoulder, and she jumped. "Are you okay?" she asked. With an effort, Carlie tore her eyes away from Rowan and nodded. "We're going to grab a cup of tea, would you like me to get you one?" her new friend asked. "We have an hour to hang out here and mingle before the program starts."

Carlie smiled. "Thank you." As the other woman walked over to the kitchen area, she felt Rowan's eyes on her, and looked back over. Shock crossed his face, then something she couldn't quite place, then he smiled and walked towards her. He held out his hand.

"Hi, I'm Rowan, it's lovely to meet you," he said, then winked at her. "I can't believe you're here, but I'm so glad," he whispered, and the love she saw shining from his eyes soothed her a little. "But oh my god, I want to hold you!"

She smiled. "Me too," she whispered back.

He stared at her searchingly. "Are you okay?" he asked, voice still low. "You look sad."

She tried to smile, but her confrontation with Rhiannon and the words she'd read in her mother's diary were swirling around in her brain. "I'll be fine. It's a long story. I just needed to be with you tonight," she replied.

He stared at her appraisingly, eyebrows raised, and she blushed. "I don't mean that! I just —"

"Rowan, welcome," a tall man interrupted them. "I'm sorry I was delayed for a few moments, but let me show you to your cabin. Do you need a hand bringing your things in? My daughter can help," he said, motioning to the pretty woman Rowan had just been talking to.

"That would be great, thank you," he told the man, shaking his hand then turning back to Carlie. "It was so nice to meet you. I hope you enjoy the weekend," he murmured, then followed the man and his daughter outside.

She nodded, forced a smile, then wandered back to Cressida in a daze. As she sat down with them and drank her tea, she let their words about how great Rowan was wash over her. She knew he couldn't make it obvious that they were together, but surely it was a bit cold to pretend he'd never met her before? He knew most of the people here, had done ritual with them a few times before, so it was conceivable that he had with her too. Yet he was treating her like a total stranger. Or was she just projecting Rhiannon's prejudices on to him, creating fears where there was no need for them?

Trying to shake off her weird mood, she joined in their chat. They all adored Rowan, credited him with changing their lives, and were so excited about the weekend ahead. She concentrated on summoning a memory of how he made her feel, the warmth and sense of security she felt in his arms, and this soothed her.

She reminded herself too that it had been love in his eyes as he'd greeted her, and he'd been genuine when he told her how happy he was to see her. She shouldn't let her mother's awful experiences impose on hers. And just because Violet realised she should have listened to her friend about her relationship, it didn't mean there were parallels there. Rowan wasn't Andre. And she didn't need Rhiannon's voice in her head trying to convince her that he was too old, too untrustworthy, too ready to cheat on her, too bad for her in general. Her friend didn't know him like she did.

By the time the ritual started she was feeling much more cheerful, and she let herself be swept away in the beauty and magic of the Yule's Eve ceremony. She could feel Rowan's energy in the circle, feel the warmth of his arms around her, and she clung on to that, hoping everything was still okay between them.

When they broke for dinner, she found herself looking around for a new table, since Cressida and her daughter were at one that was already full. A woman looked up and caught her eye, motioning to the empty seat opposite her, and she smiled her thanks. But as she sat down, the woman's face paled and she saw fear in her eyes, much like the look on Rowan's mum's face.

"Hi, I'm Carlie," she said nervously. "Um, have we met?"

The woman jumped, brought abruptly back to the present by the sound of her voice. "I'm so sorry, I'm Jasmine. It's lovely to meet you. I just… well, I apologise," she said, flustered and clearly rattled. "You're just the spitting image of an old friend of mine, but it can't be… you're from where, Australia?"

Carlie nodded, but her mind was whirring too. Jasmine had been her mum's only friend in the circle. "Do you mean Violet?" she whispered, and the woman across from her nodded, shocked.

"How do you know her?" she asked. "But this means she's okay, right? I thought… well, I never knew what happened to her – she just disappeared," Jasmine stuttered, voice cracking.

"She was my mum," Carlie replied. "And she was okay, but she died in June this year." She felt tears well. It was still all so fresh – her loss, her beginning of a new life in a new country, all the new people she'd met, and all the strange discoveries she was making about her mother, and herself.

"I'm only just finding out about her life in England – she changed her name when she got to Australia, and never spoke to me or Dad, or her best friend, about her past. I didn't even know I had a grandmother until recently, because Mum had always said her parents were both dead."

Jasmine reached out a hand and grasped Carlie's, sympathy oozing from her as she tried to hide the shock and sadness she was clearly feeling, which was mixed with relief too. "I'm so glad she got away," she said. "I always worried that he'd do something bad…" she broke off.

"You mean Andre?" Carlie asked. "I've just started reading her old diary, which explains a bit of what happened – that they were totally in love, and she gave up her family to be with him, but once they were together he changed, became violent and cruel. So much so that she was scared for her life?"

Jasmine nodded, and Carlie felt herself break all over again. She'd been hoping that her mum's diary entries had been exaggerated, made more dramatic because she was young and in love, or felt guilty for leaving home in such tragic circumstances.

"It was no exaggeration, I promise," Jasmine said, breaking into her thoughts. Carlie looked at her questioningly, heart beating faster as she sensed herself getting closer to the mystery of her mother.

"I met Violet when she started coming to our circles, and it was obvious that she loved him deeply, and that he loved her even more. They had such a strong connection, which was brilliant for both of them, at first anyway. They really inspired each other, and encouraged and supported each other, and their love brought a whole new dimension to our group work – it pushed us further and higher with our spellworkings, with our goals – and some of the rituals we performed then, and the spells we cast, were so powerful.

"He seemed really proud of her, and so enamoured with her. Violet was young and beautiful, self-confident, friendly, clever, deeply spiritual and magical from the work she'd been doing with her mother before I met her, and she had a light within her that drew people to her," Jasmine remembered.

"But then Andre became insecure and paranoid, and it was so strange. He'd always been amazing, so spiritual, so wise, so compassionate. And he was – at least he was with everyone else who'd ever met him, everyone else in our circle. It was just her that he reacted to so strongly. It was like they were playing out this past life drama where one of them had betrayed the other or something – he kept accusing her of cheating on him, of breaking his trust, of trying to destroy him and his work, but there was nothing of the sort from her.

"She was devoted to him, had eyes only for him, had been swept off her feet by his charisma and charm, and of course it didn't hurt that he was so powerful, so magical. Half the women he met fell in love with him, and I know he'd had relationships with some of them before, but never like this. He became obsessed with her, and lost all rationality. She didn't even look at or speak to any of the guys in the circle or at the retreats he led, but he accused her of chatting them up, of sneaking around with them, of having sex with them. I didn't know this until much later though, I promise, not until just before she left. They both hid it so well," Jasmine said, and there was regret and remorse in her voice.

"At first she thought it was sweet that he so clearly cared about her so much, and flattering that he was a bit jealous. But when it started blurring into obsession, she got scared. Which he sensed, and which only made him worse. More controlling, more paranoid, more unbalanced. I'd never seen him like that before, and I'd seen him with a few girlfriends, and three wives. He'd always been so considerate, and so rational. But as he became more and more obsessive, the circle started to fall apart, and people stopped coming, which isolated Violet even further. It was so sad. All the things he'd loved her for – her light, her independence, her strength – he tried to destroy, maybe so no one else would love her, maybe because he just couldn't stand the reflection of her light..."

Carlie felt a rush of love and warmth for her mum. All this time she'd thought that Violet had been so cruel to leave Rose in a purgatory of not knowing if she was dead or alive, but she'd been in a hell far worse all that time, unable to reach out to her mum. She took a sip of her tea, feeling so sad for the woman who'd been so traumatised by all that she'd endured that she'd never felt able to get in touch with her own mother, to feel the comfort and immense healing power of Rose's love.

Jasmine gazed across at Carlie and broke into her thoughts. "So, is it weird doing ritual with Rowan?" she asked, and Carlie stared at her, perplexed. She shook her head. "Should it be?"

"Well, it's just strange that Violet's daughter would want to work magic with his son," she said.

Carlie's face went white, shock robbing her of her voice and her thought process. "His son?" she finally choked out.

"Yes, Rowan is Andre's son. You didn't know?" Carlie shook her head again, mouth open and head spinning. "He would have been, I don't know, two or three when Andre left his wife and child for

Violet. Not that it was her fault," Jasmine added quickly. "He'd told her he was divorced, and had mentioned Rowan once as his nephew. She was devastated when she found out."

Oh god, that could explain why Rowan's mother had looked so terrified of her. She wondered if she'd mentioned her suspicions to her son. Was that why he'd freaked out when she'd said her mum's name was Violet at the ball last night? Had that confirmed Louisa's suspicions? No wonder he'd looked at her strangely when he saw her earlier today, that expression she hadn't been able to interpret.

Feeling his eyes on her now, she looked up. He'd just walked in to the dining room, and someone had already jumped up to wait on him hand and foot. Like father like son? She shook her head, not wanting to believe he was anything like his dad, but a wave of sadness engulfed her when he looked away and went to sit with the pretty woman from earlier, who was clearly a little bit in love with him. Her stomach turned as she watched her fawn over him, touching him way more than was necessary.

Jasmine drew her back to their conversation. "Don't let him bespell you Carlie," she said gently. "I saw what his father did to Violet, saw him turn from loving her, almost worshipping her, to acting like a wife-beating husband as he tried to break her. He thought she was so beautiful, so smart, so independent and strong-willed, such a free spirit – all traits that he loved at first. But then he became paranoid, and didn't want anyone else to speak to her, even look at her, so he tried to diminish her. She did nothing to make him doubt her, nothing at all, but that didn't matter to him, he'd convinced himself that he'd psychically seen her doing all those terrible things, so it must have been true. But they were just delusions, not psychic visions. I've wondered since if he had bipolar disorder. Certainly towards the end he was self-medicating with alcohol and cocaine, which obviously didn't help his paranoia.

"Violet went from being flattered that he loved her so much, to terrified he would destroy her. Eventually I started to realise some of what was going on, and became scared he would harm her, or worse. I'd decided that I would have to convince her to leave, or help her escape, I wasn't sure which, but by the next circle she'd disappeared.

"Of course he interrogated all of us – Where had she gone? Who had helped her? – and later the police got in touch. Apparently someone, an old friend of hers from her home town, had mentioned that Andre may have been a threat to her, so the police questioned us, and him too, but he really was genuinely worried about her. He couldn't find her, not through legal channels, not through psychic means. It really was like she vanished into thin air. She sent me a postcard though, from London airport, which just said: 'I'm safe, thank you for caring.' And I never heard from her again."

"Mum mentioned a retreat like this one in her diary – I was just reading it on the way here. It seems that what he did to her there was what gave her the courage to leave when she got the chance. But what happened to Andre? Did he hurt anyone else?" Carlie asked.

"Once he accepted that she wasn't coming back, he had a bit of a meltdown. He cancelled his workshops and teaching circles, and said he was going to South America to find himself again. I think he was actually scared about what he'd turned into, how obsessive he'd become. Someone mentioned that he'd married a young Brazilian girl while he was there, but I don't know if that's true. And I heard many years later that he'd died."

Carlie nodded. "When Rowan was twelve. They weren't close though – he doesn't speak very highly of him, if he mentions him at all," she said, then stopped, embarrassed that she'd revealed that she knew Rowan so well.

Jasmine raised her eyebrows questioningly. "When I heard that Rowan was teaching, and realised who he was, I decided to keep an eye out for him, or an eye on him, just in case."

Suddenly Carlie felt as though the room was closing in around her. "And you think that Rowan –" she broke off, unable to put her question into words, but Jasmine shook her head.

"God no, I'm sorry, I didn't mean to imply that. But it's a strange kind of responsibility and, I don't know, fame of sorts, that healers and teachers like Rowan are weighed down by. It would be very easy to have your head turned, but he seems to be handling it really well. You can tell in ritual with him, he's very calm, very balanced, very inclusive. Whereas for all his claims of being spiritually enlightened,

Andre could be a misogynistic jerk. He loved your mum's free spirit, until he decided that she belonged to him and he had to break it.

"But Rowan's not like that. His mother brought him up well, and he's a credit to her. It was the best thing that ever happened to the two of them, Andre leaving them when he did. So you have no need to feel guilty about it," she said, smiling across at Carlie, who felt a rush of relief at this revelation. She had been feeling awful that Rowan's dad had left him and his mum for her mother, and had no idea how he'd feel about it if he found out, and whether she'd be able to hide the knowledge from him. Or did he already know? Was there any way he could know?

Jasmine broke into her thoughts. "I'm so glad to know that Violet was okay, that she found happiness, and that she had you."

Carlie smiled, and suddenly realised that knowing any more details about Andre was of no benefit to her. It was in the past. And trying to draw parallels to bring the spectre of his cruelty here, in the present, wasn't fair to herself or to Rowan. But in front of her was someone who had known her mum before she became Fiona, so she had a great opportunity now to learn more about her when she was younger.

"Tell me what she was like when you knew her," she begged, and Jasmine smiled. They sat there for a long time, finishing dinner, then drinking endless cups of tea and eating cinnamon cookies, reminiscing about the past, then sharing stories of more recent times. Eventually, as the fire burned low, they bid each other goodnight.

Carlie hadn't nabbed a bed earlier in the day, but she knew there were still some bunks free in cabin three. So she headed there now, backpack in hand – but as she reached the darkened doorway she felt a hand on her shoulder and jumped, barely stifling a scream before she realised who it was.

"Carlie, oh god, I've been waiting so long to see you, hold you. Come here," he whispered, pulling her into his arms. She melted into him, felt herself relax and really breathe fully for the first time all day. "Come on," he whispered, and led her through the darkness to his little cabin, candlelight spilling out of the windows and looking so welcoming, so magical.

They walked up the two steps hand in hand, then he unlocked the door and drew her inside, arms going around her, lips finding hers and kissing her hungrily. "I've missed you so much," he sighed, and she nodded, kissing him back, as he drew her down onto the couch and into his lap.

Her body responded to his touch, but her mind wasn't quite as comfortable. So many thoughts were whirling through her mind – Rhiannon's ultimatum, all that Rowan's dad had put her mum through, the memory of the woman he'd sat with at dinner, and her hands all over him. The images started to blur, to meld with Rhiannon's conviction that Rowan would cheat on her, and her mum's description of Andre leading her back to his cabin at a retreat a lot like this one and torturing her for nine hours.

"It's been torture to see you here, so close but so far away," Rowan said, and his voice brought her abruptly back into the room, his use of the word torture sending a shiver up her spine. "I wanted to grab you in the middle of the circle, announce to everyone that I love you, just so I could hold you, and kiss you," he whispered, hand gently stroking her face, his touch so warm, and his eyes sparkling in the candlelight with love and desire.

"Why didn't you?" she demanded. She kept her tone light, like maybe she was joking, but she was curious. "Or at least concede that you'd met me once or twice before, instead of treating me like a total stranger, and going out of your way to avoid me."

"What do you mean?" he asked, and the pain in his eyes at her accusation took her breath away. But she couldn't stop herself. She might sound petty, but she felt restless and confused, and was struggling not to lash out at him.

"Today, with the retreat owner, you made a point of saying it was nice to meet me."

"I'm sorry baby, I didn't mean anything by that," he said, and she could hear the regret in his voice. "I'd just rather he didn't know about us, because it can make people a little uncomfortable. It wouldn't affect us at all, because working magic with you only makes me stronger, but some people think any romantic attachment can weaken the circle or corrupt the teachings, that it's unprofessional."

"What, like your dad was?" she challenged him, eyes fierce, shield rising around her heart.

He gazed at her in confusion. "What do you mean about my dad? He's been dead for more than ten years."

"He was pretty unprofessional with the way he treated my mum," she said, tears trembling on her lashes. She didn't want to cry, didn't want to feel weak, but all the things she'd read on the bus today, everything Rhiannon had said, the sense of injustice she'd felt when Rowan hadn't acknowledged her, and had chosen to sit with the flirty woman instead, all mingled together into a fiery blend of emotion.

Carefully, deliberately, he set her down from his lap onto the couch beside him. He was still holding her hands though, which she was glad of, and she could see his mind working, see some things registering, others being discarded. Finally he shook his head.

"Carlie, my love, forgive me please, but I don't know what you mean," he pleaded. "Tell me what's wrong."

"Didn't your mum tell you why she looked so scared of me when we met the other day at your place?" she whispered, pain crackling in her voice, even as she realised that she'd felt slighted then too. Oh god, this wasn't his fault, she couldn't hold him responsible, but it was too late now. She'd opened a wound in both of them that ran much deeper than either had known, or would have admitted.

He touched her cheek, hands so gentle still, and eyes filled with his usual tenderness. "Yes," he said softly, simply, honestly. "After I took you home last week, Mum rang, and she finally revealed a lot of things about my father, things she hadn't told me because she wanted to protect me, wanted me not to hate him. But she admitted that when I was little, Dad had an affair with one of his young students, a girl who looked exactly like you. She told me her name was Violet, which is why I was surprised last night when you said that was your mum's name. It wasn't the only affair he had apparently, but he left us for this girl, and that was new."

Carlie blushed, sensing how awful it must have felt, to have been deserted for some teenager.

"That wasn't what upset Mum though – she was actually relieved when he left," he added quickly, holding her hand tighter. "But a few of her friends from his teaching circles, from when she still used to go, had told her that he was becoming irrational, and warned her to avoid conflict with him, and keep me safe. She didn't think much of it, apparently he was civil to her when they did have to talk, but then the police arrived to question her. The girl had gone missing, and a friend of hers had mentioned Dad's name. For a while there she was terrified that my father had... done something terrible to this girl."

He looked haunted, and Carlie took his hand, suddenly desperate to reassure him, to comfort him. "He was awful to her, but he didn't kill her," she said, shuddering at the word, at the idea, that this was even a possibility. "Mum escaped to Australia, and she ended up being really happy. It wasn't the life she'd envisaged, or with the man she'd imagined, but she found love, and contentment."

"And she had you," Rowan said, voice sad, regretful, but filled with love. "Mum was also worried that if you were Violet's daughter, my father could have been yours too," he conceded, and she stared at him, horror-struck. "It's okay though, he's not!" he added quickly. "You would have had to be a few years older than you are."

She wrinkled her nose. "Finally a reason to be glad I'm so much younger than you," she muttered.

He looked at her closely. "What's wrong baby? You say that like our ages matter."

"Don't they?" she sighed.

"No," he said firmly, then stood up and paced around the room. "Tea?"

She nodded, and watched as he walked over to the sink in the bench along the wall, filled the kettle then hunted for tea bags and cups. He was trying to stay busy, trying to work off his agitation, she noted, recognising one of her traits. Once that would have made her happy, to note more similarities between them, but now she wasn't so sure.

Finally he came back over and handed her the tea. "It's just normal tea, and normal milk," he said apologetically. She shrugged. Not having soy milk or earl grey tea was the least of her worries right now.

He looked up abruptly. "But wait, how could you know he was my dad?" he asked. "And why didn't you say something before?"

"I didn't know, not until tonight. The woman I was talking to at dinner stared at me the same way your mum did, like I was a ghost or something. Turns out she was part of your dad's teaching circle too, and knew my mum back then."

He nodded thoughtfully, then seemed to be gathering his courage. "Is there something else bothering you my love?" he asked hesitantly. "You seemed upset when you got here today, before you knew it was my father, but you only said that it was a long story, and you needed to be with me tonight."

She blushed at the naked desire she saw blazing in his eyes, but the things she'd read in her mum's diary were haunting her even more now that she knew the connection between Andre and Rowan. In her mind it was Rowan doing those awful things, Rowan holding the razor blade to his wrist, holding her mum down and forcing himself on her. Panicked, she shook herself, trying desperately to get the images out of her head.

"I was reading my mum's diary on the bus trip over here, and what he did to her, it was so awful. She was so terrified. I didn't know it was your dad then, but there were already parallels – he was a healer, like you, older than her, like you. I just..."

He pulled her back into his arms, but she struggled against him. "Carlie my love, that's awful, but don't let it come between us." She stiffened as he reached out to stroke her cheek, then recoiled at the pain she saw in his eyes at her reaction. "I'm not him Carlie, you have to believe me. I would never hurt you. I'd slit my wrists before I ever allowed myself to hurt you."

"I know, I just..." her face creased as she struggled with so many warring emotions. She hadn't even known Andre was his dad when she'd read the diary, so this couldn't be about Rowan.

"What is it my love?" he asked softly, tenderly. "Talk to me. We can figure this out."

"Rhiannon came over this morning," she began, and tried not to laugh at his quick attempt to smother his annoyance. "She *is* my best friend," she said defensively.

He smiled. "I know, and I respect that. But I also know that all of a sudden she really doesn't like me, and I'm not sure why. It can't just be because of that fortune teller, surely?"

"I'm not sure either," Carlie said, shrugging helplessly. "She's so adamant that I break up with you – she claims you're too old, you're bad for me, you just want me for sex, you'll cheat on me if I don't give it to you, you'll discard me if I do. She's been drawing parallels between us and my mum and her 'older shaman guru guy' as she calls him, and she doesn't even know he was your dad yet..." She sighed.

"But you know those things aren't true," Rowan said, voice pleading, and she felt his frustration as well as his love for her and his fear of losing her. It should have reassured her, but her heart was still uneasy, and she didn't know why, or how to soothe it.

"She also said she couldn't be my friend if I stayed with you, that she couldn't watch the making of such a terrible choice, see me hurting Rose so badly, lying to people, sneaking around, and ultimately being heartbroken by you," she whispered.

He stared at her, more shocked than she'd seen him before, anger and sympathy both crossing his face too, warring for dominance. "But that's blackmail. That's not fair to you," he insisted. "And still not a single valid reason."

"Still, that's what's been torturing me. I don't want to be one of those girls who gives up her friends for a guy. I don't want to be ungrateful to her for all that she's done for me, and I don't want to hurt Rose by lying to her, going behind her back, breaking her trust. Not after all she's been through," she said, then she shivered at the look on his face. So much pain.

"And I don't think you're too old, but maybe I'm too young," she added, realising the truth of it as she said the words. "I need to help Rose in the shop and at home, and focus more on school, concentrate on getting into uni so I can study to be a counsellor."

"You could always work with me," he offered – but he knew the moment that the words had left his mouth that he'd said the wrong thing, and regret settled in his eyes.

"That's what your dad said to Mum. But I need to forge my own path, follow my own heart," Carlie replied. Tears were beginning to fall, carving out a trail down her cheeks, but despite her desperate sadness she felt right somehow. She had Rose and Rhiannon, and the magic that they wove together. And her desire to help other grieving people was becoming increasingly important to her, as a way to honour the memory of her parents. It would have to be enough for now.

Rowan's face was pale. "But you are my heart Carlie," he whispered, voice strained. "I love you so much, and I know that you love me. Isn't that enough?"

"I do Rowan, I love you more than anything, and this is killing me," she said. Taking a deep breath, she tried to hold on to the strength it had taken to make this decision, to tell him. "You have no idea how much this is hurting me, but I can't honour my parents, help Rose, study hard enough, continue my magical education, if I'm obsessed with you and wanting to spend every moment with you.

"And I can't keep lying to Rose, begging Rhiannon to cover for me, sneaking around. That's not me. I don't want to be the type of person who practises deceit, who hides her true self. I don't want to be what the woman in green said I would be, the betrayer of those closest to me," she whispered, voice haunted.

Tears formed on his lashes, and she watched them spill over and run down his face. God, she wanted to reach out and stroke his cheek, stop his tears, kiss his lips, hold him close, tell him she didn't mean it, that of course they should be together. But she couldn't. She knew she was breaking his heart as well as her own, but she also knew that it was for the best.

"I'm sorry," she said, voice cracked with pain, then picked up her bag and fled. She had no idea what she was going to do, but she couldn't stay in the room with him for another minute or she would take back her cruel words and throw her arms around him, begging his forgiveness, begging for him to keep loving her.

Through her tears she saw that the lights were still on in the dining hall, so she headed there. Maybe someone had a phone and she could call a cab. She was half happy, and half disappointed, to see Jasmine at the urn, about to make another cup of tea. But when she saw Carlie's tear-stained face she put her mug down and raced over. "Are you okay?" she asked, fear in her voice.

She nodded, though her heart was shattered, and tried to stifle her sobs as Jasmine spoke. "Tea?" she asked.

Carlie shook her head, even as she smiled at the crazy English notion that a cup of tea would solve everything.

"I need to get out of here. Do you think I could call a cab?"

"I'll drive you," Jasmine said, and she'd rinsed her cup, picked up her purse and was leading Carlie out to the car park in a matter of moments. They pulled out quickly, tyres squealing, and Carlie was shocked out of her reverie by the anger stamped across the other woman's face.

"Did he try to hurt you? Force you to do anything?" Jasmine asked, voice fierce and eyes blazing.

"It's not Rowan," Carlie said quickly. "I promise." Jasmine glanced over at her, eyes searching her face for something, and seeming to find enough to reassure her, for now at least. Carlie was touched that she was so quick to jump to her defence.

"He's the best person I've ever known, and probably no one will ever love me the way he does," she said, feeling sadness at the truth of those words, and realising as she said them the startling differences between her relationship and her mum's. Violet had been so glad that no one would ever love her the way Andre did, but Carlie was devastated at the thought that no one would ever love her as much and as well as Rowan did.

She sighed. "We're both desperately in love. It's just... too much for me. I think I'll always think of what Mum went through at his dad's hands. And I know that's not fair, but maybe my friend is right, maybe I am too young for him. Maybe I lack the courage to love him as he deserves to be loved, as he loves me. And I know it's not fair to him, to leave like this, to run away, but surely it's better that I do it now rather than later, when we fall even more deeply in love?"

She paused for breath, trying to get her tears under control, and stared out into the darkness for a while in silence.

"But don't you deserve to love, and to be loved?" Jasmine finally asked, voice gentle, hesitant.

"Oh god, please don't give me a reason to take it back!" she implored her. "Of course I want to be with him, with all my heart, but I have to be strong. Me being with him hurts the other people in my life, and I can't do that."

Jasmine held her tongue, and they drove for a long time without a word, both lost in their own private worlds, gazing out at the lonely highway.

"Um, sweetie? I don't know where you live," Jasmine finally said as they approached a large intersection, and Carlie came back to the present with a crash.

"If you could just drop me in Smithfield I should be able to get a bus from there," she said.

Jasmine leaned over and took her hand, and pain seared through her as she remembered all the times Rowan had done that. Gasping for breath, and unable to speak, she sobbed once, before she got herself under control again.

"I'll take you home Carlie," the older woman said. "You're in no fit state to be waiting for buses in the middle of the night."

Grateful, Carlie finally managed to tell her where she lived, and Jasmine eventually got a smile out of her as she recalled more memories of Violet as a teenager.

It was almost midnight when Jasmine pulled up just down the road from Rose's cottage and gave Carlie a hug and her phone number, which she insisted she could call any time she needed to talk, day or night. Overwhelmed by her kindness, Carlie hugged her back, then stole around the side of the house and in through the back door, trying not to wake Rose. She couldn't face anyone right now, no matter how well meaning and filled with love they were. As quietly as she could she tiptoed up the stairs, then she threw herself down on her narrow bed, crying into the pillow until there were no tears left.

But sleep eluded her, and her mind raced ever faster. It was even worse because she knew she'd done this to herself. She was causing so much pain to them both, and now she was torturing herself over whether she'd done the right thing or not. After tossing and turning for ages, she finally lit the candle on her bedside table and crept out of bed, over to where she'd dumped her backpack, and pulled the diary out. Maybe her mum would have some wisdom for her...

Chapter 35

Dear Diary…

I t's funny, sometimes the most insignificant of chance encounters can change your life. Can save your life. I didn't even know his name for ages, just appreciated his kind hellos whenever I saw him, his offers to help me if I was carrying heavy shopping bags. Of course I could never let him help me, or let him into our apartment, or even return his greetings, because Andre would have known somehow, and I was always terrified of doing something wrong – or anything he would consider was wrong – for fear of his anger.

Oliver lived in the same building as us, and although I barely spoke to him, too afraid to, if I'm honest, somehow an unlikely rapport developed between us. It was pretty one sided – he'd ask how I was, he'd tell me about his day, and I would stare at him, mute with fear that somehow Andre would twist even this into something ugly. He'd become so jealous, so controlling, so angry. He was convinced that I was chatting up every guy I met, from the plumber who came to fix our hot water to the guys in our ritual circle who he was certain I was having sex with. So I tried to avoid Oliver – he seemed so sweet, and I didn't want him being dragged into our drama, didn't want him being hurt if Andre ever grew suspicious.

But while I never told him anything, somehow he noticed the bruises everyone else refused to see, and saw me shrink into myself when I was with Andre, in a way no one else ever did… Somehow I'd found a *friend, in the most unlikely place, from the most unlikely country. He was a backpacker from Australia, living in London for a while, and he offered me friendship when I needed it. Maybe that's the Aussie way, I don't know. But I will forever be grateful that he persevered with me, no matter how many times I ignored and rebuffed him.*

One afternoon Andre and I had a terrible fight, worse than usual – and that's saying something! It was only a few days after the retreat where he'd forced himself on me, and I could feel myself disappearing, losing myself, becoming just a shell of a person. He said he'd overheard me on the phone to Mike, planning to escape. Which was laughable – I knew I couldn't use the phone, I knew he had it bugged, and there was no way I could call Mike, or would call Mike, and drag him into this. I'd given up hope of ever seeing him again.

But Andre didn't believe me. He screamed at me, awful, ugly accusations, said with such conviction that I started wondering if I'd really done all those terrible things after all. But they weren't true, so for some stupid reason I continued to deny them – and he threw me into the glass coffee table, which smashed, and cut me up pretty badly. I couldn't even stand up, I was in so much pain, but he came at me again, lifting me up, hand biting into my shoulder, his other hand over my mouth to smother me as I clawed at him, desperately trying to breathe. He continued his awful abuse, shouting things so cruel that I wondered what he'd ever seen in me, how anyone could ever love me, let alone him, if I was all those terrible things.

Carlie stopped, stunned. It wasn't Rowan in that fortune teller's vision, forcing her to have sex and throwing her into a glass table, it was Andre and her mum. Andre who no doubt looked a lot like Rowan, and her mum who had looked so much like her at that age. Tears blinded her. Rhiannon had been so wrong. She had been so wrong. It was never Rowan. Heart breaking a little more, but not knowing what else to do, she kept reading.

Finally I started to black out, and part of me welcomed the thought of oblivion, of release from the pain, from the mental anguish, from the fear that now consumed every waking moment. Then someone hammered on the door, and he dropped me onto the floor and stomped off down the hallway, threatening to kill whoever had knocked. He didn't come back though, and eventually I realised that the person who'd knocked had gone, and so had he.

I lay there, crumpled on the ground, shaking, crying, sending a prayer of thanks to the goddess that I'd survived one more beating, even though part of me wondered what the point was. It was inevitable that he would go too far at some point, and I would die, so what did it matter if it was today or any other day?

Then slowly I became aware that someone was standing in the room with me, and a shiver of fear and shame rocked through me. Was it a neighbour, drawn by the crash? Or had Andre come back to finish me off? But it was Oliver, so gentle, so out of place in this shambles of a room, with this wreck of a person. He winced as I turned towards him, and I raised a hand to my face and realised there was blood still pouring out of the cut on my scalp. As ever, the wound wouldn't show though – they were always well hidden.

Panicked, I told him he had to go, quickly, that he needed to escape before Andre came back, but he shook his head and came over to me. And he lifted me up, so gently, and pulled off his long sleeved t-shirt and used it to try to stop the blood. There was still some glass in some of the smaller cuts, and he pulled them out, his face contorting with emotion each time he thought he'd hurt me, but by this stage I'd become almost oblivious to the sensation of physical pain.

He wanted to take me to hospital, or call the police, but I freaked out on him, and eventually he promised he wouldn't. I became increasingly hysterical the longer he stayed though, scared Andre would come back and kill us both. Finally I got through to him, and he agreed to go – but then he said he was leaving for Australia the next day, and had actually come to say goodbye.

I'd never felt so sad, or so desperate. I hadn't realised how much I'd come to depend on him and his sunny nature, his quiet acceptance, his occasional smiles and hellos in the corridor. Then he said: "Come with me." That we could go backpacking around Australia, and he'd teach me to surf, and I could hang out with his buddies – take a bit of time out to think clearly. I shook my head, knowing it was impossible. He'd find me, he'd stop me, and he'd make this kind stranger's life hell.

"He'll kill you if you stay," he said, as though he'd heard my thought. But there was no judgement in his voice, no drama, it was just a simple statement of fact. Which I already knew, of course, and was numb to, but there was something about the way he said it, the look on his face, the compassion in his eyes, that made me suddenly cling to a skerrick of hope that there could be an escape from the inevitability of my life.

It sounded crazy, and wildly impossible, but he said a friend of his had an old passport in her maiden name, and no plans to travel for a few years, and we looked a little alike. So I became Fiona Scott, nineteen years old. I gained two years, and even got a new birthday. But I wasn't thinking about the future at all, by then I was just thinking day to day, how to survive one more day. If I thought at all, I guess I imagined that eventually I'd go back home and pick up my old life with Mum, become Violet Tyler again, and straighten out the ID issue. But that never happened.

And so I grabbed my diary, a change of clothes and three hundred pounds from Andre's drawer, then we went down to Oliver's apartment. I cut off my hair and bleached it blonde, to look more like Fiona – to look less like myself – then we left for the airport, too scared to stay in the building, even inside behind a locked door, in case Andre somehow found us. Oliver bought me a plane ticket, and we stayed the night in the gate lounge, him watching over me like a guardian angel when I finally slept for a few short hours, then we flew out early the next morning.

It was the perfect escape – even if Andre did have all those "high up" contacts that he'd threatened me with, they wouldn't be able to track me because I didn't travel under my own name. And he'd never even known Oliver existed, wouldn't know his name even if someone described him. It probably wouldn't have worked now, with whiz bang computers and high alert security, but somehow I got away with it. It did help that Fiona's passport photo had been taken when she was fifteen, so obviously she would look a bit different by now, four *years later. And who knows? Maybe the goddess granted me one last favour, even though I'd turned my back on her.*

Don't misunderstand me – although I'm recounting this calmly now, I did totally freak out, somewhere over Europe, that I was flying across the world with a stranger. Had I learned nothing?

It horrified me that the first real conversation I had with this man was on a plane to Australia with him. I was actually more dependent on him than I'd been on Andre, and it's a testament to his patience and kindness that I didn't try to throw myself off the plane somehow. So yes, of course it seemed crazy to do this – but my life was crazy. I no longer knew what normal was, what safe was. I guess I'm just really lucky he didn't take advantage of me too, that he was so trustworthy and so honourable.

We spent some time in Sydney, staying with his parents for a while. I don't know what he told them about me, but they were so lovely, and said I could stay in their spare room for as long as I needed to. It took a while for me to stop jumping whenever there was a knock on the door, or flinching when the phone rang, but they were very patient with me, gave me a lot of space, and I was indebted to them until the day they died for their gentle acceptance and immense warmth. Mum would have loved them, and loved Oliver too.

Because he was so kind. So patient. So sweet. He is so kind, so patient, so sweet. And he did everything he possibly could to reassure me that he didn't expect anything from me, that I didn't owe him anything, then or ever. He introduced me to all his friends, and encouraged me to become their friends too, especially the girls, independent of him – although I was painfully shy for a long time, overly cautious and scared of giving anything of my past away, so I didn't become close to any of them until a year or two later.

But they were all so lovely, and when a few of them said they were going to travel up north and pick fruit in Queensland through the summer, I told Ollie I'd like to go too, to earn some money and start trying to live in the world. So we all went. We didn't earn enough money to stay anywhere fancy or go out every night, but it was nice – we stayed in a hostel on the beach, sat around at night having picnics on the sand and just talking, laughing, joking, just being normal young people. It amazed me how carefree they all were – yet after a while I was even more amazed to find myself joining in.

When they drifted back to Sydney to their real lives, Ollie and I got the train south and then went across the Nullarbor, and worked through vintage season, picking grapes through the night at a vineyard on the south-west coast for two months. Then we moved on, travelling north to follow the sun, spending days at the beach, camping out and just watching the stars, slowly opening up to each other. It was amazing – after the stress of that time with Andre, just drifting from place to place, with no real job and no commitment, no pressure, was perfect. It was everything that I needed.

Ollie told me later that he'd fallen in love with me the day he rescued me, when we stood in the bathroom of his tiny London apartment and he watched me chop off my hair, bleach it blonde and gather my courage to escape. But he never told me that at the time, never let me know by word or action – was always so desperately careful to never let me feel pressured in any way.

Years later he revealed to me that when he was growing up, his next door neighbour had been a victim of domestic violence, so he'd recognised the signs when he first saw me, and felt compelled to help me because their friend had been killed by her husband. He was only twelve when that happened, and it had affected him deeply. In some way I think saving me healed the guilt he'd always felt about not intervening, the powerlessness of knowing it was happening but not knowing how to help.

We picked up bar work here and there – Ollie taught me how, and since I was apparently legal now, being suddenly nineteen, I could get jobs in pubs too. I desperately wanted to be self-sufficient, and to eventually earn enough money to pay him back for the cost of the plane fare and the time I'd spent with him in Sydney before I'd got work. We always worked cash in hand, and Ollie booked the hostels, just to be on the safe side, but I opened a bank account in Fiona's name, since the only ID I had was her passport, and slowly I became her. I went for my driver's licence in her name, I introduced myself to everyone I met as Fiona, and even Ollie called me that, because he'd never actually known my name in London.

I felt sad that Violet had disappeared, like she'd never existed, but I knew this was the opportunity I needed. No one here knew Violet, knew me, so I was free to reinvent myself, to become the person I wanted to be, to hide my shameful past from myself and everyone else. So I become Fiona – stronger than Violet, tougher, more outgoing. Fiona was less trusting certainly, less generous with her time, and far more sceptical of everything. I always shied away from the new agey events Oliver's friends invited us to, and the smell of burning sage still makes me sick to my stomach.

I wrote to Mum once, to tell her I'd found happiness, but it came back return to sender, addressee unknown, so I figured that she didn't want to see me again, or she'd moved away to start over, and perhaps I should just leave it be, let her build a new family, a new life. Now it's not much to go on, but just in case you ever need to know, her name is Rose Tyler, and she lived at 32 Meadow Lane, Summer Hill...

Carlie tore her eyes from the book, aghast. Rose lived at number 23, not 32. She'd never moved away, had stayed in the same house all these years, just on the slightest chance that her daughter might get in touch one day. Grief and such a deep sense of loss and regret overwhelmed her, and for a while she just sat there, tears running down her cheeks, eyes unseeing, as she held the book to her chest and cried. Finally though she took a deep breath and wiped her eyes, and turned back to the tear-stained pages.

This, at last, was the mystery of her mother. She was a victim of domestic violence – but she was not a tragic figure, and not a victim in the end, because more than anything she was also a survivor. She refused to have her life defined by what was done to her by a cruel man, and instead defined herself and her life by what she made of it. By how she overcame her circumstances and created a life of love and joy for herself, the man she loved, and Carlie, the child of that love.

Even her name became a conscious choice and a symbol of her empowerment. Sure, at first it was borrowed simply as a means of escape, but she took ownership of it and became the woman she wanted to be, stronger, more independent, filled with love and courage. No longer diminished, no longer scared, finally herself.

She hadn't cast off her old name as a slight to the woman who had given it to her, but as a way to pull together the shattered pieces of what Violet had become, and create a symbol of her survival, a symbol of her reweaving of her life into a woman of strength.

Carlie was stunned. She'd never known a braver woman than her mum, and she was in awe at the depth of her father, who had saved a scared young girl then helped her blossom into the warrior she had become. Many men would have liked the insecurity and weakness a woman who'd been through all that might cling to, but her dad had seen the light inside her when she was a terrified teenager diminishing herself almost to nothing – a light no one else had seen – and nurtured it, helped it grow. She prayed that she would find a man who would love her like that, then felt her eyes fill with tears as she realised that she *did* have a man like that, and she had just cruelly cast him aside.

Desperate not to dwell on that right now, she turned back to the diary. There were pages torn out, and a few blank ones, then she came to what appeared to be the end, and one final block of text. The handwriting was different – neater, stronger, less girlie – and it seemed some time had passed since the previous entries.

Tomorrow I am getting married, and I will have a new name. Not the name I was born with, or the name I borrowed to escape, but the one that represents the love I've found with a truly good man, the acceptance of his wonderful parents, which I thank the goddess for every day, and the new life of love that Oliver and I will build together. And I can't quite believe it, but today we found out that I'm pregnant, and we couldn't be happier. This is why I want to finish writing this letter to you, in case you ever get to read this, and then I will put it away forever. Because this is my new beginning. My fresh start.

I am not the girl who started this diary. I feel so much for her, and I am so grateful that she was so loved, by her parents, by her friends, by Mike, the truest friend anyone could ever have. My heart breaks for the pain she went through, the pain she caused, but to be honest it feels like all that happened to someone else. A childhood friend I'm no longer in contact with, or someone from a nightmare that used to plague me. She is not me, and I will not be defined by what happened to her. It is over, it is the past. It made me who I am perhaps, but that is all. No longer will it have any power over me. People can be defined by the worst parts of their life, or by the best. I choose the best.

So tomorrow I will become Fiona Parker, wife of Oliver, mother of our beloved child, and future lawyer. I went back to school you know, and now I'm at university. A few years ago a good man saw the potential in me, when I had lost all hope, had lost even the will to live, and he continues to encourage me to follow my heart, and my dreams, to be the best person I can be.

This is not what I ever expected my life to be like – I have a different name, a different husband, a different career, a different home country – but in many ways it's so much better. Of course I miss Mum, every single day, and I deeply regret that she'll probably always wonder if I'm dead. But I might have been, if I'd stayed with Andre, and so I try to be glad that, although she doesn't know it, I am alive, and I am happy, and I am loved.

I guess my daughter, if you ever read this, I want you to know not only of the pain and disappointment of love, but the beauty and goodness of it. Be wary, and don't let any man diminish you – and especially don't diminish yourself for any man, or any person. But even more importantly, don't lock your heart away and refuse to feel just in case you get hurt.

If you find a good man, a true man, one who loves you for who you are, not what he wants you to be, hold on to him. Don't let other people's opinions of him colour your judgement, and don't judge him harshly for one misunderstanding or mistake. People make mistakes – you will make mistakes, no doubt your loved one will make mistakes – but there's a big difference between someone who acknowledges their error, asks for forgiveness and is determined to prove that they'll never do it again, and someone who can't even see that what they did is wrong.

Be honest, be fair, listen to his point of view and his explanation, and make sure you are not responding out of fear or misinformation, turning one small misunderstanding into a catastrophic event that colours everything you see from then on.

Don't judge him on another person's idea of him, or break up with him because they said so. Everyone has a motive, everyone has a different perspective, and no one knows the real story, your story, except you. And don't let your perception of everyone be tainted by the actions of one person. Some people are cruel, yes, but one bad man does not mean all men are bad. Some people are amazing, inspiring. They will lift you up, help you grow, help you be better, help you find what it is within you that makes your heart sing, makes you feel all the amazing possibilities of this amazing life.

Don't ever let a man bend you to his will, but equally don't let a friend make your decisions for you, issue you with ultimatums or decide what is best for you. You must trust your heart. The wisdom within your soul. The light that shines so brightly within you.

And if you find someone who loves you, flaws and all, who encourages you to shine ever brighter, well, be brave enough to give your heart to them. To dive into the great unknown and risk everything for the love you will share. Because it's worth it. It's so worth it. You are so worth it.

Chapter 36

The Choice

Staring at the words on the page, Carlie pondered the wisdom her mum had left her. To follow her heart. To let her light shine. To trust her own wisdom. To not cave in to a boyfriend – or to a friend. To choose what was right, what was fair, what made her heart sing. She knew some would expect her to choose Rhiannon. Her grandma might too. Wasn't that what women were taught, that the sisterhood was more important? To never let a man come between friends?

But the problem with that was that it wasn't Rowan who was coming between them. He'd been nothing but sweet and kind to Rhiannon, helping her with her magical studies, inviting her to the festival, including her, acknowledging her importance in Carlie's life. And he'd always encouraged her to spend time with Rhi, despite the fact that he liked her a little bit less every time she tried to encourage Carlie to break up with him. Every time she tried to convince her he was capable of the awful things that her mother had suffered.

She sighed. She knew there were also those who would say she should be with the man she loved, and sacrifice Rhiannon's friendship, especially as that was the only option she was giving her. Thinking about it like that, it seemed more logical to choose Rowan. He was the one who wanted her to be happy, who encouraged her to choose the best option for *her*. She still couldn't understand why Rhiannon was demanding she break up with him in the first place.

But was this the betrayal that the woman in green had spoken of? Did she know even then that she would be faced with a choice between Rhiannon, the girl who had helped her so much in her grief, and Rowan, the man who had taught her how to love and be loved? And did Brianna expect that she would choose the guy, and betray her friend? Know even then, before Carlie had ever met him, that it would come to this? Was that what she'd meant, that she should do what Rhi wanted rather than betraying her?

But if she accepted her friend's ultimatum and broke up with Rowan – stayed broken up with Rowan – wasn't she betraying herself? Betraying her own heart? Shouldn't she be willing to risk her heart for the man who treasured her so deeply? Be brave, like her mum, and seek out the deep and desperate all-consuming love that she now knew was possible?

And why did she even have to choose? Her mum had had the love of her life as well as her best friend Sandy. Couldn't she choose both as well? Rowan accepted the importance of Rhiannon in her life – why couldn't her friend accept him? Or at least accept that she loved him. That she wanted to be with him. Because she'd realised, as she read her mum's words, that she did want Rowan, that she loved him desperately, and she was mortified that she'd let her friend's words, and her mum's old stories, turn her against him.

How could she have looked at him and seen his father? How could she have connected herself with her mother in that tragic scenario? How could she have doubted him for one moment? She'd done just what her mother had warned her against, let the actions of another man colour her perception of him. Let the words of her friend – words that had no foundation – influence the way she thought of him. But she and Rowan were not their parents. They weren't destined to play out their lives, doomed to repeat their mistakes. They could choose their own path, their own love, forge their own way forward.

Climbing out of bed, Carlie threw back the curtains, letting the waxing moon shine in on her, feeling the presence of the nearby hill silhouetted against the dark sky connecting her to the earth, to the beating heart of the planet and all that lived on it. She tried to reach out with her mind to Rowan. So often when they were apart they'd stared up at the same moon and felt connected, and she could swear he was doing that now, reaching out to her, holding her close, stroking her cheek as he whispered words of forgiveness and love. Closing her eyes, she sent out a prayer to the moon, and a prayer to him, that it was not too late. That she could reverse this mess she'd created, and take responsibility for the cruel things she'd said – and take power over and ownership of her choice. She was choosing him. And she was choosing Rhiannon. *She was choosing them both.*

Groping around on her desk until she found the cards she'd bought the other day, she climbed back into bed, smiling as Luther jumped up and settled on her feet, purring happily, as though to tell her she'd finally made the right decision. And as she gazed at her cat friend she felt her heart lighten, and knew that she had. Rhiannon had to understand that she would not choose one over the other. She loved them both, and it was time she told them that.

Dear Rowan, my sweet beloved,

As soon as I left tonight I knew I'd done the wrong thing, made the wrong choice. Because I choose you. I love you. I want to be with you. That's the truth of it, and anything else is superfluous. How I deal with Rhiannon, when I tell Gran about us, they're just details to be worked out. They don't affect the only thing that actually matters - the fact that I love you.

I'm going to come and see you in the morning, get the first bus back so that I can tell you all this myself, but I want to write it down too, right now, in this moment that I choose you, because I'm sure you will feel it. I'm sure you will know it deep in your bones, in your heart, in your soul, and you will feel my arms around you until I can be there in person to tell you, to hold you, to love you. I can feel your arms around me too, I'm sure of it - I can feel your love, and I thank you with all my heart for your forgiveness.

I deeply regret the pain I caused you, caused both of us, tonight. I let other people's opinions cloud my judgement, and allowed someone else to make a decision for me. And I'm sorry, so sorry, for thinking for even a second that you could be anything like your father. I know you're not. I feel that in every cell of my body, every beat of my heart. And I am not my mother, though I love her dearly. You and I are not fated to walk the path of our parents, but to forge our own path, our own destiny. Lives entwined, souls in harmony, hearts as one.

I choose Rhiannon too, and I hope that one day soon you'll both see in each other what I see. She is the sister of my heart, and I value her highly and deeply – but you are the love of my life, and I will not give you up for anyone or anything.

You have opened my heart to love, after I thought it would be closed forever. I thought I was unloveable, unable to love, unworthy of being loved, but your patience and compassion have transformed me. Being loved by you has made me blossom, has given me the courage to let my light shine, has made me a better person. Your mum got it wrong – it is you who has changed me for the better, not the other way round. You have transformed me. You have healed me, in so many different ways, and I am so grateful to you.

And I will love you forever,
Your Carlie xx

Dear Rhiannon, sister of my heart,
I went to see Rowan today, and I broke up with him, because of the ultimatum you gave me. But I've been thinking about it every moment since, and I know that I made the wrong decision. I will not choose between you. I love you both. I choose you both.

I appreciate that you are concerned for me, and I'm grateful that you care so much, but please know that there is nothing to fear. Rowan loves me, and he will never hurt me. I know this in my heart, in my mind, in the very bones of my body. And there's something I learned from my mother today – Rowan is my Oliver, not my Andre. He is the man who makes me more, not the one who diminishes me. He is my beloved, and being loved by him has healed me in so many ways. I hope that when you come to know him as I do, that you will see us together and recognise how much we love each other.

And I want you to know too that he has always honoured you, and your importance in my life. Even tonight, even when I told him I had chosen you.

Another thing I learned from Mum today – if Rowan didn't want to be with me, he wouldn't be. It's that simple, and that complex. He doesn't gain anything from being with me – it would be so much easier for him if he wasn't with me, if he didn't have to sneak around, and wait for me to finish school before he can see me... if his girlfriend had a car, and was free to travel with him... if she didn't have a curfew, if she wasn't too scared to tell her grandmother about him... But he loves me despite all that. He loves ME.

I love him so much, and I love you too. I hope one day you'll be able to see in him what I see, be able to spend time together with us both like we did at the Autumn's End festival. And I hope you won't carry out your ultimatum, because I would be devastated to lose you. You are the sister of my heart, my dearest friend, and I value you and want you in my life.

Much love, Carlie xx

Hand cramping and eyes feeling tired from her furious writing, Carlie finally put the cards in their envelopes and wrote Rowan and Rhiannon's names on theirs. As she snuggled down under her mum's old quilt, she felt as though a huge weight had been lifted from her shoulders, and was filled with incredible relief that she had made this decision. Now she couldn't wait to get up in the morning and rush off to see Rowan.

A tiny flicker of fear shot through her, as she wondered whether she would be too late to make amends, but she could feel his arms around her somehow, would have sworn that he was sending the same message to her. Luther miaowed, and climbed up the bed, close to her head, so she fell asleep to the sound of his purring, with a smile on her face and an incredible lightness and sense of hope in her heart.

Chapter 37

For A Short Time

The hammering on the door woke her, and she struggled up from the depths of her beautiful dream, clinging to the memory of Rowan's arm around her, his hand stroking her face, his lips warm on hers. Smiling, she dragged on a pair of jeans from the messy pile on the floor and his cosy black jumper from the end of her narrow bed, and made her way downstairs.

Excited, she pulled the door open, expecting it to be Rowan, called there by her dream, by the message of love that she'd sent him. But her smile faltered as she gazed at the man and woman standing under the stretch of blackberry vines twisting overhead. They were police officers, the man holding a package wrapped in heart-print paper, with a card with her name on it nestled under the ribbons. She stared at them, a shiver of dread racing up her spine.

"Can I help you?" she croaked, fear already tightening her throat.

"Are you Carlie?" the woman asked, and she nodded, terror clutching at her heart as she tried to wake up, tried to kick her brain into gear, tried to understand what they were doing there.

"There was an accident this morning," the woman said, voice gentle, soothing. "Do you know the young man? Long black hair, tattoo of the moon on his wrist?"

Face ashen, heart pounding, she nodded again. "My boyfriend Rowan," she whispered. "What happened? Where is he?"

"He was just down the highway, on his way here I guess, but his car must have slid off the road in the snow," the man said. "We found your address in his wallet..."

"But is he... What has... Can I see him?" She stopped, unable to bring herself to ask what she most needed to know.

"I'm so sorry," the woman said, reaching out for her as she staggered a little, clutching the door frame, trying to stay upright. "The ambulance came, but it was too late." The space around Carlie opened up, all noise receded, and time seemed to whir around her, stretching, slowing, collapsing in on her. Slowly she slid to the ground, not even aware she was falling. Not aware of anything but the crushing pain and anger swelling inside her. This couldn't be happening, not again. She couldn't lose him too. That wasn't fair. Not now, not when she still had to tell him how much she loved him.

"Carlie, what is it?" Rose asked, hurrying towards the three people standing in her doorway, catching her distraught granddaughter as she sank to the floor. A small part of Carlie felt Rose's arms around her, holding her close, holding her safe. Not safe enough though. Never safe again. That part of her was also aware of the snow falling around them, twirling in the doorway, catching in her hair. Like diamonds, he'd said. The rest of her was just numb, so numb, and cold and dead inside.

The tiny part of her that remained there in the present was relieved when Rose took charge and invited the officers inside, but she couldn't move. Didn't want to move. Thought she could just stay there, slumped and frozen in the doorway, snow in her hair, in her face, in her heart. Stay there forever. Her shattered heart had crumbled into pieces again, and there was just a gaping wound where it used to be. An endless black hole that would never be filled again.

The male officer had come back out when she didn't follow them, and he lifted her to her feet and half carried, half dragged, her inside to the warmth of the kitchen, where Rose pressed a cup of tea into her cold hands. She shuddered as she inhaled the scent of ginkgo, valerian, juniper and cayenne, her grandma's blend for shock, honey stirred into it but unable to mask the smell or the taste. But she swallowed it dutifully, too numb to argue.

She wished she could swallow something stronger, something that would end her pain forever. The officer had steered her into a chair and settled down next to her. He was asking her questions, but she stared at him blankly. She couldn't understand them, couldn't make sense of the words floating around his head, jumbles of letters moving through the air. Then finally one landed. Parents.

"His mum is Louisa, Louisa Dunbar. From Smithfield," she whispered. "His father is dead. Like everyone else," she muttered, and broke down again.

Later, she became vaguely aware that Rose had shepherded the officers out. Heard, on the edge of her consciousness, the sudden rain as it poured from the sky, the thunder rumbling across the village, and the lightning that was splitting the heavens apart. It was perfect, she thought bitterly, and wanted to run outside into the storm and let the lightning split her apart too. Tears finally came, and she felt the sobs wracking her body.

Shaking with anguish, she ran up the stairs, threw herself through her bedroom door and slammed it closed behind her. Crawling into the far corner, she crouched there, knees pulled up to her chin, arms wrapped tightly around her legs, trying to make herself smaller, trying to diminish herself in an effort to diminish the pain. She rocked, slowly at first, then less gently, as wrenching sobs shook her body, shook her world.

Through the mist of her tears, her gaze flitted wildly around the room, coming to rest on the altar she'd so carefully constructed with Rhiannon. A huge chunk of rose quartz sat in the north, mocking her with its promise of forgiveness, compassion and unconditional love. Fat lot of good that had done her.

Close to it was her athame, the ceremonial dagger she'd been gifted by a woman more mist than substance. Snatching it up, she held it in her hand, its weight a welcome distraction, grounding her in her body, in her pain. Holding the point of the blade to her wrist, she tried desperately to find one single reason not to draw it across the delicate skin, draw it through the blue vein, draw out a river of blood, and draw this painful existence to a close.

He'd promised her that he would slit his wrists before he ever hurt her, but that had clearly been a lie. Fury raged through her, red hot, and suddenly the thought of oblivion, of letting herself drown in this swirling crush of despair and never come up for air, seemed the most welcome idea in the world.

But in the end even that effort seemed too much for her, and she slumped on the floor and allowed her mind to shut down as the pain of her loss tore her heart into a million broken pieces.

For three days she didn't leave her room, didn't eat, didn't even seem aware of her surroundings. Someone had lifted her into her bed, but she didn't know who. Christmas morning dawned, then set, and she didn't even notice. Sometimes she sensed Rose, putting another cup of herbal tea in her hands, holding her head up and forcing her to take a few sips. She thought Rhiannon might have been there once or twice too, but she wasn't sure, couldn't be sure, because she also thought her mother had been there, sitting on her bed, holding her hand, smoothing back her hair, and she knew that couldn't be right. Everyone she loved left her. *Everyone.*

She thought she'd never stop crying, but eventually her body couldn't make any more tears, and she sobbed without them, great gulping breaths torn from the very centre of her soul, which wracked her weakened body until she slipped back into welcome oblivion again. Finally Rose came in, with Mike behind her for moral support.

"Sweetheart, you have to get up now, you have to eat. Can you do that for me?" Carlie stared at her, hollow eyed. Dead inside. She didn't want to ever move again. Moving hurt. Living hurt. Loving was a pain beyond all measure. Mike came and sat on her bed, and took her hands gently in his. She tried not to recoil, but it was hard. He smiled at her, sympathy and caring oozing from every pore.

"Carlie love, do you think you could get up, just for a little while? Just have a piece of toast? Even half?" He leaned in closer and lowered his voice. "Your grandma is really worried, and I'd ask, if not for yourself, that you do it for her," he said beseechingly.

Looking over at Rose, she saw her, really saw her, and her heart constricted. There were great black smudges under her eyes, and her face was gaunt, sadness etched in jagged lines across it. She was so frail, a million miles from the grand high priestess she usually appeared to be, just an old woman who had endured more tragedy than any one person should have to. Glancing back at Mike, she saw the suffering writ deep in his eyes too, and slowly nodded. He smiled at her, a small smile, patted her hand, then helped Rose back downstairs, leaving her door open so she couldn't descend back into the dark that had so consumed her.

Carlie lay in bed for a few more minutes, crippled with despair, then she forced herself to get up. Her body ached. She was stiff and sore, and her legs buckled under her as she tried to stand. Every step was a huge effort, but the memory of her grandma's face pushed her on. Gazing down at herself, she saw that she was still clad in her old jeans and his woollen jumper, the clothes she'd pulled on three days ago – or was it three years? – in that time when she'd been so filled with joy and optimism. When she'd been about to tell him that of course she loved him, as much as he loved her, and she desperately wanted to be with him forever.

Turning towards the door, she caught sight of her reflection in the mirror, and walked closer, shocked. She looked like a zombie, dark circles smudged under her lower lashes, hair lank and lifeless, lips pale, and her eyes bloodshot and deadened of all expression. No wonder Rose was worried about her.

Slowly she picked up a skirt from the floor, then dragged open a drawer and pulled out a clean t-shirt and underwear, and walked into the ensuite next door. She turned on the hot water, piled her hair into a knot on the top of her head – washing it would have to wait – and stepped into the shower. Then she stood under the stream of scalding water, hating the feeling of her body waking up. She didn't want to wake up. Being awake was too painful.

When the water ran cold she stayed there, liking the sensation of pain as it chilled her through, matching her frozen heart. But eventually she sighed, and turned off the shower, then stepped out and dried off. She dragged on her clothes, then pulled Rowan's jumper over her head. It still smelled of him, of lemongrass and vanilla, and precious moments spent together outside, and the sweetness of his hugs. She couldn't choke back the sobs or stop the river of tears as she felt his arms around her, felt his lips on her ear as he whispered how much he loved her.

Every fibre of her being ached to crawl back into bed, wanted to slip back into oblivion, but she knew that Rose was waiting for her. So, heart filled with dread, she made her way downstairs, Luther weaving around her ankles, helping her into the kitchen. Rose stood there, trapped between the sink and the bench, a piece of toast on a plate in one hand, looking totally lost.

"I'm so sorry Gran," Carlie croaked, as she fell into the older woman's arms, tears trickling down her face and soaking into Rose's hair. Her grandmother was all she had now, and she didn't even know how long she'd still be with her. "I'm sorry I didn't tell you about him, didn't let you meet him. I wanted to wait until I was sure, which was stupid. I was sure the minute I met him. He was sure the minute we met. I just..." she trailed off, tear-stained face filled with anguish and regret.

"Oh Sweetheart, I'm the one who's sorry. We're all so sorry."

Carlie looked up at her, puzzled. "Rhiannon told me about him," Rose said. "Not the misunderstanding – well, that too – but she told me how much he loved you, how protective he was of you, and how deeply sorry she is that she came between you."

When Carlie looked even more puzzled, Rose took her hand and gently led her over to the table, sat her down and placed the piece of buttered toast in front of her.

"She found the card you'd written her, and it really affected her. She feels terrible, and hopes you'll be able to forgive her."

Carlie shrugged. "I can't feel anything right now. Not love or forgiveness or empathy or anger or even the will to go on," she said, voice small. But she picked up the toast and took a bite, and forced herself to swallow it down.

"You need time Sweetheart, time to process it, time to feel it."

"But not time together," she whispered, tears welling again in her eyes, and pain exploding in her brain.

"I'm sorry," Rose whispered. "My dear girl, if I could change this, bear your grief for you…"

"Oh Gran, you must think I'm so silly. I only knew him for three months, from Mabon Eve to Midwinter Eve, just a quarter turn of the Wheel," she sobbed.

"No Sweetheart –"

"But I loved him. He listened to me, he believed in me. I couldn't tell Rhiannon all my doubts about wanting to be a counsellor, but I could pour everything out to him, and he never judged me, he just held me, and listened to me, and then made me feel like I really could do that, really could help people. And he helped us both with our coven work, with our research – he helped Rhiannon connect to more magic than she ever had in her life. And me too. The most connected I ever felt to magic was when I was with him, just sitting by the stream talking, listening to the bees, holding hands as we climbed the hill. Connecting to nature, to the earth, to each other." She rubbed her eyes impatiently, sick to the death of the tears, of the salt, of the pain.

"And he healed me," she whispered, voice shaky, but determined to let her grandmother know just what he had meant to her. "He gave me the strength to go on, to open my heart to love again, when I thought I never would, not after –" She broke off, the deep hurt naked and raw on her face.

"Yet it was nothing, really. What's three months? No one else even knew that I knew him, knew that he changed my life…"

"Carlie, look at me." Surprised by the force of her grandma's voice, she raised her head, and Rose took both her hands and stared straight into her eyes, into her soul. "You have to know that the length of time means nothing. You can mean more to somebody you knew for a single day, than someone you knew for a year. Fall in love more deeply, share more of yourself, with someone you only spent a short time with, than you ever could in a lifetime with someone else. The length of time has no bearing on the strength of the love, or the depth of the meaning, that two people have for each other, or on the power they wield to change each other irrevocably for the better.

"And I know you can't see this now, but to have someone touch your life so deeply, open your heart so wide, it's a blessing. It's more than most people will ever have. It will take time, but I know that you'll be able to see that some day," Rose said, holding Carlie's hands, holding her gaze, making sure she was listening to every single word.

"He has changed you forever, and will be a part of you forever. And to be changed by someone, to change them – to each become more than you were before, through your love – that's the rarest and greatest magic of all."

Carlie stared at her grandma, tears pouring down her face, listening but not listening. Eyes blank.

"And besides, I did know him," Rose added, eyes twinkling, and Carlie looked up at her in surprise.

"I met Rowan a few years ago at a healing course, and he was lovely. And a great healer and teacher. I'd seen him a few times since then – this industry is smaller than you'd think – and then he came into the shop last week," she said. Carlie's mouth fell open.

"He wanted to let me know how he felt about you, how much he loved you," Rose told her with a smile.

"But –"

"He said you weren't ready to tell me, that you were worried about what I'd think, but he wanted to let me know how much he respected you, and to assure me he was taking things slowly. That he would never hurt you. That you were the goddess to him, and you shone brighter than the moon and the stars."

"I just… Oh my god, I can't believe he did that," Carlie whispered. "And you didn't say anything to me?"

"This was your story to tell Sweetheart, and your responsibility, to work out when you were ready to share it with me," she replied, glancing pointedly at the toast with its one tiny bite out of it. Carlie dutifully picked it up and took one more mouthful, then she sighed, seeming to collapse back in on herself.

"How did you do it Grandma?" she whispered. "How did you manage to go on?"

"There is no secret to dealing with grief Sweetheart," Rose said, her own voice thick with unshed tears. "There's no easy solution, no map to guide you.

You just get out of bed every morning, and try to get through the day as best you can. Some days are more difficult than others, some less so. And you just keep doing that. Over and over again."

"I don't know if I can do it, not after I lost Mum and Dad too. It's not fair," Carlie said, voice broken and cracked with pain.

"It never is fair. But did you tell him how much you loved him?" Rose asked gently.

"Of course, every time we saw each other," she replied.

"Then there's some consolation in that," her grandma said. "Regret is a terrible thing to die with – and to live with. The last thing I said to Louis was to pull himself together, for Violet's sake, and it's hurt me every day since, that as he died he was replaying words of condemnation from me, not words of love."

A tear trickled down Carlie's cheek. "The last thing I said was that it was over. That I loved him but I had to end it, because me loving him was hurting the people closest to me."

Rose stared at her granddaughter, shocked.

"Rhiannon told me that she couldn't be my friend any more if I stayed with Rowan," Carlie said, voice barely a whisper, before she broke down in tears again.

Rose gathered her into her arms, patting her shoulder and holding her tight as she sobbed. "Yet it seems that both of you knew that it wasn't the end. You'd already decided to fix it, and he was on his way to see you, to fight for you. He knew."

"Thank you Gran," Carlie said, trying hard to smile, but not having much luck.

"Oh, but this is for you," Rose announced suddenly, and pushed the heart-print-paper wrapped package across to her. "You can open it upstairs if you'd rather."

Slowly Carlie reached out her hand to the parcel, tracing the love hearts with her finger, then gazing at her name scrawled across the card in his familiar looping script. Holding it gently, almost gingerly, in her hand, she stood up and stumbled back to her room in a daze.

Chapter 38

The Dark

Holding the package like it was the most fragile thing in the world, she sank down onto her bed. She sat for a long time, just looking at it, tracing over her name on the envelope. She wondered if he'd had any idea, as he'd scrawled her name, that it would be the last thing he'd ever write. More importantly, she wondered if he'd known that she'd changed her mind, that she was going to see him that morning and take back her cruel words, beg him to take her back, to forgive her, to keep loving her.

Finally, breath held, she slid the card out of the envelope. Tears welled in her eyes at the beauty of the painting on the front, two lovers holding each other tight, oblivious to the world around them. Smiling through her tears, she opened the card.

My Sweet Soul Mate and Beloved,

I'm coming to see you in the morning, first thing, to tell you how much I adore you, and beg you to change your mind, but I wanted to write it down too, hoping that you can feel every word I write as I write it, feel me thinking of you, feel my arms around you, feel my love. I want you to know, no matter what happens, how much I love you, how much I will always love you.

I hope it's not just wishful thinking, but I can feel you with me right now, your lips on my hair, your voice in my ear, whispering your love across these miles that separate us, telling me you've changed your mind.

I want to apologise to you my love – finding out that it was my father who treated your mother so badly shook me to my core, but please know that I am nothing like him. I barely knew him, and what I do know of him, what I've learned recently, I despise.

I know we haven't been together all that long, in some people's eyes, but it feels like forever, and it will be forever. I fell for you in the dreams we shared before we ever actually met. I was smitten the moment you walked up to my stand at the festival to have your painting done. And I fell hopelessly in love with you that first morning we spent on the tor, as I held you in my arms and we watched the sun rise, as we sat by the stream together and just talked, just held hands.

Every day I'm away from you hurts me physically – you are the missing piece I'd been searching for, and once found I couldn't bear to be apart. You make me feel whole.

Your love has made me a better, kinder person, with more depth than I ever imagined possible. My mum was right, she realised it even before I did, that I am more myself when I am with you, that you have helped me recognise my light and encouraged me to shine it. I feel like we're meant to be together, that we're destined for each other. Whether we were together or not in a past life means nothing, because we are together now, and that's all that matters.

I don't want to keep us a secret any more. I want the whole world to know how much I love you – our friends, my students, your grandma. How could anyone be upset by how much I love you? How could that hurt anyone?

Because I love you Carlie, and I will fight for that love. I know you long for me as much and as deeply as I love and long for you, and I know we can figure out a way to make this work. I will never give up on you, on our love, and I will be there with you soon, to tell you all of this in person.

Until then my precious beloved, my sweet goddess, know that I love you, and I always will.

Forever yours, Rowan xx

She sat on her bed for a long time, motionless, holding the card to her heart, tears pouring down her face. It was all so surreal. Then finally, slowly, she reached out for the package, and carefully untied the ribbons and peeled off the heart-print paper, folding it neatly so she could keep it always.

Gently she lifted the delicate froth of black lace from the paper and let it spill out over the bed. It was the most beautiful dress she'd ever seen, like a gothic bride's dress. A lump formed in her throat as she thought back to the Yule Ball, when she'd sat in the corner, moving his beautiful ring to her left hand, imagining weddings and honeymoons and a whole lifetime together. This was too cruel.

Running her fingers over the soft tulle of the skirt, she sobbed as she gazed at the bees embroidered on the bodice, and thought back to the first time they'd met, when he'd said that he saw bees around her. Clumsily she got to her feet and pulled her clothes off so she could slip the dress over her head. It felt so soft on her skin, and fit her like it had been made for her. Which, according to the note attached, it had been, her Christmas gift from her beloved.

Her gaze flickered back to her bed, and she saw a smaller package, wrapped in the same heart-print patterned paper. Sinking down onto the floor, she picked it up, then impatiently tore the paper away. Inside was a small box, and a note.

My Dear Sweet Goddess, who I love beyond measure...
I wanted to give you this the other night at the ball, wanted to slip it on the ring finger of your left hand and pledge to spend my life with you, but I sensed that you weren't ready. That I would have freaked you out. So I gave you the herkimer diamond ring instead, put it on the middle finger of your right hand, rather than where I wanted to see it.

But I want you to have this, to know that my promise then and now is a forever promise. Eternal. And whether you start wearing it now or it takes ten years until you are ready, please know that I will wait for you forever, and love you always, no matter what. I want to spend my life with you Carlie, I want to love you every single day, and I will.

And the day that you feel ready to wear this ring, and agree to marry me, to spend your life with me – loving each other, supporting each other, helping each other dream and scheme and grow stronger and more joyful because we have each other – I will be the happiest man alive.

I will love you forever my precious beloved,
     Your Rowan xx

Choking back tears, she opened the small box, and gasped in astonishment. Nestled on a bed of black velvet was the most beautiful jewel she'd ever seen, a deep violet amethyst that matched her mum's necklace, the one she'd worn to the ball, which already seemed so long ago, although only a few days had actually passed since that night. The precious gemstone was set on a pretty rose gold band, engraved with swirls of ivy on the outside, while inside it eight words were etched. *Lives entwined, souls in harmony, hearts as one.* The same words she'd written to him.

Quickly she slid it on the ring finger of her left hand, the finger she'd wanted the ring to sit on at the ball, and the one he'd wanted to place it on that night. It seemed a lifetime since they'd clung to each other on the dance floor, kissed under the oak tree in the snow.

As she stared at the beautiful ring, she felt her mum there, smiling at the choice she'd made. She felt her father reaching out to hold her hand, the father whose depths she'd never guessed at. And she felt Rowan whispering in her ear. "Always and forever."

Glancing up at the mirror, she stared, transfixed. Her hair was still in need of a good wash, still piled on her head in a messy top knot, and her face was gaunt and bruised looking from the black circles under her eyes. She looked years older than she was, but not in a bad way. She looked like she'd been to hell, and was perhaps still there, but would eventually return, stronger than before, with greater purpose and passion.

She looked like someone who would find a way to survive because she knew how much she was loved. Even if that was a past tense thing...

"We're stronger in the places
that we've been broken."

Ernest Hemingway, American writer

Thank You!

Thank you so much for reading this book,
and sharing the magic of Carlie, Rose and Violet's stories.
As an indie author, I rely on word of mouth and reader reviews
to get the word out. If you enjoyed *Into the Dark*, I would be
so grateful if you could take a moment to leave a review on
any book site. Reviews help improve sales and ranking,
and are of immense help to all indie writers.

If you'd like to stay in touch and receive free exclusive content,
be the first to hear about book news and events info, giveaways
and more, you can sign up for my newsletter at

www.sereneconneeley.com/subscribe.

(And don't worry, you can unsubscribe at any time...)

With love and gratitude,
Serene xx

Carlie's adventures began in...

Into the Mists

Enter the swirling mists of an enchanted land, and open your heart to the mystery...

Carlie has the perfect life. A wonderful family and a best friend she adores. A house by the beach so she can go surfing after school. A clever, rational mind and big dreams of becoming a lawyer. A future she's excited about and can't wait to begin.

But in a split second her perfect life shatters, and she is sent to the other side of the world to live with a stranger. In this mystical, mist-drenched new land, she is faced with a mystery that will make her question everything she's ever known about her parents, her life and her very self. A dark secret that made her mother run away from home as a teenager. An old family friend who is not what he seems. A woman in blue who she's not convinced is real. A shadowy black cat that she would swear is reading her mind. A deserted old cottage she can't always find. And a circle of wild-haired witches who want her to join their ranks.

Will she have the courage to journey into the mists, and into her own heart, to discover the truth? And can she somehow weave together a life that she'll want to live – or will she give up and allow despair to sweep her away from the world forever?

"I can't put this book down. It's so compelling and beautifully realised – there's so much magic. Absolutely recommended!"

Lucy Cavendish, author of Spellbound and White Magic

"*Into the Mists* is Amazing with a capital A. It's comforting, healing, empowering, inspiring and, like all the author's work, truly magical. While I was reading it I felt like the little kid in *The NeverEnding Story*, tucked into my own little world with Carlie and Rose. I absolutely loved it – it's one of my favourite novels ever. It has opened my heart and inspired the magic within me. "

Sarah Byrne, teacher

And continue in...

Into the Light

A friendship torn apart. A love lost forever… A curse to break. A mystery to solve. A heart to heal…

When her parents died in a tragic accident and her life fell apart, Carlie was sent to the other side of the world to live with a stranger. After a harrowing journey through the enchanted mists of an English village, she finally found peace with her grandmother, magic with her new friend, and first love with her druidic soul mate. But then she was plunged back into darkness. Now, haunted by loss and betrayal, and worried her shattered heart is beyond repair, she must decide if she has it in her to find her way back into the light.

In the stunning conclusion to the trilogy, the wheel of the year turns from the bleakness of midwinter to the new hope of spring. Can Carlie break a decades-long curse and save the person she's closest to? Will she unlock the mystery of the sad woman she meets late one night? Which of the Otherworldly beings can she trust? Who is the man with the raven tattoo? And how far is she willing to go to forgive and be forgiven?

For a chance at happiness, she must challenge the wise priestess and embrace her darkest fears. But is she already fated to echo the lonely life of her grandmother, or can she find the courage to open her heart again?

"I'm absolutely blown away by this book and this series. It is beautiful from start to finish – magical, realistic, gentle, harsh, sad, joyful… I've been on a total rollercoaster ride, and am now feeling so bereft at the thought that these wonderful people (not just characters, but *real people*) will no longer be part of my life. What the author has created with these books is just beautiful."

Kylie Matthews, book reviewer

Into the Mists, Into the Dark and *Into the Light*
are also available as audiobooks, narrated by
British voice actor Gabrielle Baker, from
Audible, iTunes and Amazon.

Also in the Into the Mists Series...

Into the Mists
– A Journal

Awaken your inner voice and unlock the power and strength within you......

Keeping a journal is a powerful way to make sense of the world, and of your inner universe, whether you're recording the everyday events of your life or journeying within to discover your own truths. It is a valuable tool of self-expression, self-knowledge and self-discovery, a sacred, secret place to unravel and reveal your inner being, and a mirror that will reflect back your shadows and light, showing you who you truly are, and the beauty of all that you are becoming.

Including words of wisdom from priestess Rose, the Otherworldly women Carlie encounters and other beloved characters from the Into the Mists Trilogy, these pages will inspire you to look within and express the feelings at the core of your being, encouraging you to let go of past pain, forgive yourself and others, and move forward with joy and confidence so you can achieve all that you dream of.

Whether you use it as a daily diary, a gratitude book, a travel record or a place to write your novel, *Into the Mists: A Journal* will help awaken your inner voice, unlock the power and strength within you and allow you to start seeing the magic in every moment.

"This is *divine*! The lovely quotes throughout are very inspiring, and the feel of the journal is heart-warming and comforting to me. It sits on my bedside table for writing in during the quiet times of reflection, to hold my thoughts and personal inspirations. Just beautiful."

Cheralyn Darcey, eco artist and author of Flowerpaedia

The Into the Mists Trilogy – Hardcover Omnibus

Come on a magical journey...

The Into the Mists Trilogy brings together all three of the novels – *Into the Mists, Into the Dark* and *Into the Light* – in a beautiful hardcover omnibus edition.

"I couldn't put it down. This series is healing, empowering, inspiring and magical. I loved every single page. I haven't enjoyed a story so much since I read *Heart's Blood* by Juliet Marillier."

Julia Burdock, healer

"This is a beautiful journey of healing and magical discovery. I highly recommend it. It's a transformative experience to read it, a healing journey you take with the character..."

Selina Fenech, author of The Memory's Wake Trilogy

Two Sides to Every Story...

A companion to the Into the Mists Trilogy, *Into the Storm* is Rhiannon's story, beginning before she meets Carlie. It can be read after the Mists books or as a standalone.

Into the Storm

A spell to weave. A life to save.
A heart to break. A storm to brave.

When Rhiannon's mother dies, her whole world falls apart, and she withdraws from her family, her friends and her life. As grief and anger rage within her, she connects with the wildness of the winter storms – until she's consumed by the powers they unleash. A priestess tries to help her, a woman from the mists seeks to comfort her and her little brother attempts to reach her, but she doesn't know how to find her way back.

Entwined throughout is the story of her mother, which reveals a haunting mystery. Why did her parents keep such a dark secret? How will a spell she casts in the woods one full moon night unravel her? Who is the woman in red she encounters atop the sacred hill? And what chaos will be wrought by a girl from the other side of the world with a strange link to her father?

As the darkness of her shadow self is revealed, Rhiannon must find the courage to go into the storm and face her greatest fears. But if she does, will she be transformed by its terrible power, or broken and lost in the wreckage?

"*Into the Storm* takes you on such an emotional journey, and makes you believe in real magic. I loved it."

Selina Fenech, author of *The Memory's Wake Trilogy*

Coming soon...
New Into the Mists Chronicles, featuring other
beloved characters, including *Into the Fire*
and *Out of the Shadows*.

The Wheel of the Year

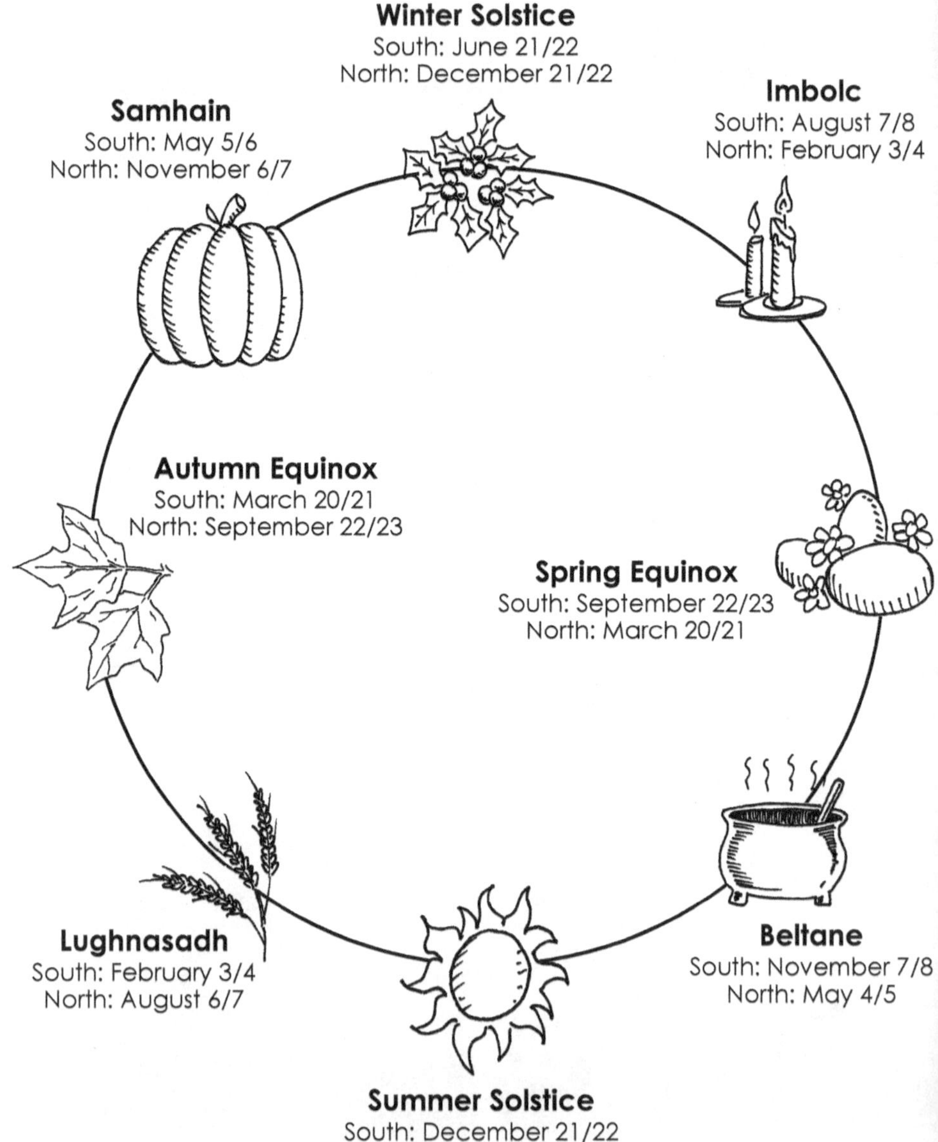

arlie's grandmother Rose and her witchy friends celebrate the eight sacred sabbats, or festivals, of the Wheel of the Year, as the ancient priestesses did, and modern pagans still do.

In *Into the Mists*, Carlie took part in her first ritual, the harvest festival of Lughnasadh, where she met Rose's circle of magical, supportive women friends and saw her grandmother as a powerful, loving priestess for the first time.

And in *Into the Dark*, she celebrated Mabon, the autumn equinox, with Rhiannon at London's Body Mind Spirit festival, where she met Rowan, then with Rose's circle back in Summer Hill the next night. She honoured her lost loved ones at the Samhain feast of the dead at Mike's house, then did a deeper ritual with Rhiannon in the ruins of an old temple. And tragedy visited her again at the winter solstice.

> "The old seasonal festivals offer a framework within
> which we can connect to the earth, ourselves and each other.
> Each season affects us differently, and each season is
> an opportunity for us to flow in harmony with the
> underlying energy of the life force, as well as celebrating
> the many changing wonders of our beautiful earth.
> By celebrating the eight seasonal festivals we become more
> rooted in our environment and our selves. We keep in touch
> with our spiritual development, and where our emotions
> are leading us, through the unfolding cycle of the year."
> *Glennie Kindred, British pagan, artist and author*

powerful way to become more aware of your inner world is to harness the natural magic of the cycles of the seasons. The shifting energies of the earth's turning have been celebrated and utilised for thousands of years, and even today, when we are so far removed from nature, you can still tangibly feel the introspection of winter, the crisp change of autumn, the potent energy of summer and the vibrant power of spring.

Attuning yourself to the vibrations of the eight sacred festivals that make up the enchanted Wheel of the Year will fill you with strength, magic and a sense of grand possibility and potential. You'll become more in sync with your inner self and your intuition, and start to connect with your own emotional tides as you connect with the earth's.

These special days, determined by the position of the earth in relation to the sun, mark the beginning, midpoint and end of each season, and are measured today by astronomers and scientists. In the past they were calculated by druids, the philosophers and scientists of their age, and recorded in stone circles and cairns, or by shamans who created calendars in pyramidal structures. These events have been honoured for thousands of years in cultures throughout the world, so the imprint of their energy can be tapped in to and absorbed.

Long ago, when life revolved around agriculture, and the sun and moon were considered deities to be worshipped, the Celtic peoples of Europe, and many others around the globe, were in tune with nature. They had to know when each season began and how long it would last so they could plant and harvest crops, hunt migratory prey and prepare for the harsh winters. They divided their year by seasons, not months, and honoured each change, celebrating eight festivals that marked the turning of these seasons and the cycles of the earth.

There are four astronomical and four agricultural festivals. The astronomical celebrations are determined by the position of the earth in relation to the sun. These include the spring and autumn equinoxes (Latin for "equal night"), which occur when the sun is directly above the equator and the length of day and night is equal, and the summer and winter solstices (Latin for "sun stand still"), which occur when the sun is at its northern or southernmost extreme, the furthest it ever gets from the equator. These four events are the midpoint of each season – thus the summer solstice being referred to as Midsummer's Day and the winter solstice as Midwinter.

The agricultural celebrations are known as cross-quarter days, because they fall midway between the astronomical festivals. Traditionally they were tied to agricultural events such as the sowing and harvesting of crops, and they mark the beginning of each season.

Even today, when we no longer live in harmony with the earth's rhythms or agricultural cycles, people celebrate the Wheel of the Year as an honouring of nature and an acknowledgement of the continuing cycle of life, death and rebirth, both literally and symbolically.

Literally this refers to the changing seasons – the fertility and vibrant life force of summer, the harvest energy of autumn, the introspection and endings (death) of winter, and the rebirth of spring. Mythologically it was tied to the story of the god and goddess. At the spring equinox they meet and court, before consummating their love during the rites of Beltane. At the summer solstice the goddess blooms into the mother, pregnant with new life, and the sun god reaches his energetic peak. From then he weakens through the harvest time of Lughnasadh and the autumn equinox, before going to the underworld at Samhain to learn new wisdom, then being reborn at the winter solstice when the goddess gives birth to the infant sun god and the Wheel turns again, playing out the cycle on and on through time.

Once this creation story was accepted as fact. Today some still think of it as a literal retelling of a historical truth, while others feel it's simply a parable that humanises nature. Either way, it's now the symbolic meaning that's most relevant to our lives – planting the seeds of our dreams in the metaphorical spring, watching them grow and manifest in the world before we give thanks for our literal harvest, allow the things that no longer serve us to die off or be released, then start all over again with new dreams as we celebrate our own rebirth.

Becoming aware of the seasonal shifts and the patterns of nature wherever you live, and celebrating these ancient but still relevant festivals, is a simple way to tap in to the magic of the earth and start to connect with nature and your inner self.

Channelling this energy and creating meaningful rituals in your life doesn't conflict with any religion or require a belief system, as it's a celebration of the science of nature and the cycles of the planet. Many pagans, like Rose and her friends, do call on gods and goddesses, and have a personal concept of the divine as a universal creative force, but others don't believe in any form of deity, simply revering nature as sacred and as the source of life, and believing that divinity is an inner not an outer power, an energy within themselves and every other person alive.

Lughnasadh : First Day of Autumn : Gratitude

Lughnasadh, also known as Lammas, is celebrated in the first week of August in the northern hemisphere and the first week of February in the southern hemisphere, and marks the end of summer and the beginning of autumn. It's the first harvest festival, traditionally a time of feasting and of thanksgiving for the life-giving properties of the grain and nature's bounty, as well as a recognition of the cycle of sowing and reaping of the crops.

It is also the time to honour the things you have grown and created in your life, a day to harvest the fruits of your labours and acknowledge your successes and what you've achieved in the past year. Celebrate the goals you've reached and have your own festival of gratitude, in whatever form that takes. Toast your success, throw a party or do something special to mark the occasion – maybe reward yourself for your hard work with a gift you've long wanted, or some precious time off to rest and chill out. Make a list of all the things you've gained over the past year – the gifts you've been given, the new talents you've developed, the friends you've made, the experiences you've had, the healings you've received – and give thanks for it all.

Then, out of gratitude and in the spirit of the ancestors who shared the bounty of their harvest with those less well off, pay your good fortune forward. Donate to a local charity or collect food for the homeless, as Rose and her friends do, lend to a business in the developing world, or give your time to help someone, ensuring the energy of abundance continues and is strengthened. Give joyfully, with no expectation of receiving anything in return. And work out small ways in which you can make a difference to the people around you all year long as well.

As the energy begins to subtly slow, this is also a time to be patient and to trust that everything is as it should be, because there are still harvests to come. Not everything has to be achieved right now – some things take longer to manifest. The lesson of the Wheel of the Year is that everything continues, everything happens when it should, and everything is eternal.

Mabon : Autumn Equinox : Harvest

The autumn equinox, known as Mabon and celebrated on September 22/23 in the northern hemisphere and March 20/21 in the southern, is characterised by the length of day and night being equal as the sun travels back across the equator to the other hemisphere. From this point on, the days will become shorter and cooler, but this is a moment of balance in nature and within – a point of harmony and calm.

Vibrationally Mabon is a season of withdrawal, of being alone to meditate, recharge, reassess and ponder where you're at in life. The energy of the earth retreats and goes within, as does your personal power, but from this cycle you will emerge with immense strength and wisdom. It's a time to honour your achievements, experiences and growth, and to ensure balance by integrating all parts of your self. Acknowledge and celebrate what you've reaped in your own life. Feel fulfilment from each goal reached, releasing what no longer serves you in order to move forward. In the wild, old growth is cleared. In your life, cut out anything that's holding you back or preventing new life and love from flourishing, whether it's work, people, a belief system, regret or the past.

On this day, when all is balanced, witches traditionally renewed their magical commitments, and you can renew any vows you've made or pledge a new one, be it to do with magic, love, friendship, career or anything else. As the shadows lengthen, it's also a good time to scry for insight into your future. If you can, light a fire and stare into the flames, allowing your mind to go blank and your vision to blur a little, or go outside and watch the clouds scuttling across the sky, analysing the shapes and symbols you see within flame and cloud. Without over-thinking it, write down what they mean to you.

Pyromancy (fire reading) and nephomancy (cloud reading) are forms of divination that have been used for millennia. You should develop your own dictionary of symbols, as you know better than anyone what any shape or image means to you, but you can begin with standard readings, such as a heart indicating romance, a cat referring to a need to trust your intuition, a tree meaning you will make new friends and a plane foreshadowing travel.

Samhain : First Day of Winter : Death

Samhain, which is celebrated in early November in the northern hemisphere and early May in the southern, is a cross-quarter day marking the end of autumn and the beginning of the cold and dark of winter. Symbolically it is about rest and renewal, of preparing for what's ahead and withdrawing a little to conserve your energy, and releasing the things you've been holding on to in order to ready yourself for new challenges and experiences. It's also the night when the veil between the worlds is said to be at its thinnest, when people honour their ancestors and try to commune with the dead. Some set a place at the dinner table for any loved ones passed over, as Rhiannon's dad Mike did at their Feast of the Dead ritual, while others cast spells to bring their spirit back, or perform mediumship rituals to converse. This magical time and its purpose has been conserved in modern-day Halloween, which celebrates ghosts, witches and restless spirits.

The beginning of winter is a period of reflection, so spend time in contemplation. If you've lost someone close to you, light a candle and remember them. Look at photos or letters and feel their presence with you. This shouldn't be morbid – you're celebrating their life and all they meant to you. Also honour those who are here now. Call your mum and dad, visit your grandparents, or write to someone who meant a lot to you when you were growing up and thank them.

Long ago, Samhain was the end of one year and the start of the next, so it's also a powerful time to let go of the energy of the old year and old memories so you can move forward with lightness and strength. Light another candle, and by its flickering illumination, write out all the worries, frustrations, regrets and seeming failures you've held on to over the previous twelve months. See the candle flame burning them away and leaving you purified and refreshed, and breathe in this positive new energy. Then burn the list in the flame, releasing your attachment to those emotions and their power over you.

This is the time to prepare yourself for the rebirth you'll experience at Yule, but for that to happen there must be death – the death of fears and doubts, and anything holding you back.

Yule : Winter Solstice : Rebirth

The winter solstice, known to pagans as Yule and Midwinter, falls around December 21/22 in the northern hemisphere and June 21/22 in the southern, and marks the middle of winter. It's the shortest day and the longest night of the year, and marks the transition between dark and light, both emotionally and physically. It's the lowest point of the Wheel in terms of daylight and energy, with the sun rising later and night falling earlier. The land is barren and cold, there is less light, and energetically people feel tired and unmotivated.

Winter is a time to rest and reflect, to acknowledge sadness and loss – of dreams, of friendships, of parts of your self – and conserve your energy. But the solstice is the turning point in this time of darkness, introspection and dreaming. Considered the dark night of the soul, it also marks the period when the dark half of the year relinquishes its hold to the light half. From this time forward, the days will start to lengthen, the sun will become stronger, and the energy within and without will start to increase and build.

In pagan times an evergreen tree was brought inside as a symbol of the hope of spring's return, and Yule was a time of feasting, celebration and gift-giving in honour of the birth of the sun god – traditions that live on today in the Christmas tree we decorate, the presents we put under it, the huge family meal we cook, and the celebration of the birth of the son of God.

To attune yourself to this festival of rebirth, light a candle on solstice eve to symbolise the sun and its activating energy, and list your dreams for the coming year. Traditionally people stayed up all night to await the return of the light, but if you can't do that, get up for the sunrise to toast the dawn and give thanks for this energetic reawakening. Open yourself to the promise of new growth and achievement, and the rebirth of your own self and your creativity, as the sun is also reborn. Symbolically and energetically it's a time to honour your inner wisdom, consider the lessons you learned during winter's introspection, and integrate them into your life so you can start to initiate change and prepare for the rush of growth of the coming springtime.

Imbolc : First Day of Spring : Purification

Imbolc, which is celebrated in the first week of February in the northern hemisphere and the first week of August in the southern, is a cross-quarter day marking the end of winter and the start of spring. It celebrates the return of light to the land, and to our own hearts, and is a time of hope, renewal and fresh starts after winter's sluggishness.

Energetically it's a time of awakening, rebirth and re-emergence. Nature fills with life force and begins to quiver with the energy to grow again, and we start to emerge from the chill of winter, shaking off our lack of motivation and re-engaging with the world, making it a great day to sow the seeds of what you want to achieve in the coming year.

Imbolc is dedicated to Bridie, the goddess of inspiration, creativity and fire, who was later supplanted by Saint Bridget, whose festival is also celebrated at this time. Talk to Bridie – or Bridget, or the higher-self aspect of yourself – or write her a letter, and tell her what you want to create in the next twelve months. Meditate on your goals and what you hope to achieve. Don't worry about how to do it, as that will be revealed later in flashes of inspiration, guidance or outside help.

Physically it's a time of purification and cleansing after the long dark of winter, so clean your house and clear your space, sweeping out old energy and thoughts so the new can thrive. It's a good time to write about your beliefs and examine how you feel about your spiritual path too, exploring the reasons you think the way you do and perhaps questioning if there are other viewpoints you might also embrace. It's also about new beginnings, and in some magical traditions it is the day chosen for initiations and rededications, so if you want to make a pledge to a new path or a new goal, or a personal vow of any kind, you will be supported by the energy of the season.

You may like to ignite a candle to represent the coming back of the light and do some candle magic. Stare into the flame as you concentrate on what you want, then blow it out, sending your desire out to the universe. Making a wish as you blow out the candles on your birthday cake is a magic that has survived from pagan times, and is a potent way to manifest your wishes into reality, whatever day it is.

Ostara : Spring Equinox : Blossoming

The spring or vernal equinox, known to pagans as Ostara, is celebrated around March 20/21 in the northern hemisphere and September 22/23 in the southern. It's one of only two times in the year when the length of day and night is equal, as the sun sits directly above the equator on its journey north or south, creating equal light and dark in both hemispheres.

This equinox is about growth, passion and the unfurling and release of the immense potential you have within you. On both a universal and a personal level, it's a time of balance and harmony, of union between the physical and the spiritual, and the integration of your heart and soul. This can be harnessed to anchor your dreams in reality and enhance your own inner harmony as the balance of universal outer energies is reflected within. Relationships are harmonious now too, making it a good time for weddings and for healing rifts.

It's a time of growth and fertility, when new crops are sown, new shoots break through the earth, buds on the trees open, birds build nests and lay eggs, and new life is celebrated. Thanks was traditionally given to the fertility goddess Ostara, whose symbols were an egg and a hare, and who is still honoured around the world today, albeit unknowingly, in the form of chocolate eggs and the Easter bunny.

Energetically it's also a very fertile time, as the seeds you sowed of your goals at Imbolc begin to sprout and gain momentum. Paint some hard-boiled eggs with symbols that represent your desires, or buy or make the chocolate version, meditating on your own metaphorical fertility and your ability to manifest dreams into reality. Choose an affirmation relating to your desired outcome, write it down and pin it up where you'll be able to see it every day.

Go outside during the day and breathe in the fresh spring air, filling your heart with new inspiration as you fill your lungs with oxygen. In many ancient cultures, including the Roman one whose calendar we have based ours upon, the spring equinox was the first day of the year, and the sense of new hope and optimism reflected in this time remains today. It's a celebration of new life, hope, passion, growth and energy.

Beltane : First Day of Summer : Growth

Beltane, celebrated in early May in the northern hemisphere and early November in the southern, is a cross-quarter day marking the end of spring and the start of the heat and energy of summer. Evidence of new life is everywhere, in abundant blossoms, the hatching of birds and bees pollinating flowers, showing that time is moving forward and life is progressing. Women bathed their faces in the dew gathered from their garden on Beltane morning to harness the energy of youth, and flowers were brought inside to symbolise fresh beginnings and the power of nature.

Beltane was the major fertility festival. Handfasting rituals were conducted, and lovers leaped over bonfires then came together in sacred union in the fields to bless the crops with fertility. Maypole dancing, representing the union of the god (the pole) and the goddess (the ribbons), was performed to join the forces of masculine and feminine, and May Day remains a popular day to wed in the northern hemisphere.

It's a time of lovers and spells to attract love, and celebrating the fertility of life, not just physically, but also of your dreams and ambitions. Symbolically this day marks the igniting of the fires of creativity and passion, of the fertility of your dreams being made manifest, and is the time to take steps to achieve what you want. Check in on the projects you started at Ostara, and write about their progress and the ways in which they've sprouted into reality. If you need to fine tune anything, learn a new skill or let go of one aspect so it can germinate further on its own, the energy of this day will support you. Make a commitment to yourself – start a new project, apply for a new job or take up a new hobby, knowing the universe is bursting with raw energy and power that you can tap in to.

It's also a powerful time to repledge your love to your partner. You don't have to build a bonfire and leap over it, although you can! Simply lighting a red or gold candle as you stare into each other's eyes and speak your love and commitment will invoke the power and passion of the element of fire. If you're single, make a commitment of some kind to yourself, nurture a friendship, or if you seek love, sing your intention and wanting of a romantic partner to the universe.

Litha : Summer Solstice : Fruition

The summer solstice, known to pagans as Litha, is celebrated around June 20/21 in the northern hemisphere and December 21/22 in the southern. It's the longest day and the shortest night of the year, and marks the peak of energy and solar power for the year. On this day the sun reaches its northern or southernmost latitude before it turns and heads back towards the equator, so near the poles daylight lasts for twenty-four hours – the sun just doesn't set for weeks at a time. In nature, everything is ripe and abundant, and life is blooming.

It's a time of high, hot and active energy. Creativity and expression is at a peak, so stand in your power and express your needs, saying what you want rather than assuming that people know. Whereas the winter solstice is slow and introspective, its opposite is fast and effective. Make use of the active energy – this is a time to do, to get out there and harness the energising earth power and make things happen.

Follow your passion, take a chance, say yes to new opportunities and express your creativity and your inner self. This is not the time to be withdrawn or shy, it's for getting out amongst it and making your dreams come true. It's also a time when relationships – and you – will mature, and you'll apply new wisdom and forethought to your passion, so give thanks for the lessons you've learned, and allow the person you are maturing into to unfold.

It's a time of celebration too, of acknowledging how far you've come and what you've achieved. Enjoy the happiness and abundance of this season and soak up the sunshine and festive atmosphere. Traditionally people stayed up all night on solstice eve, partying around bonfires or within sacred circles of stone, then watched the sun rise the next morning, feeling it bathe them in warmth and light.

At dawn, stand with your arms outstretched and breathe in the sun's life-giving power. Let it wash over you with its healing energy and burn away anything you no longer need. Take note of how your dreams and goals are manifesting into the world, and meditate on anything that could be blocking your progress. Be open to letting go of whatever isn't working so you can move forward in a new direction.

The Magic of the Moon

Rose works with the phases of the moon in her spellcasting and her healings, and performs rituals at the new moon, dark moon and full, and witches, druids and shamans have long harnessed its power too.

Using the energy of the moon phases can help you bring a goal to fruition, and connect you to the energy of nature and the earth. Lunar phases are printed in newspapers, moon diaries and websites like www.sunrisesunset.com, and you can also determine the phase of the moon by its shape, as well as by the time it rises, which occurs about fifty minutes later each day. It can be remembered by the old adage: "The new moon rises at sunrise, and the first quarter at noon. The full moon rises at sunset, and the last quarter at midnight."

As the moon progresses from dark to full it's the waxing or growing period, a time of new beginnings and increasing energy. As it goes from full back to dark it's the waning period, a time of lowering energy and introspection. Magical practitioners use the cycles of the moon to increase the power of spellworking. So do fishermen, who understand the pull the moon has on the tides of the ocean and its creatures. Gardening also operates to lunar rhythms, which enhance or hinder growth. To boost it, sow crops that produce above the ground between new moon and full, as light and energy increases, and crops that produce below ground, such as root vegetables, between full moon and dark.

Surfers understand its power too. The full moon magnifies weather patterns, so a winter full moon will bring stormier swells and bigger waves. The tides are more extreme at both the full moon and the dark moon – high tides are higher, and low tides lower. These two phases have an intense influence on the ocean, heightening conditions and drawing huge swells – or, if the ocean is flat, making it even flatter. Surfers going to Indonesia for a wave-riding safari book around a full moon, so they'll have optimum conditions and even bigger waves.

The moon affects tides, plants, animals and human behaviour. Some can't sleep during the full moon, others feel more emotional or have strange dreams. It's common to feel more energetic during the waxing phase, and more tired when it's waning. Today the moon's journey across the sky is obscured by buildings and artificial light, but it still impacts our energy and emotions, and can be used to influence the outcome of rituals, and empower any project you want to complete.

Phases of the Moon

One lunar cycle runs for 29.5 days, beginning with the tiny crescent of the new moon, building in energy through the waxing phase to the full moon, then decreasing and withdrawing through the waning period to the dark moon, before starting a new cycle. Here are some ways to take advantage of the phases of the moon to set your goal or intention and watch it grow to beautiful, abundant completion.

New Moon: Day 1

The new moon rises just after dawn and is up all day, often unnoticed in contrast to the sun and the bright sky, and sets just after sunset. From the moment the tiny new crescent moon is first sighted and for a day or two afterwards is a time of heightened energy and new beginnings. It's a good time to start new projects, make resolutions and vows you want to stick to, go in a new direction, invite something new into your life or look for a different job. This is the time to plant seeds, both literally and metaphorically, be it in the garden or in your life, sowing the seeds of new ideas, dreams and hopes. Magical workings are most powerful during the day, when the moon is visible; during this phase there is no moon at night.

A simple yet powerful new moon ritual is to sit outside as dawn breaks, watching the sun rise and feeling the energy of the new moon as it peeks above the horizon, and write down your wish for the coming month. Work out an affirmation to support it, and keep it somewhere you'll see it often. You can also invoke maiden lunar goddesses such as Rhiannon, Bridie and Persephone to add sweet, innocent yet powerful energy to your intent.

Waxing Moon: Days 1 to 14

During the two weeks from new moon to full, the energy is strong and positive, so concentrate on attracting and drawing things to you. It's the optimal time for magical workings to manifest love, abundance and new career opportunities, and for learning new things, expanding your outlook, increasing spirituality and boosting fertility. In the waxing period the lunar energy continues to build, so whatever seeds you planted at the new moon will sprout rapidly. It's an energy of gathering, growing, strengthening and increase, so if you need to release something while the moon is waxing, reverse the intent of the spell so it fits with the energies. Rather than giving up smoking by releasing your addiction, create a ceremony to attract willpower.

If you're doing healings, draw good health to you when it's waxing, and release illness when it's waning. Maiden goddesses can also be invoked, such as Bridie, Artemis, Athena, Aphrodite and Aine.

Full Moon: Days 14 to 16

The full moon rises as the sun sets, which is why it's so obvious and clearly seen, because it sails across the sky all night, contrasting with the velvety blackness, before setting around dawn, just as the sun is rising. The three days of the full moon – the day of, day before and day after – can be used to boost any intention or project. It represents achievement, culmination and abundance. The world is filled with energy and potential, so it's a great time for healing and manifestation.

Midnight is the most powerful time, as the moon is directly overhead. Stand beneath the golden orb and give thanks for what you've achieved so far, and breathe in the energy and power so you can harness it for self-expression and strength. Perform a Drawing Down the Moon ritual, bringing the energy of the moon, and the moon goddess, into your heart and soul. This is also a great time to charge crystals and amulets and cleanse your own physical and etheric bodies. And psychic abilities are thought to be at their strongest, so practise any divination methods you are drawn to, looking within to find answers to your questions and clues to your future.

The full moon is the high tide of power in a lunar cycle, so cast spells for completion, things you want to achieve, and anything requiring a boost of intensity, such as healing work, job hunting or love. You can also invoke mother goddesses Arianrhod, Isis, Selene, Diana, Lakshmi, Quan Yin, Demeter, Ishtar and Mama Quilla, who embody the full moon, motherhood, fertility, the earth and creation.

Waning Moon: Days 16 to 29

During the two weeks from full moon to dark, the energy is slowing, so it's a time for banishing and release work. Do a ritual to let go of anything that no longer serves you, such as a past relationship, a bad habit, a trait like procrastination, or any material objects or issues weighing you down and blocking your progress. If you need to attract something while the moon is waning, reverse the intent. Rather than doing a spell to draw love to you, which works against the energy of this phase, cast one to banish loneliness. This is a time of retreat and withdrawal, when you can invoke darker crone energy goddesses such as Ceridwen, the Morrigan and Grandmother Spiderwoman, who hold the wisdom and power of transformation, endings and rebirth.

Dark Moon: Day 29

The dark moon rises at dawn, with the sun, and sets at sunset. It is between the earth and the sun the whole time, making it invisible to us. While some people take the dark moon as a day off from magic, others use it to go within, using the introspective energies to examine their feelings and thoughts and delve deep within their psyche.

It's a powerful time to scry and divine to uncover hidden truths, and for getting in touch with your inner wisdom and approaching the Mysteries. This energy helps you explore the darkest recesses of your mind and your heart, and acknowledge your passions, your fears and your anger so you can release them to the approaching light.

This is a time to rest and renew your strength, and evaluate your life and progress. The transforming energy of the dark moon is internalised, so be aware of your thoughts, avoiding focusing on negativity in case you manifest the fears you're supposed to banish. The dark moon celebrates the crone, so invoke the energies of Ceridwen, Kali, the Cailleach, Hekate, Baba Yaga or Nephthys to help you descend to your metaphorical underworld and examine the layers of your subconscious.

About the Author

Serene Conneeley is an Australian writer with a fascination for history, travel, ritual and the myth and magic of ancient places and cultures. She's written for magazines about news, travel, health, spirituality, entertainment and social and environmental issues, been editor of several preschool magazines, and contributed to international books on history, witchcraft, psychic development and personal transformation.

She is the author of the Into the Mists Trilogy – *Into the Mists, Into the Dark* and *Into the Light* – and is finishing a new series in that world that includes *Into the Storm* and *Into the Fire*. She also wrote the non-fiction books *Seven Sacred Sites, A Magical Journey, Witchy Magic, Mermaid Magic* and *Faery Magic*, and created the meditation CD *Sacred Journey*.

Serene is a reconnective healing practitioner, and has studied magical and medicinal herbalism, bereavement counselling, reiki and many other healing modalities, plus politics and journalism. She loves reading, rainbows, drinking tea with her friends, and celebrating the energy of the moon and the magic of the earth. Her pagan heart blossomed as she climbed mountains, danced in stone circles, wandered through ancient cathedrals and stood in the shadow of the pyramids on her travels, and she's also learned the magic of finding true happiness and peace at home.

www.SereneConneeley.com

NaNoWriMo...

Into the Mists began as a fun challenge with a few friends – to write fifty thousand words in thirty days for the 2012 National Novel Writing Month (nanowrimo.org). After publishing five non-fiction books, I was curious to discover whether I could write fiction, and this seemed the perfect way – no time to edit as I went, or let my doubts stop me, and if at the end I hated it, well, I'd only wasted thirty days. It wasn't easy, but I committed myself to doing it, and sacrificed time for other things so that I could – and I did it! Fifty-one thousand words by November 30. And while I spent several months afterwards adding, rewriting and revising, Carlie's story was definitely born in that single month, and the first draft wasn't all that different from the final one...

A few of us decided to do it again in 2013 – and I figured that the fact I'd be travelling with my sweet husband through Scotland for the whole of November was no reason to back out. Lots of people said I was crazy to attempt it, but I always love a challenge ☺ And so I spent my days dancing in stone circles, crawling into ancient burial chambers, climbing snow-capped mountains (and, just like Carlie, seeing snow for the first time!), watching the full moon rise over Callanish, sailing across the ocean to Orkney and the Outer Hebrides, meeting up with a dear friend in Glastonbury – and spending mornings and nights scribbling in a notebook or tapping away on a crappy little laptop, fuelled by pots of tea and the odd shortbread biscuit, and averaging seventeen hundred words a day, give or take.

But although I made my fifty thousand words by November 30, probably only half of them ended up in this book, and I spent several months afterwards writing new chapters, changing a major plot line, introducing a new character and generally messing with poor Carlie's head. It ended up longer and darker than *Into the Mists*, but after not liking it for the longest time, I'm finally happy with how *Into the Dark* turned out. Carlie may not be – but I promise she'll have a happier time in book three...

With Thanks...

I am so grateful, as always, to my sweet husband, for his immense love, endless patience, encouragement, inspiration, support and belief in me, for making me countless cups of tea to keep me going, and for not complaining when I would banish myself to my little purple office and write for days...

I am grateful to book editor and friend Kylie Matthews, for constructive feedback, encouragement, and for understanding Carlie and Rhiannon, and what they might do and feel, and when, and for giving me faith I'd done these characters justice.

I am indebted to gorgeously talented and adorably sweet and generous artists Selina Fenech and Daniella Spinetti.

I am inspired every day by so many wonderful people... My workout buddy Claire, who has encouraged, supported and pushed me every day for the last eighteen months – working out together every morning has kept me sane, especially towards the end of this deadline, and feeling physically strong has made me feel stronger emotionally too... Kate Forsyth and Debora Geary, who taught me something about myself and my writing... Sarah Addison Allen, JK Rowling, Philip Pullman, Juliet Marillier, Richard Dawkins, Sam Harris, Jillian Michaels, Bob Geldof and Bono, who weave magic with their words and deeds... All the people who stand up and fight for the rights of everyone to have food and shelter, to be safe, and to have equality in all areas, from refugee advocates and anti-poverty campaigners to social rights activists and environmental warriors... And Platinum Brunette, Michael Monroe, U2, Alanis Morissette, Weddings Parties Anything, Divinyls, Hole, Bif Naked, The Almighty, Green Day, Joan Jett, Everclear and countless more artists that I listened to while I wrote...

And I'm proud of, and grateful to, my inspiring NaNoWriMo buddies – Laura, Karen, Miri, Jaz, Kylie, Paulette, Annalie, Johoanna, Bel, Cynthia and Sharne... Same time this year?

With much love, Serene xx

Also by Serene Conneeley

Seven Sacred Sites: Magical Journeys That Will Change Your Life is part spiritual adventure story, part history, part travel guide. Discover what makes these places sacred, when to go and how to get there, the fascinating histories, the rituals that were performed there, the cultural and magical significance of each sacred site, both now and in the past, and the many ways in which they still inspire, touch and initiate growth and learning in all who visit.

> *"By far the best travel book this year. Her style evokes the great travel writers like James A Michener, who weave cultural anthropology into an entertaining traveller's tale – a recipe for pure reading pleasure. And it's absolute gold for those interested in the spiritual traditions that shape our world."*
>
> Joanne Lock, Spheres magazine

A Magical Journey: Your Diary of Inspiration, Adventure and Transformation combines a diary where you write the story of your life with a guidebook that includes the physical, mental and spiritual health benefits of journalling, and tools to release emotional blockages and unleash your authentic self. Make a wish come true using the cycles of the moon, celebrate worldwide festivals, and create magic in your life by harnessing the ancient, sacred energy of the seasonal turning points of the year.

> *"This helped me connect to self, and venture forth with boldness and compassion. I am so much more aware, and I thank the author from the depths of my heart and soul for the opportunity to grow."*
>
> Marissa Clarkson, bereavement counsellor

Sacred Journey: A Meditation to Connect You to the Magic of the Earth is a CD of seven guided meditations set over beautiful music. Each runs for around seven minutes, and can be done on its own, or all together as a fifty-minute meditation journey. Attune yourself with the sacred elements and energies of the earth to soothe your soul, uplift your spirit and heal your heart.

> *"A gem to treasure. Serene is a gentle, loving, wise teacher of wisdoms we can all benefit from. This takes us on a sacred journey into the earthly and heavenly elements and realms, and into history, spirituality and self-love too."*
>
> Lucy Cavendish, creator of As Above, So Below CD

Sacred Sites: The Pocket Guides to Your Magical Journey are seven mini books that are perfect for travelling, or collecting. They include each of the places in *Seven Sacred Sites*, with extra practical information and websites added, plus pages for your notes, the better to plan your magical adventure.

Witchy Magic (with Lucy Cavendish) is an enchanting adventure into the Craft of the Wise, with clear guidance on how you can access this ancient knowledge to create the life you dream of. It is an earth-honouring spiritual path and an empowering, beautiful way to be at one with the universe, taking responsibility for your life and transforming every word and action into an alchemical tool of change. Step into the world between the worlds and the wisdom of your inner witch to create an inspiring, magical life.

"This is a definitive reference for the would-be witch, and entertaining and enlightening for the witch-curious... For the history buff, ritualist and nature lover to the magician, pagan or spiritualist – and well beyond."

Kylie Matthews, freelance book reviewer

Mermaid Magic: Connecting With the Energy of the Ocean and the Healing Power of Water (with Lucy Cavendish) is brimming with sea magic, inner journeys, marine conservation and rich research, and will help you develop a deep connection with the element of water. Work with the ocean and its creatures, learn about tides and lunar phases, divine your future with sea oracles, absorb the healing energies of sacred wells and springs, become an eco warrior, and discover the beauty of mermaid lore and love.

"This is a wonderfully inspiring read. It really made me want to shed my twenty-first century shackles and dive into the ocean to embrace its wonderful healing powers. Thanks magical ladies for the journey!"

Sabina Collins, freelance writer

The Book of Faery Magic (with Lucy Cavendish) is rich in tradition, history, research and lore, and is filled with whimsical interactions with the fae, grounded guidance on how to work with them, and beautiful ideas for reconnection with nature and the magical realms. Whether you believe that faeries are truth or fantasy, *Faery Magic* is your portal to a state of being where fun and healing energy will help you fulfil your dreams, transform your life, and improve your relationship with the earth, your self and others.

"The ultimate guide to all things faery – entertaining, informative and enthralling. Whether you believe in faeries or are just curious, there is much to learn in this book, from their history and legends, their magical gifts and nature sites, to the unique beings from around the world."

Larissa Chapman, Good Reads

www.BlessedBeeBooks.com

www.ingramcontent.com/pod-product-compliance
Lightning Source LLC
Chambersburg PA
CBHW030659120726
47905CB00001B/278